THE PAYBACK GIRL

JONATHAN DUNSKY

The Payback Girl
Jonathan Dunsky
Copyright © 2018 by Jonathan Dunsky
Cover by Deranged Doctor Designs
Cover photographs © Elovich/Shutterstock (Grunge texture); Plume
Photography/Shutterstock (Factory); Neo-stock (Woman)

For Dan

BOOKS BY JONATHAN DUNSKY

1

Amber-May hurt like hell.

The pain was everywhere. A stabbing sensation on the inside of her chest. A hammering in her skull. A nasty ache all over her face. And, worst of all, a jagged, burning pain that started in her genitals and radiated fire into her stomach.

She was drowning in blackness. Not like in sleep, but as if she'd been tightly wrapped in some thick material that blocked out all light.

She willed her eyes to open but felt no reaction. She strained her ears but picked up no sound. The silence was as deep as the blackness enveloping her. *Am I dead?* she wondered.

That most terrifying of questions was followed not by a thought of herself, but by one of her grandmother. If Amber-May were dead, who would care for Grandma Betsy?

She banished the thought from her mind. She couldn't be dead. There was no way death could hurt this much.

She tried to cry out, both to call for help and to simply hear the sound of her own voice. But either she was unable to make a sound, or her ears were not working.

Panic gripped her heart in an icy fist. She started to hyperventilate, which only made the pain in her chest worse. It was as if someone had worked a razor blade inside her and was scraping it against her ribs.

What's happening to me? Where am I? How did I get here?

A tsunami of questions flooded her mind. If they didn't stop, she would drown in them. Because she had no answer to any of them. And the pain made it impossible to think.

Amber-May imagined a dam blocking the flow of unanswerable questions. Then she pictured a sun burning brightly in a clear blue sky, drying out the questions that had already flooded her consciousness. It was a trick her mother had taught her when she was little. A visualization technique to control her thoughts and emotions. Sometimes it worked; sometimes it didn't. This time it did.

As her mind began to clear, Amber-May focused on her breathing. *Slow down*, she told herself, and, gradually, her lungs obeyed, inflating and deflating at a normal pace. Now her chest hurt a little less, and she turned her attention to her ears. *Work, damn it! Come on!*

At first the utter silence persisted, but then she picked up something—a drumming sound, very close to her ears.

Her heart. She was hearing her heartbeat thudding against her eardrums. An unsteady, erratic rhythm, but music to her ears all the same. It meant her hearing was still functioning. Up to a point at least.

She diverted her attention to her other senses. At first there was nothing, no sensory input, but then she smelled something.

A coppery scent, like that of blood. And pine needles. She smelled pine needles. The smell was very faint, but unmistakable. Was she in a park? A forest? She couldn't remember any reason for her to be in either.

She couldn't remember other stuff, too. Like what day of the week it was or what had happened over the past few hours. Her memory was clear up to a time she was sure was some days ago—a week maybe—but fuzzy after that. Like an impenetrable fog.

Amber-May shivered. She was freezing. And something hard was pressed against her back, buttocks, head. She realized that she was lying on a hard surface. Hard and uneven. Like dirt or bare earth.

Then came another sensation—chilled air moving on her skin. Wind. A cold wind was caressing her legs, stomach, breasts. Wait—was she naked?

She had to be, because the wind touched her everywhere and she couldn't feel any clothes.

The panic surged back, a black wave of fear and anxiety, eager to consume her mind, to push her under and never let go.

Oh, my God. Why am I naked in the middle of nowhere? This is bad. This is really bad.

It was like a scream in her head, repeating itself over and over, louder and louder.

Amber-May gritted her teeth against the onslaught, grinding them hard into each other. They felt strange, misshapen. Her gums flared with sharp pain that radiated across her jaw. It helped her refocus her mind on what was positive. She was regaining control of her body, and her senses were coming back to life.

In her mind, she added height to the dam warding off the panic, strengthening it. She was still terrified of what was happening to her, but she was able to think; she was not lost.

Again she strove to open her eyes. The blackness held, heavy, dispiriting, but Amber-May did not give up. She might be blinded for good, for all she knew, but she was not willing to accept such a fate. Not yet, anyway. Not without giving it her all. She directed all her energy, everything she had, at her eyes, ordering them—begging and pleading—to open.

The darkness broke. A sliver of yellow light appeared off center, to the right. Amber-May realized only her right eye had opened. This could mean that she was half-blind, but she was not going to think about that now. Right now, she was going to be positive. She was going to hold onto that sliver of light, hold onto it for dear life.

As if it felt her need, the sliver of light widened, brightened, dazzling her right eye so it filled with tears. But she didn't clamp her eyelids shut. She was so grateful to have sight; she wasn't about to give it up, not even for a fraction of a second.

As she grew acclimated to the light, she caught sight of lofty tree-tops swaying gently against a backdrop of a cloudless blue sky. A bird flitted across her field of vision, chased playfully by another. It was beautiful, tranquil. But how did she get here? And why was she hurting so bad?

Then she heard them—two voices, chattering, approaching fast. Female voices.

Amber-May struggled to call out. Silence. Her mouth felt as dry as old paper, her tongue as heavy as a bowling ball. The two voices drew nearer, accompanied by the sound of rapidly pounding feet on tarmac.

She knew that sound. Five times a week, in the early morning hours, she would strap on sneakers and a running outfit, slip on her earphones, turn up the volume on her music player, and produce the exact same sound for three miles, sometimes more.

Jogging. The two women were jogging. Very close now.

Couldn't they see her?

The way her head lay, she was staring straight up. The two women, however, were somewhere to her left. She tried angling her head, but the sharp stab of pain in her neck made her stop. Her breath caught in her throat, her vision spun, and for a second she was sure she was going to pass out. Then the pain subsided, her vision cleared, and she was able to breathe normally again.

Okay, let's try again.

Slowly, gradually, she swiveled her head to the left. Her neck hurt this time as well, but she was ready for the pain and didn't stop until she was peering sideways.

Through a jumble of foot-high bushes, she caught glimpses of tarmac—a path cutting through the woods, ten, maybe twelve feet away.

The two women were almost upon her. She could make out their words. One was telling the other about a bad date she'd had.

Amber-May opened her mouth, commanded her lips and tongue to vocalize the word *Help!*

Nothing came out.

She tried again, and this time a moan, high-pitched and pitiful, unrecognizable as her own voice, emerged from her lips.

The running footsteps pattered to a stop. First one pair and then the other.

"What is it, Mary?" one of the women asked.

"Did you hear that?"

"Hear what?"

A pause. Amber-May could see their legs through the bushes. She had to get their attention. She could not let them get away.

Again she moaned.

"That," Mary said. "I think it's coming from here."

Mary came closer, feet off the tarmac and now crunching on grass. Amber-May could see her. Tall, Caucasian, medium build, mid-thirties, long dark hair pulled back in a ponytail. Mary saw her, too. She stared at her, aghast.

"Oh my God, Susan. It's a girl."

The two women—Mary and Susan—came toward her. Susan had her hand pressed to her mouth, looking close to fainting.

"What—what happened to her?"

Mary crouched down beside Amber-May, reached for her hand, and held it in both of hers. To her friend, she said, "Don't lose it now, Susan. Get your phone and call for help." She turned to Amber-May, tried on a smile, but it kept slipping off her lips. "It's okay, honey. Hold on now. Help is coming. You're going to be fine. You hear me? You're going to be fine."

Mary's distressed expression told Amber-May that she was lying. She wanted to tell her to stop bullshitting, but the darkness was once again closing in at the edges of her vision. Her strength ebbed. She felt herself drifting, falling, plummeting into a black well of nothingness.

"Thank you," she tried to mutter, but had no idea whether she'd succeeded before she passed out.

2

Amber-May woke in darkness.

The darkness was incomplete. She could see twinkles of red, yellow, and blue electronic light on both sides of her. The soft hum and buzz of machinery was the only sound in the room.

She was lying on something soft, and a thin blanket covered her to her neck. She felt cold, and under the covering her arms and chest had sprouted goosebumps.

On her left was an IV stand, a bloated bag of transparent liquid hanging from it, a line running from the bottom of the bag under the sheet into her arm. On her right, on another stand, was a small screen, across which ran a white squiggly line. A heart monitor. Keeping track of her heartbeat. Every so often it beeped.

She realized where she was. A hospital room.

The memory came rushing back. Her lying naked in the woods and being found by the two women—Mary and...for a moment the name eluded her, but then she had it. Susan. The other woman was called Susan. She was the one with the phone.

Amber-May's mouth was devoid of moisture. She worked up a tiny bit of saliva and swallowed. It hurt a little. That made her remember the pain.

It was gone. Well, not entirely, but almost. She could sense it just on the edge of her consciousness, as though it were forcefully held back. It lay there, lurking like a ravenous predator waiting for the opportunity to sink its claws into her again.

What day was it? How long had she been in the hospital? What sort of shape was she in?

She felt disoriented, lost, scared. Her head weighed a ton, and something was wrapped around it tight. She was more tired than at any other point in her life. It was a struggle to keep her eyelids from closing, but she didn't want to sleep. Not just yet. She wanted to know what was happening. Running her gaze around the small austere room, she discovered only her right eye was working.

Okay, don't panic. There'll be time for that later. First, let's see how bad things really are.

She tried moving her fingers and let out a sigh of relief when she felt them shift a little on top of the sheet. She tried the same thing with her toes, but there was no response. No sensation, either. From her hips downward, she felt nothing at all.

The heart monitor started beeping faster, and the squiggly line showed higher peaks. A tiny red bulb began pulsing. Amber-May's chest tightened. Her throat constricted in terror. Was she paralyzed from the waist down?

A wedge of bright yellow light spilled into the room. Through the open door entered a woman dressed in a nurse's uniform. She closed the door behind her and flicked a switch. A single ceiling light came on, bathing the room in a lambent, soothing glow.

The nurse was beaming at her. "You're up, I see. Thank you, Lord, thank you." She had a full, melodious voice. She came toward the bed. A plump black woman, early forties, with a pleasant round face and curly hair held back by a red headband. She stopped by the heart monitor, gave it a frowning glance, and laid a hand on Amber-May's arm, over the blanket. The hand was warm. "Hush now, dear. It's all right. You're safe now. Don't you worry about a thing."

Whether it was her mellow voice, her warm touch, or her mere presence Amber-May couldn't say, but she felt herself relax. The squiggly line calmed down as well.

The nurse smiled again. She had the sort of smile that could brighten the deepest of darknesses and kind eyes the color of walnut. "There. Good girl." She patted her arm. "I'm so happy to see you awake. You had us worried there for a while."

Amber-May opened her mouth to speak. Her throat was so dry that her words came out in a low croak. "Where am I?"

"St. Augustine's hospital. My name's Jolene. Hold on for a sec. Let me get you some water."

Jolene pressed a button and the top half of Amber-May's bed lifted to a reclining position. She brought over a glass with a straw and Amber-May sucked greedily, the water cool and wonderful down her parched throat.

"My, my, aren't you thirsty," Jolene said when Amber-May had finished the water. "Well, it's no wonder. You haven't had a proper drink in quite a while."

"How long have I been here?" Amber-May barely recognized her own voice. The water had done away with the hoarseness, but now she sounded nasal, as though her nostrils were congested.

"In the hospital? Four days. You spent the first day and a half down in intensive care. Then you were moved up here. You've been my guest for three days. More water?"

After draining the second glass, Amber-May found that she felt a little better. The drowsiness had evaporated, and her head no longer weighed like a truck. But she knew that meant little. She was in bad shape.

She said, "I don't remember getting here. I don't remember the past four days at all."

"Well, you were unconscious pretty much the whole time. First couple of days, you were out cold. Yesterday and today, you'd come to for a few seconds here and there, then drift off again. But I knew you'd come through. I took one look at you and I told myself—that girl, she's a fighter, she's strong, she's not a quitter."

At that particular moment, Amber-May felt anything but strong. She doubted she could have beaten a kitten in a one-on-one fight. She dreaded learning the answers to the questions she knew she had to ask.

"What happened to me? What's my condition?"

Jolene's face turned somber. "It's almost eleven p.m. Why don't you get some rest? Dr. Wilkerson will see you first thing in the morning, I'll make sure of it. He'll answer all your questions."

"No. Please, Jolene, I want to know now. Whatever it is, no matter how bad, I gotta know." Amber-May could hear the desperation in her voice and feel her anxiety mounting. She hated the way she sounded, whiny and pitiful, like a weepy child. The heart monitor started acting up again.

Jolene put her hand on Amber-May's shoulder. "Don't get upset, please. Just keep calm, okay? You just remember everything's all right now." But Amber-May could hear the lie in Jolene's voice. It was a kindhearted lie, one based on good intentions, and that scared her even more. It was clear Jolene was trying to shelter her from some horrible truth.

"You don't remember how you got hurt?" Jolene asked.

"No. It's all a blank. Please tell me."

"It would be best, I think, if you weren't alone. Is there anyone I can call? Maybe your parents?"

"They both died years ago."

"Oh. I'm so sorry. Any other family?"

"Just my grandmother, and she's in a home. She can't help me. Not in her condition. Just tell it to me straight. I can handle it."

The nurse chewed on her lower lip for a moment, as if unsure of how to begin. Then she drew a chair close to the bed and sat down in it heavily. She reached under the blanket, clasped Amber-May's hand tightly in hers, took a deep breath, and began talking.

"There's no easy way to say this, so I'll just say it plain. You were attacked. Someone attacked you and—" Jolene paused for a second, hesitating before forging ahead, the words tumbling out of her mouth as if she were eager to get rid of them "—raped and beat you. Then that animal dumped you in the woods with no clothes on. Want me to go on?"

Amber-May's windpipe felt as though a rock had been shoved inside it. Unable to utter a single word, she responded with a jerky nod.

"Your nose is busted, and so are your left cheekbone and two of the fingers on your left hand. You've lost five teeth. Three of your ribs are broken and three more are cracked. You suffered a head injury, a concussion, so you may be feeling groggy and have headaches. You have a bunch of cuts, contusions, and bruises on your belly, arms, and face. Some of the cuts were pretty bad and needed stitches. You also have some injuries related to the rape itself. There were some internal injuries and bleeding. The doctors—they had to perform surgery, they had to remove your spleen. I'm so sorry, dear."

It was almost too much to bear, and it took Amber-May several moments to find her voice. "What about my legs? I can't move my toes. And my left eye, am I half-blind?"

"Oh no, your sight is undamaged; it's just that your left eye is swollen shut. Once the swelling subsides, you'll be able to see fine. As for your legs, I don't see why there'd be a problem. There was no spinal injury. Let's run a quick test, okay?"

Jolene rose and folded back the blanket at the foot of the bed, exposing Amber-May's feet. From the breast pocket of her uniform, she produced a capped pen and said, "Can you feel this?" and pressed the pen to the sole of Amber-May's right foot.

Amber-May held her breath and then released it in a relief so profound that it made her head swim. Her right eye welled with tears. "I feel it. I feel it."

Jolene asked her to move her toes, and together they saw them wiggling. Amber-May almost smiled. Jolene said, "You remember nothing about the attack?"

The dam broke then, the one holding back her tears. They spilled like a waterfall of liquid salt, carving wet lines down her face. Because she did remember. In a flash, it was all back in her head. Every horrific second of it.

"I remember," she said through her tears.

"Do you know who did this to you?"

"Yes," Amber-May said. "I remember them all."

3

Jolene said the police had been called when Amber-May first arrived at the hospital. A rape kit had been administered and taken for analysis. The police would want to speak to her, but it was too late to call them at that hour. In the morning, she'd be able to see them.

"Will you be here?" Amber-May asked, and when she saw Jolene hesitate, she added, "I've got no right to ask it of you; I suppose it's not your shift. It's just that I have no one else, and I don't want to talk to them alone."

Jolene smiled and nodded. "I'll be here, I promise. Don't you worry about it."

"Thank you," Amber-May said and asked Jolene to bring her a mirror. Jolene said she thought it wasn't a good idea, but relented when Amber-May insisted.

Amber-May held up the mirror in her right hand and gazed at her reflection in the glass.

The face reflected back at her was a ruin. Her nose was bandaged, but she could see it had been knocked askew. Her left eye was a closed line in a flaming mess of distended red and purple tissue. Her right eyebrow was also swollen; a black scab marked its middle. A thick bandage was wrapped around her head. She noticed that her hair had been cut short, probably by the medical staff to make her easier to treat.

Her face was no longer symmetrical. The left side had been pummeled out of its previous contours. Her cheekbones no longer matched. Cuts and bruises and scabs marked her face. Some of the cuts had been stitched. She didn't know much about such things, but she suspected that some of the cuts would be forever imprinted on her face as ugly scars.

It was the pitiful face of a battered wife, the traumatized face of an assault victim, the face of a stranger. Even her right eye, the one she could see with, looked alien to her. A part of her mind rebelled against the notion that the haunted look of fear and misery in that eye really belonged to her, but there it was.

She would never look the same. She would never be the same. She had been altered and deformed, both physically and emotionally.

She lowered the mirror to her lap with a trembling hand and sat gazing at nothing.

Jolene hovered worriedly at her side. "Are you okay? Can I get you something?"

Amber-May didn't answer.

"It will look better in a few days," Jolene said, but Amber-May could hear the effort the nurse was making in an attempt to comfort her. She wasn't lying; she just wasn't telling her the whole truth. Some of her wounds would not heal completely. Some of the damage would be permanent.

Amber-May handed back the mirror. "Thank you, Jolene. I think I'll go to sleep now."

Jolene nodded. "Okay. Do you want a tranquilizer? A sleeping pill?"

Amber-May said she didn't and thanked the nurse again. Jolene left the room. Amber-May was once again alone with her dark thoughts and bleak memories.

She began weeping. Violent silent sobs shook her body, making her head throb.

It took a long while for the sobbing to cease. When it did, she lay motionless, staring at the dark ceiling, feeling empty, deprived of vitality. She thought about meeting the police in the morning and felt some of her energy return. She would get back at them. At all four of them. She would see to it that they paid for what they did to her.

The decision buoyed her spirit enough so that she was able to gently rub the residue of tears off her wounded face. She wished it were morning already, so she could tell it all, drain some of the poison out of her system. She knew it would not be the end of it. She would have to appear in court, be questioned and probed. Her life would be scrutinized, challenged, misrepresented. It would be hard, but she would do it. She would not back down.

4

She hadn't slept long. She knew that the instant she awoke. And she knew something else, too: she was not alone in the room.

A man was sitting quietly in a chair on the right side of the bed, his legs crossed and his hands clasped in his lap. A solitary ceiling fluorescent cast its light directly downward on his head, making his bald scalp gleam a sweet pink. The fringe of hair he had left was a light-brown laced with gray. He was gazing right at her with a pair of shrewd eyes, amber and small, set a bit too close together behind a pair of large black-rimmed glasses.

Amber-May gasped in startlement. The drowsiness of recent wakefulness evaporated. She was wide awake now and alert. *Get Jolene*, she thought, then remembered that Jolene's shift had ended shortly after their conversation. Another nurse, then. Where was the emergency switch that would alert the duty nurse?

The man, sensing her agitation, said, "Don't be alarmed, Miss Jackson. I'm not here to do you any harm."

He wore a dark three-piece suit, perfectly pressed, and a bow tie —white dots on a dark blue field—perfectly centered beneath his sagging chin. Black loafers encased his feet. His clothes looked expensive. With his chubby face, unimposing pale features, and casual, good-natured expression, he looked harmless enough, but he gave her the creeps all the same.

She had never seen him before in her life. What was he doing in her room? What did he want?

"Who are you? How do you know my name?"

The man smiled broadly. The smile lent his face an innocent, almost childlike quality, but Amber-May wasn't fooled. He was here because he wanted something from her, and she had a feeling it was something she wouldn't like one bit.

"My name is Garland Pickens, and I'm a lawyer." He spoke with a lazy Southern drawl—Louisiana or Alabama, something in that neighborhood—and his voice was a smooth baritone that could easily carry across a large hall and command the attention of everyone therein. Of course, this would only happen if he made full use of it. At the moment, he was speaking softly, his words meant for her and her alone.

He had fat lips, a small mouth, a weak jawline, and a double chin. Fifty extra pounds crowded his waistline, ballooning his suit jacket. Amber-May pegged his age at fifty-five.

Garland Pickens said, "I am here to make you an offer, Miss Jackson, one you'd be wise to accept. This offer is only good until the moment I step out of this here room, so I advise you to listen closely to what I have to say. If you raise your voice or call for the nurse, my offer will be immediately withdrawn, and you would soon have cause to regret it. I guarantee you that."

Her right hand had been moving while he spoke, brushing along the sheet in search of the rectangular plastic call switch. She found it, held it up, and made sure he saw it in her grasp. It felt good to have it. It gave her some power over this intruder. Her thumb was poised over the call button. "You still haven't told me how you know my name."

"It's my business to know, Miss Jackson, and I have the resources to do so. I know quite a bit more about you than just your name. It's amazing the extent of information proficient private investigators can uncover these days just by tapping their keyboards. Simply put, I had you checked out."

"Why? You say you're a lawyer, who do you represent? Tell me now or I'll press this button and get hospital security to throw you out."

Pickens smiled amiably, as though the only effect her threat had on him was to induce amusement. "My client—my one and only client—is Patrick MacBaxter. Perhaps you've heard of him? He is the father of Emmett MacBaxter. I assume you know who he is."

Amber-May froze. For a few endless seconds, the entire world seemed to stand still. The call switch slipped from her hand, bounced once on the mattress, and fell over the edge of the bed, dangling at the end of its looped cord like a hanged man. Pain lanced through her skull, sudden and powerful enough to elicit an anguished moan from her lips. Her breathing accelerated, making her tortured ribs throb. She clenched her right hand until the pain subsided to a level that made speech possible. She looked over at Garland Pickens. He was the picture of calm composure. Witnessing her suffering had made no change to his tranquil, country-club expression.

"No deal," she said.

"But you haven't yet heard the particulars of—"

"I said no deal. I don't care what you plan on offering me to buy my silence; it's not for sale. I am not for sale. Mark my words, Mr. Pickens, I'm going to make sure Emmett MacBaxter goes to prison for what he did to me. Him and all of his buddies. I hope they rot. Now get out of here and tell your client you failed in your little errand."

She was breathless after that little speech, but pleased to have said it all in a determined, unwavering voice. Garland Pickens, however, did not appear to be moved. He remained in his seat, unperturbed.

"Miss Jackson—" he began, speaking with the same mellow tone he'd been using throughout their conversation.

Amber-May cut him off. "Didn't you hear what I said? I want you to get—"

"Shut your mouth, you stupid girl, and don't interrupt me again!" The abrupt shift in his tone stunned her into silence. It was as if his voice were a whip that had thus far been coiled at his side, but had now, without warning, lashed out at her face. Pickens had both feet on the floor and was leaning forward, his face hard. "Do I have your undivided attention? Good. I'll have you know that I like to finish my sentences, Miss Jackson, and I get quite upset when I'm repeatedly hindered from doing so. Trust me when I say you do not want me upset. I am, though you may fail to believe it, the best friend you got in the world at the moment. Now, are you going to let me say what I've come here to say?"

He waited for her to reply, but Amber-May offered him neither word nor gesture. Inside, she was seething with anger, on the verge of erupting at this arrogant, rude agent of evil, but a more rational part of her brain advocated a different course of action.

Pickens was her enemy, and it was always good to know as much as possible about one's enemies. No harm would befall her if she listened to whatever he wanted to say. It might even prove beneficial. She could tell the police about this meeting. The mere fact that Emmett MacBaxter's lawyer had made her an offer in exchange for her silence would be viewed as an admission of his client's guilt, wouldn't it? Amber-May could feel the onset of a smile tugging at her bruised lips. She quickly quashed it. Best to keep Pickens in the dark as to her thoughts.

Garland Pickens waited a few more seconds; then his lips stretched into a wide smile, all the hardness melting off his doughy face. He reclined in his chair. "There. That's better. Now we can be friends again."

"Enough of that," she said. "Just get on with it."

"Very well, Miss Jackson. As I said, I am here as Emmett MacBaxter's lawyer. But, for the purposes of our little chat, you should consider me the representative of all four men who were involved in the, eh, incident."

"You mean rape."

Pickens waved a hand dismissively. "Whatever you wish to call it is all right with me."

"Not to mention assault and battery. Do you know what your clients did to me, Mr. Pickens?"

"I read your medical file quite thoroughly."

Again she found herself momentarily speechless, though this time by his words, not the tone in which he'd delivered them. "How did you get access to my file? That's private information."

"Nothing is truly private in this world. Suffice it to say that I wanted to know what your condition was, so I took the necessary steps to gain that knowledge."

A horrified sort of curiosity took hold of her. "What else do you know about me?"

"Quite a few things. For instance, I know that you were born on May 22, 1998, making you twenty years old. You were born in Detroit. Your father served in the Army Special Forces, earned a number of commendations, and worked as a security consultant following his honorable discharge. Your mother was a schoolteacher—a very good one, apparently. She was once voted Teacher of the Year in the state of Michigan." Pickens sounded genuinely impressed, but Amber-May couldn't help but suspect it was merely an act designed to make her more amenable to the offer he was planning on making her. "You're an only child and an orphan. Your parents died together in a head-on collision with a truck when you were eleven. The truck driver was intoxicated."

Pickens paused, his eyes on her, trying to gauge her reaction. She kept her face blank, determined to show him not a hint of her emotional state—which was pure, unadulterated rage. It was bad enough that Pickens had pried into her life and history. But the fact that he'd also had her parents investigated, including the manner in which they'd died, was worse—it was sacrilegious. That was hallowed ground, and he had soiled it. She felt like ripping his eyes out.

He continued, either unaware of her menacing thoughts or indifferent to them. "Your grandmother took you in. Her name is Elizabeth Mallory, but everyone calls her Betsy. She was also a teacher. Taught first grade at the same school for forty years."

"Forty-one."

"Forty-one," Pickens said, inclining his head. "You were a good student, had the necessary grades to go to college, were even accepted at a few good ones, but financial difficulties kept you from attending. It was due to your grandmother. Two years ago, shortly before you turned eighteen, she was diagnosed with Alzheimer's. A particularly virulent kind. Her deterioration was exceptionally swift. You cared for her at home for a while, but that soon proved impossible. She requires round-the-clock supervision. You had no choice but to move her to a home. You could have had her admitted to a state-run facility; that wouldn't have burned a hole in your pocket. Why didn't you?"

"Have you ever been to one of those places, Mr. Pickens? I wouldn't wish them on my worst enemy. Not even you."

The dig had no apparent effect on him. He went on, "You found her a private nursing home, a good one, and expensive. Your grandmother was a thrifty woman, but her savings quickly ran out. You sold her house and cashed in your college fund, but that money was soon gone as well. You got a job as a waitress and never turned down a chance to put in an extra shift. You cleaned houses and washed cars to supplement your income. But whatever you pulled in, it was always exceeded by the cost of your grandmother's care. You needed a way to earn a lot of money. You settled on taking your clothes off in front of strange men."

Garland Pickens paused to push his glasses up his nose with a thick forefinger. He crossed his legs. "You found a website that allows young women in that line of work to set up a profile and offer their services. You uploaded a few revealing pictures that, while not showing your face, left no doubt as to your physical shape and attractiveness. You began to get referrals. The money you earned went toward paying your grandmother's medical bills. I'm curious, did you limit yourself to taking your clothes off, or did your services extend beyond that?"

It was clear what he meant by that. Amber-May felt a flush spread across her cheeks and hated herself for it. She was aching all over now, a steady pain that pressed around her like bandaging around a mummy. It made her feel small, or maybe it was Pickens who did that. Maybe that was why he'd asked her that question. But she wasn't small or weak or helpless. She was going to defeat Pickens. She was going to send his clients to prison.

"Your clients can answer that question for you," she said. "Ask them how much they offered me to have sex with them."

"Perhaps I will."

"Then ask them what they did to me when I refused."

"I have a pretty good notion already."

"Then you know your clients are animals, that they belong behind bars."

"I can see why you'd think so. As their lawyer, my perspective is naturally different. That is what I'm here to discuss with you."

She gave him a long look. He did not seem even slightly empathetic to her suffering. "How can you represent such people?"

Pickens sighed. "Let's not waste time by discussing my morality, Miss Jackson. Why don't we get on with the business at hand? In exchange for you agreeing to put this sordid incident behind you, to not identify any of my clients to the police or the media or anyone else, and to never press charges or accuse them of any wrongdoing, I am authorized to offer you the annual sum of forty thousand dollars. That's tax-free dollars, Miss Jackson. Each year, for the next fifteen. How does that sound?"

"Fifteen years—why? Is that the statute of limitations on rape in this state?"

Pickens hoisted both eyebrows and gave Amber-May an appraising look, as though he had suddenly discovered something that prompted him to reconsider his earlier assessment of her.

"I may not have gone to college, Mr. Pickens, but I'm not a fool."

Pickens gave a curt nod. "Well?"

"The answer is no. Now it's time for you to leave."

"Will upping my offer change your mind?"

"No. I want your clients in prison. It's as simple as that."

Pickens breathed loudly through his nose and gave a tiny shake of his round head. An odd expression came over his face. He looked faintly melancholic. "I hate to break it to you, Miss Jackson, but there is no chance my clients will ever go to prison."

"Then why are you here?"

"To save them, and yourself, a great deal of pain and embarrassment. To safeguard all of your reputations. Allow me to describe what will happen if and when this case ever makes it to trial. You'll be exposed as a stripper and a prostitute. It won't matter whether the latter is true or not; I will have witnesses and evidence that will ensure the jury will believe that it is. I will paint you as promiscuous, degenerate, and money-hungry. I will plant the idea that your injuries are the result of a scheme by you and an accomplice, your pimp perhaps, to extract money from my clients in civil litigation or a pretrial settlement. None of the four men involved have criminal records. All are students with bright futures ahead of them. All come from good families—affluent, if not rich. Who do you think the jury will believe? A stripper and prostitute or four upstanding young men?"

He let the question hang in the air. To Amber-May it felt like the blade of a guillotine poised above her outstretched neck, ready to sweep down and slice off her life. The pain in her head and sternum rose a notch. She grabbed a fistful of bedsheets in her right hand, balling her fingers around the fabric.

Pickens said, "Our defense team will have the finest experts, all ready to testify on behalf of my clients and against you. By the time we get to jury deliberations, the jury may be more inclined to have you imprisoned rather than my clients."

Amber-May willed the pain to subside. It didn't. She drew on some inner reservoir of strength and said, "Your experts won't be able to explain away the rape kit that was taken from me. It will have your clients' DNA."

"Maybe it would have, but we'll never know. You see, a mishap at the police forensic lab has rendered the samples taken unusable as evidence. Contamination." Pickens shrugged. "That kind of thing shouldn't happen, but sometimes it does."

Amber-May could read the unspoken message Pickens was sending her. *I had someone at the lab contaminate the samples the same way I got access to your hospital files. Through bribery.*

She had no doubt he was telling her the truth. If she pressed charges, there would be no forensic evidence to support her accusations. The entire case would rest on her testimony, her character, and how the jury perceived her. Her work as a stripper would make it easy to paint her in a bad light. She squared her shoulders, took a deep breath, and directed her steady gaze at Pickens. When she spoke, it was with a voice steeled by resolve.

"Then I'll have to make sure the jury believes me, not you or your clients. I'll take that risk. Now get the hell out of here and don't show your face around here again."

Pickens made no move to leave. "Suffer my presence for a minute or two longer, Miss Jackson, as there are some things you are either unaware of or have failed to consider."

"What things?"

Pickens counted them off on his fingers. "One, while you are in the hospital, you are unable to work. Yet the monthly payments due to the nursing home do not halt. Two, the damage you suffered in the incident, especially to your face, will prohibit you from resuming your previous line of work after you're discharged. There's not much call for strippers with scarred cheeks and crooked noses. Three, your medical insurance will not come close to covering the costs related to your hospitalization, convalescence, and the extensive plastic surgery you will need. Four, you failed to disclose the income you derived from your stripping on your IRS forms last year. That means you committed a felony. I have some connections with the IRS. I will make sure they investigate you."

"I don't care," she said, hiding her fear. "I'll handle all of that. I'll manage somehow. It will be worth it to see your clients locked up."

Pickens raised a fifth finger, his hand like a stop sign informing her that she'd reached the end of the road. "Five, as of two days ago, the nursing home in which your grandmother resides is owned by Patrick MacBaxter. If you and I don't come to an agreement right now, I'll have your grandmother thrown out by the end of the week."

The silence that followed was almost as heavy as the one that had enveloped her when she woke up naked and hurt in the woods a few days earlier. She felt a great weight of panic pushing down on her, almost robbing her of breath.

In a tiny, incredulous voice she asked, "You would stoop so low as to throw a helpless, senile old woman out on the street just to get your rotten clients off?"

Garland Pickens did not even bat an eye before saying, "If you force me to, I will."

The panic-induced pressure around her increased. Soon it would crush her to a pulp. It was like a malevolent being, intent on destroying her. She closed her eyes and imagined herself healthy and whole and with gigantic biceps, sort of like the Incredible Hulk. Moving like a whirlwind, she punched at the invisible force that was closing around her—right hook, left jab, right uppercut—and each of the blows landed with resounding force. Yet the pressure did not yield, the panic did not abate. The old trick her mother had taught her had this time failed her.

For a second, she was certain blood was seeping past the bandaging on her head, but it was only sweat trickling down her forehead. Which was strange, because the rest of her, from the neck down, felt icy cold.

"And if I agree, what will happen to my grandmother?"

"She will not only be allowed to stay, but I'll make sure to upgrade her to her own room. And Mr. MacBaxter will bear all the costs. You wouldn't have to pay a penny. I have no wish to see your grandmother harmed in any way. Regardless of what you may think, I am not a monster, Miss Jackson."

"No," she said. "You only represent monsters."

Pickens ignored the insult. "Mr. MacBaxter will also pay for the best plastic surgeons in this state to make sure that all the cosmetic damage you suffered will be erased. You will have your face back, Miss Jackson. You'll be able to look forward to a bright future."

His voice was like a swarm of insects droning incessantly in her ears. It made it difficult to think. "Be quiet for a moment," she said with her eyes closed.

Pickens held his tongue. He let her consider her position in whatever form of peace she could find under the circumstances.

Amber-May ran the entire conversation through her mind, ignoring his offers, focusing instead on his threats. There was no denying that they scared her to death, but she decided she was willing to face them all for the chance of seeing the four men who had raped and beaten her go to prison. She was even willing to live for a while—perhaps a long while—with deformed facial features. She would work hard, save up, do whatever was needed, and eventually get the funds to have the damage fixed. Life would be a torment, but she would survive somehow.

What she was unwilling to do was to allow Grandma Betsy to be thrown out of her care facility. She would not be able to afford another of a similar quality. And she owed her grandmother so much. She deserved to live out her days in as much comfort as possible.

She opened her eyes. "How do I know you'll keep your end of the bargain?"

To his credit, Pickens did not smile or show any outward sign of reveling in his triumph. He merely replied, "You have my word, that's all. As for me, I insist that you sign an agreement that stipulates my clients have done you no harm." He reached inside his jacket and withdrew a folded document. From another pocket he produced a pen, which he proceeded to uncap. He handed both to Amber-May. "Just sign your name at the bottom of each page."

Amber-May took the pen and document. She set the pen on the bed beside her and began to read the agreement. She ran her eyes over the text, trying to focus on the words through the blur of tears welling in her one functioning eye. She was not crying because of what had been done to her, but because of what she was prevented from doing. She would not be allowed the basic right of having her wrongs redressed, of seeing justice done on her behalf. In a way, it was even more humiliating than the rape and assault themselves.

She was not aware of the manner in which her hand had closed into a fist, crumpling the agreement, until she heard Pickens's voice. "Miss Jackson. Miss Jackson!"

She blinked, looked at her hand, released her grip, and smoothed the agreement as best she could on the sheet. She picked up the pen and signed her name as Pickens had instructed. It was done. She felt a deep cold settle into her bones. Her empty hand was once again balled into a fist. It was all she could do to stop from visibly trembling.

"There," she said, striving to keep her voice level, "you can congratulate yourself on a job well done. Maybe you'll get a bonus."

Pickens retrieved his pen and the signed agreement, but did not put them away in his jacket. Instead, he gave Amber-May a long, contemplative look. Amber-May met his gaze without flinching.

"Is there a problem?"

Pickens kept staring at her for almost a minute, his thick lips pursed. Then he said, "One more thing. It's not written in the agreement, but consider it a requirement, just the same."

"What?"

"Once your recovery is complete, I want you to leave Boston and not return."

Amber-May's lips parted in surprise. "Why?"

"I think it would be best if you were not in the same locale as my clients. Best for all concerned."

Amber-May felt her stomach tighten. Her heart stuttered in her chest. "But I won't be able to visit Grandma Betsy."

"Unfortunately, that's correct. But rest assured, she'll receive the finest care available. You have my word on that. And besides, she doesn't remember your visits. It will make very little difference to her if you stop coming."

But it would mean a world of difference to me, she thought. Somewhere deep inside her mind a small voice—the voice of an eleven-year-old girl who had just learned both her parents had died in a car crash—was screaming, "No, no, no, NO!"

She was on the verge of pleading with him, of begging him to change his mind, to not demand this of her, to not leave her all alone in the world. But no way in hell was she going to do that. She wasn't going to give the bastard the satisfaction of seeing her grovel. Then a thought occurred to her. "You had everything planned in advance; you knew what I would say and how to counter it. The agreement was already written and ready to be signed."

"That's what good lawyers do."

"But you hadn't planned on asking me to leave the city. This is something that just came to you now. Why?"

Pickens shrugged. "I should have thought of it beforehand, I suppose. Be that as it may, I must insist on it."

She wasn't going to get a truthful answer from him. Not that it made any difference. It didn't matter what had led him to set this new condition. She was beaten. She had no choice but to accept his terms. For Grandma Betsy's sake.

"Fine. I'll leave. But I have a condition of my own."

His eyes narrowed. "And what might that be?"

"Relax, Mr. Pickens. It's a small thing. After the doctors fix me up, after I recover, I want to visit my grandmother one last time. I want to say goodbye and see that she's all right. Then I'll go away. Agreed?"

Pickens slid the signed agreement and pen back inside his suit. He nodded. "Agreed."

5

After Pickens had left, Amber-May was dead tired but couldn't fall asleep. She stayed awake as night gave way to dawn, as the early morning sun brightened the hospital room but did nothing to lighten the blackness of her mood. Shortly after eight that morning, a police detective named Theresa Sanchez came to take Amber-May's statement. Jolene came with her. Sanchez had soft feminine features and deep brown eyes. She told Amber-May she was safe now, that she could trust her, that she was there to listen to whatever Amber-May had to tell her.

Jolene gave Amber-May an encouraging smile. It made Amber-May sick to her stomach to have to disappoint her.

"I don't remember what happened to me," she said.

Sanchez frowned. Her eyes flicked to Jolene. Amber-May deduced that the nurse had told the detective to expect Amber-May to give her a complete report, including an identification of her assailants. "It was my impression that you knew who did this to you."

Amber-May shook her head. "I don't. I'm sorry."

"But..." Jolene began, "but last night you told me you did."

Amber-May could hardly bear looking at her. "I made a mistake. I was confused."

Sanchez said, "If you're scared someone's going to hurt you, Amber-May, I assure you we can keep you safe."

No, you can't, Amber-May thought. *You can't do anything.*

"I'm not scared. I just don't remember. I wish I did."

She could tell the detective wasn't buying it. For the next ten minutes, Sanchez tried to coax the information from her. At one point she said, "You know they'll do the same thing to other women. You can help prevent that. You can put them away."

But Amber-May kept repeating that she did not remember the attack, and finally Sanchez stood up with an exasperated sigh that said she had seen this kind of thing before but had never gotten used to it. She gave Amber-May her card. "If you change your mind, call me. Anytime."

Amber-May took the card, feeling ashamed. Hoping against hope, she said, "What about the rape kit? Couldn't that tell you who attacked me?"

By the way Detective Sanchez's eyes dropped to her shoes, Amber-May could tell that Pickens had told her the truth. All the samples taken with the rape kit were worthless. There was no evidence apart from what existed in her head, and she had signed away the right to share it with anyone. She was all alone with her pain and suffering. The realization was like sinking into a fathomless well, midnight black and soul smothering.

The look Jolene gave her after Sanchez left the room almost broke Amber-May to pieces. She was grateful when the nurse said nothing, walking out while shaking her head in sadness or disgust or both.

Jolene did not stop by again, not even to say goodbye later that day when Amber-May was wheeled out of her room, down the hall into an elevator, out of the hospital lobby, and into a waiting ambulance. The ambulance whisked her to a private hospital, where she was given a room on the fourth floor.

The room was big and spotless. Framed reproductions of watercolors adorned the walls. The equipment and furniture all looked shiny and new. The large window by her bed afforded a breathtaking view of a park with a pond at its center. Swans swam lazily across the water. Birds soared overhead. Sunlight made the lawn sparkle.

It was a view to calm even the most troubled of hearts, but it did little to soothe hers. As the sky darkened with the onset of night, she descended deeper into dejection. A little after midnight, she permitted herself the privilege of weeping. She wept until she was all cried out, and only then did she fall asleep.

But sleep did not bring with it any form of escape. It brought nightmares instead. Amber-May did not wake. She twisted and thrashed on the bed, pleading with the men who in her dreams reenacted their attack on her. She did not scream or raise her voice loud enough to arouse the attention of any of the hospital staff. She faced her demons all alone, as she knew she would have to do for the rest of her life.

6

Patrick MacBaxter stood at the window of his spacious office, thirty-nine floors above the downtown area, with his hands in his trouser pockets and his back to Garland Pickens. He said, "How did it go?"

Pickens stood before the immense oak desk, his hands clasped behind his back, his loafers sinking into the plush wall-to-wall carpeting. "According to plan, sir. She signed the papers and told the police she did not recall the attack."

"Will she keep her mouth shut?"

Pickens could have shrugged, but what would have been the point? With MacBaxter's back to him, no one would have seen the gesture. "I believe so, yes. But there is just one way to be absolutely sure of that."

MacBaxter turned sharply on his heel and leveled his tired gray eyes at his lawyer. His expression was stern. "We do many things, Garland, but killing women is not one of them. You know that."

Pickens accepted the rebuke by lowering his gaze in apparent contrition. In truth, he found the sight of Patrick MacBaxter hard to take. His boss, whom he loved as some men love their fathers, was waning fast. His six-foot-one frame, formerly as erect as a lamp post, now had a bend in it. His shoulders, once broad and straight, had narrowed and curled inward. His face, which had on many occasions graced the covers and inner pages of magazines and newspapers, had lost its manly, carved-rock lines. His cheeks were sunken, his eyes bottomed by puffy folds of skin the color of used teabags, his complexion sallow. Pickens knew that the suit his boss was wearing had been made to measure just two weeks earlier. Now it hung baggily on MacBaxter's dwindling frame.

Patrick MacBaxter was sixty-seven, fifteen years Pickens's senior, but until six months ago, he might have easily been mistaken for the lawyer's contemporary. These days, he looked an ailing eighty. Seeing the transformation never failed to strike gloom into Garland Pickens's heart.

MacBaxter said, "Is it the money that'll keep her quiet?"

"No, that wasn't it. And it wasn't our offer to pay her medical bills, either. It was the threat to her grandmother that made her see the wisdom of acquiescing to our demands."

"It's a good thing you found out about her, Garland."

As always when MacBaxter favored him with a compliment, Pickens felt a surge of pride. "It wasn't difficult; she wasn't keeping it secret. Once I realized how close the young lady felt toward her grandmother, I knew I'd found the perfect leverage."

MacBaxter stepped over to his desk chair and slowly lowered himself into it. Wincing, he adjusted his seating position. He rarely displayed any sign of the pain his illness was causing him. He was a strong man who disliked showing weakness. Over forty years of experience in the cutthroat world of American business had instilled in him the belief that showing weakness invited attack by one's competitors.

Leaning back gingerly in his chair, MacBaxter said, "Let's toast your success, Garland. There's an unopened bottle of Macallan over there. Fetch it, will you?"

Pickens went over to the well-stocked drinks cabinet, found the bottle, and brought it and two empty tumblers to MacBaxter's desk. He uncapped the bottle and poured two generous measures. Taking one of the drinks, he seated himself in one of the two chairs before the desk. The scotch held the pleasant aroma of barley and aged wood. Its color was golden brown. Pickens knew that the bottle had cost upwards of three thousand dollars. Worthy of a special occasion.

MacBaxter held up his tumbler. "To you, Garland."

Pickens accepted the toast in humble silence. He sipped his drink. MacBaxter downed half of his in one swallow. He gazed thoughtfully at Pickens from across the desk. "It's a dirty business sometimes, isn't it?"

Pickens nodded. "Often it doesn't work any other way. As you taught me, first you offer a sweet carrot, and if that doesn't work, you bring out the heavy stick."

MacBaxter smiled. Pickens noted how, in the hollow gauntness of his boss's face, the smile held an eerie resemblance to the vacant grin of a toothy skull.

The cancer that had spread its poisonous tentacles throughout MacBaxter's body had first made itself known nearly two years prior during a routine checkup. An aggressive strain, it resisted all the treatments the doctors prescribed, conventional and experimental, until they were forced to concede defeat. They gave MacBaxter six months to live.

That had been nine months ago. One might be forgiven for feeling hope due to the fact that MacBaxter had proved the doctors wrong by surviving past his expiration date, but Pickens was under no such illusions. His boss and mentor was at death's door. One of these days, the door would swing open and MacBaxter would be snatched to the other side.

And once that happened, Pickens would have to serve a lesser master.

MacBaxter took another sip, the smile gone from his lips. "How badly hurt was the girl?"

"A few broken bones, some internal injuries, scars and cuts on her face."

"Anything they can't fix?"

"Most of it they can, but they had to remove her spleen."

MacBaxter shook his head. "Goddamn it. Does it mean she's an invalid, not having a spleen?"

"No. She'll have to make some adjustments, but overall she'll be able to lead a regular life."

"Good. That's good. Garland, I want you to make sure she gets the best treatment available. No skimping, you got it? This is our responsibility."

"I'll make sure of it, sir."

MacBaxter downed the rest of his scotch and motioned for Pickens to refill his glass. He took a sip from the fresh drink and sighed—whether in contentment or irritation, Pickens wasn't sure. "And I'll have a talk with Emmett. This kind of thing, it can't happen again. It won't."

Pickens raised his glass to his mouth, obscuring his face, but MacBaxter caught his expression.

"Did I ever tell you the story about my grandfather Duncan?"

"Which one? I've heard and read quite a few." Duncan had featured prominently in several books that had been written about the MacBaxters and the ebb and flow of their fortunes in the nearly two centuries of their presence in North America.

"Well, you haven't heard this one, I bet. It's not the sort of thing we publicize. As you know, when Duncan assumed control of the family business following his father's death, there wasn't much of the business left. Duncan's father was a wasteful, good-for-nothing imbecile. He had a natural instinct for bad deals. It's a good thing he died relatively young or the family would've gone bankrupt."

MacBaxter took another swallow of scotch and smacked his lips. One of the things that had not deteriorated along with his health was his voice, which remained strong and full. If Pickens closed his eyes, he could imagine that MacBaxter's cancer was nothing but a bad dream.

"Duncan is remembered as the man who revitalized the family company and became a titan of industry and a renowned philanthropist. Plaques with his name adorn buildings across this country to this day. All this I'm sure you know."

Pickens acknowledged the truth of that assumption with a nod.

"What you're probably not aware of is the sort of man Duncan was before he took the helm of the company. He was, to use a word more common in those days, a scoundrel. He drank heavily, made all sorts of mischief, patronized prostitutes, and bedded any woman he could lay his hands on. In all likelihood, his methods of courtship included tactics that today would be considered criminal. In one instance, they surely did."

MacBaxter finished his second drink, but did not ask for another. He held the empty tumbler in his right hand, resting it on the arm of his chair. With the left he rubbed his jaw.

"The girl's name is not important. She was young, pretty, and from a good family, though not an affluent one. She was undoubtedly a virgin. In those days most unmarried women of her age were. I don't suppose this girl, the one you talked to, is a virgin. I wonder if that makes it easier on her."

"I wouldn't know, sir."

"No, how would you? Anyway, the girl I was telling you about, Duncan took her against her will. Forcibly. He left her defiled and hurt. I don't know precisely what her injuries were, but they were severe. It took a good deal of money, back-scratching, and arm-twisting to keep the whole thing hushed up. Just about what you did with the girl Emmett mishandled."

You mean raped, Pickens thought, remembering how Amber-May Jackson had corrected him when he referred to what had happened to her as an *incident*.

"The girl never fully recovered," MacBaxter said, "and my grandfather was never the same either. When he told me about this secret episode of his life, he said it was like a hammer had come down on his head, knocking all of the youthful stupidity and selfishness out of him. He became a different man, a better man. The sort of man he needed to be to revive the family business. He also became generous, kind, and giving. Do you understand what I'm getting at, Garland?"

Pickens opened his mouth to answer, but MacBaxter was already forging ahead.

"Emmett can be the same. He will be the same. He made a mistake, committed a terrible sin, but he's young, just twenty-three years old. I don't want one horrible mistake to ruin his life, to stop him from becoming the man he's destined to be. Do you see, Garland? Do you see?"

Pickens didn't like the keen desperation in MacBaxter's voice. He'd never heard it before in the twenty-five years in which he'd been the man's lawyer, adviser, and confidant. Was it another symptom of the disease that was ravaging MacBaxter's body? Or a weakening of spirit in the face of impending death? Or maybe it was a desire to believe something that MacBaxter worried was not true. Either way, Pickens didn't like it. Nor did he like the wide-eyed, distraught expression on the older man's face. He took a long sip, corralled his agitated thoughts, and replied simply, "Yes, sir. I think I do."

"Good," MacBaxter said, his face returning to its familiar controlled countenance. "Because I've been cheating death for quite a while now. I doubt I'll be able to continue doing it for much longer. And when I'm gone, I want Emmett to take over MacBaxter Holdings. I want the company to remain in the family, the way it's been for five generations."

Pickens knew all that. He had drafted MacBaxter's will himself. All of the stock his boss owned was to go to Emmett. Since MacBaxter owned nearly all of the stock in the company, Emmett would become president and CEO of MacBaxter Holdings.

"So I want you to stay on top of this thing, to control the situation in case the girl suddenly has second thoughts about staying quiet."

"I'll see to it."

"I'm counting on it. And I'm also counting on you to help Emmett when the time comes. I've taught him quite a bit, as much as I could given this rotten disease, but things will be different when it becomes his responsibility, when he has to make decisions himself."

"I'll help in any way I can, sir."

"You'll have your work cut out for you. Emmett is young and inexperienced, and as this mess with the girl shows, he needs to learn how to control his impulses. In an ideal world, he'd have finished his graduate degree and joined me for a few years to learn the ropes properly. But there won't be time for that. And he's my son, which means that it's his destiny to take this company forward. I want him and the company to succeed and grow together."

Pickens said nothing. Not for the first time, he wondered if he'd erred in not revealing to his boss the other instances in which he'd intervened on Emmett's behalf. Like the time he got a young woman so drunk she had to be hospitalized, or when he broke a guy's jaw when the guy tried to stop Emmett from hitting on his girlfriend. Pickens had kept those incidents to himself, thinking that they'd prove an unnecessary burden on MacBaxter, given his illness. After each such occurrence, Emmett had promised Pickens that he'd stay out of trouble from then on, but obviously those had been empty words.

MacBaxter leaned forward, resting both forearms on the desk and snaring Pickens's eyes with his own. "Swear to me, Garland, that once I'm gone, you'll serve my company and my son. Swear."

Pickens had the urge to tell his boss the whole truth about his son —that he was an unstable, prone-to-violence young man, but he knew it was no use. Emmett was an only child, the solitary fruit of MacBaxter's third marriage, after the first two had failed to produce any offspring. All of MacBaxter's legacy—the continuation of his line, the preservation of his family name, the future success of his business—hinged on Emmett. He wouldn't accept anything that got in the way of that vision. Not even from his most trusted adviser.

Besides, what choice did he have in the matter? Emmett was going to be the owner of MacBaxter Holdings, and Pickens had given his whole professional life to advancing and expanding the company's fortunes. He would either be there, at Emmett's side, or he would cease to be a part of the company he loved. That was a fate he could scarcely bare to contemplate.

Which meant that to continue serving the company, he would need to serve Emmett as well.

Pickens drew a deep breath and said, "I swear."

Then he knocked back the rest of his scotch.

7

The first two days she wouldn't eat.

It wasn't that the food was bad. Whoever said hospital food was lousy had obviously never spent a day in the private hospital Amber-May was in. She just wasn't hungry. It was as though that need had been shut off, erased, cut out of her system.

She knew it was a symptom of her mental state. She was depressed. It wasn't the rape or having to look forward to spending months in the hospital. It wasn't the pain that flared up whenever her pain medication started to wear off. It wasn't even the fear that she would spend the rest of her days with ugly scars on her face. It was surrendering to Pickens that had laid her low. It was the knowledge that the four men who had molested her would remain free, without a blemish to their names, that had cast a pall on her.

The nurses tried to bring her out of it. They told her she had to eat, to regain her strength, to give fuel to the recovery process. When that didn't work, they called in a psychiatrist to talk to her. The psychiatrist was Asian and gentle in both features and voice, and she probed and pried into Amber-May's state of mind and did her best to persuade her to start eating.

Which Amber-May did on the third day. But it wasn't due to the nurses' cajoling or the psychiatrist's coaxing—though she rapidly tired of both. And it wasn't because she suddenly felt hungry again. It was a decision she came to rationally. It was a form of defiance.

If she didn't eat, she would be sabotaging her own recovery, and this would be punishing no one but herself. Worse, it would be a further capitulation to her tormentors. Besides, she hated the fact that every day she was in the hospital was a day she was living on Patrick MacBaxter's dime. She wasn't going to refuse the treatments he was paying for; she had a right to them, and she knew she needed them. But what she wanted more than anything was to be through with her recovery and out of the hospital. She wanted to see Grandma Betsy, and then she wanted to get on with her life as best she could.

So she ate, hardly tasting the food, not deriving much pleasure from it. It was sustenance, nothing more, building material that her body needed to repair itself. Once she could get out of bed on her own, she took to going on long meandering solitary walks up and down the hospital corridors and out in the gardens that surrounded it. She was weak at first, but she gradually regained her strength.

She underwent a number of cosmetic surgeries to fix the damage done to her face. The doctors reconstructed her cheekbone, straightened her nose, and smoothed out the scars that marred her chin, forehead, and cheeks. They implanted false teeth in place of the ones that had been knocked out of her mouth during the attack. She spent much of the next three months with one sort of facial bandaging or another, in constant dread over what she'd look like once the surgeries were finally over and done with. A part of her wanted to be ugly so no man would ever bother her again. But that was a small part. Mostly, she wanted to return to the way she'd once been, to regain her beauty.

She kept mostly to herself during her stay. Having her own room meant she didn't have regular contact with other patients. Those she passed in the corridors or in the gardens she greeted with a short "hello" or "good day," but never initiated any conversation beyond that. In the few times in which another patient tried to engage her in a chat, she quickly extricated herself, making up some excuse—an appointment with one of the doctors, having to replenish her supply of pain medication, not feeling well and going to lie down in her room.

The medical staff were all nice, polite, and caring. A couple of the nurses inquired as to her history and what she planned on doing once she was released from the hospital. Amber-May kept her answers vague. She trusted none of the staff. She suspected one or more of them was on Pickens's payroll. Anything she said was likely to reach the lawyer's ears before long.

In truth, she had no plans. Nothing definite. All she knew was that she'd go visit Grandma Betsy one last time, to say goodbye and make sure that Pickens was keeping his end of the bargain. Then she would leave Boston.

Apart from not being able to visit Grandma Betsy, she had no problem with leaving. The city held no emotional significance to her. Her attack overshadowed all the good times she'd had there. Now it was a place she wanted to forget, to be somewhere far away, where she could hopefully feel safe again.

Her mood swung between dejection and rage. At times she felt like staying in bed for the rest of her life, with the curtains drawn and the lights off. She wanted to see no one, talk with no one, to be left alone to wallow in her misery. Every now and then, she had bouts of intense weeping that shook her body and left her exhausted. At other times, the anger she felt was like a high-voltage current, buzzing through her system, making her muscles clench to the point of aching.

She hated herself for having been assaulted. She blamed herself for disregarding the signs that indicated the four men who'd hired her to strip in their little party had in mind a different sort of entertainment. She felt guilty for failing to stop the attack, for not fighting hard enough. The rational side of her knew she was not at fault. She had fought, and fought hard, which was how she'd sustained her injuries, but what hope did she have against four men?

Her rage was not directed merely at herself. Some of it was aimed at her attackers. In her dreams, she saw their vicious faces, heard their cackling laughs, felt the repulsive touch of their sweaty hands. A few times, when she was trudging along the footpaths on the hospital grounds, she was sure she spotted one or more of them. An acute fear gripped her then, a certainty that they had come to finish the job, to beat her until she was dead. She usually froze when that happened, robbed of breath, until she saw that the persons she mistook for her attackers were just a pair of doctors or a patient out for a stroll with a visitor.

Her rage was augmented by her impotence. She could do nothing to these men. She had given up her right to have them prosecuted for their crimes. She knew she had made the right decision—for Grandma Betsy's sake—but that did not alleviate the pulsing helpless anger that consumed her. If she wanted to rebuild her life, she would have to cope with this anger. She doubted she would ever be able to let it go completely, not to mention forgive and forget, but she would need to learn how to live with it. She hoped that one day she'd be able to do that, but it was too soon. She would worry about that after she got out of the hospital, after she left the city.

Her final surgery took place ten weeks after her admittance. The bandages came off a week later. Without warning, a nurse held a hand mirror in front of her face before Amber-May could avert her eyes. The sight of her reflection made her wince. Her face was puffy and full of purple splotches. The doctors assured her that once the swelling receded, she would look better. All the surgeries went well, they claimed.

One evident improvement was her hair. It had grown back and now fell past her shoulders in a lush cascade of wavy, jet-black tresses. Running a tentative hand through it, she found it to be dry and tangled. Upon her request, the nurses supplied her with a top-line conditioner, a moisturizer spray, and a hairbrush. She took to caring for her hair each morning after breakfast and each night before she turned in, until she'd returned it to its former glossy glory. She found the routine soothing; it took her mind off other things.

She avoided looking at the mirror, remembering the bruising and swelling she'd seen after the last bandages had been removed. She dreaded seeing the final results of her surgeries, knowing that, whatever they were, she would have to live with them.

But one day, after her doctor informed her that all the swelling was gone, she could postpone it no longer. She climbed out of bed and walked shakily into the adjoining bathroom and raised her eyes to the mirror over the sink. Her breath caught as she witnessed the new her.

The face that stared back at her was not that different from the one she'd possessed before the attack. Her nose was a trifle thinner, her cheekbones a bit more pronounced, the skin a touch tauter. But it was clearly her face. No one who knew her from before would mistake her for anyone else.

She examined herself from multiple angles, scrutinizing every inch of her face. All the scars were gone and the color of her false teeth matched that of her natural ones. No overt sign of her trauma remained. Her face was unmarred. And beautiful. In fact, she couldn't make up her mind which face was more beautiful—the new one or the old.

And after several minutes in which she eyed herself, looking for signs of wear and tear and finding none, she did something she hadn't done since the day she entered the hospital. She smiled.

It felt strange, as though she were a baby taking its first uncertain steps. Like a muscle that hadn't been used in a long while, her lips took their time to find their path as they stretched. The surgeons had done good work; the smile looked natural and very attractive.

Relief washed over her, making her legs unsteady so she had to brace herself on the bathroom sink. She lowered her head, eyes closed, and took deep breaths. The emotional scars could not be smoothed by any scalpel, but she wouldn't be deformed for life. She had that, at least.

8

Garland Pickens was in his office, going through that day's large pile of paperwork at his usual, tornado-wind speed, when his phone rang. The voice on the other end was female and middle-aged. He recognized it instantly. It was one of the nurses from the hospital where Amber-May Jackson was staying.

"You asked to be informed as to any developments. She's being released tomorrow morning."

Pickens thanked her and promised that her final payment would be wired to her account later that day. He hung up but didn't set down the phone. Instead he tapped in a number, waited while it rang twice, and asked the man who answered to come by his office as soon as he could.

"Clear everything, Freddie. I got a job for you. Top dollar."

Freddie Sheehan said he was currently out of the city. They agreed to meet in ninety minutes.

As usual, Freddie was punctual. Eighty-eight minutes after their conversation ended, Pickens's secretary buzzed the private investigator into the office.

Freddie had a cigarette burning. Pickens heard his secretary rebuke the detective for smoking in the building, to which Freddie responded by blowing a jet of smoke in her general direction before shutting the door and turning toward Pickens. He was wearing black jeans over a pair of steel-toed boots that elevated his five-ten frame by two solid inches. His jacket was black and unbuttoned. Under it, he had on a dark gray cotton T-shirt. He wore no tie.

He strode toward Pickens's desk and dropped onto a chair without a word of greeting. He lounged in the seat, his legs stretched out in front of him. He drew in a drag, blew out a puff of gray smoke, and said, "What's on your mind, Mr. Pickens?"

Pickens slid an empty saucer across his desk. "Here. Don't get ash on the carpet."

Grinning, Freddie tapped some ash onto the saucer. "You said you had a job for me?"

Pickens eyed the man critically. He didn't like Freddie Sheehan all that much. He didn't like his clothes or the way he oiled and slicked back his hair or the dusting of black stubble on his cheeks and chin. When Pickens had still possessed hair of his own, he had always kept it short and parted neatly on the side and never put a drop of oil on it, not even in his more rebellious teens. And each morning before he left home, he made sure to run a razor over his face.

He also didn't like Freddie's eyes—murky and crafty—like a rodent always on the lookout for more food to scrounge. Particularly, he didn't like his wise-guy attitude, as if Freddie found everyone he encountered a cause for mocking, barely concealed amusement.

But Freddie was damn good at his job, and he worked alone and knew how to keep his mouth shut. Which was why Pickens had turned to him instead of the detective agency he'd hired to probe into Amber-May Jackson's life the day he learned of what Emmett MacBaxter and his pals had done to her. Back then he'd had no choice. He'd needed quick results, and the only way to get them was to employ a large team. This time, he didn't want a lot of people involved. The more people who were in on something, the greater the chance of it coming out.

And Freddie could handle this assignment on his own. It wouldn't even be hard.

"There's someone I want you to follow," Pickens said.

Freddie said nothing. His eyes, half-open, peered at Pickens through the smoke, waiting for him to continue.

"A young lady. Her name is Amber-May Jackson. Here's a picture of her." He handed Freddie a head shot of the girl. Freddie took a look, and Pickens noted how his eyes widened as he absorbed the beauty of Amber-May Jackson's face. "I'm told she looks almost exactly like that picture."

Freddie gave him a questioning look. "What does that mean?"

"She's had some plastic surgery done. I don't have a current picture, but I understand the differences are minimal. Besides, I'm going to tell you where she'll be tomorrow morning, so you can see her for yourself."

Freddie studied the picture again. "A woman like her, she's got no need for surgery."

There was a question there somewhere, but Pickens ignored it. There was nothing to gain by providing Freddie with the details of Amber-May Jackson's injuries and what had led to them.

"She's being released tomorrow from the hospital. Her car is in the parking lot." He gave Freddie the address of the hospital and the plate number and make of the car. "She's got one stop to make. After that, she's supposed to leave the city."

Freddie asked where she was headed, and Pickens said he didn't know. "It's not important to me where she goes, only that she does. That's why I'm hiring you, to make sure she leaves and stays away."

Freddie took a final pull on his cigarette and crushed its life out. He scratched his neck, where the top curve of a coiling blue and red tattoo was peeking over the collar of his shirt. Was it a snake? Pickens couldn't tell for sure. "Anything I need to know about her to do my job?" Freddie asked.

This was what Pickens liked most about Freddie Sheehan. He was only as curious as he needed to be, and he wasn't a man prone to idle talk. Though Pickens had known Freddie professionally for over eight years, he had no inkling as to the man's hobbies, tastes, or any of the myriad trivial details people tend to reveal about themselves in the course of regular conversation. Freddie kept his life to himself and didn't pry into anyone else's—unless he got paid to do so.

"No. And you don't need to do any digging, either. I know all I need to know about Miss Jackson. You just keep an eye on her and report to me where she goes, what she does, who she sees. That's all."

"How long you want me to tail her?"

Pickens had asked himself the very same question, and he gave Freddie the answer he'd settled on. "I don't know yet. Consider this an open-ended assignment."

Freddie had his eyes once more on the picture. His lips curled in a sly smile. "Fine by me. Most people I follow don't look half as good as her."

Pickens raised an admonitory finger. "Just so we're clear: you are not to talk to her under any circumstances. I don't want her to know she's being followed. Got it?"

The smile stayed on Freddie's lips just a little too long for Pickens's liking. Then the detective slid the picture inside his jacket, giving Pickens a glimpse of a large-caliber pistol hanging in a shoulder holster. He stood up. "You know my fee, right? And you'll cover my expenses?"

"You'll get your money, Freddie. Have we ever had a problem?"

"Nah, you're all right." Freddie raised two fingers to his forehead in a mock salute. "Don't worry, Mr. Pickens. I'm on it."

Then he turned and left the office, a fresh cigarette lit by the time he walked by the desk of Garland Pickens's secretary.

9

The next day, there was a sealed manila envelope waiting for Amber-May at the nurses' station. Her name was printed on the back in large block letters.

"Who left this for me?" she asked the duty nurse.

"I don't know. It was here when I started my shift."

Amber-May took the envelope and found a deserted corner with a few chairs clustered around a low table. She sat down and opened the envelope. Inside was a ring of keys and a folded piece of paper. She recognized the keys. They were for her beat-up 1998 Ford Fiesta. She unfolded the paper and read it.

It was printed and unsigned and lacked a letterhead, but she knew who it came from. Garland Pickens. The note explained that her car was parked in the hospital parking lot and that her clothes and other belongings were in the trunk. The rent on her apartment had been paid in full, as had all her outstanding utility bills. Her first payment of forty thousand dollars had been deposited in her new bank account. The account number and access code were listed, followed by a recommendation that she memorize them and destroy the note so it wouldn't fall into the wrong hands. It ended with a brief, formal line wishing her a bright and successful future.

And that was it. No mention of the rape, the assault, the months of painful and fear-ridden hospital stay. Not a word of apology or concern for her well-being. Just a cold, emotionless message—like a company memo. Or a notice of termination.

Teeth clenched, Amber-May tore the paper into tiny pieces, then dumped them in a nearby trash can. She didn't go through her room one last time. There was nothing she could have left behind. She marched to the elevators, ignoring the nurse's anxious calls asking her to wait for an attendant to wheel her out in a wheelchair. She didn't want to wait. She couldn't stand the thought of staying in that hospital one second longer. She walked as fast as she could out of the building and onto the sun-baked asphalt of the parking lot.

The note had told her the exact spot where her car would be. It infuriated her that Pickens had sent someone to her apartment, to pack her things into her car and drive it to the hospital—all without her knowledge or consent. It was another violation, an added insult. Perhaps it was intended to convey the impression that Pickens was all powerful, that his people could go wherever they wanted, enter wherever they wished. She told herself it was no use losing her temper over this. Compared to everything else that had been done to her, this was but a minor offense.

Whoever had driven her car had taken the trouble to have it washed. It didn't improve its appearance much. There were too many dents and scrapes for that, too much faded paint.

The door was unlocked, the interior spotless and smelling like fresh pine. Amber-May felt a sudden bout of dizziness as the scent hit her nostrils. It was all too similar to the smell of the woods where she had regained consciousness naked and alone all those months ago. She leaned against the side of the car, eyes screwed shut, until the dizzy spell ended. Then she climbed inside.

The keys were under the floor mat on the passenger's side. The car started without a hiccup. She hadn't driven for months, but the old car was as familiar as a broken-in pair of running shoes. She followed the exit signs, barely noticing the sigh that bubbled out of her the instant she was finally off the hospital grounds. A chapter had closed. A dark one. She hoped the one that was now beginning would prove to be brighter.

The day was sunny and balmy. She drove with the windows open, the fresh breeze feeling good on her face. The roads were not busy and she made good time, arriving at the nursing home where Grandma Betsy lived in just over thirty minutes.

She parked and locked the car and entered the building. Riding the elevator to the fourth floor, she realized how much she had missed Grandma Betsy and that she hadn't allowed herself to feel that way throughout her hospitalization.

The duty nurse, a soft-faced lean woman in her early fifties called Martha Mitchum, looked surprised to see her.

"Aren't you a sight for sore eyes. How long has it been, Amber-May? You used to come visiting so often; I was worried something had happened to you."

"I've been away," Amber-May said, putting on a false smile. She liked Martha Mitchum. She was a good nurse, caring and affectionate, and she treated Grandma Betsy with kindness. Amber-May disliked having to lie to her, but the truth was out of bounds.

Martha peered closely at her. "Something's different about you, but I can't put my finger on it."

"I've lost a couple of pounds, that's all. Is Grandma awake?"

"She was the last time I stepped by her room. It's the new one we moved her to a while back, in the corner with a good view of the trees." Martha eyed her speculatively. "You must be doing well; that's quite an expensive room."

Amber-May said nothing, which Martha mistook for a rebuke.

"I'm sorry, Amber-May. I didn't mean to snoop."

Amber-May told her it was all right and started walking toward Grandma Betsy's room. Idly, she wondered where Martha thought her newfound wealth had come from.

Probably thinks I've got a rich boyfriend. Or a sugar daddy paying my bills in exchange for sex. She felt her lips curl in a humorless smile. *You're right in a way, Martha, but you also couldn't be more wrong if you tried.*

The new room was twice as big as Grandma Betsy's old one, and she didn't have to share it with another resident. On the wall opposite the bed hung a large TV, and off to the left by the windows was a seating set that included a two-seater couch and a couple of cream-colored easy chairs. Grandma Betsy was sitting quietly on the couch, facing the large windows. Sunlight streamed in through the glass, bathing her diminutive form in warm illumination. Amber-May stood transfixed in the doorway, a lump the size of a baseball forming in her throat, as she gazed at her grandmother's half profile.

Grandma Betsy's hands were folded in her lap. Her eyes were closed and her breathing was slow and steady. Amber-May wasn't sure what to do—should she go inside and wake her grandmother or wait outside the room for her to wake on her own?

The decision was made for her. All of a sudden, as though alerted by some sixth sense, Grandma Betsy's eyes fluttered open, and she turned her head to peer in Amber-May's direction. Her eyes—an eternal, youthful blue—blinked twice. Then a broad smile spread across her face, as warm as a down comforter.

"Amber-May, is that you?"

Amber-May couldn't speak. She nodded shakily.

Grandma Betsy stretched out her hand. "Well, why are you standing there like a frightened kitty? Come in, dear."

Amber-May entered and clasped her grandmother's hand in her own. Grandma Betsy's fingers felt tiny and fragile, her skin paper-thin. Amber-May released the hand, sat down beside her grand-mother, kissed her wrinkled cheek, and pulled her into a long, tight embrace. The old woman's breath tickled the side of her neck. She smelled like soap and the citrus-scented perfume she dabbed on herself every day for as long as Amber-May could remember. But more than that, she smelled like love and family.

When she finally let go, Grandma Betsy laughed delightedly and said, "That was the nicest hug I've had in my life." She patted Amber-May's cheek with abundant affection. "Thank you, dear. Now tell me, how did your math test go today?"

Inexplicably, the disease that had robbed her grandmother of much of her memory, and made a jumble of all that remained, had never deprived her of the ability to recognize people, her grand-daughter among them. Everything else, including her sense of time, was shaky and vagrant, here one day and gone the next.

Amber-May didn't know which math test Grandma Betsy was referring to. It could have been one she'd taken in the seventh grade or her senior-year finals. Her heart sank. She was familiar with her grandmother's wandering mind, but she'd never gotten used to it.

"I'm finished with school, Grandma."

A look of bewilderment came over Grandma Betsy's face. Then she smiled. "Of course you are. You'll be going to college soon. I'm very excited for you, dear. You're going to have a wonderful time."

Amber-May smiled back. She couldn't bring herself to shatter her grandmother's delusions. If she told her she'd had to cancel her plans of attending college, she would have to explain why. She didn't want to saddle Grandma Betsy with guilt. She was going through enough as it was.

"Did your mother call, by any chance?" Grandma Betsy asked suddenly, frowning. "She told me she would be back in half an hour, and that was three hours ago. The turkey I made will get cold."

Amber-May could feel her eyes grow moist. Grandma Betsy not only had a shaky sense of time, but also of place. She must have been thinking she was at her old house, the one Amber-May had been forced to sell to cover part of the cost of the nursing home. "Mom's passed away, don't you remember? In a car accident. Nine years ago." She knew that what she was doing was futile, but she couldn't help it. A tiny ridiculous part of her never gave up hope that her grand-mother would one day snap out of her illness, regain her mind and memory, and return to be the sharp-witted woman she once was.

This would never happen. There was no recovery from Alzheimer's, no improvement, just continued decline. But she still clung to the irrational belief that a miracle would happen, that Grandma Betsy would one day be healed. This was why she kept reminding her of reality, because she hoped that would somehow do the trick.

Sadness clouded Grandma Betsy's eyes. She lowered them to her hands. "Oh. You're right, of course. It...it slipped my mind."

Amber-May put her arm around Grandma Betsy's thin shoulders and kissed her on the side of the head. "It's okay, Grandma. It's all right."

Grandma Betsy took a deep breath, looked out the window for a moment, then turned back to face her. The sadness was gone. She'd forgotten all about the accident. She looked pleasantly surprised. "Amber-May? I didn't hear you come in. It's so nice to see you."

Amber-May swallowed and faked a smile. "You too, Grandma."

"I was thinking about you earlier today. I had a feeling you'd stop by. How have you been? What's new?"

Amber-May felt an intense desire to tell her grandmother everything that had happened to her, to cry on her shoulder like she used to do in her teens whenever something dreadful had occurred. But what would be the point? Grandma Betsy could no longer help her. And the only thing opening up to her would do was hurt her. She would soon forget what Amber-May told her, but Amber-May did not wish to inflict even a minute's worth of pain on her grandmother. It would be selfish and purposeless.

She was so immersed in her thoughts that she failed to register what Grandma Betsy had said to her. "Huh?"

A look of deep concern was etched on Grandma Betsy's face. "I asked what was troubling you, dear."

"Oh, it's nothing, Grandma. You don't need to worry about me."

"Is it the Duggins boy again?"

Amber-May frowned. "What?"

"Is Sam Duggins bothering you again?"

It had been five years since Amber-May had last thought about Sam Duggins and six since she'd last seen him, but she remembered him very well. He had been in her class in junior high, a big kid with bad skin and eyes that were only slightly less mean than his disposition.

Sam Duggins had bad grades and few hobbies other than terrorizing his schoolmates. He mostly bullied the smaller, weaker boys, but on occasion he targeted girls, too. In fact, it appeared that as Sam Duggins entered puberty and discovered girls, he sensed the years of female rejection that were likely to befall him and was taking out his frustration in advance. One of the girls he set his sights on was Amber-May.

She never knew why he'd chosen her. Perhaps it was due to her breasts, which at age fourteen were already full. The one time she asked him why he was bothering her, a look of stupid confusion came over him, and he gave her the only answer he could probably think of. "Because I feel like it, that's why."

He proceeded to taunt her mercilessly. He called her names, some of which stuck and were echoed by other kids. He made nasty remarks about her looks and speculated on her being sexually promiscuous. He pulled her ponytail a few times and got into the habit of sneaking up behind her to snap her bra straps painfully. He knocked her books out of her hands and, one time, accidentally-on-purpose, spilled his carton of milk on her back during lunch hour.

She endured his bullying without complaining to the teachers. That was a social taboo in her school. She wasn't very popular; she would never have been able to live with being tagged a snitch. He would soon tire of her, she told herself. He would turn to another victim.

But the days dragged into weeks and he didn't relent. In fact, his name-calling only became more toxic, the sneer on his face when-ever he caught her eye more threatening. With an odd sense of shame, she turned to Grandma Betsy for help.

At first Grandma Betsy was adamant about talking to the school staff about Sam Duggins; she didn't work at that school, but she knew some of the teachers. It took Amber-May an entire evening to talk her out of it.

Grandma Betsy knew the Duggins family and had taught some of Sam's siblings. His mother had left home when Sam was little, and his father was a foul-mouthed drunk who was probably the reason Sam had turned out the way he did. There was no point in appealing to him to rein in his son.

"I can put the scare into the little shit if you want," Grandma Betsy said.

Amber-May stared at Grandma Betsy in shock. She could not remember her clean-spoken grandmother ever using that word before.

"But," Grandma Betsy continued, "it would probably be better if you did it yourself."

"Myself?"

"Yes."

"But he's so much bigger than me."

"So what? That doesn't mean you shouldn't face him. That's what you do with people like Sam Duggins—you face them, you fight them, you hurt them so they'll leave you alone."

Like a hot coal, the notion that she could, and should, confront Sam Duggins stayed with Amber-May for the following week, but it likely would have guttered out if not for Duggins himself.

This time when he crept behind her, he didn't limit himself to snapping her bra but reached around her to cup her breasts. She jumped, nearly tripping, and spun to face him. They were in the schoolyard, not a teacher in sight, a gaggle of pupils already forming a ring around them, sensing that something interesting was about to occur.

Amber-May could feel the red flush that colored her cheeks. She felt naked in front of the crowd of spectators. Sam Duggins was grinning, puffing out his chest, basking in all the attention.

"Don't do that," she said, her voice vibrating with fear and humiliation.

His grin widened, exposing a set of teeth badly in need of braces. "Why? You like that, don't you, you little cunt."

Some of the gathering pupils gasped, and some snickered. Amber-May felt her face grow hotter still. Her legs were trembling. She wanted to run away, but in her mind she heard Grandma Betsy's voice, exhorting her to stand her ground, to fight.

Sam Duggins took a step toward her and then another. He reached out a large hand, making a squeezing motion. She took a step back. He laughed. Something dark entered his eyes. He took another step forward. He was close, almost within touching distance.

Amber-May couldn't say what it was, but something came over her. Her sensory field narrowed, becoming focused on Sam Duggins. She no longer saw or heard the watching crowd of schoolmates. All she saw and heard was the boy coming to torment her. Her muscles tensed like a taut rubber band. Rage boiled in the pit of her stomach, a pressure that begged to be released, and without thinking about it, she let it loose by drawing her foot back and kicking forward and up.

Her shoe connected solidly with Sam Duggins's crotch. His mouth formed a perfect oval, emitting a half-stifled groan. He folded in half, falling to the ground on his side, his hands clutching his crushed privates as he squirmed in pain, finding no comfort.

Then came a wave of sound. A hundred teenagers laughing together. Not at her, but at the hurting boy on the ground. A few even clapped. Someone whooped a cheer. A teacher finally appeared, too late to see all that had happened, and took her by the arm to the principal's office.

There she waited until Grandma Betsy came. The principal chastised her for resorting to violence, but Grandma Betsy had her back, and she got off with just two days' suspension. At home that night, she and Grandma Betsy ate ice cream together and Amber-May told her all that had happened. Grandma said she'd never been more proud of her.

And Sam Duggins? He ceased bothering her and did his best to avoid making eye contact. A few months after she fought him, Sam Duggins's father got a job in another state and took his son with him. Amber-May never saw him again.

She found herself smiling at the memory.

"You just kick him again where it hurts," Grandma Betsy said. "Maybe he's the sort of boy who needs to learn every lesson twice."

Amber-May's smile melted. What she was facing now was no adolescent boy of subpar intelligence. Her enemy was much more formidable. And this was a fight she'd already lost. Retreat was all that was left to her.

"No, Grandma. It's not Sam Duggins. I'm just tired, that's all. Don't you worry about me, all right?"

She stayed with Grandma Betsy till ten that night, two hours past the official visiting hours. Then, with Grandma Betsy visibly exhausted and the evening shift nurse standing at the doorway and pointing emphatically at her wristwatch, she finally said her good-byes, kissed Grandma Betsy, and left.

She sat in her car for a long time, surprisingly dry-eyed, as the darkness of night deepened around her. It came to her that she had no plans, no destination. She wasn't expected anywhere. She could go wherever she wished.

Exhaling loudly, she turned the key in the ignition and started the car. She began driving, not knowing where the night would take her.

10

Amber-May's first stop was at an ATM, where she withdrew four hundred and twenty dollars, leaving just two dollars and thirty-seven cents in her bank account. She didn't want to touch the forty thousand given to her as part of the devil's bargain she'd signed with Pickens. That money was tainted. If she had no other choice—if she were starving, for instance—she might degrade herself sufficiently to use it, but she was not at that point yet. She would do her utmost to never be.

She drove southwest on I-90 before switching to I-84, the Ford putting on a brave front as she pushed the old engine past the speed limit, until the night lights of Boston could no longer be seen in her rearview mirror. Then, after stopping at a service station to fortify herself with a cup of blisteringly bad coffee, she opted for a slower pace, driving for three hours straight before spying a blinking VACANCIES sign and pulling into the weedy parking lot of a seedy motel.

The clerk at the desk was young, pierced, and unwelcoming. In exchange for thirty dollars, she gave Amber-May a key and a lukewarm "Enjoy your stay." Then she turned her dull eyes back to the vapid reality show she was watching.

The room smelled. A mixture of mildew and the pungent odor of reefers. She cracked open a window, hoping to air the room. The bathroom was surprisingly clean. There was ample hot water. Not perfect, but certainly good enough for one night.

After showering and brushing her teeth, Amber-May got into bed. The mattress was too soft, the pillow lumpy. The hum of traffic infiltrated through the open window. Somewhere close by a night bird squawked. Amber-May lay on her back, thinking of the day that'd passed, figuring it would be a while before she managed to drift off. But her body, exhausted and worn-out, had its own ideas. Two minutes later, she was fast asleep.

Early the next day, she stopped at a roadside diner for breakfast. Her appetite was poor, so she only had buttered toast and coffee and was back on the road by eight o'clock. At a Walmart she purchased a cheap prepaid mobile phone. Her previous phone had been lost along with the clothes she'd worn the night of the attack. She tapped the number of the nursing home into the phone's memory. That was the only connection she had left to her previous life.

Driving on, she drifted through a medley of small towns, stopping every so often at restaurants and diners to see if they were hiring. At the fourth such place, a restaurant with gigantic deer antlers over the bar, she got a bad vibe from the owner. He hardly looked her in the eyes, instead alternating his leering gaze between her breasts and groin. Licking his lips, he said, "Sure thing, honey. You can start today. Just come on back into the office; I'll get you your uniform."

Amber-May turned around without a word, scurried to her car, and peeled out, the Ford's tires raising dust.

That night she slept in another motel, this one run by an old couple with matching Coke-bottle glasses and thinning white hair.

The following day, she stopped for lunch at a town called Crumley Creek, halfway between Knoxville and Chattanooga. The diner was run by a bosomy, plump-cheeked woman in her fifties, with short dyed-blond hair and loop earrings. She was generous with the coffee and her smiles, which she lavished on each and every one of her customers, keeping up a steady, cheerful patter as she served them. Old-style country music played in the background—plenty of banjos and fiddles—and the walls were festooned with pictures of cattle, horses, dense fields of grain and corn, and open plains stretching out to an endless horizon. The place was lively with laughter, banter, and the sound of people eating and drinking. The aroma of grilled meat, French fries, and an assortment of freshly baked pies wafted enticingly about. Amber-May was surprised to feel her mouth watering. She was famished. She found an empty stool at the counter and learned that the woman's name was Susie Mestecky.

Amber-May ordered a hamburger and fries, both of which were excellent, and drank a diet Sprite. As she ate, she noticed how Susie had to keep hustling without a second of respite, just to deliver the orders her short-order cook was pumping out.

She ordered a second bottle and, as Susie was uncapping it, asked whether she could use a little help.

"My lord, could I ever," Susie said. "My regular waitress upped and quit on me last night. No notice, no nothing. Told me she found the love of her life and was off with him to Alabama. Nothing makes a young girl's head spin like a hunk in a pair of tight jeans. Excuse me."

Susie hauled a plate heaped with hash browns to a couple in one of the booths. When she returned a moment later, she said, "Why d'ya ask? You looking for work?"

"Yes."

"Ever worked at one of these madhouses?"

"For over a year."

"Things can get a little hectic around here, as you may have noticed."

"That's all right. I'm not afraid of hard work."

"When can you start?"

"How about now?"

Susie's face broke into a smile of pure joy. "Now would be perfect. Get yourself over on this side of the counter and say hi to Jimmy while I fetch you an apron. If you need to pee, go now, 'cause you won't get a chance for the next couple of hours."

Amber-May hurried to the bathroom, did her business, and just had time to introduce herself to Jimmy the cook before Susie thrust an apron at her. Then time became a blur of activity—taking orders, pegging the orders to the ticket holder at the kitchen window, carting plates and cups and bowls to hungry customers—all of whom were as nice as could be, wanting to know her name and wishing her luck on her new job.

It was the first time since she'd regained consciousness in the hospital that her mind became completely, blissfully free of any thoughts of the rape. She just kept moving, serving, pouring, clearing tables and setting them again. She didn't have time to think. It was liberating.

It was only later, at about half past two, when the lunch crowd finally thinned, that she started feeling her feet. They were hurting like crazy. Susie noticed. "Go park yourself in that booth in the corner and put your feet up. Take your shoes off or keep them on, whatever makes you more comfortable. Don't mind the upholstery; it's seen worse. I'll get you some tea and a piece of pie and we'll talk."

And so they did, getting to know and like each other in the process. Susie wanted to know how long Amber-May planned on staying in town. Amber-May said that as long as she had a good job and a decent place to live, she had nowhere else she wanted to be. Susie said she might be able to help out in the accommodation department—one of her regulars had a vacant garage apartment, and she was sure the rent would be reasonable. "We'll go see him together later tonight. Once he hears you're the new waitress, he'll knock ten percent off the rent." As for the job, Amber-May could get as many shifts as her heart desired, and as long as she worked as she had today, Susie would be happy. Amber-May expected to get minimum wage, but Susie surprised her by offering an hourly wage that was twenty-five percent higher.

Susie explained, "I'm doing okay, and I like my employees to do okay, too. Besides, that way, when a stud in tight denim starts making goo-goo eyes at you, you'll think twice before hitting the road with him. So what do you say? Ready to join the team?"

Susie stuck out her hand across the table. Amber-May took it. The older woman's grip was warm and strong. Amber-May could feel herself smiling.

"Count me in."

11

Freddie Sheehan had no trouble keeping track of Amber-May. After Pickens had given him his assignment, he drove straight to the hospital parking lot, located the crappy Ford the girl was driving, and clamped a tracking device behind her rear bumper. The device sent a signal to a tablet computer he had in his car, allowing him to monitor wherever the Ford went.

Still, he wanted to get a close look at the girl, so the next day he was in his car, watching the Ford as the girl approached it. He whistled softly when he saw her. Pickens had been right. Whatever plastic surgery she'd had, it hadn't changed her much. She was a hot piece of ass.

Freddie wondered why she'd had to have plastic surgery in the first place. Judging by the picture Pickens had given him, there had been nothing about her looks that required improvement. So that left only one explanation: she had suffered some sort of injury and had to have surgery to fix the damage.

The bigger question, though, was why Garland Pickens wanted him to follow her. Early on in his career, Freddie had learned the benefits of appearing to be supremely incurious. It made clients relax and trust him more. In truth, he was quite the opposite. Freddie liked knowing things, secrets most of all. It was what had led him to become a private investigator. He knew information was currency and that the right nugget of knowledge could prove to be the key to fast riches. So he kept his eyes and ears open, looking for ways to further himself. Now he wondered what the connection was between Pickens and Amber-May Jackson.

Was she Pickens's mistress? If so, the fat ugly lawyer had better taste than Freddie had suspected. But in that case, why was she leaving town? Maybe she'd gotten pregnant or Pickens had tired of her for some reason. Maybe Pickens had given the girl a sum of money with the understanding that she leave and not return, and now he wanted Freddie to make sure she kept her end of the bargain.

But if any of that were true, why would she need plastic surgery?

Freddie drummed his fingers on the steering wheel of his Toyota, replaying his conversation with Pickens in his mind. From the way the lawyer had spoken, Freddie didn't think Amber-May was his lover. Pickens had never struck him as the sort of man who prowled after young flesh, but he supposed it was possible. More natural than not. Still, the idea of Pickens and this stunning girl being intimate together didn't sit right. There was something else going on here, and he wanted to know what it was.

When the Ford pulled out of the hospital parking lot, he followed, making sure to keep a few cars between him and his quarry at all times. Pickens had said the girl had one stop to make before leaving town, and Freddie wanted to see where she went, whom she met. He was surprised when the Ford swung into the parking lot of a fancy-looking nursing home and Amber-May walked inside. He didn't follow her in. A nursing home isn't the sort of place you can just barge into and start asking questions. Not without raising a few eyebrows. But he wasn't worried. He could find out later who the girl visited.

Freddie decided to wait in his car. He could track the Ford electronically, but the professional thing to do was to keep his eyes on the prize, or as close as possible, during the first hours of a job.

He didn't expect Amber-May to stay as long as she did. By the time she emerged after ten o'clock that night, he was hungry, thirsty, and thoroughly irritated. He was muttering a string of profanities as the Ford's headlights finally came on and the old car cut a path to the highway, with him shadowing.

He stayed half a mile behind, knowing that as long as the Ford kept moving, he didn't need to keep it in his line of sight. When Amber-May pulled into a service station, he went in after her, sliding his Toyota into a shadowy parking space between two panel trucks. He watched as she visited the restroom and then bought herself a coffee. After she drove out, he purchased four cans of Red Bull and some snacks and followed her.

He spent the night at the same motel as her, four doors down from her room. As he lay in bed, he pictured her lying in hers. He imagined her sleeping nude and had the urge to go out, sneak to her window, and peek inside to see how closely her body matched the enticing picture he had painted in his mind. He laughed at himself. He was like a horny teenager, head full of dumb ideas. He watched TV for a while—a stupid movie with plenty of unrealistic shootings and car chases. Then he slept.

He awoke to the sound of his tablet beeping, alerting him that the Ford was on the move. He didn't rush. He didn't need to. When Amber-May stopped for breakfast, he stayed in the diner's parking lot, watching her through the window. She talked to no one but the waitress, ate her food, paid her check, and left. Once she did, he went inside and sat at the same table as she had. He hoped that she'd left her scent behind, but his nose picked up nothing but the stale, air-conditioned smell of the diner. He ordered a big breakfast, wolfed it down, and got back on the road.

The day quickly fell into a rhythm. She drove; he followed. She stopped to pump gas, grab a bite, or visit a restroom; he did so, too, or used the opportunity to stretch his legs. They cut through a number of towns, the Ford going at a slow pace through the main commercial streets. A few times she stopped, went into diners and burger joints and restaurants, exchanged a few words with the managers, then got back in her car and drove on. A couple of times he went in after she'd gone and asked some questions. One manager eyed him suspiciously and told him to get lost; another said the girl had asked about a job.

"I told her she could start right away, but she just turned around and walked out. Crazy girl. I'm probably better off."

That night he slept in a different motel, a mile further south from the one she'd picked for herself. He didn't think she'd seen his car, but he didn't want to take unnecessary chances. He was starting to believe the girl didn't have a destination in mind. She might keep driving for weeks before settling somewhere. That was all right. Pickens was paying top dollar and the girl was easy on the eyes.

In addition, his curiosity was growing. Sitting behind the wheel for miles on end, his mind kept raising possibilities as to why Pickens wanted the girl followed and why she'd had to get her face fixed. Did she have an accident? Or had someone attacked her? Pickens? That seemed even less likely than the two of them being romantically involved.

Around noon the next day, in a midsized, middle-of-nowhere town called Crumley Creek, the girl stopped for lunch at a diner bearing the uninspiring name Susie's Joint. The parking lot was full, so Freddie parked across the street. He stayed in his car, the radio blaring a song about love, loss, and youthful desperation. Looking around at the low wooden buildings of Main Street, he thought that this was the sort of place where nothing ever happened. He fired up a cigarette, blowing smoke out his open window, as he waited for the girl to come out. When half an hour elapsed and she didn't, he got out and sauntered over to the front window, giving the place a quick sidelong scan.

He saw her, a bright red and yellow apron over her jeans and white T-shirt, hoisting a tray piled with dirty dishes toward the kitchen behind the serving counter. She said something to a pudgy middle-aged woman with fake blond hair before exchanging her cargo for a pitcher and two tall glasses, which she ferried over to a table by the door.

Watching from the corner of his eye, he kept his face averted from the window, but in truth, he didn't need to. She never turned her eyes toward him. She was too busy. And there was something different about her. The way she moved. Her steps were lighter than at any other time since he'd begun trailing her, as though before she'd had weights tied to her ankles. And she was smiling. He hadn't seen her smile before. The smile dug sexy, schoolgirl dimples in her smooth cheeks, exposing a set of perfect white teeth that gleamed between her curved full lips.

Goddamn, she was a foxy little thing, but what the hell was she doing waiting tables in this dump of a town?

He went back to his car, chugged a can of Red Bull, and munched on some chips. Ten minutes later, figuring that the girl would stay put for a while, he drove off, stopping at a gas station four miles out of town, where he replenished his depleted supply of cigarettes, Red Bull, and junk snacks. He had lunch in a dingy restaurant nearby.

Returning to Susie's Joint two hours later, he saw the girl sitting in a booth. The blond woman was sitting across from her. They talked for a long while, at one point shaking hands with an air of finality, as though a momentous bargain had just been sealed.

He smoked a few more cigarettes, barely listening to a couple of vacant-brained political pundits hurl abuse at each other on the radio. He watched as Amber-May got up and went back to work. Customers came and went. Daylight waned. A half-moon ascended into a sky more starry than any you'd see living in a big city.

Around eight thirty, he saw Amber-May, the blond woman, and a lanky guy moving about inside, tidying things up, lifting chairs onto tables. The guy left first; the two women a couple of minutes later. The blond woman got into a white GMC pickup; Amber-May into her Ford. The Ford followed the pickup down Main Street, hooked a left, another left, a right, and stopped in front of a ranch house with a detached garage. Freddie glided his car to a stop in the canopied darkness of a mimosa tree diagonally across the street. The two women went to the house together. A beer-bellied, gray-haired man in baggy pants and suspenders let them in. They emerged ten minutes later, the man leading the way to the garage. He unlocked the door. The three of them went inside. A short while afterward they came back out. The girl shook hands with the guy, looking pleased with life. He handed her a set of keys, mumbled something to her and the blond woman, and lumbered back into his house. The two women hugged.

The night was still and windless, so Freddie, parked nearby, caught their conversation through the open car window.

The older woman said, "See? I told you it would work out. Gary's a sweet old guy. Likes his football, hunting, eating burgers at my place, and minding his own business. You'll get along fine."

Amber-May said, "I hope so. The apartment is very nice."

"His baby girl and her man lived there for a while before they moved to Georgia. So all the work that went into it was a product of love. And it's less than ten minutes from work. Heck, I have to drive longer than that." She paused, tapping a finger on her chin as though weighing a new idea. "Come to think of it, maybe I should move in here and you could take over for me at my house. You'd love it. Cooking for two teenage boys is so much fun, not to mention cleaning up after them."

Amber-May, grinning, raised her hands palms out. "No. No. I wouldn't dream of depriving you of all that family bliss. Especially after you gave me a job. I'll just have to settle for being here by my lonesome."

"You won't have to be by your lonesome for long. With your looks, I'm sure you'll have a string of beaus lined up to have you on their arms."

Freddie saw the grin slide off the girl's face like blood off a sidewalk on a rainy night. He heard her say, "I'm okay with being on my own for a while."

The blond woman cocked her head. "You got man trouble, Amber-May?"

"You could say that."

"Anyone who might suddenly make an appearance?"

"Oh no. Nothing like that."

"Good. But just in case that changes, you let me know, you hear?"

"I hear."

"And if you want to talk about your troubles, my dainty little ears are at your disposal."

Amber-May laughed. "Thanks, Susie. For the job, for finding me this place, for...well, just thanks."

"Heck, I should be thanking you. You saved my bacon today. But if you're still thinking you owe me any thanks, I'll just say that you're most welcome, Amber-May." Susie patted the girl on the shoulder. "You get some sleep, okay, and I'll see you bright and early tomorrow morning."

"I'll be there. Good night."

The blond woman got into her pickup and drove off. Amber-May waved goodbye. After the pickup rounded the corner, she remained standing in the driveway, her eyes sweeping around her new street. Freddie slid lower in his seat. The girl's eyes did not penetrate the shadows where he sat.

Finally, he saw her take a deep breath and walk to her car. She removed two gym bags from the trunk and lugged them into her new apartment. After she closed the door, he waited for twenty minutes for her to come out. When she didn't, he turned on his car.

"I know where you live now," he said softly to himself with a grin, then drove off in search of a motel.

12

Emmett MacBaxter leaned his arms on the balcony railing of his penthouse apartment. A chill wind buffeted his half-naked muscular body, ruffling his shock of dark brown hair. He gazed up at the night sky, at the blinking lights of a soaring jetliner. Lowering his eyes, he stared twenty-nine stories downward at the street below. Cars as small as cockroaches, pedestrians like mindless ants, hurrying to and fro, looking ready to be stomped. He smiled at the thought.

Behind him he heard drapes flapping softly in the wind. Then bare feet padding closer. His smile contracted, his lips now set in a tight, grim line.

He sniffed her scent. Sweet perfume and body lotion mingled with the musky smell of recent sex. And his odor too, imprinted on her body, and within it as well. He didn't turn to face her. He waited until she came to stand beside him.

She was blond and slim, with long legs and high, firm breasts. A frilly white negligee covered her body from her shoulders to the middle of her thighs. Her skin showed through the sheer fabric. Taut, smooth, pale, young. Her nipples stood out, the areolas pink and just the right size. She'd told him her name was Linda. Which was probably a lie, but he didn't really care.

"This is some view," Linda said.

He didn't reply. Beneath his forearms, the railing was cold and hard. He noticed his fingers were clenched into fists. He forced them open.

"You want me to get you another drink? There's some left."

"No," he said. "I'm fine."

"I can still feel it," she said, giggling coyly. "I take a tiny sip and...whoosh, it goes straight to my head. Feels good, but not half as good as you made me feel, baby."

He said nothing, moving his eyes left to right. He caught sight of her toes. Small, dainty, the nails glossed and pedicured to perfection. He liked small feet on a woman.

Linda might have been lying to make him happy, stroke his ego, but it hardly mattered. His pleasure was what counted, not hers. Still, it was possible she was being truthful. Judging by her groans and moans, he'd made her climax just before he came inside her. Then, when she'd risen from the bed to go to the bathroom, he slid on his pants and walked out onto the balcony, where the wind made his sweat-drenched skin tighten.

She shifted her feet, perturbed by his reticence. Shivering dramatically, she hugged herself, her enclosed forearms pushing her breasts higher and closer together. "It's cold out here, isn't it?"

"If you don't like it, go back inside."

She licked her lips, unsure of herself. She smiled a sultry smile. "Why don't you come inside with me? After all, we've got time to burn."

She had a point. It was just after midnight. Daylight was hours away. He could have her a second time and then a third and a fourth. He was in great physical shape and his sexual appetite was such that it usually afforded him the ability to go multiple times a night. But tonight was not like most nights.

He turned his head to look at her. Pert nose flanked by deep green eyes, made larger by the deft appliance of eye shadow and false eyelashes. Shapely lips that closed in a perfect spoiled-girl's pout. Hair that fell loosely a few inches past the line of her shoulders. Delicate jawline, slender neck, collarbones that stood out under her white skin. Good, sexy body, and she knew what to do with it.

She'd done everything she was supposed to, had used her hands and lips and tongue on him with tremendous skill. Yet it had taken his body a long time to respond accordingly, and were it not for her perseverance, he might have failed to become erect at all.

As soon as he was, he thrust himself inside her, feeling profound relief and finding her slick and willing and energetic. Not a cold fish like some of them. This one wasn't content to simply lie there. She moved beneath him and then on top of him, pumping with her hips and pelvis, grinding against him, deepening each penetration.

It felt good, but not as good as it should have. Like the difference between a scratch and a cut, she only managed to touch the surface. It made him angry, and a little afraid, especially when he began to feel his erection weakening inside her. That was when he rolled her over on her belly and lay on top of her, one hand closed around the back of her neck, pushing her head into the pillow while he thrust himself inside her as hard and fast as he could, pumping with frantic urgency until he came a minute later.

When he finished, he stayed on top of her quivering body for a moment, catching his breath. Then he rolled off her and onto his back. She smiled at him, her face flushed. "That was—" she searched for the right word and finally settled on "—intense."

He said nothing, averting his face, not wanting to look at her or be looked upon by her. He suspected that she'd felt his transient softening, and though he'd been able to recover from it, it shook him that it had happened at all.

But maybe it shouldn't have. There had long been signs that something was wrong. Two months ago, at a dance club he partially owned, he had taken a woman customer to a storage room in back. She'd been drunk and dazzled by his money. It hadn't taken much to get her in a compliant mood. In less than a minute he had peeled off her dress and positioned her just right, bent over a table. He'd been hard but not as excited as he usually was in the seconds preceding a fresh conquest. Though the woman was attractive and eager, the sex had been no more than adequate. When it was done, he was left wanting and unsure why.

A similar thing had happened three times since, with three different women. Two were students, the third a waitress called Marilyn. He'd performed well enough with the two students, but had gotten just token pleasure from each encounter. With Marilyn the waitress, disaster nearly struck. They had been kissing and feeling each other's body for a few minutes, and he'd already removed half of Marilyn's clothes, when he became aware that his penis remained flaccid in his pants. He usually hardened quickly, without much coaxing, but now he was getting no reaction whatsoever.

It might have proved embarrassing if Marilyn hadn't gotten a sudden call from her babysitter, alerting her that her boy was feverish and wailing for his mommy and that she needed to get home as soon as possible. Marilyn had been effusive with her apologies, and he had pretended to be disappointed, but in truth, he was relieved to see her go.

He took a monthlong break from women after that, thinking that he'd been too active, had run the batteries low. Then earlier today, feeling horny as a horse, he had rung the number of an exclusive service he had used a few times before and asked them to send their best girl to his apartment. They sent Linda. Her price for one night was four thousand dollars. He didn't care about the money; he was rich, and soon, when his dad finally did the world a favor and died, he'd be even richer. He wanted someone hot who knew what she was doing. He wanted to have a great time, to get back in the saddle.

It should have worked, but it didn't. Standing now on his balcony, with the gorgeous Linda at his side, he realized that he had known for a while the reason for his flagging enthusiasm but had done his best to ignore it. Why had it taken him so long to accept what was happening? Was a part of him in deep, perhaps fearful, denial of the truth?

If so, that was a part he would soon squash to nonexistence. It was something no real man should tolerate. Life was about having as many of the things you wanted, and a man was judged by his ability and willingness to take those things for himself, even when that meant depriving others of them.

What he now wanted was to slake his sexual thirst utterly and completely. And if he needed to do it a specific, unconventional way, then so be it.

He turned to Linda, flashing the wide, good-boy smile he'd perfected over the years, both as a way to charm people and to hide the darker depths of himself. That smile had earned him frequent appearances in the pages of gossip magazines, where he was touted as one of the hottest rich young men in America. He said, "Sure, babe. You lead the way."

She took his outstretched hand and pulled him inside after her, swishing her hips seductively. Staring at her ass through the see-through negligee and knowing what he was about to do, his skin started tingling. His cock twitched, hardened, fattened. The nature of his smile morphed, turning hungry, predatory. Just before they reached the bed, as Linda began turning to him, he shifted his grip from her hand to her wrist, pulling her arm behind the small of her back, his left arm encircling her waist and pressing her tight against him. She looked over her shoulder at him, confusion in her pretty eyes, but no fear. Not yet. His lips by her ear, he said softly, "Fight me."

Linda frowned, her confusion deepening. And there was the fear, just a hint, but enough to send a jolt of excitement through his system. She tried yanking her arm free, but he held on tight. He jerked her arm higher up her back. Her face contorted in pain, and she let out a moan. Now the fear was shining in those green eyes like a tropical blaze. Fighting the pain, she put on a brave smile. "Hey, what—"

He shoved her hard onto the bed. She flopped on her front, her limbs flailing. By the time she turned over, he had already shed his pants. He hurled himself on top of her. His crushing weight knocked the air out of her lungs. She lay half-dazed as he straddled her, grabbing a fistful of her negligee in each hand and ripping the flimsy material like tissue paper.

He stared down at her naked, pale body, at the frantic rising and falling of her chest, at her wide eyes and gaping mouth. He waited for her to buck, to try to throw him off, to scratch at his face, but nothing of the sort happened. Like a deer in headlights, she had frozen, seeming to shrink into her own skin, striving to make herself as small a target as she could.

He could feel his excitement wane at her passivity. The stupid woman was not playing the part he wanted her to. She was ruining things.

"Fight me," he commanded.

Linda's eyes, huge and bright, were blinking frenziedly. On her face, shock and confusion combined to give her a pathetic, moronic expression.

"What?" she whimpered. "Please, I don't—"

"I said fight me," he growled. He pinched one of her nipples between thumb and forefinger, twisting it.

She yelped, jerking her upper body sideways. He grinned and let go of her, expecting her to continue struggling. But once she was free of the pain, she disappointed him by just lying there, panting, measuring him with her eyes. She seemed to arrive at a conclusion of sorts and arranged her mouth to form a lascivious smile. "Don't be so rough, okay, baby? There's no need for that. Didn't I make you feel good earlier?" and she reached a hand for his penis.

He shoved her hand away and slapped her face. She cried out. Redness spread across her struck cheek. Tears spilled out of her eyes, smearing her eyeshadow.

He grabbed her jaw with one hand, shouting into her face, "Resist me, you bitch. Come on."

Face pale and wet, she begged, "Don't. Please, stop. I'll do whatever you want. Just tell me what to do, and don't hit me."

Which was not what he wanted to hear. He didn't want her to be the accommodating whore, to play a role in some fake fantasy game in which she'd pretend to fight him in order to enhance his arousal. He wanted her to feel real fear, true pain, and to fight him as if her life depended on it. Anything less would not give him the rush he needed, the satisfaction he craved.

He bent down until their eyes were mere inches apart, until the only thing she could see was him. "Fight me or you die." He shook her head hard. "Do you understand me, you stupid whore?"

She did. She fought. But he had sixty pounds of muscle on her, and his excitement gave him added strength. The struggle didn't last nearly as long as he wanted. She was not a fighter; she soon tired, her spirit crumbling under the assault of his punches and slaps. By the time he entered her again, she was a motionless bundle of bone and flesh. The only indication she was still there, in the moment, were the tears that kept seeping from her eyes.

It was still the best sex he'd had in months. When he finished, he was gasping for air, grinning victoriously, his mood soaring on adrenaline and endorphins. He raised himself on his hands, looking down at Linda. Her breasts were red and raw with teeth marks, her belly, shoulders, and arms discolored where he'd hit her. But apart from the one slap, he'd left her face untouched, knowing that inflicting damage on it might prove problematic. Facial injuries were hard to conceal and took too long to heal. She would not be able to ply her trade until they did. He did not want trouble with her employers, not too much of it, anyway.

Besides, after what had happened with the stripper, Garland Pickens had taken him to task, telling him in that you-better-listen-now-boy tone of voice he employed far too often for Emmett's liking that such an occurrence must not be repeated.

"It's not so simple to make these things go away, Emmett," the lawyer said, "not when hospitalization and the police are thrown into the mix. Soon, when your father passes away, you will be the owner of the company, under the watchful eye of more reporters and media than you can chase off with a stick. Have you any notion what a sex scandal, even one that never makes it to court, can do to the valuation of the company? To the reputation your father has worked so hard to establish? So keep your pecker in your pants, or only whip it out when the young lady in question is fully, and I mean fully, willing. Do you get my drift, Emmett?"

Emmett had thought of instructing Pickens to refer to him as Mr.

MacBaxter, but he held his tongue. As long as his father was alive, Pickens was acting in his name. Emmett had never understood why his father valued the bloated Southern lawyer as much as he did. Sure, Pickens had brains and a knack for making pesky problems disappear, but there must be dozens of such people, as long as you had the money to buy their services.

Emmett hated Pickens. The lawyer had never failed to give Emmett the impression that he considered him to be a lesser man than his father was, an unworthy heir to his fortune. Pickens did not show him the proper deference, and it took a lot from Emmett to restrain himself from putting the man in his place.

But that didn't mean it would never happen. Emmett could be patient. His father had one foot solidly in the grave. It wouldn't be long before he went to whatever hell awaited him. When that happened, Emmett would be the boss. He would be the one giving orders.

Emmett had little doubt that Pickens intended to act as his close adviser—or maybe chaperon was the better word for it—when he took control of the company. In all likelihood, his father had a similar idea—to have Emmett go through a protracted period of tutelage under the benevolent guidance of Pickens. Emmett knew his father considered him to be young, inexperienced, unruly, and brash. But that was all right. He didn't care what his father, or Pickens, thought of him. Once his father finally croaked, he would never have to suffer through one of his long-winded lectures ever again. And once he was in control of the company, Pickens would be his underling.

Perhaps he would simply get rid of the son of a bitch. Or maybe he would let him stick around but cut him off from any real power. Because Emmett planned on running the company his way. He would show everyone that he was not merely his father's match but his superior. He would enhance the company's valuation, expand it a hundredfold, and make it, and himself, a household name.

And when he was boss, he would live life as he wished, without constraints. He would not let Pickens, or anyone else, tell him what to do. He would take what he wanted when he wanted, and he would have the money and power to do so without fear of repercussions.

He rolled off Linda and sat up on the bed. She curled over on her side, her legs tucked close to her belly. She was sobbing ever so quietly.

If she'd fought him harder, his pleasure would have been greater. But he now knew that she'd given him all she could. It was not her fault that he needed something else, something he could not get from her. He was actually appreciative of her. She'd helped him open his eyes to the truth. Without her, he might have kept on being blind to himself and his true desires.

"Don't worry," he told her. "In a week, all the bruises will be gone. You'll be good as new."

Her eyes flicked to his, glistening and full of hate and humiliation. Her voice was low and brittle. "You had no right to do what you did. No right."

He ignored her nonsensical words. "Twenty thousand."

Linda frowned in incomprehension.

"Cash, right now, just for you. All you gotta do is keep your mouth shut. And I'll square things with your boss, tell her I'm hiring you for a full week." She began shaking her head, opened her mouth to refuse, but he held up a silencing hand. "You won't need to actually come here. I'm done with you. I don't ever want to see you again. Take a week off, go someplace nice. Travel first class, stay at a five-star hotel. Twenty thousand can go a long way. But breathe one word of what happened here tonight, and I'll hire some people to pay you a visit, and they won't be as gentle as I was."

Her face, pale to begin with, blanched to the color of bone. Her lower lip trembled.

"Do we have a deal?"

She swallowed. "Okay. Yes."

"Good." He got up from the bed, stretched his arms over his head, and yawned without covering his mouth. "Want to take a shower before you head out?"

She shook her head. Earlier, she'd taken off her clothes and laid them, folded neatly, on a nearby couch. Her eyes twitched in their direction, but she made no move to get them.

"Go on. I won't bite." He grinned. "Not anymore."

She rose hesitantly, scurried over to her clothes, and hurried into them, balling her stockings and stuffing them in her purse instead of putting them on. She held the purse before her like a shield and looked at him, uncertain.

He smiled. "If you're anxious to leave, there's the door. Or would you rather wait for me to get you your money?"

She looked at her shoes. "I'll wait."

He laughed, walked out of the bedroom, and went over to his study. Behind a framed picture was a wall safe. He opened it and counted out ten stacks of cash. He found a bag from a men's clothing store and dropped the cash inside. Back in the bedroom, he handed Linda the bag. "Here's your money."

She snatched the bag away from him with a quick movement, as though afraid he'd pounce on her. She opened the bag, peeked inside, then squeezed it shut, clamping it to her chest. She didn't move. He was standing between her and the door.

"Get out. You know the way. And don't forget: you tell one soul about tonight, even your mother or a girlfriend or a priest, if you've got one, and you're dead. And not quickly."

She scuttled past him. He heard the door close behind her. He surveyed the bedroom. The blanket was tossed on the floor, the bedsheets tangled and dotted with blood. The shredded remains of the negligee hung off the edge of the mattress like torn strips of skin. He stripped off the bedsheets, rolled them and the negligee together, and jammed them into a garbage bag.

He took a long, steaming shower, then got into a thick terrycloth robe. He poured himself the remains of the vodka bottle he and Linda had shared earlier and ambled once more onto the balcony. He drank slowly, his muscles relaxed, but his mind kept churning.

Why had it taken him so long to figure out what he truly wanted? What he needed? A man should be more aware of himself.

Raping Linda the whore had given him pleasure but not the rush he had been longing for. It had not been as disappointing as his other recent sexual encounters, but it was still undeniably lacking. Compared to what? The answer was as clear as the two fingers of vodka in his glass.

The stripper. The one he and his friends had taken by force.

The attack had not been premeditated. Russ had hired her to do nothing but dance at their little get-together at Shane's house. But as soon as she walked in the door, Emmett knew he would not be satisfied with merely feasting his eyes on her. He badly wanted to have her. And he could tell that his three friends—Billy Raddick, Shane Erickson, and Russ Koenig—wanted her too.

But none of them would have had the balls to act without his lead. Emmett had assumed the stripper could be had for money. The difference between exposing your body and selling it did not seem all that great to him. Nothing that money couldn't bridge.

But the stripper—she'd given them the name Sandy, but he learned later that her real name was Amber-May Jackson—had adamantly refused, even when he'd offered her thousands of dollars for each of the four guys. She said she was not a prostitute, which he now knew was the truth. But by then, he'd been too aroused to take no for an answer.

So when he reached out a hand to touch her bare thigh, which was against the rules she'd set before she began her dance routine, and she responded by slapping his hand away and admonishing him in a sharp tone, he shot up from his chair and pushed her tumbling to the floor. Then, his friends watching, he lunged at the girl.

They grappled on the floor for a hectic minute, the girl putting up a hell of a tough fight. She was like a wildcat, scratching, punching, slapping, even biting at his face. It surprised him and made him even more excited. He got more violent, but she wouldn't give up, not even when he backhanded her across the face or punched her in the belly. He couldn't subdue her. Not until he called his pals for help.

Russ didn't hesitate, but Emmett had to yell twice for Billy and Shane to lend a hand, saying that if they wanted the girl, too, they needed to pitch in. With some reluctance, especially on the part of Shane, both did.

Russ went to grab her arms, the other two a leg each. Still she fought like a madwoman. Only after they beat her up some more—with fists and kicks and stomps—did they manage to overcome her resistance and have their way with her.

It was only when they were done that they became aware of the damage they'd done to her. Each had a different reaction. Shane got sick and had to wobble off to the bathroom to throw up. What a pussy that guy turned out to be. Billy looked a little green, and Emmett thought he was about to faint, but he didn't. Russ, the crazy dog, actually had a grin on his face. Drunk and doped out of his mind, he was whooping and howling, doing a wild jig—funny because his pants were bunched around his ankles, impeding his movements, and his limp dick was waggling side to side in rhythm with his dance moves. "Oh man, oh man, we got her good, didn't we? Look at her. We got her so good." And he actually raised his hand for Billy to high-five him.

Billy didn't seem to notice. He mumbled, "I think she's dead."

That managed to wipe the grin off Russ's face. He stopped jiggling, brushed his long black hair off his face, and stared down at the girl, open mouthed. Emmett looked too. The stripper was not moving. Her eyes were closed. Her chest did not seem to be rising and falling with breath.

Shane came back from the bathroom, wiping his mouth with the back of his hand. He looked terrified. When he spoke, he sounded ten, not twenty-three. "What's going on?"

Emmett crouched down beside the girl, reached a hand for her neck, and felt around for a pulse. He couldn't find one.

Billy, Shane, and Russ seemed paralyzed, completely at a loss as to what had to be done. Emmett, the natural leader, took command of the situation. He told his friends they had to get rid of her, dump her someplace. Someone suggested the woods. Looking back, that had been a pretty dumb idea, one Emmett should have rejected out of hand. But you live and learn with each mistake, and, as it turned out, no harm befell any of them.

They bundled the girl into a sheet and hefted her to the trunk of Billy's Lexus. Billy was shaken, so Emmett took the keys and drove them to the woods. They were deserted at that time of night, full of shadows and animal sounds, sort of creepy, like a cheap horror movie set. Maybe that was why they didn't go very far into them. They found a place that seemed right and unrolled the stripper onto the ground. Then they left, taking the sheet with them.

It was a shock to learn that she wasn't dead. Shane was the one who broke the news. He'd been glued to the news sites from the second he got home, bouncing from one to the next, waiting to see when someone found the body. Which happened sometime the next morning, only it wasn't a body they found.

Learning that the stripper was alive, Billy and Shane had gone into full panic mode. Russ had reacted by getting even more wasted than usual. Only Emmett held his shit together, which was another sign that he was made of the right stuff to lead MacBaxter Holdings, that he was the sort of man who would one day be thought of as great.

Emmett told his friends he'd take care of everything, that they had nothing to worry about. Then he did something he very much detested. He went to Garland Pickens for help.

Pickens listened intently as Emmett told him what had happened. He interjected here and there with questions—where they'd found the stripper, the time they'd dumped her in the woods, the sort of damage they'd inflicted on her—and made some notes on a legal pad. Emmett could tell by his expression that Pickens was displeased with him. Disgusted even. That only made Emmett hate the bastard even more. Especially when, after he'd finished telling Pickens everything, the lawyer leaned back in his chair, removed his glasses, pinched the bridge of his nose, and sighed deeply. Then he launched into the sermon Emmett had known was coming.

It was similar to the ones Pickens had given him after he'd smoothed over previous episodes of misbehavior on Emmett's part. It included a reminder of his position, both present and future, and a warning that there were limits to Pickens's power, that one day Emmett might do something that could not be fixed. Emmett pretended to listen, seething inside at Pickens's impertinence. Who the hell did Pickens think he was, lecturing him? He was an employee, a hired hand. That was all he was ever going to be and only if Emmett wished it. When Emmett took over the company, he would be the master and Pickens the servant. He would give orders and it would be Pickens's responsibility to carry them out. For the moment, he had to sit there and listen to the lawyer bleat his admonishments, like a schoolboy being reprimanded by the principal. But he would remember this affront. Oh yes, he would.

When Pickens was done preaching, Emmett said, "So can you make this thing go away or what?"

Pickens frowned his bushy eyebrows at him, pursing his blubbering lips. "I need you to talk to your friends, Emmett, and tell them they must not say a word of what happened. Not to anyone. Tell them I'm taking care of it."

"Good," Emmett said. "Thanks." He'd added that last word without meaning it. He didn't believe he should be thanking Pickens for merely doing his job, but he thought it prudent to act the grateful, abashed brat for now. He had no power over Pickens at the moment, and he needed him. But soon things would be different.

They shook hands, Emmett noting that Pickens did not rise from his chair but merely extended his hand across his desk. Pickens told him to keep his phone close by so he could reach him at any time. Emmett didn't like being told what to do, but he simply nodded, thanked him again, and went home.

To his credit, Pickens had delivered big time.

A few days after the rape, Pickens had called to inform Emmett that everything was taken care of. The girl had been paid off. She would file no charges, nor would she talk to anyone in the media. Whatever evidence the police had collected had been compromised. Emmett and his friends were in the clear. For the first time in as long as he could remember, Emmett had actually felt something like fondness toward Pickens. Then the fat bastard had to go ruining the moment by giving him that spiel about how difficult it was to cover such things up and how Emmett needed to be better behaved, finishing up with that bit about keeping his pecker in his pants.

What an insufferable, sanctimonious sack of shit.

Now, standing on his balcony with a vodka in his hand, Emmett thought of Amber-May Jackson. He could see her clearly in his mind —her gorgeous face, her luscious body. He remembered how she had moved as she danced, the way her muscles had rippled under her unblemished skin, the fuck-me-now look in her smoldering eyes, the full lips, the perfect natural tits. And he remembered with exquisite detail how she had felt when he was on top of her, inside her. The memory was getting him hard again.

She was special. He wasn't sure why. Her beauty had something to do with it, and her indomitable spirit also. Thinking back, he realized that, though he and his buddies had eventually taken her against her will, her spirit had not been broken. Otherwise, she would have died in those woods. She would not have recovered from her injuries.

He took a long swallow of vodka. The taste of alcohol mingled in his mouth with the memory-taste of Amber-May Jackson's skin.

After Pickens had told him that everything had been taken care of, Emmett had not given her much thought. He had no idea what had happened to her or where she was now. He did not know whether the injuries she'd suffered that night had left her scarred or otherwise spoiled. Maybe she was no longer a ravishing beauty. Maybe he was getting all excited over something that no longer existed.

The possibility gave him a pang of remorse. Not for the girl's sake —her well-being counted for nothing—but for his own. Because he now knew with absolute clarity what he needed, what he wanted, what he had to have.

It was her. Amber-May Jackson. No other woman would do. The way she had made him feel, the way just thinking about her now was making him as hard as a bull, he knew he wanted to experience that feeling again and again. He wanted to fight her, and he wanted to conquer her. He wanted her to be his and his alone. He wanted to possess and own her, body and soul.

He did not give a second of consideration to morality, the law, or Pickens's warnings. He was his own man, and, like a king, he made his own rules. He wanted Amber-May Jackson, and he would have her. As simple as that.

But to do that, he first needed to find her.

13

Freddie Sheehan was not a computer whiz.

Some in his profession were. There were investigators who never stepped out of their office. They prowled the internet, mined information from various electronic databases, collated this detail and that fact, and presented their clients with a complete picture of whoever it was they were hired to investigate. Often, those guys got to know more about their target than the target knew about himself.

Freddie was not that sort of detective. He was a field investigator. He followed people. He took pictures. He asked questions. Sometimes he would break into houses or businesses to search through papers or plant listening devices. The law posed no moral barrier as far as he was concerned, and breaking and entering was so inconsequential as far as crimes went that he hardly considered it as such. In his youth, he'd been into much heavier stuff. For a time, he'd worked as an enforcer in the service of a protection racket in San Diego. Later, he had been employed as a bouncer at a mid-level brothel. In both positions he'd had to break a few arms and legs. Twice, he'd committed murder.

Fortunately, he'd gotten out of that life without getting arrested even once. Looking back, he knew he'd been damn lucky to escape police notice. These days, he broke the law rarely, and only on jobs that paid very well. And when he did, he was always careful about it and had never come close to being caught.

While Freddie didn't know much about tech stuff, he did know how to perform basic internet searches. Which he did a few days after arriving at Crumley Creek and becoming certain that Amber-May Jackson was going to stay there. He searched her name and came up with a Facebook profile that had last been updated two years earlier. In it were pictures of Amber-May dating back to when she was fifteen. He clicked through them, examining each closely. She'd been a ripe peach at an early age, a succulent fruit. The boys must have followed her like dumb dogs, tongues lolling out of their mouths. If she'd been one of the girls at the brothel he'd worked at all those years ago, they'd have had horny guys lined up all the way to the next block.

One picture, of Amber-May wearing a two-piece bathing suit and a smile that could have dazzled a blind man, kept drawing him back. She'd been seventeen then—of legal age, he thought with a sly smile —and, though her pose was anything but suggestive, she oozed sex appeal. The curves of her body were perfect, her stomach flat. Her hair was wet and strands of it clung to her naked shoulders like lizard tongues. She glowed with youthful, carefree happiness. It was an enticing picture, provocative in its overflowing innocence. She looked like a girl unaware of her beauty, ignorant of the lewd thoughts she aroused in the minds of men who saw her.

The pictures were great, but they gave him no pertinent information. Neither did the public posts on her profile. Abandoning Facebook, he returned to Google, scrolling through the first four pages of results for the name "Amber-May Jackson." Some involved a woman by the same name who owned a fishing store in Alaska. She was in her fifties and dumpy. Other results were for women with similar names, such as Amber Jackson or Amber May or May Jackson. There were also results that appeared to have no relevance at all.

He clicked News on the Google menu at the top of the search page and was rewarded by a string of more irrelevant results. But at the bottom of the second page, he came upon a nine-year-old article from a local paper in Michigan that reported on the death by accident of James and Simone Jackson. The couple were survived by one daughter, Amber-May, eleven.

"Tough break," he muttered.

He lit up a cigarette, leaning back in the cheap knockoff chair in his motel room. He was disappointed. The Facebook pictures were nice and all, but he had hoped to learn what had happened to Amber-May recently, not when she was eleven.

He called the hospital where he'd begun following Amber-May and talked to a nurse, trying to weasel information regarding Amber-May's stay there. It was like talking to a prerecorded message—the nurse kept telling him she was not authorized to share medical information. He called again the next day, got a different nurse, and this time presented himself as a police detective. That garnered the same dismal result as the day before, though this time the nurse was more polite.

Ending the call, he got up from the chair and began pacing the room, thinking.

The only reason he could see for Amber-May to undergo cosmetic surgery was if she'd suffered some sort of physical trauma. That meant an accident or being the victim of a violent crime. Either way, there was a good chance the police would be involved.

He tapped a number on his cell phone. A gruff voice came over the line.

"Sergeant Malone."

"Hey, Leonard. This is Freddie Sheehan."

"Yeah, I could tell it was you by the way my ulcer started acting up."

"Ha, ha. You're wasted on the force, Leonard. Comedy, that's where your strength lies."

"Don't I know it. What do you want, Freddie?"

"Some info. I got a name here I'd like you to run through your system."

"You know I'm busy, right? I got a job and cases and everything."

"Sure, I know. But I was thinking you could do with a couple of extra fifties, unless you're too busy to fold a pair of bills and slip them in your pocket."

Malone grunted. "What's the guy's name?"

"It's a woman, actually. Amber-May Jackson, twenty years old."

"What am I looking for? A criminal record?"

"If you find one, I'd like to know about it, but that's not what I'm primarily interested in. What I want you to see is whether she was a victim of a crime or an accident, car or work-related or whatever. Something that left her physically injured, including facial injuries."

"Got a time frame?"

"Past year."

"What's your interest?"

"She's part of a case I'm working on."

"You saying physical injuries makes me think it's an insurance fraud, but if that was it, you'd know how she got injured, wouldn't you?"

"You've got one hell of a deductive mind, Leonard, anyone ever tell you that?"

"Screw you, Freddie. I'll take a look through the computer later today, right after I work on some real crimes, like a real detective."

"You do that. When should I call you?"

Malone told him he should have something by the next morning, told him to screw himself again, and hung up.

Right after breakfast the following day, Freddie called Malone again.

"You got something for me, Leonard?"

"Yeah, I do," Malone said, sounding more solemn and serious than his usual brusque self. "According to the computer, an Amber-May Jackson, twenty, was the victim of rape and aggravated assault and battery a few months ago." He read Freddie the date. "She was uncon-

88

scious for a few days after being found naked and close to death by a couple of joggers. After regaining consciousness, she was questioned by Theresa Sanchez, a detective from the Sexual Assault Unit. Sanchez went to interview her at the hospital, where Jackson told her she had no recollection of the rape. She said she could not identify any of the attackers. Sanchez noted that she believed the victim was lying."

"Why'd she think that?"

"Sanchez talked to one of the nurses at the hospital. The nurse said—and swore to it later, after Sanchez interviewed the victim— that the previous night, after Jackson came to, the two of them had a long conversation during which Jackson said she knew who had raped her. Sanchez wrote she believed the nurse."

"Any idea why Jackson would lie?"

"Who can say? Maybe she didn't want to go through a trial. You know what those defense lawyers scumbags do to rape victims, the way they run their lives through a microscope. Or maybe she was close to whoever had raped her and didn't want to get them into trouble. It happens sometimes, especially if it's one family member raping another. In this case, though, that's less likely. Sanchez wrote that Jackson had no male relatives. Her only family is a grandmother, and she's in a home."

So that was who Amber-May had visited at the nursing home. Freddie scratched his ear, then remembered something Malone had said. "You said them."

"Huh?"

"You said she didn't want to get *them* into trouble. There were multiple rapists?"

"Yeah. The scumbags. I'd like to wring their necks, whoever they are."

"How do you know there was more than one?"

"The rape kit they took at the hospital showed semen from multiple men."

"How many? Can you ID them through DNA?"

"I can't say, and no. The sample got tainted. Probably some moron at the lab with a PhD in chemistry and the clumsiness of a drunken chimpanzee. You know how often those geeks screw up? More than you'd ever guess watching those CSI shows, let me tell you. Man, do they go over the top with their fancy science and slides and all that crap. If only the department had the budget for all those gizmos, maybe then my job would be easier."

Freddie was barely listening to Malone ramble. He was thinking about Garland Pickens. He had little doubt that Pickens was behind the mishap at the crime lab that resulted in the sample taken from Amber-May being tainted. One of those geeks, as Malone had called them, had probably gotten a fat envelope stuffed with cash for his efforts.

He was also certain that the reason Amber-May had developed a sudden case of amnesia was due to Pickens. The lawyer had gotten to her somehow, had offered her money for keeping her trap shut. Evidently, she had accepted his offer.

Freddie wondered how much money she had gotten. Whatever it was, it likely had come on top of Pickens footing the bill for all those plastic surgeries. Part of the deal was that she had to leave the city and not return. Pickens wanted to make sure of that, which was why he'd hired Freddie.

He said, "Did Sanchez have any suspects?"

"No. Nada. She went around, talked to some people where Jackson worked, but got nowhere fast. Jackson was a private person, worked around the clock, no close friends, no boyfriend. Besides, with no physical evidence, the only way to get a conviction would be if Jackson's memory made a miraculous recovery. Like any detective with other cases to clear, Sanchez wouldn't waste much time on such a lost cause." Malone paused. "Do you know who did it, Freddie?"

"Me? No. Not a clue."

"You sure about that? This is serious stuff. I saw some of the pictures they took at the hospital. Those assholes did a real number on her. They deserve to have their balls cut off for what they did. You know something, you need to tell me."

"I don't know who raped her, Leonard. Swear to God, I don't. I didn't even know she was raped until you told me."

They talked some more, Freddie promising Malone his money the day he got back to the city. When they hung up, Freddie sat for a long while, thinking. Who was Pickens covering up for? And was there a way Freddie could use that information to his advantage?

14

Amber-May took a while getting used to her new life.

It helped that she was busy. She worked six days a week at Susie's Joint and would have worked seven if Susie hadn't put her foot down and told her flatly that she was not to show her face at the diner on Tuesdays.

"Rest. Sleep. Watch a movie. Go out and have fun. Just don't come back here till Wednesday morning," Susie said, shooing her away with a wave of a napkin and a smile.

Amber-May knew she could use the rest, but she didn't want to sleep. Sleep brought dreams. Not the sort you wake up smiling from, but nasty ones, of the rape and her attackers. Each night, she would wake up at least twice, sweating or shaking, staring petrified at the unfamiliar dark corners of her new apartment. So on her first day off since arriving in Crumley Creek, instead of catching up on her sleep, she went running.

Running had been part of her routine before the attack, and she returned to it with gusto. She ran each morning before work, usually for three or four miles. On that Tuesday, and those that followed, she upped her distance to six.

She also began lifting weights regularly. Gary's son, a Marine sergeant stationed in Korea, had been into weight training and had left his dumbbells behind when he went into the service. Gary had gladly offered her the use of them.

The exercise helped burn some of her anger away. But not all of it. It was always there, like a low fire that can never be extinguished, ready to flare up into a blaze if you fed it the right fuel.

The dreams were worst during the first two weeks in Crumley Creek. They improved during the third; she woke only once each night by then. By the fourth week, she was getting the occasional night of uninterrupted sleep. That, along with her strict fitness regimen and her improved appetite, made her feel and look healthier, stronger, and, she noted with a melancholic sort of satisfaction, more attractive than at any other time since the attack, and possibly even before it.

Often in the early days after settling in, she would study herself in the bathroom mirror, peering closely at her face, surveying it from various angles. Not out of vanity, but as a way of getting to know the new her. It took her a while to decide that she could live with her new face, that she, in fact, approved of it.

When she wasn't waitressing or working out, she read books she got from the library or from Gary's impressive collection of paperbacks. She also watched television, mostly sports. She shied away from the news, fearing reports about rape or sexual assault that might make her relive her ordeal.

Twice a week, she would call the nursing home and inquire with Martha Mitchum as to how Grandma Betsy was doing. She wanted desperately to talk with her grandmother directly, but that was impossible. Grandma Betsy was incapable of talking on the phone. One of the peculiar symptoms of her dementia was that she was unable to recognize voices. Unless she was face-to-face with whomever she was talking to, she believed she was speaking with a stranger. This invariably made her agitated to the point of panic. Amber-May had learned this the hard way. The separation from her grandmother was the hardest part of her life. It made her even angrier than the rape itself.

The rest of her free time she spent taking long walks around town, getting to know her new home. She traversed the streets, the small parks, the sprawling meadows. The only place she avoided were the woods that abutted the southern edge of the town. They were beautiful, but she couldn't bring herself to enter them.

The one thing she didn't do was go out on dates, although there had been numerous offers. She wasn't ready for dating. She hoped one day that would change, but she didn't think it would be any time soon. Just the thought of being intimately touched by a man made her skin crawl, her stomach cramp, and her heart begin to palpitate. She could stand casual, friendly touching—she was able to shake a man's hand—but anything romantic was out of the question.

She knew Susie wondered about her. More than once, when a customer got flirty, she caught her boss studying her, noting how she rebuffed each compliment and advance. Susie never came right out and asked her about it, but that didn't mean she wasn't curious.

Amber-May did not resent Susie's curiosity. She knew it came from a good place. Susie was like a mother hen, and she worried over Amber-May as though she were one of her chicks. Amber-May liked Susie a lot, but she had no intention of telling her about the rape. She did not want to talk about that with anyone. She wanted to put it behind her as much as possible.

The best thing about her time in Crumley Creek was how friendly the townsfolk were to her. It was as though being hired by Susie had instantly conferred upon her the status of a longtime resident. The customers were very nice. Even the grumpy ones, those who could find fault in anything, weren't too bad. So she went to work with an eagerness she had not experienced in any previous job. It was as though Susie's Joint had become a refuge where she could let go of her nightmares, fears, and anxiety for a few hours and just be alive.

She made no plans during those first weeks. She simply lived each day as it came, gradually getting stronger, less anxious, and more at home. It was only as her first month in Crumley Creek was drawing to a close that she began to think that this was a town she might like to stay in indefinitely.

That all changed the day she noticed the car.

15

Garland Pickens filled a glass with cold water and gulped it down. There was a purified water dispenser in Patrick MacBaxter's hospital suite, but Pickens had opted to walk the eighty feet to the water cooler in the staff kitchen. He needed a moment to himself, away from his boss.

The call had come at three thirty in the morning, wrenching him out of a shallow sleep. It was MacBaxter's private nurse. She informed him that MacBaxter had taken a turn for the worse and had to be rushed to hospital. Pickens wasted no time. He dressed quickly and drove with uncustomary recklessness, arriving at the hospital shortly after four.

By that time, MacBaxter had already been stabilized, sedated, and deposited in the finest suite the hospital had to offer. Pickens had met with the doctor and was comforted to learn MacBaxter was breathing without assistance. That was surely a good sign, but he knew full well that the overall picture was bleak. His talk with the doctor only confirmed this. MacBaxter, the doctor said, was in critical condition. "He might hang on for days, or he might pass away at any moment. Knowing his history, he might surprise us all and walk out of here on his own two feet tomorrow. But I need to be honest with you. It doesn't look good."

"But he's not comatose, is he? He's going to wake up?"

"I think so, yes. Probably late this afternoon, once the drugs wear off. But understand that I'm not making any guarantees. He's very weak. It's a miracle that he's survived as long as he has. You and those closest to him should say your goodbyes, just in case."

Normally, only close family members would have been allowed to see MacBaxter, especially at that hour. They made an exception for Pickens. One reason was that MacBaxter had donated generously to the hospital over the years. Another was that Pickens was on a first-name basis with half of the hospital's board of directors. Consequently, word had come down from management that anything Pickens asked for, he should get.

He didn't need much. Just to be in his boss's presence. He sat in a padded armchair by the bed and watched Patrick MacBaxter's ravaged body, covered to the neck with a thin hospital blanket.

The past few months had not been kind to MacBaxter. His complexion had grayed. His face had wizened. His muscles had dwindled, loosening his skin. Even his voice, which had seemed impervious to the effects of his illness, had finally succumbed. It was now the thin, reedy voice of a sick old man.

His health had declined to the point that he never ventured out of his house anymore, conducting his business by phone or via Pickens. Pickens began each day by going to MacBaxter's sprawling mansion. There the two of them—the mentor and the disciple—would sit together in MacBaxter's home office and go over company reports, discuss possible deals and ventures, and decide on the various actions that were to be taken that workday. Each night, after the workday was done, Pickens would report to MacBaxter in person. As always, Pickens marveled at MacBaxter's razor-sharp intellect, his grasp of details, his clarity of mind. The disease, which was daily consuming more and more of him, had yet to sink its venomous teeth into his mental faculties. That, at least, was a blessing, Pickens thought on the frequent occasions when his mood turned dark.

Pickens kept silent vigil by the bed for over an hour. Then he succumbed to his fatigue and drifted into sleep. He was working harder and longer hours than ever before and sleeping very poorly. When he worked, he did so in the knowledge that time was running out, that soon the company would be deprived of its captain. The more things he got done now, while Patrick MacBaxter was still around to steer the massive ship that was MacBaxter Holdings, the better the company would be when it entered its transition period under the control of Emmett.

In addition to his regular duties, Pickens was also responsible for training Emmett. This was not easy. The company was involved in so many ventures across so many fields that there was a tremendous amount of information to convey. And it all had to be done fast. Emmett had to be brought up to speed as soon as possible so he could slide into his new position with minimal friction.

Pickens conducted much of the training himself, though other executives and managers also did their share. At first, he had not looked forward to spending much time with his future boss. But his impression of the young man had improved as time went by. He was gratified to note that Emmett had a quick mind. He absorbed facts quickly and easily, asked pertinent questions, and showed a healthy interest in the workings of the company. He was also capable of seeing the big picture, not just the small details. These were all good signs.

However, Pickens had noticed that Emmett also appeared to be high-strung, distracted, sometimes short-tempered. He had asked him about it, but Emmett just said he had a lot on his mind.

Perhaps Emmett was feeling the pressure of his upcoming eleva-tion to the head of MacBaxter Holdings. It was understandable; he was young, after all. Perhaps Emmett was also gearing himself emotionally for the death of his father and, as men often did, keeping his emotions bottled up inside him. Pickens had noted with approval that Emmett had paid his father more frequent visits over the past months. "The boy's got a head on his shoulders," Patrick MacBaxter had told Pickens after one such visit. "Every time he comes over, I teach him more about how to be a good man, in business and out, and I can see that he is listening closely, taking it all in. He's going to do fine. You'll see, Garland. He's going to make my ghost proud."

Emmett had certainly done well at college, graduating with high marks. And there had been no more trouble. No fights, no women too drunk to remember their names, and, most important, no sexual assaults following the incident with Amber-May Jackson. Perhaps Patrick MacBaxter was correct. Perhaps what had happened with Jackson was simply a horrible mistake on the part of a man not fully matured. Perhaps like his forebear Duncan MacBaxter before him, the man Emmett would become would do much good, enough to offset one terrible youthful sin.

Pickens still did not think Emmett was the man his father was, but he had to admit that he was showing signs of growing into his role. Pickens was starting to believe that Patrick MacBaxter's faith in his son was not as misplaced as he had feared. Emmett would make his share of early mistakes; Pickens supposed that was unavoidable. But he hoped they would not be too costly. He would do his best to make sure they weren't. All in all, he was feeling more confident in the future of the company under Emmett's leadership than he had ever thought he would.

When Pickens awoke in the armchair, his back was sore and his throat parched. Sunshine was pouring in through the large east-facing windows opposite the bed. The light fell on Patrick MacBaxter's face, making his skin look like ancient parchment. It was a sight that made Pickens's heart sink. He heaved himself to his feet and massaged his back in a futile attempt to relieve the pain. Then he exited the suite and went to the staff kitchen in search of water and a few moments of not having to witness MacBaxter's decline.

After drinking the water, he scratched his cheek, his fingers brushing stubble. He had not shaved after being rousted from bed by the nurse's call. He made a mental note to head down to the drugstore in the lobby and buy himself a razor and shaving cream later that morning. Then he phoned Emmett.

When Emmett answered, Pickens told him about his father's

condition and said Emmett might want to come over as soon as possible.

Emmett said, "Is he...is the end near?"

"They're not sure. But it's possible, I'm afraid. You should come see him before it's too late."

"Of course. But I'm out of the city at the moment. It'll take me a few hours to get there."

"Where are you?"

"Up north. I'll be by as soon as I can. Call me if, you know, if something happens."

Pickens promised he would. Then he returned to the suite and resumed his vigil, waiting for MacBaxter to wake up. Or die.

16

Emmett MacBaxter was furious. He could barely stop himself from yelling into the phone, "What do you mean, you've got nothing? You've been on this for more than three weeks."

The voice on the other end was male, deferential, and sincere. "I realize this is taking longer than you wish, sir, but I assure you we have our very best people working on this."

"How good can they be if they can't find one goddamn woman?"

"I understand your frustration, sir, and I share it."

"Maybe you don't. Maybe you think I'm some rube you can charge by the day indefinitely."

"I assure you that's not the case. It's just that these sorts of assignments can take time."

"How much time? How much longer?"

The man babbled something about not being able to guarantee a successful outcome by a certain date, and that he and his team were making every effort on Emmett's behalf, but Emmett tuned him out. He ground his teeth, wanting to reach his hand through the phone and sink his fist into the man's face.

The man was Nicholas Brunnert, the CEO of a company called Folssom Investigations & Security. Folssom had a reputation for discretion, competence, and a willingness to take on nontraditional, unsavory, and even illegal assignments without asking inconvenient questions. Emmett had been paying them eighteen hundred dollars a day for over three weeks, and so far they had nothing to show for it. Emmett had no problem spending money, but he sure as hell wanted results.

"You've got nothing? Nothing at all?"

"As I said during our talk two days ago, sir, we know the young lady in question spent some time in the hospital, first at St. Augustine's and later at Kleinman Medical Center. She was discharged a month ago. We know she visited her grandmother at her nursing home the same day. We know she emptied her bank account through an ATM withdrawal shortly after. We still don't know where she went after that, but we're working on it. She'll surface, sooner or later."

Which wasn't good enough for Emmett. He didn't want later. He didn't even want sooner. He wanted Amber-May Jackson found right now. He couldn't stand waiting much longer. He had been sure Folssom would have no trouble locating her quickly. That had obviously been a mistake. His frustration was intense, as was his anger at Nicholas Brunnert for his company's lack of success. So far, he hadn't told Brunnert what he planned on doing with Amber-May. That would come later, if and when his team managed to find her.

"Find her, damn you," he growled into the phone. "You know who I am. You know the position I will soon hold. If you want my business, you will find her for me. And fast."

He hung up before Brunnert could respond, and was on the verge of hurling the phone at the opposite wall when he managed to restrain himself. He needed the phone. News might come at any moment from Garland Pickens. News Emmett had been secretly longing to hear for a while.

His father had taken a turn for the worse during the night and was admitted to hospital. It wasn't the first time this had happened. Several times in the past year, his father had seemed on the brink of death but had pulled off an unexpected recovery. The stubborn old asshole was strong, both physically and mentally; Emmett had to give him that. He clung to life like a leech to skin. He might make it through another downturn. But if he didn't, Emmett wanted to hear the good news straight away.

Emmett was going to visit his father later that day. He didn't want to, but he knew he must. If and when his father came to, he would ask about him. He had to kiss the old man's ass a bit longer to ensure he wouldn't get any crazy ideas about changing his will at the last minute. Just the thought of seeing his father filled his mouth with a bitter taste. But you had to make sacrifices to achieve your goals. Every man who'd ever amounted to anything knew that.

He went into the kitchen, got a bottle of beer from the refrigerator, popped the cap, and took the bottle with him to the veranda. He sipped from the bottle, gazing absently at the wide expanse of lawn and shrubs and trees that surrounded him. The country house had been in the MacBaxter family since the 1950s. It was located in the center of a fifty-acre lot, which was bordered by dense forest on three sides and a river on the fourth. The nearest neighbor was miles away, out of sight and earshot. The property was off the beaten track, unfrequented by hikers or sightseers. And since the house was rarely occupied, there were no live-in servants. It was secluded. Private. Just what he needed.

The beer helped wash some of the bitter taste off his tongue. He guzzled the rest of it, went back into the house, and tossed the bottle in the trash. After taking a fresh bottle, he exited the kitchen, walked halfway down a hall, and stopped before an oak door. He fished a key ring from his pocket, found the right key, and unlocked the door. He flicked the light switch on the wall behind it. A bulb came to life, illuminating a wooden staircase descending into darkness.

Emmett went down the fourteen steps, reaching the basement. It smelled musty and stale down here, even though he'd left a window open. When he'd arrived at the house four days ago, a film of dust covered everything—the shelves, the furniture, even the doorknobs. An industrious spider had spun a complex web in one corner. In another lay a dead mouse, its body decomposed. Emmett then did something he had never done before in his life. He cleaned.

He stuffed the dead mouse into a plastic bag and dumped it in the trash. He tore down the cobwebs. He wiped the dust off every surface. He vacuumed the couches. He mopped the floor. He made the bathroom sparkle. He didn't enjoy the cleaning, nor did he resent it. Like visiting his father, it was a means to an end, something he had to do. A real man did not grumble or pout. He pulled up his shirtsleeves and got busy.

The basement was divided into a number of rooms. There was a bedroom at one end and an expansive living space in the middle. The living space was paneled in wood and had a parquet floor. It held a large-screen TV, two couches, an assortment of chairs, a table, and shelves filled with books and children's games that Emmett used to play with years ago whenever he'd stayed in the house.

There was also a modernly equipped kitchenette. As long as you had the proper supplies, you could live very comfortably down here.

At the far end of the living space, down a short hallway and an additional eighteen stairs, was another door. Emmett swung it open. He had to put his whole body into it. The door was made of steel, very thick and heavy, and set right into the concrete wall. Beyond it was a twenty-by-twenty high-ceilinged room. A double bed stood against one wall, a bunk bed against another. A door in one corner led into a small shower and bathroom. Another opened onto a storage room, with shelves crowding all four walls. The shelves were empty now, but decades ago, during a time in which Americans lived in fear of nuclear war with the Soviet Union, they had carried a variety of canned goods, enough to live on for months, if not years.

The walls were reinforced concrete a foot or more thick. The entirety of the bomb shelter was below ground level, so there were no windows. The only light came from ceiling light fixtures. The shelter had been built to withstand a nuclear blast. Emmett had no idea whether it would have worked. What he did know was that the thick walls and door and the subterranean positioning of the shelter made it impossible for any sound to escape from it. Add to that the isolation of the house and it was perfect for what he had in mind.

He still had had to put in some work to get things ready. He'd spread the purchases of the tools and materials across a number of stores, none of which was in the vicinity of the house. He'd paid cash for everything. No one could make the connection. Nothing could be traced to him.

He had never used a power drill before, but he watched a few how-to videos on YouTube and got the hang of it pretty quickly. Still, he'd screwed up the first time he tried to drill into the concrete and had to shift half a foot to the left to try again. In the end, he'd gotten it done, and when he stepped back and surveyed the results of his handiwork, his lips spread into a smile that was all teeth and fevered anticipation.

Bolted into the wall were four metal chains, at the end of which were shackles. Two of the shackles were intended to encircle wrists, the other two ankles. The ankle chains were long enough to allow whoever was shackled to them to reach the bathroom and shower, but not the shelter door.

Everything was ready. Ready for her. For Amber-May Jackson. For his and her reunion. Only this time, he would not let her go after one night. He would feast on her again and again. He would take all the pleasure she had to give. He would stretch it out over a very long time. Months, perhaps years.

Would he share her with anyone? Any of the other three?

No. He didn't think so. Their friendship had frayed in the months following the rape. That was all right with him. He didn't need them anymore. They had been good company during college, all studying business management together, all coming from wealthy families, but none of them was like him. None of them had greatness in him. The smartest thing was to keep this whole arrangement to himself, and to keep Amber-May Jackson to himself as well.

Amber-May Jackson.

His mouth went dry at the thought of her. The blood quickened its flow through his veins and arteries. His head swam with manic desire. He wanted her here, in this house, in the bomb shelter, shackled to the wall, at his mercy. He could picture her, hear her anxious cries, smell the sweet fragrance of her fear, taste her skin. His need for her was turning him into a pressure cooker, ready to explode. If he had to wait much longer, he would go mad.

Feeling as though his head might burst at any second, Emmett launched the beer bottle at the wall where the shackles hung empty. As the bottle disintegrated in a spray of brown liquid and green glass, he screamed at the echoing walls of the makeshift prison cell, "Where the hell are you, you bitch!"

17

It took Amber-May nearly a month to notice the car. This meant she was rusty as hell. Which was understandable. She hadn't played the Car Game in years.

The game was her father's idea. When Amber-May was eight or nine, she got to asking her father about his time in the military. She wanted to know what he'd done, what it had been like. She remembered how his face had clouded over, how he'd tried steering her to other topics.

When he saw she would not be diverted, he smiled and pulled her onto his lap. Pointing out the bay window of their house, he said, "Want to know one of the things I learned as a soldier, Ambie?" That was what he'd often called her. Ambie. "I learned how to pay attention to my surroundings, to notice things. In particular, I learned to notice cars. That's because you never know who might be hiding in them. And a soldier should never allow himself to be surprised." He turned his back to the window and told her to ask him the make, model, and color of the cars parked on their street. She did, and he got everything right, in the correct order. He also knew which car belonged to which neighbor. There weren't a lot of cars, but it still impressed her. So they began playing the Car Game regularly. When they were home, at a MacDonald's, in the playground, anywhere. Amber-May got quite good at it.

"Good enough to be a soldier?" she asked one time.

Her dad smiled and said, "Sure thing, sweetheart. If that's what you want."

After her parents died, she stopped playing the Car Game. But for a long time afterward, she still noticed things, especially cars.

As the years passed, this ability faded with misuse. So she might have failed to notice the car at all were it not for Nurse Martha Mitchum.

It was during one of her regular calls to the nursing home. After telling her that her grandmother was fine, Martha said, "Someone was asking about you."

"About me?"

"Yes. A woman. She said she worked with you."

"Did she give a name?"

"Janet something. I'm sorry, but I don't remember her last name."

"Janet Cranston?"

"That's it. You know her?"

Janet Cranston was one of the other waitresses in the café where Amber-May had worked prior to her attack. Amber-May got along well enough with Janet, but she wouldn't say they were friends. They never met or spoke with each other outside of work. It seemed odd that Janet Cranston would be asking about her.

"When did she call?"

"Oh, two or three days ago."

"What did she say?"

"That she was trying to locate you, that you two used to work together, but then one day you didn't show up for work and she hasn't seen you since. She said she knew your grandmother lived here, so she wondered whether you'd been by. When I told her I'd last seen you about a month ago, she asked whether you'd called or if I knew where you were. She said she was worried about you."

Amber-May racked her brain trying to remember if she'd ever told Janet Cranston about Grandma Betsy. If she had, she had no recollection of it. As she held the phone to her ear, she felt a chill creep up her spine. Something didn't smell right about this whole thing.

"What did you tell her?"

"That I haven't spoken to you since your last visit and that I had no idea where you lived." Martha lowered her voice. "I got an odd feeling talking to her—I don't know why. I didn't feel it was my place to tell her anything about you. I didn't know if you'd want me to."

Amber-May let out a breath. "Thank you, Martha. That was a good call. If she phones again, please tell her you still haven't heard from me."

"I will." Martha paused, then asked, "Amber-May, are you in some sort of trouble?"

"Don't worry about me. I'm fine."

"If you say so. If there's anything I can do to help..."

"Just take care of my grandmother. That's all I need from you," Amber-May said, a little ashamed of how brusquely she was responding to Martha's offer of help.

"You can rest assured I'll do that as best I can," Martha said, her tone formal and distant. Then her voice softened. "You just...just take care of yourself, all right? And I hope that you'll come visit again soon. Seeing you does your grandmother a world of good, even if she doesn't remember it for very long."

"I'll try. Thank you for everything." Amber-May ended the call, feeling her eyes moisten.

She sat on the small blue couch in her apartment for a long time, gazing out the window at the street outside. She didn't think Janet Cranston cared enough to worry about her, not to mention go to the trouble of trying to locate her. And the more she thought about it, the more convinced she became that she had never discussed Grandma Betsy's living arrangement with any of her co-workers, Janet included.

That meant that whoever had asked Martha Mitchum about her was someone pretending to be Janet Cranston. Whoever she was, she'd done her homework, learned that Amber-May had worked with

Janet, and decided to use her name while trying to learn where Amber-May was.

Why?

The answer was clear. In case Martha told Amber-May about the call. The caller hoped that if this happened, Amber-May would fall for her ruse. The caller had obviously talked to Janet Cranston. Maybe Janet had made herself out to be a close friend of Amber-May, someone Amber-May might believe would inquire after her. It was just like her. Janet was the sort of person who liked to be seen as more important than she really was.

But who was the woman who had talked to Martha Mitchum?

It wasn't Detective Sanchez or any other policewoman. A policewoman would have identified herself. It wasn't anyone Amber-May knew, for the same reason. It was someone who wanted to know where Amber-May was. Someone who wanted to find her.

Or someone who'd been hired to find her by some other party.

Garland Pickens, for instance.

But why? Why would Pickens want her found?

She was ruminating over this, when her gaze alighted on the car.

It was a metal blue Toyota, a common make and color, parked across the street diagonally from her apartment, in the shade of a large tree. It had tinted windows. She couldn't see whether there was anyone inside.

The street where she lived contained medium-sized houses, each with its own carport or garage, mostly large enough for one or two cars. Some of the households owned more vehicles than could be parked on their property, but even so, there was always plenty of parking space along both curbs. Consequently, the residents parked their cars as close as possible to their homes, usually in about the same spot.

But not the Toyota.

With her sense of vigilance heightened by her talk with Nurse Mitchum, Amber-May's latent ability to notice cars came back to life. As she stared at the Toyota, she became convinced that the car had been parked on the opposite side of the street the day before as well, but not in the same spot. Yesterday, it had stood two hundred yards up the street, also in the shade of a tree. And that had not been the first time she'd seen it. Last week—she wasn't sure on which exact day—the Toyota had been there as well, that time a few houses south of the one in front of which it now stood.

If the car belonged to one of the street's residents, why would it be parked in front of different houses on different days?

Now that the car had finally registered in her mind, she began to wonder how long it had been around, how long she had missed it. She took a few deep breaths and closed her eyes, willing her body to relax and her mind to clear. It wasn't easy—her heart was drumming in her ears, and her mind was choppy with darting thoughts. She did her mental trick, imagining herself sitting on the crown of a sunny hilltop, with a brisk, yet pleasant, wind swirling around her. The wind brought with it the calming scent of jasmine, and its flow dispersed the chaotic thoughts that were churning through her brain. She felt her heart rate slow to a steady, tranquil rhythm. She focused on the image of the car and let her memory work.

Her memory was by no means perfect, but after marshaling every ounce of her concentration for several minutes, she opened her eyes, certain that she'd seen the Toyota several times since her arrival in Crumley Creek. The first time had been more than two weeks ago. It might have been around since shortly after her arrival at her new home. And her street was not the only place she'd seen it. It had also been in the parking lot of Susie's Joint. More than once.

She strained her brain, trying to match a driver to the car, hoping that the bells ringing in her ears were raising a false alarm. Her mind failed to produce a face to go with the vehicle. If the Toyota belonged to one of the customers who frequented the diner, she couldn't say which one he or she was. Which didn't mean all that much. Crumley Creek was not big, but it wasn't the smallest of towns either. And Susie's Joint enjoyed the patronage of many residents of neighboring towns and also folks who were just passing through.

Gnawing her lower lip, she pondered what all this meant.

There might be an innocent explanation for the car. Her rape might have made her more prone to seeing danger where none existed. She wanted to believe this was the case, but both her mind and her gut told her this was not so.

What, then?

She did not like the answer her brain supplied, but she could not argue with it. She could not lie to herself.

What the car signified was that someone had followed her to Crumley Creek and was now keeping track of her. Someone who worked with the woman who had called the nursing home and talked to Martha Mitchum.

But wait, this didn't make sense. Whoever was driving the car, whoever had been watching her since her arrival in Crumley Creek, if not before that, could not be working with the woman who had called the nursing home. If he were, the woman wouldn't have tried eliciting information from Martha Mitchum. She would already know where Amber-May was.

Which meant that there were two parties involved. One already knew where she was; the other was trying to find out. Garland Pickens could be one of them but not both.

Which begged the question: Who else wanted to know where she was?

18

After a month of surveillance, Freddie Sheehan was officially bored out of his mind.

Each day was the same. He'd wake up in his motel room, have breakfast, check his tablet to make sure Amber-May Jackson's Ford had not moved during the night, and surf the net or do a quick breeze through the channels on the TV. Then he'd climb into his Toyota-now equipped with a set of Tennessee plates he'd filched from a junk-yard—and head out to do his surveillance in Crumley Creek.

The more time he spent in the town, the less he liked it. Nothing interesting ever happened, and it didn't seem like anything ever would. And this was also true of his target. Amber-May spent most of her days at the diner and never left her apartment at night. She did not have anyone over, nor did she go out on dates. What she did do was take long and apparently aimless walks throughout Crumley Creek and its surroundings, and each morning before work she would run.

She looked hot in her running shorts and top, her calf muscles bunching and releasing with each springing step, her ponytail swinging side to side along her lovely neck. But seeing it day after day wore the novelty off quick.

She never drove out of town. The only places she went with her car were the diner, the library, and the grocery store. If she had anything worth noting about her life, Freddie didn't see it.

So, yeah, he was bored stiff.

After his talk with Sergeant Malone, he dedicated considerable thought to Amber-May and the question of whom her attackers might be. Since he doubted Pickens himself was involved, it had to be someone he was connected with. Freddie knew that Pickens worked as the personal attorney of Patrick MacBaxter and was his right-hand man in MacBaxter Holdings. So Freddie figured whoever Pickens was covering up for was connected to that company or to the MacBaxter family. That meant that one or more of the rapists could be a high-ranking executive in one of the corporations MacBaxter Holdings controlled. Or they might be personal friends of the MacBaxter family, or even members of that family itself. Hell, Patrick MacBaxter himself might be one of them.

Freddie read extensively about MacBaxter. The guy was a bit old, and recent rumor suggested he was not well. But maybe months ago, when Amber-May Jackson was attacked, he was in better shape. In addition, MacBaxter had a history of dating younger women; his second and third wives had both been much younger than him. Maybe he and a few of his rich buddies had put the moves on Amber-May and she had rejected them. Rich guys don't get turned down often; their money usually buys them any woman they want. So maybe MacBaxter and his pals got mad enough to beat Amber-May up in the course of raping her.

MacBaxter's son, Emmett, was another possibility. Freddie had found pictures of Emmett and read a few kiss-his-ass articles on him. The kid was twenty-three, much younger than his dad. Tall, well-built, with an I-know-I'm-a-stud kind of shit-eating grin plastered across his wide face.

No hint of any improper behavior on Emmett's part in any of the articles, but Freddie supposed that meant little. Pickens had enough cash and pull to sweep a lot of dirt under the rug. Maybe Emmett had met Amber-May at a party somewhere and did not appreciate her not putting out on the first date. Maybe he lost control of his temper. Maybe he had a few friends around and they joined in when he jumped her. When you're young and stupid and horny, that kind of thing can happen.

But Freddie wasn't sure it mattered whether either of the MacBaxters was one of the men who had put Amber-May in the hospital. Because the more Freddie thought about it, the more it seemed to him that he couldn't personally benefit from such knowledge.

Let's say Patrick or Emmett MacBaxter had raped Amber-May. So what? What could Freddie do? Threaten to inform the police? Do a little blackmailing?

It was possible, but blackmail was a risky business, especially when you targeted really powerful people. You might end up in a ditch somewhere with a bullet in the back of your head.

Besides, the only person the rapists really needed to worry about was Amber-May. And since Pickens had succeeded in paying her off and persuading her to go away, she was unlikely to finger her assailants to the police.

So Freddie had reluctantly arrived at the conclusion that he would have to settle for the money Pickens was paying him for keeping an eye on her. Which was pretty good, all things considered. Pickens paid well, and the job itself was far from hard.

Apart from being excruciatingly boring.

It was either his boredom or his curiosity that caused him to go to the diner. He knew it was stupid, but he figured one time couldn't hurt. Besides, he wanted to see Amber-May up close. Maybe he would spot something he'd missed before.

Yeah, right. He knew that was just an excuse. The girl was hot and he was bored. That was all.

He took some precautions. He chose the busiest time of day and parked the Toyota a block away from the diner and himself on a stool at the counter, where the older woman served. Amber-May was handling the booths.

He ordered a burger and fries and a pie. He'd put on a baseball cap and pulled it low over his eyes. He sat huddled over his food, his head tilted downward to further hide his features and obscure where his eyes were pointed.

He snuck glances at Amber-May whenever he could without being obvious. She wore tight-fitting light-blue jeans and a red shirt with two buttons at the neck, both open, showing a wedge of bright skin. Her apron went down a little past her knees and had a pocket for an order pad and pens.

She moved through the diner like an ice-skater, her feet gliding across the linoleum floor, her back straight, her head up. Maybe she'd taken dancing lessons as a kid. Or maybe it was all the running and walking she did.

He noted how firm her ass looked in her jeans, the way her breasts pushed out the top of her apron, the tautness of her arms. No loose skin on the underarms. No, sir.

She didn't show any sign of being recently raped and beaten. Nor did he spot any scars left by the surgery done on her face. Her skin was smooth, rosy, and fresh. She smiled easily and often. Her voice was clear and just a little bit throaty. He wondered how she smelled.

He wanted to keep watching her but decided not to push it. He'd already taken a chance going into the diner. Once he was done with his food, he wiped his mouth with a napkin, threw some money on the counter, and left.

The short-lived rush of excitement he got from seeing Amber-May up close had already faded by the time he got to his car. The boredom was creeping back in. Goddammit, this assignment had better be over soon or he might go crazy.

19

Back in his motel room, Freddie called Pickens.

"Good day, Mr. Pickens, this is Freddie Sheehan calling in with a report."

"Yes, Freddie. Go ahead. I'm listening." The lawyer sounded tired as hell, like he hadn't slept in a week.

"It's the same as two days ago. She goes running, then to work, then to the library or shopping or home to her apartment. She doesn't visit anyone's house, and she gets no visitors at her place."

"She doesn't meet with anyone?"

"She meets lots of people in the diner where she works, but no one like you mean."

"I see."

"Once she's off work, she seems to prefer being alone."

"All right. Good."

The motel television was on with the sound off, a talk show flickering on the screen. A black guy in a gray suit and a blond woman in a blue dress were interviewing a fat balding white man. The interviewee was talking animatedly while holding up a book like a street vendor, so Freddie guessed he was a writer hawking his latest creation.

Freddie said, "If she's up to something, I'm not seeing it. Of course, if you told me what to look for..."

"There's nothing specific, Freddie. I just want to know that she's far away from here and get a general sense of what she's doing."

"She's not doing anything, far as I can tell. In fact, I think she's settled in for the long haul."

"Oh?"

"Yeah. For one thing, she hasn't left this town once since the day she got here; for another, the day before yesterday, she put up new curtains in her apartment."

"I see. Any other signs of domestication?"

Freddie, whose attention had been drawn to the television, where the anchorwoman had uncrossed and recrossed her legs, showing a good deal of thigh in the process, had only half heard the question.

"Huh?"

"Is there any other indication that she's going to stay there for a while?"

Freddie thought for a moment before saying, "She borrows books from the library, so she must have taken out a card. That's something, isn't it?"

"Yes," Pickens said contemplatively. "Yes, I think you're right."

On the TV, they broke for commercial. Some guy holding a tooth-brush in one hand and a tube of paste in the other was flashing a goofy, all-white smile. Freddie pictured how he'd look if someone knocked a few of his teeth out.

He turned his attention back to the phone. "How long you want me to keep shadowing her?"

For a few seconds, Pickens didn't answer. Then he said, "How does she seem?"

"What do you mean?"

"How does she look? Happy? Depressed? Healthy?"

Freddie shrugged at the phone. "She looks fine to me. Like I said, she looks like she's at home."

Another pause. On the other end, Freddie thought he heard a door open, faint voices in the midst of a conversation; then the voices were muted as the door was shut. He heard Pickens say hello to someone. Followed by: "Give me a second to finish this call. If you want some coffee, there's a machine over there."

Then Pickens was back, "All right, Freddie. Give it till tomorrow, then pack it in. It sounds like she's not going anywhere."

"As you say, Mr. Pickens."

"And call me when you get back. There'll be a bonus waiting for you."

The bonus had better be big, Freddie wanted to say, considering how boring this assignment turned out to be, but he managed to keep the words unspoken.

20

Emmett MacBaxter fought to mask his emotions as Pickens ended his call and turned to shake his hand. He molded his features into a doleful expression, inclining his head toward the hospital bed where his father lay unconscious.

"How is he?"

"Not good. He's under sedation. He'll likely be out for a few more hours." Pickens sighed. "He might not come out of it at all."

"Can you give me a few minutes alone with him?"

Pickens nodded. "I'll go grab myself some lunch. Would you like me to get you anything?"

"No. Thank you, Garland."

He kept his eyes firmly on his father so Pickens wouldn't be able to read the eager anticipation on his face. He had cast his voice low, aiming for a somber tone. Just how a devoted son worried about his much-beloved ailing father would sound. He didn't want Pickens to suspect anything.

After Pickens had mumbled something and left the room, Emmett counted slowly to one hundred. He wanted to make sure the lawyer wasn't about to make a surprise reappearance. Then he whipped out his phone and made a quick call. Three minutes later he had the phone number he sought. He called it.

The voice on the other end was weary and impatient. In the background Emmett could hear a television playing.

"Yeah?" the voice said.

"Freddie Sheehan?"

"Yeah. Who's this?"

Emmett ignored Freddie's question and asked one of his own. "Do you know where Amber-May Jackson is?"

On the other end there was a pause. The television was turned off. Then Freddie Sheehan was back on the line, sounding tense and wary. "Who is this?"

Emmett balled his fist and opened it slowly. He wanted answers. He had no patience for questions. "My name is Emmett MacBaxter. Now answer my question."

When Freddie spoke next, all the wariness and tension were gone from his voice. He sounded utterly relaxed. Emmett was certain the man was smiling.

"Why, yes, Mr. MacBaxter. Indeed, I do."

Emmett closed his eyes and a broad smile stretched his lips. He couldn't believe his luck. He had found her. Just like that. And to think how close he'd come not to. If he'd arrived at the hospital one minute later than he did, he would have missed hearing the tail end of Pickens and Freddie Sheehan's conversation.

But he had been there on time. As if he'd been destined to.

Fate.

It was fate propelling him toward Amber-May, a hunter toward a rare exotic quarry. His domination of her was meant to be.

And if Pickens hadn't said exactly what he had, mentioning Freddie's name and saying something about a woman not going anywhere, things might not have clicked in Emmett's brain. Even so, the fact that they had must also mean something, because he easily could have failed to make the connection.

He'd heard about Freddie Sheehan a while back, perhaps a year or so ago. Pickens or his father had mentioned him in passing;

Emmett didn't remember the context. What he did remember was Freddie's line of work. He was a private investigator, and there was a hint of shadiness attached to him. Nothing definite, nothing concrete, but enough to make an indelible impression on Emmett's memory.

Of course, it could have been another Freddie that Pickens had been talking to. Or if it were Freddie Sheehan, his job for Pickens might have had nothing to do with Amber-May Jackson. But the buzz of excitement that had started sounding in Emmett's ears told him it was neither of those things. It told him that Pickens had been talking to Freddie Sheehan, and that they had been discussing Amber-May.

And just like that, his luck had flipped. An hour ago, he'd had no clue as to where Amber-May might be, and was beginning to lose hope that Folssom Investigations & Security would ever find her. Now he knew her location. But that wasn't enough. He needed to know one thing more.

He asked Freddie, "How does she look? Does she have any scars on her face?"

"No. Nothing like that. She's as perfect as they come."

Emmett's grin widened further. He bunched his left hand into a fist and pumped it in the air like a basketball player after making a last-second winning shot. It was going to work. She was going to be his.

But there was something that had to be done for that to become a reality.

He said into the phone, "This is your lucky day, Freddie. I have a job for you. If you do it right, I'll make you rich."

Two minutes later, after he had explained to Freddie exactly what he wanted him to do, he hung up the phone, feeling elated. He wished he had some vodka or champagne with which to toast his good fortune. He felt like partying all day and all night.

Then he heard the rustle of bedsheets behind him.

He whirled around and saw his father awake and staring at him with those judgmental gray eyes of his.

The old man looked terrible, half alive and half dead. But those eyes, they still held immense power. How Emmett hated those eyes.

From as far back as he could remember, those eyes had always made him feel small, inadequate, weak, less than what he should be. He could feel himself shrink under the weight of their scrutiny.

Oh God. Had his father heard his talk with Freddie Sheehan? Had he heard what he'd asked the investigator to do?

When his father spoke, Emmett got his answer.

"You," Patrick MacBaxter began, his voice weakened by his illness but made resonant by his indignation, "are a despicable, revolting, filthy excuse for a man. What are you planning to do to that girl?"

Emmett didn't answer. He couldn't. His throat had seized up. His body was rigid with panic. Catastrophe. This was a catastrophe. His father had heard everything. And this time there would be no forgiveness. This time there would be no more chances. He would be cut off from the will. He would not get the money or the company. He would be left with nothing. Fear made his bowels contract painfully and his eyes sting with welling tears.

A shrill voice started screaming incoherently in his head. His eardrums felt like they were about to burst from the inside out. His skull began aching. He couldn't tear his eyes away from his father's.

Though his vision was blurry with unshed tears, Emmett could see that his father's thin lips were curled in a sneer of abject disgust. His eyes looked huge in his emaciated face. They bored right into him.

MacBaxter said, "Never mind. You don't need to say anything. I can guess well enough what you have in mind. I don't need to know for sure. And it doesn't matter, because I won't let you do anything else to that poor girl. You've hurt her enough already. I should have let her tell the cops everything. I should have let them lock you up in a cage like the animal you are." His eyes flicked about the room. "Where's Garland?"

The second his father's eyes left his, it was as if a tight vise had let go of him. Emmett sprang forward, his brain sending one urgent message to every cell in his body. "Stop him now!"

MacBaxter, seeing that Pickens wasn't in the room, was reaching a frail hand toward the call switch hanging on the side rail of his bed. His fingers touched the plastic, but Emmett gripped his wrist.

"Oh no you don't," Emmett said in a tear-choked voice. "Don't you dare." And he gave his father's wrist a twist and wrenched his hand away from the switch.

MacBaxter grimaced, but he didn't let out a sound. Emmett was now bent over his father. He could smell the stringent scent of medicine wafting from the old man, mingled with the rank odor of disease.

Emmett had the advantage of youth and weight and health, but Patrick MacBaxter showed no sign of fear. His eyes held nothing but naked contempt for his son.

"I'll see you locked up with other rapists to keep you company if it's the last thing I do."

"No," Emmett said, baring his teeth. "You won't."

And he slid the pillow from under his father's head and put it over his face, covering his mouth and nose, cutting off his access to oxygen. And as he did so, the tears started flowing from his eyes.

21

Opting to remain close by, Pickens chose to eat in the hospital's cafeteria. He ordered ravioli drenched in cream, a small green salad with olive oil, and a large black coffee with plenty of sugar. He had just filled his mouth with the third forkful of ravioli when his phone chirped.

The doctor's number flashed on the screen. Pickens felt his heart skip a beat. Had MacBaxter woken up?

He swallowed and set his fork down and answered the phone. The instant he heard the doctor's solemn tone, he knew it was bad news.

"Are you in the hospital, Mr. Pickens?"

"Yes. Downstairs, in the cafeteria. What is it?"

"You'd better come up to the suite."

"Why? What's going on? What's wrong?"

There was a pause. The doctor said gently, "I'm afraid he's gone."

Pickens closed his eyes and sat for a moment in complete silence. Then he said, "I'm coming up. Five minutes."

There were medical staff milling about the open doorway to MacBaxter's suite. A burly male nurse was pushing an emergency cart toward the far end of the hall. Two female nurses were talking in soft tones. They fell silent as Pickens approached.

Inside the suite there were just two other living persons. Emmett was sitting on the couch, weeping openly, his shoulders quaking as he sobbed. The doctor was standing by the bed. On it lay Patrick MacBaxter. The covers had been pulled down his body, and his scrawny chest was exposed. Pickens supposed this had been done in an attempt to resuscitate him. MacBaxter's mouth was open. His eyes were closed, his chest motionless. There was no doubt that he was dead.

Pickens found a chair and plopped down onto it. He lowered his head. He did nothing but breathe in and out for a full minute. Then he raised his eyes to the doctor. "What happened?"

The doctor shrugged his thin shoulders. "His body just gave in."

"But why now?"

"I told you it might happen at any moment. He was strong. He stayed alive longer than any of us expected he would. But there's only so much the body can withstand."

"You said he would wake up."

"I hoped he would, but I told you there were no guarantees. We tried to save him, but it was no use. He was already dead by the time we came into the room."

Pickens said nothing. He knew the doctor and medical staff weren't to blame. They had done all they could. The doctor shifted his feet and said he'd let them have a moment alone with the body. After saying how sorry he was, he left the room.

Pickens rose and stepped over to the bed. Looking down at his boss's body, he felt as though his life had been cleaved in half. There was what came before and what would now come after. He felt like crying, but he didn't. He wanted to shout his lungs out, but he didn't do that either. Instead, he pulled the hospital blanket back over MacBaxter's torso and gently closed his mouth. That was better. More dignified. More in keeping with the man's life and character.

Suddenly aware of the silence in the room, Pickens turned his gaze to Emmett. The younger man had ceased crying. He sat on the couch, hands on knees, staring at Pickens with wet eyes.

"You were here when it happened?" Pickens asked.

"Yes."

"Did he wake up? Did he say anything before he died?"

Emmett ran the sleeve of his jacket over his face and shook his head. "He opened his eyes, but he didn't speak. He gave a couple of labored breaths, and then he just stopped breathing." He paused for a second and added, "I didn't know what to do. I yelled for the nurses. They worked on him for a few minutes, but there was nothing they could do. He was dead."

Emmett got up and came over to the other side of the bed. He looked down at his father. Pickens expected him to start crying again, but he didn't. "I'm glad I was here, Garland. I'm glad I was with him when he passed."

But I wasn't, Pickens thought bitterly. *I was at his side for years, through many challenges, setbacks, and triumphs, but not at his final moment.* He rubbed the back of his neck. "I'm glad you were here, too, Emmett. Though it must have been hard for you to see him die."

Emmett simply nodded, averting his face. Wordlessly, he walked into the bathroom. Pickens heard the sound of running water. When Emmett emerged, his face was washed and dried. His expression was calm and collected. Were it not for his red-rimmed eyes, one would not have guessed that he had been weeping uncontrollably two minutes before.

Emmett said, "What happens now?"

"I'll handle all the hospital paperwork. I've already made the funeral arrangements months ago. We'll have it three days from now if that's all right with you. That way, your father's foreign associates will be able to attend."

Emmett nodded. "I meant what happens with the will, the company, his estate."

"Oh," Pickens said. "Right. Well, we can have the formal reading of the will any time you wish. There are no surprises. You are his sole heir."

"Let's do it tomorrow." Emmett looked at Pickens, then added quickly, "I think it would be best if I started working as soon as possible. It's best for the company, don't you think? He would have wanted it that way."

"Yes. I believe he would have."

"You foresee any problems with administering the will? Any other claimants who might pop up?"

"No. He had no close relatives besides yourself. No one with any conceivable claim."

"Good." Emmett let out a loud breath and ran a hand through his hair, smoothing it against his scalp. He slapped his hands together. "I could sure use a drink. You got something here?"

"No. Nothing."

"I'll go hunt something up. I'll be back soon." Emmett took a step toward the door, then stopped and came back to the bed. He touched his father's face with his fingertips and said, "I'd almost started to believe he was going to live forever, you know? It feels...different now that he's truly gone."

Pickens said nothing. He could not have agreed more.

Without another word, Emmett turned and left the room, leaving Pickens completely alone.

Pickens sat once more in the chair. Things were moving too fast for his taste, but Emmett had a point. It was best for the company that its new leader take up his position as soon as possible. MacBaxter would have wanted it.

Pickens laid his eyes once more on his former boss. He recalled the oath he'd sworn to him, to serve the company and to serve Emmett.

"You can count on it, sir," Pickens said softly. "You can count on it."

22

Freddie spent the next two days shopping.

For the girl, he bought duct tape, a pair of handcuffs, zip ties, and, after some difficulty, a small bottle of a contraband drug that surpassed Rohypnol in its potency. A mouthful would render a grown woman incapacitated for a few hours.

For himself, he purchased six large bottles of mineral water, two six-packs of energy drinks, a carton of cigarettes, and enough snacks to carry him through a long drive up north. He estimated that it would take him about twenty-four hours of hard driving to get to where he needed to go.

Once he left Crumley Creek, he did not plan on stopping for anything save the occasional piss by the side of the road. Not until he got to his destination. Which was why he'd also bought two five-gallon cans of fuel and placed them in the footwell of the backseat.

He put none of his supplies in the trunk. He had another purpose for it. He went over it carefully, removing the jack and the tire iron and making sure it contained nothing that could be used as a weapon. If he didn't screw up, the girl would be in no shape to fight, but it was better to be safe than sorry. He also disabled the interior trunk release. Now it could not be opened from the inside.

Once he had everything ready, he treated himself to a steak dinner at the fanciest restaurant in the area. The motel clerk had recommended it. He drank wine—an expensive brand—and had chocolate cake for dessert. The waitress was a looker, so he flirted with her and left her a large tip. He was feeling generous, on top of the world.

One million dollars.

He repeated the sum under his breath as he savored the wine and cake, smiling or even chuckling when he did so. An unbelievable amount of money. But that was what that crazy son of a bitch Emmett MacBaxter had offered him. At first, he couldn't believe it. He thought he'd misheard him, or that Emmett was playing some sick joke. But no, the man was serious. Crazy, yes, but also dead serious.

"Bring me Amber-May Jackson," Emmett had said soon after Freddie had assured him that Amber-May's face was unmarred by any scars.

"Bring her? Where?"

Emmett gave him an address in a rural part of Maine. Freddie had never been in that area, but he could find it. He didn't bother asking whether the girl would agree to come. It was clear she wouldn't.

"How do you want her?" Freddie asked.

"What?"

"In what shape? Alive? Dead? Either?"

"Alive," Emmett said quickly, "and unharmed. I don't want a scratch on her. Especially not her face. You must leave no mark on her face. Understand?"

"Yeah. I get it. But it's possible I'll have to get a little bit rough with her, you understand?"

"Okay. Just as long as nothing happens to her face and she sustains no other disfiguring or debilitating injuries. She has to look the way she looks now. That's crucial. Can you do it?"

"Yeah, I can do it. But something like this...it's not what I normally do."

"I'm willing to pay for it."

"It won't be cheap."

Emmett didn't hesitate. "Do this for me, and I'll pay you one million dollars. That should be enough, I think. Do you agree?"

Freddie agreed. He would have done it for much less.

"How soon can you deliver her?"

Freddie considered this. "Give me a week," he said, giving himself a two-, three-day cushion, just in case.

"Can't you do it sooner?" Emmett asked, and Freddie noted the eagerness in his voice.

"I can if I got to, but I'd rather do it right. It's better for you and me both."

A short pause. Then: "Okay. But remember, she's got to look as perfect as she does now. If not, our deal is off."

"All right, all right. I understand."

After their call had ended, Freddie sat for a while, thinking. He wondered what Emmett MacBaxter wanted with Amber-May Jackson, but he didn't need to wonder for long. It was pretty obvious. Emmett was one of the men who had raped Amber-May, and, for some reason, he wanted her again.

Why she would be worth a million dollars to him was something Freddie couldn't begin to speculate. He didn't think any woman was worth that much. Apparently, however, Emmett MacBaxter thought differently. Which was all right, as far as Freddie was concerned. More than all right; it was fantastic. It was going to turn him into a millionaire.

He considered what Emmett had in store for Amber-May. For what the man was paying, it had to be something special, more than simply another rape. Freddie didn't dwell on it. It was best not to think too much about certain things. Better to stay focused on what he had to do.

He also asked himself where Garland Pickens fit in all this. It was Pickens who had gotten the girl to not blow the whistle on Emmett, but Freddie didn't think Pickens knew what Emmett now had in mind. Not for a second did Freddie consider informing Pickens as to what Emmett had hired him to do. Pickens paid well, but nothing close to a million dollars. That kind of money was a once-in-a-lifetime opportunity. And he wouldn't even have to work too hard to earn it.

Freddie doubted Amber-May would prove to be much of a challenge. He was stronger than her, he had experience with violence, and she had no clue he was coming for her. He also had a gun. He'd told Emmett that he might need to get rough with her, but he now thought there was a good chance that wouldn't be the case. The girl would likely freeze at the first glimpse of his pistol. Guns made most people wonderfully cooperative.

He started planning. He had to choose the right spot. A place with no witnesses, somewhere he could stash his car close by. A secluded spot where no one would hear if the girl started screaming for help. All the boring surveillance he'd done over the past few weeks was finally proving useful. He knew the girl's routine down cold. He knew when her workday started and when it ended. He knew the route she drove to the diner and back to her apartment. He knew when she did her grocery shopping, when she visited the library. And, most important, he knew when and where she did her walking and running.

It didn't take him long to decide where he would set up his ambush. It was perfect. The location also gave him the time. Two days from now, on Tuesday, Amber-May's day off from the diner. The day when she ran farthest out of Crumley Creek and passed right by where Freddie would be waiting for her.

23

The day after she first noticed the Toyota parked across the street from her apartment, Amber-May used her break to visit the only pawnshop in Crumley Creek. The proprietor was a grizzled man named Clive Penter. He was a regular at Susie's Joint. He also smoked a lot, so his store smelled thickly of burnt tobacco, and when he smiled at Amber-May, he showed a mouthful of yellowing teeth.

"Good day to you, Amber-May," he said, in a voice made gravelly and low by all his smoking. "You selling or buying?"

"Buying, I hope."

She walked up to the counter and glanced around the cluttered walls of the small store. On the loaded shelves were old radios, table lamps, dinner sets, wristwatches, cuckoo clocks, and a whole mess of other items. "Do you have a switchblade or a folding knife for sale?"

Clive raised both graying eyebrows at her. "You planning on skinning a deer or something?"

Or something, Amber-May thought. "I'm not into hunting. I'm looking for something small that I can carry on me when I run, something that won't be easy to spot."

Clive pursed his lips for a second; then he tapped a finger on the counter, saying, "I got something just like it somewhere around here."

He bent down and rummaged around behind the counter. A minute later he came up with a small folding knife in his wrinkled palm. It had a faded red stock with a thin metal ring at the bottom. "This is so you can attach it to a keyring," Clive said. He pointed at a round metal button near the top of the stock. "You press this to release the blade. Like this." A one-and-a-half-inch blade sprang out. The metal looked a bit weathered. The knife was obviously far from new. Clive folded the blade back into the stock and handed it to her. "You try it."

It felt small in her hand and barely weighed anything. She pressed the button and felt the tiny vibration as the blade locked into place. She looked at Clive. "Is it sharp enough?"

Clive got a paper bag from under the counter. Inside was a sandwich. He took the knife and sliced the bread in half. He wiped the blade clean and gave it back to her.

"It ain't much. More a kid's knife than anything else, but it still does what it's supposed to."

Amber-May bought it.

She began carrying it with her wherever she went. It fit easily in the pocket of her jeans. Her workout shorts were another matter, but she gave it some thought and managed to come up with a solution. There was a small pocket on the inside of her shorts on the right side. She placed her keys there when she ran. She sewed a similar pocket on the left side, slightly larger than the other, and put the knife in it. It was an imperfect fit. The knife bounced around, banging against her thigh with each step. But it made her feel safer, so she kept it with her.

She did this even when she realized she hadn't seen the Toyota for three days straight. She looked for it everywhere—when she was home, at work, or out and about—but she didn't see it. It had gone. Perhaps whoever had been following her had been called off. Or maybe something else was going on, something she could not guess at. Either way, she decided to remain vigilant. And armed.

She'd never used a switchblade before. She practiced drawing it until she could do it fifty times in a row without it snagging on the fabric of her pocket. The more she studied the knife, the less confident she felt that it would do much good—it looked awfully small. But anything bigger would show and be cumbersome. This knife would have to do.

She told no one about the Toyota, not even Susie. She knew that if she said something, she would have to explain why someone was following her. This she did not want.

She did not change her routine. She saw no reason to. Whoever was driving the Toyota, he or she seemed content with simply watching her. And she had nothing to hide from anyone, even someone sent by Garland Pickens. The knife was simply an added layer of security, a means by which she could feel safer. So she went to work, got books from the library, did her shopping, lifted her weights, and went on her walks and runs. Same as always.

The weather was perfect for running—sunny, but not too hot. She ran without music. She liked the small-town noises of Crumley Creek and the quiet of its surroundings. She liked the freshness of the air and the abundance of birds she saw as she ran.

Tuesday, four days after she'd last seen the Toyota, was her day off. The sky was a brilliant blue without a wisp of cloud. The weather was mild, with just a whisper of breeze. Amber-May rose early after a night without dreams. Her body was bubbling with energy that begged to be burned off. She got into her running shorts and tank top, laced up her shoes, and left her apartment. The knife was in its pocket, thudding against her thigh. The Toyota was nowhere in sight.

She ran her usual day-off route. She started off going north, waving hello to whichever neighbors happened to be out and about, then cut west at the second intersection. The houses on this street were slightly larger and older, the trees taller. Dogs barked at her as she passed, and a couple trotted by her side for a while before they got bored and scampered back home.

She kept running west for a mile, enjoying the sensation of her feet pounding tarmac. Her breathing was unlabored, her heartbeat steady. She felt a deep sense of satisfaction at how fit she was. She upped her pace a beat and started to feel sweat gather at her hairline.

She veered north again, running through the older section of town. This was an area in decline. Houses with peeling paint, weedy lots, buckling sidewalks, and potholes in the road. Crumley Creek was in better shape than many other American towns of its size, but it too had seen better days. Folks at the diner talked about this openly and often, so Amber-May had a good picture of what was going on. Employment wasn't what it used to be, and many young people were trying their luck elsewhere. It wasn't a crisis, at least not yet, but it was a dark shadow looming over the town.

Fifteen minutes after leaving the residential area, she came upon one of the monuments to the town's more prosperous past.

It was the sprawling relic of an auto-parts factory, silent and abandoned, emptied of purpose. Gray stone buildings stood vacant of people and activity behind a chain-link fence that was coming apart in places.

The road Amber-May was running on stretched right by the fence, and she glanced into the deserted compound. Here and there, she could see signs that people still visited this place. Crushed beverage cans, an empty bottle of wine, cigarette butts, a stained old sofa someone had dragged in from somewhere, with a few metal chairs scattered around it. High-schoolers, probably. Using the place to smoke and drink and make out. Whatever got them away from the prying eyes of their parents.

That morning, though, there was no one in sight. Only a group of ravens perched on a gutter pipe high on one of the buildings. A couple flapped their wings at her. One squawked loudly. The sound made Amber-May uneasy, though she couldn't say why.

She turned her head forward and accelerated. Soon she would leave the old factory behind. Past that were open meadows and fields. As a city girl, she never got tired of the sight and feel of all that open space. She enjoyed running there more than anywhere else.

She was passing by a couple of small buildings that stood outside the fence perimeter when a flash of sunlight reflecting off glass stabbed her eyes. Dazzled, she nearly tripped, but managed to retain her footing. Still running, she turned her head leftward, seeking the source of the flash.

Then she saw it.

The Toyota, parked behind one of the small buildings. The light that had dazzled her had bounced off its windshield. She couldn't see past the glare. She couldn't tell whether the car was occupied.

Amber-May felt her heartbeat jump. What was the car doing here?

She didn't know the answer, but she knew one thing for certain. It was there because of her. It was there *for* her.

With panic making her breathing ragged and her chest ache, she did a quick spin, intending to sprint back to town.

Then she saw the man, the man who now stood on the road, blocking her path. The man with the grin on his face and the gun in his hand, pointed right at her.

24

His grin was that of a cartoon hyena, wide and toothy, happy at the sight of helpless prey. His mouth was large, his lips thin, his teeth small and sharp. His black hair was slicked back; it glinted in the sun. His eyes were flat and very dark. Creepy eyes that glistened like oil. He was lean and a little taller than she. There was something faintly familiar about him, as if she'd seen him before, but not more than once or twice, and never for too long.

He wore scuffed cowboy boots, low-slung jeans, a blue shirt, and a black jacket. The jacket hung open, exposing a leather belt with a rectangular metal buckle.

His stance was casual, relaxed, self-assured. He held the gun chest high, with his arm half-bent. His head was tilted a few degrees to the right. He looked like a man without a care in the world. When he spoke, his voice held a mocking edge.

"Good morning, Miss Jackson. Or maybe I should call you Amber-May? What do you say? Is that all right with you?"

Amber-May didn't say anything. All her attention was centered on the gun. The hole in the muzzle was blacker than a starless night sky. *He's here to kill me*, she thought. *Pickens sent him to shut me up for good.*

The man chuckled. "I think I'll call you Amber-May. I feel like I know you pretty well, after all."

Amber-May's stomach contracted to a hard, frozen knot. Her heart was thumping an erratic rhythm against her breastbone. She'd been a fool, thinking that Pickens would let her live. As long as she was alive she was a threat to his clients. What would happen to Grandma Betsy when she was dead?

Her eyes darted left and right. There was no one around. Would anyone hear her if she shouted for help? Unlikely. And even if they did, they wouldn't be able to get to her before a bullet did. With effort, she managed to say, "Who are you? What do you want?"

"My name's not important. As for what I want, that's simple. I want you to lace your fingers on top of your pretty little head and walk over this way. Slowly."

Amber-May didn't move. She couldn't even if she'd wanted to. Fear had turned her legs to lead. If someone pushed her, she would simply topple over.

The man's grin turned mean and ugly. He stretched out his arm. The gun looked even more menacing now. Bigger and deadlier. His voice dropped an octave, and his tone became pure threat. "You'd better do what I say, understand? Don't make this harder than it has to be."

Still she didn't move. His mouth became a grim line. He took a step toward her, and another. He was twenty feet away and closing the distance. And still she couldn't move.

The panic was making it harder to think. It felt like a hurricane was blowing through her brain, making it impossible for any thoughts to coalesce into something meaningful.

She took a deep breath and tried her visualization technique. She imagined a clear sky, with not a cloud in sight. She imagined houses with their windows thrown open, without storm shutters. She pictured vibrant trees standing tall, unbending. She envisioned people walking about, children playing outdoors, birds flitting to and fro. The sort of scene a hurricane doesn't fit in.

It worked. The hurricane whispered out. Her mind calmed and

cleared. In the mental tranquility that followed, she was once again able to think. And the first thought that came to her was that if this man had been ordered to kill her, he would have already done so. He would have shot her in the back when she'd run past him, or right here where she stood. The fact that he hadn't meant that he was after something else.

"Who sent you? Pickens?"

The man laughed. His laughter was low and scratchy. He was a mere ten feet away now. Nine. Eight. This close she could see a small scar on his upper lip and a mole just under his left eye. "Don't worry," he said. "You'll find out soon enough."

He's here to take me somewhere, Amber-May thought. *He's not going to kill me.*

And as this realization crystallized in her mind, she felt the excess weight fall off her legs. Her paralysis broke. She turned to flee.

And was yanked back before she managed to take a single step. Her scalp felt as though it were on fire. Her head was pulled back and down, so she was staring straight up at the sky. Her back arched backwards painfully. Her legs folded beneath her.

The man had her ponytail in his fist and was pulling it like a rein. His face was close to her ear. His breath smelled of caffeine and peanuts and potato chips. "Don't bother fighting. You're coming with me." He gave her ponytail a hard yank and began dragging her backward. Amber-May cried out. Her feet fought for purchase, but to no avail. Her shoes scuffed along the tarmac as the man pulled her after him. Pain radiated down all over her face and neck. She tried slapping at the man, at the hand holding her hair, but the angle was all wrong and her arms flailed through empty air. He was beyond her reach.

He was panting, cursing her for making him work hard. He was dragging her off the road, toward the Toyota. Once he got her to the car, it would be over. She wasn't sure what would happen, but he'd probably tie her up and gag her. It would be almost impossible to escape.

Her instinct was to keep on struggling, but she knew it was hopeless. Thrashing or trying to twist away only amplified the pain in her scalp. But she still had one chance. She stopped trying to hit him. She gathered her breath and begged, "Please stop. I'll do whatever you say."

The man let go of her hair. She fell to the ground, almost weeping with relief. Her scalp still hurt, but nothing like before. The man was breathing hard. His face was red with effort. He held the gun on her. "Come on. Get up. Walk to that car. Don't give me any more trouble."

When she didn't move, he cursed again. His body tensed. She was struck by a sudden fear that he would kick her or hit her with the gun. He did neither. Instead, he bent toward her, grabbed her under one arm, and began pulling her up.

"Listen, you fucking bitch. No more bull—"

His words were cut off by a yelp as Amber-May slashed his hand with her knife. He let go of her and she scrambled away from him across the dirt. Looking more bewildered than hurt, he stared at the bloody cut on the back of his hand. It ran from his wrist to the soft meat between thumb and forefinger. Blood oozed from the slit skin. He turned his eyes to look at Amber-May, who'd already gotten to her feet. Anger replaced the bewilderment on his face. He raised his gun. "Why, you dirty little—"

Amber-May didn't linger long enough to hear the rest of it. She whirled around and ran. She ran as fast as her legs would carry her. Her back prickled in anticipation of a bullet. It could come at any second, blow a hole right through her, take out her heart or a lung, kill her in the blink of an eye.

No shot came.

After a few seconds, she chanced a glance over her shoulder. The man wasn't aiming his gun at her. He was chasing her instead.

He's not here to kill me, she reminded herself. *He's here to kidnap me.*

But that didn't mean he wouldn't shoot. If he thought he couldn't catch her, would he try wounding her? Shoot her in the leg? He'd probably prefer that to letting her escape.

He wasn't far behind now. She could hear his heavy breathing over the pounding of her feet on the road. She was in good shape. She could run for miles. But she couldn't outrun a bullet.

There was no cover on the road. She felt exposed. Ten feet ahead and to the left was a gap in the wire fence of the abandoned factory. She veered toward it, ducking inside. She ran across the cracked weedy pavement of the factory courtyard as if the devil himself were on her tail. Her heart was thumping so hard it felt like it might burst out of her chest. Sweat flowed down her face.

She ran toward the closest building. It was a two-story stone hulk, with broken windows and a stained exterior. Its door hung open on rusting hinges. Shadows waited inside.

The man had followed her into the compound. He was panting hard somewhere behind her. "Stop, you cunt, or when I catch you, I'll..."

He didn't complete his threat. Maybe he lacked breath. Amber-May kept running. Whatever he had planned on doing to her beforehand, her fate would be much worse if he caught her now, after she'd cut him. She realized with a start that the knife was no longer in her hand. She'd dropped it somewhere, perhaps right after slashing the man. *Stupid, stupid!* Now she had nothing with which to defend herself. She ran through the open doorway and into the dark building, hoping to find some way to escape.

25

Freddie knew a lot of curse words. He'd acquired this particular subset of his vocabulary growing up in the wrong neighborhood with the sort of people who were more likely to spend a portion of their lives behind bars than in college or a steady workplace. The only language he could speak fluently was English, but he could curse like a champ in half a dozen others. As he ran after Amber-May, his mind rattled off a string of profanities that would have made the most foul-mouthed sailor in the world blush.

He'd come close to doing more.

When the girl had cut him, his first reaction was astonishment. It took him a second to realize what had happened. Then a question popped up in his head: Where the hell did her knife come from?

As he stared at the blood seeping from the wound, astonishment gave way to fury. He wanted to punish her. He wanted to put a bullet in her head, destroy that pretty face of hers so thoroughly that whoever found her body would feel nothing but revulsion. He came close to doing it; his finger had slipped past the trigger guard and was putting some pressure on the trigger itself. Just a little more and the hammer would fall, the bullet would fly, and Amber-May's face would turn to a bloody pulp.

Then he remembered the money.

The money was what mattered, not some little cut. He wanted that million, and he had to have the girl to get it. She was of no use to him dead. He had to take her alive, and relatively unscathed, to collect his bounty.

So he held his fire. And when Amber-May turned on her heel and started running away, he didn't shoot her in the back. For a split second, he considered shooting her in the leg, but immediately discarded that notion. Emmett MacBaxter had said the girl must not suffer any debilitating injuries, and a gunshot wound, no matter where, was more than likely to be just that. Worse, the bullet might hit an artery. If that happened, the girl would bleed out in minutes.

He couldn't shoot her. He gave chase instead. And as he ran after her, he cursed her in his mind.

He also made plans. Nasty ones. He imagined what he'd do to her when he caught her. Her face was out of bounds; Emmett had been crystal clear on that score. But as for the rest of her, there he had some leeway.

Freddie wasn't a sadist. He didn't get a kick out of hurting people. But no one cut him and got away with it pain-free. There was a principle involved. So when he caught Amber-May, he'd make sure to cause her some serious pain. There were ways to do that without spilling blood or leaving bruises. She'd wish she'd never pulled that knife on him.

But first he had to catch her. And, damn it, she could run. He had the longer stride, but not by much. And she was fit as hell. Also, she didn't smoke. Twenty-five strides into his sprint and he could already feel his lungs straining and was cursing himself for not going for his car instead of chasing her on foot. He was also in boots and jeans, and she was in running clothes and shoes. If he didn't push himself, she might outrun him.

He couldn't let that happen. He gritted his teeth, lowered his head, and ordered his muscles to work harder. And it was working. He was gaining speed, gaining on her. Still, he wasn't used to running. He needed to catch her fast.

Then she did something stupid. She shifted direction, ran off the road, and dove through a hole in the chain-link fence surrounding the old factory. She might have been able to lose him if she had kept on the road. It would be harder for her to do that here. He hurtled after her, getting through the fence five seconds after she did. She sprinted straight into a massive decrepit building to the left. Huffing, the side of his chest aching, he followed. She disappeared into the open doorway. He got there a few seconds later, stopped on the threshold, and looked inside.

The entire ground floor was one gigantic room, 150 feet long and half as wide, with a line of thin support columns running down its center. The only light came from small windows set high in the walls, half of them missing their panes. No sign of Amber-May.

Freddie could see another door set into the middle of the opposite wall. He grinned. The door was secured by a length of chain and a padlock. She couldn't have gotten out that way. In a far corner was a stairway leading to the upper floor. Piles of junk blocked the lower five steps, reaching almost to the ceiling. You might be able to climb above the junk and access the stairs, but it would be hard and make a lot of noise. Freddie had not heard anything to indicate that Amber-May had chosen that route. This meant that she was somewhere here, in this massive room, and the only way she could get out of it was through the door where Freddie now stood.

"Game's over, little girl," he called, his voice echoing strangely. "You got nowhere to go. Be nice and come on over here, and I promise to take good care of you."

He waited. In the faint light he could see dust motes and dark particles floating through the air. The room smelled of rotten wood, trash, and decay. Junk was stacked or scattered here and there. Old metal cabinets; tables and chairs with missing legs; lengths of wood, warped by weather; and all sorts of unrecognizable trash. Someone had heaped most of it in fifteen or so piles spread across the floor. Plenty of places a young woman could hide behind.

But not for long.

Still, Freddie didn't want to go into that room if he didn't have to.

The floor was dirty as hell and probably full of animal shit. He didn't want to step in anything like that. Not with his favorite pair of boots on. Besides, the girl had showed a willingness to fight. He'd seen the knife fall from her hand after she'd sliced him, but she could still prove troublesome. Much better if she came to him than if he had to seek her out.

"Come on. Don't make me come find you. You've already made me mad with that knife stunt you pulled. You don't want to make me angrier. Trust me on that."

Still no answer. Freddie shook his head in frustration. His hand hurt, and so did his feet from the running. Sweat was making his shirt stick to his skin. More of it streamed down his forehead. Goddamn her. He rotated the gun, holding it by the barrel. He wasn't going to shoot her, but he could use the gun as a club. Conscious or unconscious, she was coming with him.

He crept forward slowly, ears straining to hear any noise she might make, eyes going left and right. She wasn't going to surprise him a second time. No way in hell.

With the gun gripped tightly in his hand, he peered behind every stack of junk and had cleared half the floor when he heard the noise.

26

Amber-May realized her mistake before taking five steps into the building. There was no way out. She was about to turn back to the door when she heard the rapid thud of the man's approaching steps. He was almost there. She wouldn't be able to slip past him.

With no other choice, she ventured deeper into the massive grimy room. She scanned her surroundings. The staircase was blocked. The second door was chained shut. Her eyes sought another exit, but there was none. The windows were set high in the walls, beyond her reach. She was trapped.

There was no time to waste. She scuttled behind a tall pile of discarded furniture and crouched down, catching her breath. She wished she still had the knife. Losing it was an unbelievable act of carelessness. She hoped desperately it would not cost her everything.

There was a two-inch gap in the pile of desks, tables, and chairs, about two feet off the floor. Through it, she saw her pursuer pausing in the doorway. She couldn't see his face, just the middle of his body. Still, it was obvious he was looking for her.

She didn't budge when he ordered her to give up and come to him. Instead, she looked around frantically for a weapon. All she saw was junk and dirt. She could maybe pull out one of the chairs wedged in the middle of the pile and use that, but it might cause the rest of the old furniture to come tumbling down on her head. It would also make a hell of a racket.

Peering again through the gap in the furniture pile, she saw that the man had begun searching the room. He did so slowly, methodically, cautiously. His head rotated side to side, and Amber-May could tell he was keeping his ears pricked to catch any sound she might make. The gun was in his hand. He wasn't taking any chances with her. And he wasn't about to suddenly give up on kidnapping her.

Why hadn't he killed her? Why would Pickens want to kidnap her? Or was this man working for someone else?

She had no answers, and now wasn't the time to try to figure things out. She would worry about that later. If there was a later.

She struggled to quiet her breathing. She shivered with cold. Fear was turning her blood to ice. She bit her lip, hoping a plan would come to her.

The man had finished searching the first third of the room. He was now just thirty feet away and steadily closing the distance. He no longer bothered trying to convince her to surrender. The only sound apart from her breathing was the scuffing of his boots on the grimy floor.

Twenty-five feet. Twenty.

She had less than a minute to find something she could use to defend herself with. Otherwise, she would have to fight him bare-handed, and she doubted that would get her very far.

Casting her eyes around again, she spotted something she'd missed earlier due to the poor lighting. A length of pipe lying on the floor six feet to her right.

Too far away.

She couldn't reach it without exposing herself. The man would be upon her before she got her hand on it.

She nearly jumped when something hairy brushed her calf. She looked down and saw a rat. Black, furry, and huge. The size of a small cat. Its head was tilted leftward as it regarded her with its two black bottomless eyes. It had a curious expression on its face.

Amber-May had an innate fear of rats. So powerful was it that for a couple of heartbeats she totally forgot about the man with the gun. All her attention, all her dread, was focused on that single large rat standing a few inches from her unprotected calf.

For a second neither she nor the rat moved. They stared at each other like two cowboys ready to draw their revolvers. Then Amber-May swung her hand at the rodent. She missed and almost cried out, sure it was going to sink its teeth into her leg.

Instead, the rat took off running, as scared of her as she was of it. It sprinted headlong into the shadowy base of another pile of junk fifteen feet to Amber-May's left, its flank brushing a discarded hubcap as it went. The hubcap had been standing upright, leaning against a metal plate of some kind. Disturbed by the rat, it fell over with a clatter that echoed across the entire room.

Amber-May winced at the sound. Then she heard something else. The thump of boots approaching fast. It was the man, alerted by the noise.

He came into view, his back to her, as he faced the source of the noise. She didn't dawdle. This was her chance. She scrambled across the floor toward the pipe and gripped it tight. It was solid metal, about the length of a forearm and the width of two fingers. It fit perfectly in her hand.

She rose and turned and rushed straight at the man's back. He must have heard her coming because he was already turning to face her. There was surprise in his eyes and a twitch of fear. He began raising his arm, either to shield himself or to strike her down with the gun.

Or to shoot her.

Either way, he was too late. She swung the pipe. It let out a satisfying thunk as it met the side of his head.

The blow reverberated up her arm, shaking it from fingertips to shoulder. Her grip loosened and the pipe fell from her hand, clanging away across the concrete floor. It didn't matter. The man's eyes rolled back in their sockets. He fell over, landing hard on the floor. He didn't move. He was either out cold or dead. Amber-May did not try to determine which.

Instead, she fled the abandoned building. She ran across the deserted factory courtyard and through the opening in the chain-link fence. Only when she was back on the road did she turn to check if she was being pursued.

She wasn't. The man was nowhere in sight.

Maybe he's dead, she thought. *Maybe I killed him.*

Her fingerprints were on that pipe. When the police found the body, they would also find the pipe. Should she go back and get it? Hide it somewhere?

She didn't dare to. Because there was a chance the man was just unconscious. He might come to at any second. When he did, she wanted to be far away. She was more scared of him than the police.

Should she call them, tell them about the attack?

No. If Pickens had hired the man, he would simply pull some strings and make sure the case never made it to trial. If it was someone else—well, she had no idea how powerful they were. Regardless, she had zero confidence in the police at the moment. They could be bought. If she went to them for help, they would know where she was. One of them might reveal her location to whoever had hired the man to kidnap her. The same man, or a replacement, would be sent to finish the job. Only this time his orders might be to kill her.

She kept on running until she got back to her apartment.

Once there, she didn't waste a minute. She didn't take a shower or change her clothes. She didn't even pause to catch her breath or calm her stampeding heart. She just threw some clothes into her two bags, carted them to her car, got inside, and burned rubber out of there. She was trembling so hard her teeth rattled. But at least she was alive. At least she was safe.

27

It took two hours for Amber-May's heart rate to return to normal. During that time, she drove west, one eye glued to the rearview mirror in search of the Toyota.

One time she was certain she'd seen it, and her stomach flip-flopped. But when she took another look, she saw that the Toyota in question was driven by a woman, and that in the passenger seat sat a teenage girl.

A short while later, she stopped at a service station to use the restroom. Some of her anxiety had worn off. She had put some distance between herself and Crumley Creek and had seen no sign of the man who'd attacked her. He was either dead, or he had no idea where she was.

In the service station diner, she bought coffee and a Danish and sat by the window looking at cars streak by on the highway. She considered what to do next. The abduction attempt changed everything. She could no longer hope to put the rape behind her. She would not be allowed to rebuild a normal life for herself. Someone was out to get her. The question was, who?

The likely suspect was Pickens, but maybe it was someone else. After all, someone had sent the man in the Toyota, and another person was behind the woman who had pretended to be Janet Cranston when she called the nursing home. Only one of them could be Pickens, and she couldn't think of a reason why he would want to have her kidnapped. Killed, maybe—though he could have arranged that months ago.

Who, then?

Her eyes alighted on a newspaper someone had left behind on a nearby table. It was open to the business section. The name "MacBaxter" caught her eye. It was in the headline of a short report stating that Emmett MacBaxter had been named president and CEO of MacBaxter Holdings following the recent demise of his father. A small picture of Emmett, smiling broadly, was included. Anger flooded Amber-May's body at the sight of his grinning face. She squeezed the paper into a crumpled, misshapen ball, stomped over to the bathroom, and hurled it in the trash. Then she stood by the sink, before the mirror, her hands clamped into tight fists at her sides, her face hot, fuming.

When she returned to her table, she buried her face in her hands. She sat like that for a long time as memories of what Emmett MacBaxter and his friends had done to her flashed through her mind like an endless horror movie. She felt like crying, but told herself not to. She was done being weak.

When she finally lowered her hands, it was with a sudden, horrific realization. If Pickens hadn't hired the man in the Toyota, it could only be one of the four men who had raped her. And while she couldn't think of a reason Pickens would want to have her kidnapped, she could imagine why one of those sick bastards would.

She shivered. She felt cold, scared, breathless. She didn't notice the waitress until she was standing by her table.

"You okay, hon?"

Amber-May blinked at her. The waitress was in her fifties, with stringy red hair and round shoulders.

"What? Oh, yes. I'm fine."

"Want me to pour you a fresh cup?"

Amber-May glanced at her half-full cup. The coffee had gone cold. "Yes. Thank you."

The waitress smiled, took away the cup of cold coffee, and returned a minute later with a fresh one. "You just holler if you need anything, okay?"

"Okay," Amber-May said.

She took a sip of the new coffee. Its warmth banished some of the cold out of her system. But not all of it. A stubborn icy residue remained, deep in her bones, as if it had been embedded in her marrow.

She weighed her options. The police were useless. The press would likely prove the same. She could either keep running and spend a lifetime looking over her shoulder or...

The decision, when it was finally made, did not induce shock or horror. Instead, a sense of deep, unwavering conviction spread throughout her body. It felt right. It felt just. It felt like what she should have done the day she stepped out of the hospital.

Amber-May gulped down the rest of her coffee, left the waitress a large tip, got into her car, and started driving. Only this time, she was heading north. To Boston.

Her heart was beating fast again. Now, though, it wasn't due to fear, but because she was excited.

"Sam Duggins," she muttered as she tore up the interstate. "Here I come again."

28

When Freddie opened his eyes, he found himself staring at his hands.

No, he realized after a moment. It was one hand. He was seeing double.

He shut his eyes and for a solid minute did nothing but take long, deep breaths. When he opened them again, his vision was back to normal.

This was good. What was bad was the pain in his head. It hurt like a son of a bitch. Very slowly, he shifted one hand and fingered the side of his head. He winced. The spot was tender, and the hair over it was matted and wet. The bitch had clocked him good. Knocked him out in one blow. What had she used? A stick? A metal rod of some kind? He was lucky to be alive. That kind of blow could crack a skull.

He was lying on his stomach in the grime that blanketed the floor of the giant disused room. So much for worrying about his boots. His pants, jacket, and shirt were probably all covered in dirt, dust, and animal droppings.

He sat up gingerly and looked around. He was all alone. Amber-May Jackson was long gone.

Trying to stand up, he got dizzy and fell down hard on his ass. He sat with his head down and the world somersaulting fast around him for what felt like an eternity. He wanted to get up again, but he didn't think his legs were going to obey him. They were on strike. His stomach was lurching. It was a miracle he managed to keep from vomiting.

Finally, the world slowed down and he tried getting up again. Once more the dizziness struck, but this time he managed to reach one hand and lean against a junk pile and did not fall down. Still, he had to take a moment before his legs stopped feeling like noodles. He spotted his gun two feet away. He wobbled toward it, bent down cautiously, picked it up, and holstered it. He wondered why Amber-May hadn't shot him with it.

How long had she been gone? He looked at his phone and was surprised to see that it was 8:03 a.m. Forty-five minutes had passed since she'd knocked him out. He couldn't have been out nearly that long. No more than ten minutes, probably. Any longer than that, and the only way he would gotten off that floor was on a stretcher. It was that nasty dizzy spell, the one that had dropped him on his ass and kept him sitting on the floor with the universe whirling around him. It had lasted for over thirty minutes.

A sudden jolt of fear cut through him. Why wasn't the place swarming with cops? Why wasn't he in handcuffs? The only answer he could come up with was that, for some reason, Amber-May had not called the police. Still, he'd better get out of there real quick.

With tiny, hesitant steps, he staggered out of the forsaken building, across the factory courtyard, through the hole in the fence, and the rest of the way to his car.

When he got there, he stared at himself in the mirror. He was a mess. One side of his face was grimy with dirt. On the other, his hair was clotted with blood. His clothes were streaked with filth. He used an entire bottle of water to wash his face, hair, and the cut on his hand. The way his day was going, the wounds would probably get infected. He needed to find a drugstore.

With his head injury, he knew it wasn't safe for him to drive, but he didn't want to hang around there a second longer than necessary. He got in the car, started it, and began driving away.

Out in the sunlight, he discovered that his vision was off. The world looked less sharp, a bit out of focus. His entire body felt weak, less solid. He drove very slowly, clutching the wheel hard, leaning forward in his seat and squinting through the windshield so he wouldn't have an accident.

A mile away, on the side of an old empty road that was crumbling along its edges, he stopped the car and powered on his tablet. Amber-May's Ford was moving. She had left Crumley Creek and was heading west. So instead of calling the police, she had decided to flee. Freddie wondered why, but his head hurt too much for him to dwell on it. It was good news, that was all he cared about.

With a splitting headache, trembling limbs, and imperfect vision, he was in no condition to go chasing after her. He might end up wrapping his car around a tree. And even if he did manage to catch her, he wouldn't be able to subdue her. She could push him off his feet with one hand.

His head felt heavy. He wanted to sleep more than anything. He was in no hurry to go after Amber-May. He could track the Ford no matter where it went.

He drove a little further, found a dirt road that ended in a clearing, switched off the car, lowered his seat, and fell into a deep sleep.

When he woke up, he felt almost normal. His head still hurt, but nowhere near as badly as before. His vision was clear. He was as thirsty as he'd ever been and drank a full bottle of mineral water in a series of long swallows. He checked the time and discovered he had slept for four hours. It was 12:58 p.m.

He climbed out of the car, urinated against the base of a tree, then pulled out his bag from the backseat and changed into clean clothes. He got out his tablet, powered up the tracking software, and discovered that Amber-May had switched direction. She was heading north now. Her Ford was one hundred and fifty miles from his location. He grinned. The little bitch had no idea he was keeping track of her. She was in for the biggest surprise of her life.

He wanted to start after her right away, but he needed to do a couple of things first. He removed the stolen Tennessee plates from his Toyota, hurled them into the brush surrounding the clearing, and screwed the original plates back on. Then he drove in search of a drugstore.

He found one at the first town he passed through and bought disinfectant, gauze, and medical tape. He cleaned his wounds as best he could and bandaged his hand. The cut was not deep. He didn't think it needed stitches. Neither, he hoped, did his head wound. But just to play it safe, he'd go see a doctor after he delivered the girl to Emmett MacBaxter.

By the time he got going again, the Ford was two hundred and ten miles away. It didn't matter. As long as the tracking device was attached to her car, Amber-May could not disappear on him. He'd told Emmett it would take a week to deliver the girl. He had three days to make good on his promise.

As he drove, he tore open a bag of Cheetos and stuffed a handful into his mouth. Munching on the cheese-flavored snack, he pictured the horrified look on Amber-May's face when she saw him again. Only this time, she wouldn't be able to do anything about it. This time, he would knock her out and dump her in the trunk, where she belonged.

"I'm coming for you, girl," he said as the car whizzed up the highway, the radio blaring a punk rock tune. "Freddie's coming for you."

29

As she drove north, Amber-May began thinking over what she'd need. The first thing was money. She searched the internet on her mobile phone for the nearest branch of Bank of America and headed there. She parked the Ford across the street from the bank, opened the trunk, and dumped the contents of one of her gym bags. She took the empty bag with her into the bank.

Inside, she went straight to one of the teller windows, presented her driver's license, and gave the teller the bank account number that had been written on the note Pickens had left for her in the hospital. She'd memorized the number before tearing up the note, just in case an emergency came up. The situation she now found herself in certainly qualified as such.

The teller clicked some keys on her keyboard, nodded at her computer screen, and smiled at Amber-May. "All right, and what can I do for you, Miss Jackson?"

"What is the balance?"

"Forty thousand dollars exactly."

Amber-May nodded to herself. She felt relieved. She'd half expected the account to be empty. If Pickens had sent a man to kidnap her, it stood to reason that he wouldn't leave her with access to so much money. Then again, maybe to Pickens forty thousand dollars was like pocket change. Or maybe he assumed she wouldn't get the chance to make use of it.

"Good," she told the teller. "I'd like to make a withdrawal."

"What amount?"

"All of it."

The teller's plucked eyebrows jumped an inch. "I'm sorry?"

"I want to withdraw all the money in the account."

The teller glanced again at her monitor, as though she'd forgotten the balance. Then she gave Amber-May an uncertain smile. "All forty thousand of it?"

"That's right."

The teller frowned. "Can you wait a moment, please? This kind of withdrawal, I'll have to ask the manager."

Amber-May waited, her empty gym bag at her feet. The teller's discomfort did not surprise her. She knew coming in to the bank that this kind of withdrawal was uncommon. She knew there might be some questions. She would have to be firm, confident, assertive.

The bank manager turned out to be a forty-something Hispanic woman dressed in a cream pantsuit. She asked to see Amber-May's identification. She said, "You understand, Miss Jackson, this is somewhat unorthodox."

"That may be," Amber-May said, surprised at how calm she sounded, "but this is what I want. It's my money, after all."

"Of course. But still, withdrawing forty thousand in cash, it's practically unheard of. Wouldn't you feel safer taking a cashier's check?"

"No, I wouldn't. I prefer it all in cash."

"I see." The manager took a meaningful pause. "May I ask why you need such a large cash amount?"

"No. It's none of your business." Amber-May was pleased when the manager flinched. "Now, I'd like to be on my way."

For a moment, the manager seemed about to say something more, but then she let out a low breath and nodded at the teller. "Take Miss Jackson to one of the back offices and give her her money."

Amber-May followed the teller to a small characterless office. She sat in a chair by a desk while the teller left the room. She returned with a cash-counting machine and a large metal box. She asked Amber-May what denominations she preferred. Amber-May hadn't considered the question. "Vary them, please. Twenties, fifties and hundreds."

The teller nodded. She opened the box and took out several large wads of cash. Amber-May forced her expression to remain neutral. It was more money than she'd seen in her life.

The teller began running banknotes through the machine. It whirred as it counted them. It took several minutes to count forty thousand dollars. When all the money was accounted for, the teller asked Amber-May if she wanted a bag for it.

Amber-May cleared her throat. "No. I have one with me."

The teller watched with a furrowed brow as Amber-May put forty thousand dollars in cash in her bag. Amber-May wondered what was going through the teller's mind. *Probably thinks I'm a drug dealer or something.* She wondered if the police or someone else in authority would be informed of this transaction. It was too late to worry about it now. Besides, she would soon find herself in much more serious potential problems with the law.

When she'd finished putting the money inside the bag, Amber-May zipped it shut and slung it over her shoulder. It was heavier than she'd expected. Somehow the thought of paper money having weight had never crossed her mind. She thanked the teller and exited the bank at a brisk pace. Outside, she clutched the bag to her body and quickly crossed the street to her car. The money made her nervous. She'd make a dream target for a mugger.

Once inside her car, she locked all the doors and quickly drove away. Every few seconds, she glanced at the bagful of money on the passenger seat, as if she weren't sure it was still there.

But it was.

Now she just had to figure out how to best use it.

30

Garland Pickens was in his office when he got the call. He was going through some papers. In the days since Patrick MacBaxter had died, he had submerged himself in work. Keeping busy was the best way for him to ease his grief.

Taking care of the funeral arrangements hadn't consumed much of his time. He'd done most of it well beforehand. The funeral itself was an ordeal. Watching MacBaxter's ornate coffin being lowered into the ground was a difficult moment. Still, it was gratifying that the funeral went off without a hitch. It was dignified, solemn, and well attended by all the important people. The press coverage had been good.

Emmett had given a short eulogy. Pickens would have said much more, would have waxed poetically about MacBaxter's many achievements and fine qualities, but he supposed that was a matter of personal style, and Emmett's eulogy was certainly respectful enough.

Two days ago, MacBaxter Holdings' board of directors had met and formalized Emmett's accession to the head of the company. A couple of discourteous financial reporters had commented that Emmett was a bit young for his new position, but other than that, there hadn't been a whisper of criticism over his appointment.

Pickens was scheduled to join Emmett for a work meeting the next morning. They had a lot of important matters to discuss. Which was what Pickens had been working on when his phone rang.

"Mr. Pickens?"

"Yes?"

"This is Marshall Dougherty." The voice was low, almost conspiratorial.

Pickens was so absorbed in his work, scribbling notes in the margins of a contract draft, that he failed to remember who Marshall Dougherty was. "Yes, Mr. Dougherty, what can I do for you?"

"Sir, you asked me to report to you if Amber-May Jackson accessed her bank account."

Now he remembered. He stopped scribbling and laid down his pen. "Go ahead. I'm listening."

"Well, sir, it appears that Miss Jackson made a substantial withdrawal from her account earlier today."

"How substantial?"

"Forty thousand dollars. The entire account balance, in fact."

Pickens sat up straight. He had fully expected Amber-May Jackson to make use of her hush money; in fact, he wanted her to use it because it would further cement their bargain. But he hadn't expected her to withdraw the entire sum all at once. Frowning, he asked, "By withdrawal, you mean she took it all out in cash?"

"Yes, sir. That's precisely what I mean. It's quite unusual, as you may imagine. I thought you'd like to know about it immediately."

"You're right about that. I appreciate your call, Mr. Dougherty. Tell me, at what time did she make this withdrawal?"

"Fifteen minutes ago, at 16:38 p.m., to be precise."

"And where is the bank she used?"

Dougherty's answer started alarm bells ringing in Pickens's head. He had never visited the place, but he knew his geography. It was nowhere near Crumley Creek, Tennessee.

He thanked Mr. Dougherty and ended the call. He sat in silence for a minute, his eyes twitching rapidly behind his thick eyeglasses, his mind racing.

What was she doing so far away from her new home? And why did she need forty thousand dollars in cash?

He tapped a number on his phone and waited three rings before it was answered.

"Yeah?" Freddie Sheehan's voice had an echo to it. In the background Pickens could hear the whooshing of wind and cars. He realized Freddie was driving and that he was on speaker.

"Freddie, this is Garland Pickens. Are you alone?"

"Yeah. What's on your mind, Mr. Pickens?"

"Are you by any chance still in Crumley Creek?"

There was a short pause. Then: "No. I packed up my things and left. As we agreed, I was through with that job."

Pickens rubbed his forehead. He had so many things on his plate, having to deal with another was most unwelcome.

Freddie said, "Why do you ask? Has something changed?"

"Yes. It appears that Miss Jackson has upped and left Crumley Creek. Where you told me she looked to be all settled in."

"I gave you all the facts as I saw them, Mr. Pickens. If you'd told me to stick around some more, I would have."

Pickens didn't say anything for a moment. Freddie was right. It had been his decision to have him end his surveillance. A decision that now appeared to have been premature.

"Mr. Pickens," Freddie said slowly, "how do you know she left Crumley Creek? You got another pair of eyes on her?"

"I know because she withdrew some money from a bank hundreds of miles away. In Harrisonburg, Virginia." Pickens paused, then asked, "Where are you now, Freddie?"

"I'm in Virginia myself, as it happens. Just crossed the Tennessee-Virginia border five minutes ago."

That was good news. Freddie wasn't too far from where Amber-May had been just a short while ago. But that didn't mean he would be able to find her anytime soon. Not without knowing where she was headed. Pickens's fine mind chewed on this for a moment. Then he said, "Let's assume she's heading back this way. Can you pick up her trail?"

"I can try."

"Do more than try, Freddie. Find her and I'll make it worth your while. Double your regular pay, all right? With a five-thousand-dollar bonus thrown in."

"Gee, that's mighty generous of you, Mr. Pickens. I'll do my best. Just one question: why do you think she's heading back to Boston?"

"Maybe to visit her grandmother, but I don't know for sure. Which is why I want you to find her as soon as you can. If you don't come upon her on the road between your present location and Boston, I want you to stake out her grandmother's nursing home. If you need to bring in an extra man or two, that's fine. I'll cover the expenditure."

After Pickens hung up, he leaned back in his chair, thinking. Something had changed; something had made Amber-May Jackson decide to leave Crumley Creek and take out forty thousand dollars in cash and start driving north. It was by no means certain that she was heading back to Boston, but his gut was telling him that she was.

For what purpose? Was it indeed to visit her grandmother? Or was it something else entirely? Or was his gut mistaken and she was heading to some other location?

And, most important, what had made her suddenly leave her new home?

31

Freddie had nearly burst out laughing when Garland Pickens had offered him that five-thousand-dollar bonus. He had to work hard to sound serious when he thanked the clueless lawyer for his generosity. Pickens had no idea that Freddie was working toward a much bigger prize.

Pickens was also ignorant of the fact that Freddie knew full well that Amber-May Jackson had made a stop in Harrisonburg, though he hadn't known it was to withdraw funds from a bank. Freddie had never told Pickens about placing a tracking device on Amber-May's Ford. Pickens had never shown an interest in how Freddie did his job, and Freddie was not keen on discussing his methods.

For a second there, he'd hesitated before telling Pickens his location, fearing that the lawyer would find it odd that Freddie happened to be so close to Amber-May's last known whereabouts. He'd ended up telling him because he wanted to know what Pickens knew. That information had proved to be worthless. It made no difference to him that Amber-May had visited a bank. Though, come to think of it, it might turn out to be good news. The more money she had on her when he caught her, the better. He was going to take every cent.

He would have to disappoint Pickens. After he delivered the girl to Emmett, he would call the lawyer and tell him he had failed to find Amber-May. He'd have to act all apologetic, tell him she could have gone anywhere, that it was like finding a needle in a haystack. It was going to be fun playacting. Everything was more fun when you had a million dollars to your name.

Freddie took a final drag on his cigarette and flicked it out the window. Cool air was blowing in, buffeting his face. The air felt good, even though it made the wound in his head sting a little. A Bon Jovi song was playing on the radio, and he sang along, wildly off-key and not caring a bit. Traffic was flowing up I-81, and he was cruising along, feeling fine, knowing he didn't need to hurry. The girl was way ahead, in Maryland, but that was all right. Sooner or later she'd make a stop, and he would gain on her. And if Pickens was right and the girl was heading to Boston—well, that would make his job even easier. Because she'd have to stop somewhere for the night, and she wouldn't be expecting him. And after he finally had her handcuffed in the trunk of his car, he wouldn't have far to go before he handed her over to Emmett. Then he would take a nice vacation. Someplace with sandy beaches and loose women in bikinis. Hawaii, maybe, or someplace in the Caribbean. He sure as hell deserved some time off, in style.

He was deep in these happy thoughts when his phone rang.

"Yeah?"

"It's me. Emmett MacBaxter."

Freddie grimaced. Emmett had called him three times over the past few days, asking for a status report. It was annoying as hell, but Freddie hadn't complained. A million dollars was worth a bit of aggravation.

Still, hearing Emmett's voice soured his mood, reminding him of his painful failure to nab Amber-May. He wished the son of a bitch would just wait to hear from him, instead of calling all the time. He didn't like having to report to anyone. He turned off the radio and closed the window so he could hear Emmett more clearly.

"Good morning, Mr. MacBaxter," he said, affecting an obsequious tone. "How are you doing this fine day?"

"Never mind that. Tell me when you'll be here."

Emmett sounded impatient, his voice as taut as a tripwire. *He can't wait to get his hands on her*, thought Freddie. *The wait is killing him.* "Two days. Three tops."

"Not tomorrow?"

"No, I don't think so. Maybe."

There was a silence. "So you don't have her yet?"

Freddie gritted his teeth. He gripped the wheel hard enough to make his knuckles shine through his skin. Who was this bastard to criticize him? And a week hadn't even passed since they first spoke. Freddie was still ahead of schedule. "I will tonight."

"What's taking so long?"

Now Emmett sounded like a whiny rich kid bitching because he wasn't getting his way right this second. His tone grated on Freddie's ears.

"I told you it'll be a week, didn't I? Well, that's how long it'll take. This sort of thing has to be done right, unless you want the cops involved." He paused, telling himself to relax, to soften his tone. He had to remain on this asshole's good side if he wanted to get his million bucks. Soon, he would never have to hear Emmett's irritating voice again. He'd be rich himself. Not as rich as Emmett, not even close, but rich enough so he wouldn't have to take shit from anyone. "Listen, Mr. MacBaxter, you need to trust me. I know what I'm doing, all right? I've got some experience in this sort of thing."

Emmett was breathing heavily. He sounded like a dog panting to cool himself. "All right. Just remember, no damage to her face."

"Don't worry, I remember. I'm on it."

"Okay. I'll see you up here in three days or less."

"You can count on it," Freddie said.

He turned on the radio, reopened the window, and lit another cigarette. The wind sucked the smoke out of the car so fast, he hardly had time to smell it.

He stopped in Harrisonburg, on the same street where Amber-May had stopped. She was long gone, of course, but he got a strange kick out of being in the same spot where she'd been. He would have gone into the bank and had a look around had it been open.

Knowing that Amber-May might recognize his Toyota, he stopped at a rental agency and rented an unobtrusive white Hyundai sedan and moved all his gear into it. The Hyundai was sparkling clean and had a chemical fresh woodsy scent. The first thing he did, even before starting the car, was light up a cigarette.

Checking his tablet, Freddie saw that Amber-May's Ford was still moving north. She was rapidly approaching the Pennsylvania-New York border. Maybe Pickens had it right. Maybe she was going to Boston. Maybe she was going to pay Emmett MacBaxter a visit, tell him she forgave him for raping her. The thought made him laugh out loud.

Evening traffic slowed him down some as he neared Harrisburg. He broke free from it only to get caught in a traffic jam due to an over-turned truck. Amber-May, he saw, did not have such problems. The red dot on his tablet that indicated her location was climbing rapidly up the highway. As the sky blackened with the onset of night, she crossed into New York State. At eight thirty, she stopped.

By that time, Freddie was past the traffic jam and speeding after her. His body was stiff from being stuck in a car seat for so long, and his mouth felt like a heap of burnt charcoal from all the cigarettes he'd smoked. He hoped that Amber-May had found a motel and was settled in for the night.

She wasn't. The red dot was moving again.

But it stopped a little after eleven. An hour later, it was still in the same spot.

"Jackpot," Freddie said softly. "Sweet dreams, little girl. Your wake-up call is fast approaching."

32

The motel was one story, shaped like an L, with the office and laundry room on the short arm and guest rooms on the long. Amber-May paid for her room in cash. As she hoped, the clerk did not insist on seeing her ID. Nor did she require a credit card. Just three hundred dollars in cash as a deposit, in case Amber-May did any damage to her room.

The room was on the farthest end of the motel from the reception office. She parked her Ford just outside its door. It was small and tidy and smelled clean. The bed was queen size with a tall headboard. The mattress was springy and covered in white sheets and a sky-blue duvet.

Having not showered since the night before, she still had the sweat of her early morning run on her skin. She took a long hot shower, using up the two small shampoo bottles that came with the room. She emerged, hair wet and skin pink and clean, twenty minutes later.

She dried her hair and put on clean clothes. A flat-screen TV was bolted to the wall opposite the bed. Amber-May turned it on, watched a ball game and a few minutes of an inane sitcom with actors more attractive than funny, and switched it off.

She'd had dinner a few hours before, but now she felt hungry again. She went out of her room, ambled over to the front office, and bought two Mars bars and a can of Pepsi from the vending machine. She wolfed down the chocolate bars and chugged the Pepsi in three long swallows. The sugar rush made her a bit light-headed, but she was no longer hungry.

Back in her room, she dumped her car keys on the tiny nightstand, switched off the lights, kicked off her shoes, and lay on the bed, still in her clothes, on top of the covers. The only illumination was a wisp of yellow light peeking through the sliver of glass between the drawn curtains, leaving the room in near total darkness. Fingers laced under her head, she stared up at the shadowy ceiling. She stayed that way until half past midnight. Her body was tired, but she knew she would not be able to fall asleep. Her brain was in overdrive. Since the moment she'd turned the car around and started driving north back to Boston, she'd not allowed herself to think about the decision she'd made. Now she found herself unable to put it off any longer.

Her mind was a jumble. Thoughts raced here and there, with no order or reason to them. She asked herself whether she'd gone mad and decided she hadn't. Or if she had, it was a good sort of madness, a madness with a just purpose. What she had decided to do was extreme and would put her in grave danger, but she thought it was the right decision nonetheless. And she didn't feel that she had much choice.

That didn't calm her down any. Her nerves were all keyed up. A current of hectic energy was running through her system. She needed a plan, or at least the beginning of one, before she could turn in.

What should be her first step?

The answer was clear: she needed to make sure Grandma Betsy was safe. Without that taken care of, she could not proceed. She couldn't let her stay in the nursing home. Once she got started, Pickens, or whoever had sent the man in the Toyota after her, might try to get to her through Grandma Betsy. Amber-May needed to arrange somewhere safe for her to stay.

She gave this some thought and after a while came up with an idea. She was by no means certain it would work, but it was worth a try.

And if it did?

Then the real work would begin. Then she would start getting her revenge, and maybe her life—some sort of life—back in the process.

For that she'd need the money. How much, she wasn't sure, but a good deal. Her lips curved in a lopsided smile as she thought of Garland Pickens.

"You thought your money will keep me quiet and make me go away," she said to herself. "Now I'll use it to make more trouble than you ever imagined possible."

Suddenly, she needed to see the money again, to feel it in her hand. She sat up, reached down, and hoisted the bag of money onto the bed beside her. She unzipped it, pulled the mouth of the bag open, reached inside, and grabbed a stack of bills. It felt substantial and reassuring. Still holding it, she rotated her body, stretching her free hand to flick on the reading lamp that stood on the nightstand. The small bulb came to life.

Which was when the motel room's door burst open, and the man in the Toyota charged straight at her.

33

Before Amber-May could react, the man was upon her. He shoved her down on the bed, straddling her, pressing a knee to each of her arms, pinning them to the mattress. She bucked and twisted, but failed to throw him off her. She tried pulling her arms free, but to no avail. He was too strong, too heavy. His weight was crushing her arms. She opened her mouth to scream, but he clamped a sweaty hand over her parted lips, stifling her cries, pushing her head down hard against the bedcover.

Teeth bared in a victorious grin, he leaned closer. His breath reeked of burnt tobacco. It nearly made her gag.

"Hey," he said, his voice low and scratchy and gleeful, "you didn't expect to see me again, now did you? Did you really think I'd let you get away from me so easily?" He chuckled softly. His free hand was bandaged where she'd cut him. With it, he brushed away a few strands of hair that had fallen across her face. "Don't worry, if you behave yourself, I won't hurt a single hair on your head. If you give me any trouble, though..." He grabbed a fistful of her hair and tugged. Amber-May moaned against the hand covering her mouth. She tried biting his hand, but he held her head down so strongly, she couldn't find the right angle to sink her teeth into his flesh.

How had he found her? How was she going to get away from him?

The man let go of her hair and reached inside his jacket pocket. His hand came out with a small red-capped bottle. He held it before her eyes. "This here is for you. A special present from me." He jiggled the bottle a little. Dark liquid sloshed inside. He stuck the top end of the bottle between his teeth, twisted off the cap, and spit it out. He gave her a hard stare with his flat, dark eyes. "When I remove my hand, you're gonna open that pretty mouth of yours and swallow this, understand? Don't worry. It'll make you feel good and calm. If you make any noise, I'll hurt you bad."

He slowly slid his hand off her mouth and brought the bottle closer to her lips. She clamped them shut. Grunting in exasperation, he gripped her nose, closing her nostrils, cutting off her air.

Amber-May felt pressure building inside her chest and head. She wanted to shout for help, but that would have required opening her mouth. If she did that, he would pour the contents of that bottle down her throat. She didn't know what was in it, nor what it would do to her, and she didn't want to find out. Because that was what he wanted, and nothing he wanted was any good for her.

Again she tried jerking her arms free, but he adjusted his position, putting even more pressure on them. The pain was immense. She was sure the bones in her arms were about to snap under his weight.

But the real problem was lack of air. Ingrained instinct was shrieking at her to open her mouth, to suck in some oxygen. Every cell in her body was wailing desperately for air. Shutting her eyes, she sharply twisted her head sideways, and for a split second, one of her nostrils was clear. But before she could draw in a breath, the man's rough fingers had closed it again.

"Oh no you don't, you little—" His voice broke off mid-sentence. His grip on her nostrils slackened, as did the pressure his knees were exerting on her arms. She pulled in a frantic breath, then snapped open her eyes and saw what had caught his attention. It was the stack of bills she'd been holding when he'd busted through the door. It had fallen from her hand when he'd pushed her down on the bed and was now lying on the duvet a foot to her left.

Amber-May seized her opportunity. She slid her right arm free from under her assailant's knee, drew it back, and jabbed it forward fast, her fingers held rigid and straight like stilettos, aimed at the man's eyes.

Two of her fingers struck something springy; two others the hardness of bone. Pain shot up her fingers, hand, and arm like a bolt of lightning. The man cried out and reeled backward, coming off her and falling off the side of the bed, slamming against the wall. He writhed on the floor, clutching at his eyes, moaning like a wounded dog.

Amber-May shot off the bed and onto her feet, ignoring the flaring pain in her fingers. Some of them might be broken, but now was not the time to find out. Now was the time to get the hell out of there before the man recovered.

With her left hand, she grabbed the bag of money off the floor and fled the room, not bothering to put her shoes on. Outside, the parking lot was nearly deserted. There was just her car, a white Hyundai, and another vehicle parked by the reception office, at the other end of the motel.

Amber-May turned toward the Ford, then remembered she'd left the keys on the nightstand in her room. She swore. No way was she going back in there. She ran toward the reception office, the rough tarmac scratching the soles of her feet through her socks. A light was burning inside. She yanked on the door. Locked. Peering through the glass, she saw no one. The office was empty. Where was the clerk? She pounded on the door, rattling the glass, but no one came.

She glanced over her shoulder toward her room. The door hung open. There was no sign of the man. It wouldn't be long, though. He'd come out any second.

With mounting desperation, she turned, scanning her surroundings. There was no one outside. No one who could help her. On the road, a car streaked past much too fast to be alerted. She would have to make a run for it.

Then she saw it. A bus stop, a hundred yards up the road. And trundling into it was a bus. She ran toward it, seeing its doors swing open. No one came out, though, and Amber-May saw the doors beginning to close. She accelerated, her heart thumping, and shouted as loud as she could for the driver to wait.

Apparently, the driver didn't hear her. The doors closed, the turn signal started blinking, and the bus began angling back onto the road. She was going to miss it.

Giving it all she could, she launched herself forward, desperation lending her an extra burst of speed, and got to the stop just as the bus was pulling out of it. Breathless, she pounded her fists against the side of the moving bus.

Either the driver or one of the passengers must have heard her, because the bus halted with a sudden brake. The door swung open. She hurled herself inside and lay on the floor, catching her breath.

The bus wasn't moving. She raised her head. "I'm fine," she said to the driver, who was peering at her, eyebrows raised. "I'm fine. Just go. Give me a minute and I'll buy a ticket."

He shrugged and stared forward. The bus started moving again. There were three other passengers, none of whom appeared to show any interest in her. Amber-May crept onto an empty seat and peeked out the window. She saw the man standing outside her hotel room, his hands fisted at his sides, his head moving, searching for her. She ducked down and stayed that way for two full minutes, until she was certain the bus had left the motel well behind.

34

When Amber-May had jabbed her fingers into his eyes, Freddie Sheehan had jerked back and fallen off the bed, smacking the side of his head against the wall of the motel room, on almost the exact same spot where she'd clocked him in that abandoned factory building.

Consequently, he'd been dazed for a few moments, unable to do much more than probe his smarting eyes and try to silence the bells tolling in his throbbing head.

When he finally got to his feet and staggered out into the parking lot, he saw no trace of the girl. Not that he could see too well or too far, his vision still blurry from the girl's sharp fingernails.

But he did see well enough to instantly spot her car. It hadn't moved, and she wasn't in it.

At first, he considered that to be a stroke of good fortune, thinking that she had to be somewhere close by. But his opinion soon changed for the worse as he began scouring the motel and its surroundings for the girl, not finding her anywhere.

She was gone. And even with his vision restored, he could find no clue as to how she'd made her getaway.

What he did know was that she hadn't taken her car. Which meant that he had no way of tracking her location. She could be anywhere. The longer he waited, the more distance she put between them.

He cursed. Both her and himself.

He couldn't believe it. Twice he'd had her cornered, and twice she'd managed to escape. It was embarrassing, infuriating, all the more so because he only had himself to blame.

The first time, when she'd cut his hand and knocked him out, was bad enough. The second time was inexcusable.

He'd already had her subdued; that was the enraging thing. He had caught her by surprise, had her immobilized on the bed, and needed only to pour some of that quick-working anesthetic down her throat, and he would have been home free. He would have stuffed her in the trunk of his rental and driven straight to the address Emmett MacBaxter had given him. Emmett would have gotten the girl, and Freddie would have been a million dollars richer. Now the only things he had to show for his trouble were a cut hand, a bruised head, and a pair of aching, reddened eyes.

Oh, and a stack of bills, two thousand dollars' worth, that Amber-May had left behind when she'd fled the room.

Those damn bills.

If anyone had ever told him that he would be cursing the moment he found a couple of grand lying around free for the taking, Freddie would have said they were nuts. But now he was doing just that. He was standing in the motel's parking lot, the bills stuck in his jacket pocket, and foul language was spewing from his mouth like sewage from a busted pipe.

Because those bills were what had caused him to loosen his hold on Amber-May. He'd been so surprised when he saw them lying there on the bed, crisp and lovely, that he'd lost focus and allowed his attention to drift—just for a split second. But it was enough of an opening for the girl to turn the tables on him.

Goddamn her. She was causing him so much trouble.

He had to give her credit, though. She was a fighter. She didn't quit or surrender. Most other women would have broken down in tears, started pleading with him not to harm them. Some would have even offered sex in exchange for mercy.

So he had to admit that Amber-May Jackson had earned his respect.

Not that it changed anything.

She was still his ticket to a million-dollar payoff. He was still determined to find her, grab her, and deliver her to Emmett MacBaxter. Only she might arrive into whiny rich boy's hands in less than the pristine shape that Emmett wanted her in.

Because that was why Freddie had failed to nab her twice. He'd been hampered by Emmett's instructions to leave her unmarked, to not have her suffer any debilitating injuries. This had forced him to play it safe, to not use overwhelming force to subdue her. And twice it had allowed her to elude capture.

He would not make that mistake a third time.

When he found Amber-May again, he would not hesitate, he would not be gentle. He would come down on her like a pile of bricks, so that before she even realized what was happening, she'd be unconscious or too hurt to offer any resistance.

And if this resulted in her being injured, then so be it. Freddie was done playing games. He was pissed off. He could not stomach the thought of a third failure.

Emmett would be displeased if Freddie delivered Amber-May Jackson to him all bruised and battered, but he would just have to live with it. And if he tried to welsh on their deal, he might get a taste of Freddie's rage as well. Emmett would just have to accept the fact that in the real world, things did not always go one hundred percent according to plan, and that sometimes you didn't get what you wanted exactly how you wanted it.

Besides, Emmett had been waiting long enough to get Amber-May. If he had to wait a few more days for her to recover from whatever injuries Freddie inflicted upon her, before he began doing whatever it was he planned on doing to her, then no big deal. He would just have to suck it up like a big boy.

Of course, that all depended on Freddie being able to find and this time succeed in kidnapping Amber-May.

This might prove to be more difficult than he liked to admit, now that he had no way of tracking her.

But hope was not all lost.

He recalled his conversation with Pickens a few hours earlier. Pickens believed Amber-May was heading back to Boston. It might be true or it might not be, but Freddie had reason to believe the lawyer was right. People often returned to familiar ground. And there was also the fact that Amber-May Jackson's one and only kin, her grandmother, was in Boston. And Freddie knew exactly where.

He jumped into his rental, gunned the engine, and resumed driving north, hoping with all his might that Pickens had guessed right.

35

Amber-May got off the bus in the Trailways Station in Albany, New York. It was the middle of the night. The only place open for business was a small lunch counter that served coffee and crusty pastries that might have been fresh early the previous day.

She bought herself a cup of black coffee loaded with sugar and nursed it for half an hour. She massaged her fingers as she drank. They still ached, but it was clear the bones were intact. That was a lucky break.

As was her escape from the man who'd attacked her. While on the bus, Amber-May had racked her brain, trying to figure out how the man had found her. The answer—one she could not prove but was certain was true—came to her toward the end of the ride.

Her car. He'd tracked her car.

She'd seen it done in countless movies and TV shows. You attached a small tracking device to a vehicle and then you could know where it was at all times. You could follow someone from afar, with no chance of ever being spotted.

This might be how the man had first followed her to Crumley Creek without her noticing him until she had settled in. He had shadowed her car from a distance.

This meant that she'd been lucky a third time. By leaving her car keys behind in the motel room, she'd deprived her pursuer of the means by which he'd been tracking her. She could now move freely.

Or maybe she couldn't. Maybe the man had noticed the bus, figured she might have been on it, learned its destination, and would soon arrive at the station where she now sat.

With panic-induced goosebumps dotting her arms, Amber-May hastily made for the nearest exit. Idling at the curb was a taxi. She took it to the train station, glancing repeatedly through the back window. No one seemed to be following her.

In the train station, she waited a few hours for the stores to open. In a clothing store, she bought new socks, a pair of sneakers, and a jacket. She left the store, then stopped, went back, and picked out a plain baseball cap and a pair of large sunglasses. Wearing both cap and glasses, she checked her reflection in one of the store's floor-to-ceiling mirrors. Enough of her face was now obscured to make quick identification of her difficult. It made her feel a bit safer.

After throwing her old, and now dirty, socks in the trash, she boarded a train to Boston by way of Providence. All through the ride, she sat with her bag of money on her thighs, hugging it. Her body craved sleep, but she didn't dare close her eyes. She stayed awake by sheer willpower, scrutinizing the face of each new passenger who passed by her seat. She did not see the man who'd attacked her.

She arrived in Boston a little after seven that evening.

36

After leaving the motel where Amber-May Jackson had slipped through his fingers, Freddie drove all night and most of the next morning. His car chewed up the miles as he sped his way north, cutting through New York State and into Massachusetts.

It was only toward midday that his failure-induced anger finally gave way to heavy fatigue. His eyelids felt as heavy as boulders. He could barely keep them apart.

Swearing, he turned off the highway and found a shaded spot by the side of a rural road. He parked his rental, set the alarm on his phone for two o'clock, reclined the driver's seat as far as it would go, and closed his eyes. He was out in less than a minute.

When the alarm blared, he was jerked out of sleep. He felt dazed. It took him a moment to remember where he was and how he got there. His mouth was dry, his tongue thick and coated with a foul taste, like an old gym sock. He opened the car door, leaned out, and spat onto the dirt. Then he swigged from a bottle of mineral water, washing away what remained of the bad taste. He splashed some water on his face and hair. It was cool and helped clear away the cobwebs.

He fired up the ignition and resumed driving. He was on the outskirts of Boston at a little after four.

Congestion worsened as he neared the city. Cars filled the freeway, moving slowly, jostling for position in the rat-race contest to see who would get home a minute ahead of the other. Freddie banged on the wheel and leaned on his horn more than was useful. He wanted to get to his destination. He wanted to find Amber-May Jackson. He tried his best not to think about what he would do if she wasn't there or if he came to the conclusion that she wasn't coming.

A million dollars were riding on him being right. He would not consider the alternative.

He got to the Golden Sunrise Nursing Home shortly before five. There was ample parking space. He chose a spot that was off to the side but one that still afforded a clear view of the main doors. Then he fished out his phone, Googled the number of the nursing home, and dialed it.

It was picked up after four rings. The voice on the other end was young and female, with a distinct Boston accent.

"Golden Sunrise Nursing Home. Good afternoon, how can I help you?"

Adopting a cultured, East Coast accent and a slightly apologetic tone, Freddie said, "This is Mark Calvert from Social Security. Sorry to bother you, but I need some information today."

"Yes, Mr. Calvert, what sort of information?"

"We had a minor glitch in one of our systems over here and I'm trying to sort it all out." Freddie chuckled sheepishly, as though embarrassed by the system's faultiness. "Our latest records indicate that you have a resident in your facility, an Elizabeth Mallory, age seventy-nine. Is this right? Does a woman by this name reside with you?"

The woman on the other end asked him to hold for a moment. He heard the soft tapping of keys. Then she was back.

"Your records are correct. We do have an Elizabeth Mallory living here."

"Great. Is it possible for me to talk to her? I'd like to make sure the details we have on file for her are correct."

"I'll connect you to the nurses on her floor."

"Thank you very much."

Muzak sounded for a few seconds, and then the phone was picked up. This time the voice was middle-aged and tired. The woman identified herself as Nurse Harris.

Freddie repeated his lie about working for Social Security and asked if it were possible to talk to Elizabeth Mallory.

"I'm sorry, but no," said Nurse Harris. "Mrs. Mallory doesn't handle phone conversations very well. If you need to confirm any information regarding her, you'd have to speak to her granddaughter."

"Her granddaughter? Would that be a Miss Amber-May Jackson?"

"Yes. That's right."

"And does she happen to be there at the moment?"

"No, and I don't know when she will be. She hasn't been by for quite a while." Nurse Harris said that last bit with a dose of indignation in her voice, as though she were outraged by the fact that Amber-May hadn't recently visited her grandmother.

Freddie let out a low breath. He wasn't too late. "Thank you very much, ma'am. You've been most helpful."

Dumping the phone back in his pocket, he settled in to wait. He waited for four hours, but Amber-May Jackson did not show. He checked the website of the nursing home and found that visiting hours ended at nine p.m. She wasn't coming today.

Still he waited. But when eleven o'clock came and went, he decided to call it a night. He drove to his apartment. Once inside he took a long shower, changed the bandage on his hand, and climbed into bed. He set his alarm for five thirty a.m. He wasn't taking any chances. He wanted to be back in that parking lot before visiting hours started.

He wanted to be there when Amber-May showed up.

37

Amber-May sat in the shadows of the front porch, leaning against a wall, as a gray Mazda pulled into the driveway. The headlights were turned off. It was nine p.m. A chill wind was whispering through the elms lining the sidewalk. She hugged herself against the cold. In the windows of the house across the street, she could see the flickering glow of a television.

The woman in the Mazda took a minute getting out of the car. She wore loose white clothes under a long blue jacket. A large brown bag was looped over her shoulder. She locked the car and walked tiredly to the three steps leading up to her porch. She was on the second when she noticed Amber-May.

For a fraction of time, fear took hold of her face. Then it was supplanted by surprise.

"Amber-May? Is that you?"

Amber-May grabbed her bag and stood. "Yes. Sorry for startling you. I shouldn't have sat in the dark."

"What are you doing here?"

"I was waiting for you. I need a favor."

"What sort of favor?"

"A big one. Can I come in, Martha? I'd rather talk about this in private."

Martha Mitchum frowned in hesitation. Then she seemed to make up her mind and moved to unlock the door. "All right. Let's talk."

Martha hung her jacket on a wall hanger by the door, then led Amber-May into the living room. It was neat and tidy, with furniture that was in good condition, though twenty years out of style. Pictures of Martha alongside a bespectacled man and a pair of children took up the majority of one wall. Another was hung with framed embroideries. The room gave off a comfy, homey vibe. It reminded Amber-May of how her old living room, the one in the house she'd shared with Grandma Betsy, used to feel. It was a good feeling. This would do nicely, provided Martha agreed to help her.

"Is this your family?" Amber-May said, gesturing at the pictures.

"Yes. That's Morty, my husband—my late husband, I should say. And these are Robert and Grace, my two darlings. Both grown now, of course."

Amber-May walked over to the embroideries. Each depicted a different animal. "Did you make these?"

"Yes. It's just a hobby. I'm not very good, I'm afraid." Martha chuckled self-consciously.

"Yes, you are. These are lovely."

Martha smiled. The compliment had obviously pleased her.

They stood in silence for a moment. Curiosity played across Martha Mitchum's soft features. She obviously wondered what Amber-May was going to ask her. Amber-May was searching for a way to begin, and so far coming up empty. This was turning out to be harder than she'd anticipated. Shame was choking off the words. She knew she had nothing to be ashamed of, but that didn't change how she felt.

It was Martha who broke the silence. "The last time we spoke, I asked you whether you were in trouble, and you told me you weren't. That wasn't true, was it?"

"No."

"Does this have something to do with the woman who was asking about you?"

"Yes."

"This trouble is the reason you stopped visiting your grandmother?"

"Yes."

"Do you want to tell me what it is?"

"No. But I think I may have to. Otherwise, you probably won't agree to do the favor I'm about to ask you."

"I see." Martha appeared to think for a moment. Then she said, "Why don't I make us some tea? Maybe that would make it easier to talk."

Amber-May sat on the sofa as Martha puttered about in the kitchen. She emerged bearing a tray with some cookies and two mugs. Wisps of steam rose from each mug.

"I've put in some honey," Martha said. "I find honey very soothing."

Amber-May took one mug and held it in both hands, enjoying its warmth. Martha sat in a stuffed armchair, munching on a cookie and looking at her.

"Why don't you start by telling me what you want me to do?" she suggested after a moment.

Amber-May took a tiny sip of the hot tea before setting it aside on an end table. She fixed her gaze on Martha Mitchum and said, "I have to take Grandma Betsy out of the home, and I need someone to look after her."

Martha's eyebrows shot up. "What? Why?"

"Because some bad people might hurt her if she stays there."

"Bad people? What bad people? If someone is about to harm your grandmother, you should tell the police."

"The police can't help me. These people, they're powerful. They've got connections with the police."

Martha took a minute to digest this. Her brow had furrowed, and there was a hint of fearful suspicion in her eyes. Slowly, she said, "Why would anyone want to hurt your grandmother? Because of something you did?"

"No. Because of something that I'm going to do, and something that was done to me."

Amber-May licked her lips. Her heart was pounding. It was now or never. She would either tell Martha Mitchum everything or she would have to leave empty-handed and come up with another plan. And she wasn't sure there was one. She rose from the sofa, moved closer to Martha, and knelt down before her. Brushing her hair away from her left ear, she folded the ear forward, exposing the skin behind it. "Do you see the scars?"

Martha leaned forward, squinting. "Plastic surgery? So that's why you seemed different to me. But why would you need surgery? You're so pretty."

Amber-May returned to the sofa, rubbed her hands together for warmth and reassurance, and began talking. She talked for a long while and did not stop until it was done.

Through it all, Martha sat listening intently. At times her breathing got quicker, deeper, but other than that, she didn't make a sound. When Amber-May described the rape, Martha gasped and covered her mouth with her hand. But other than that, she didn't move.

Telling it all was easier than Amber-May had expected. At first she couldn't meet Martha's gaze. After a while, she raised her eyes and kept them on the nurse's until she got every word out. She didn't keep anything back. Not a single nasty detail.

When she was through, she sat back and took stock of how she felt. She had expected to feel lousy, sharing this with another person for the first time. She was surprised to learn it was the opposite. It felt good not being the only one who knew.

She looked at Martha Mitchum and waited for the other woman to say something.

Martha lowered her hand from her mouth. Her face bore a

stunned, mournful expression. "You poor child. I can't believe you went through this whole thing by yourself. And it shocks me that this man—this lawyer—would threaten you this way. You say they now own the nursing home?"

"Yes. That way, they can threaten to evict Grandma Betsy if I tell anyone."

"And I work for these people," Martha said softly, perhaps to herself. She shuddered. "But why would they want to hurt your grandmother now after they agreed to pay for her stay in the home?"

So Amber-May told her what she was planning on doing. "Once I get started, they'll come for her. They'll want to use her to get to me."

This was the hardest part. Earning Martha's sympathy was easy. Getting her to agree to help her once she knew Amber-May's plan was an entirely different matter.

Martha was quiet for a long time. There was a clock on one wall, above a window, and its ticking was the only sound in the room. It ticked more than a hundred times before Martha Mitchum spoke.

"If the police catch you, they'll lock you up for good. Or worse."

"I know."

"You don't sound scared of that possibility."

"I am, but I'm more scared of being captured by whoever sent that man after me."

"Still, there has to be another way."

"If there were, I'd have chosen it. But there isn't. Maybe I should have talked to the media in the beginning, but I couldn't stand the thought of Grandma Betsy being thrown out of the home. Now that's no longer an option, not when they're trying to catch me."

"Why do you think they want to do that?"

"I prefer not to think about it. It scares me even more than if they were trying to have me killed. Which is what will happen if I talk to the media. Then Grandma Betsy will be all alone. Or dead, too."

"But what you're suggesting...have you ever done such a thing before?"

"Of course not. Never."

"How will you do it?"

"I don't know yet," Amber-May said. "I'll find a way. You don't need to know how. It would be best if you don't. That way, in case the police ask you about it, you can say you know nothing."

"You think they'll believe that?"

"If you stick to your story, they won't be able to prove otherwise. What you'll say is that I paid you to take care of my grandmother. When you asked why, I didn't answer. I just said it was temporary. And you wanted the money."

Amber-May's bag lay on the floor at her feet. She picked it up, opened it, and turned it upside down over the couch. Stacks of money tumbled out. Martha Mitchum's jaw dropped.

"My God," she whispered.

"That's all of it," Amber-May said. "Thirty-seven thousand and three hundred dollars and change. All that's left of the forty thousand I got as hush money. I'll need some of it for my expenses, but the rest you can use to care for Grandma Betsy. And I'm willing to pay you for your time, of course." She paused before adding, "I know I'm asking a lot, Martha, but I have nowhere else to turn. I need a nurse to care for my grandmother, or I won't be able to do what I must. I don't trust any of the other nurses in the home. It's you or no one."

Martha's eyes went to her. For an endless moment she said nothing. Then, all of a sudden, tears came to her eyes and spilled down her cheeks. She wiped her face with her hands, muttered "Excuse me," and hurried over to a windowsill, on which stood a box of Kleenex. She dabbed at her eyes, then stood at the window looking out, her shoulders trembling slightly.

Seeing her distress, Amber-May felt her hopes being dashed. What did she expect? That Martha Mitchum, who was in truth nothing more than an acquaintance, would be willing to risk her career and freedom to help her carry out her vendetta? It sounded ludicrous because it was.

Clenching her jaw with frustration, she stuffed the money back into the bag, hefted it, and stood. "I'm sorry, Martha. I can see all this is too much for you. I was a fool coming here. I'll leave right now, okay?"

It didn't seem that Martha had heard her. Still staring out the window, she started speaking in a low, distant voice. "When I was a girl, just eighteen, I dated a boy from my high school. He was tall and handsome, a football player. Very popular. Out of my league. I was surprised and pleased when he showed interest in me. I was never as pretty as you are, you see. Anyway, for our third date he took me in his car to a drive-in. Things got steamy. He wanted to go further than I was willing. But when I told him to stop, he seemed to accept it. On the way home, he turned off the road down a dirt path and parked the car in a clearing. It was very dark. Huge trees all around, just the moon and stars for light. And then...then..." Her words faltered. The tremor in her shoulders intensified. She began crying again. "You are not the only one this has happened to, Amber-May. It wasn't as horrible as what you went through, but it was still the most terrible thing that has ever happened to me."

Amber-May watched the older woman's narrow back. It too was now trembling. She felt like crying alongside Martha Mitchum. She felt guilty. "I'm so sorry, Martha. Sorry this happened to you, and that my coming here has made you relive it."

Martha Mitchum turned from the window. She looked anguished. "You don't need to apologize. You didn't do this to me. If anything, I am to blame, because I chose to say nothing. I didn't go to the police. I didn't even tell my mother. I kept it all to myself for all these years. I allowed that horrible young man to get away with what he did to me. Do you know why I kept silent?"

Amber-May shook her head.

"Because I was scared, that's why. I was scared that people would think badly of me, that I'd get called names. I was afraid that people would say it was my fault, that I'd led him on, that I'd been a tease." Martha's voice nearly broke when she added, "I didn't even slap the bastard's face."

Then her legs started shaking, and she might have fallen if

Amber-May hadn't moved quickly to steady her. She steered Martha to the sofa and asked whether she could bring her anything.

"Just the tea," Martha said, and she took a big gulp from it. She looked into the mug for a moment before raising her eyes to Amber-May's. "It's too late for me. I can no longer do anything to make sure the man who raped me gets punished. What I can do is help you in any way I can. You can bring your grandmother here, Amber-May. I'll take care of her until you finish killing them all."

38

"There's just one problem," Martha Mitchum said.

They were sitting side by side on her living room sofa. They sat close to each other, almost touching, bonded by their trauma and their plans for vengeance.

"What?" Amber-May asked.

"Your grandmother needs round-the-clock supervision. And I have to work. Once you start hunting them down, they'll come looking for her. If I stop showing up for work, they'll figure out she's here, won't they?"

"Yes," said Amber-May, thinking that such a coincidence wouldn't escape Garland Pickens's notice.

"So we need another nurse to be here when I'm working. You said you didn't trust any of the other nurses in the home. I can't say I do either, not with something like this."

Amber-May thought for a moment. "I know someone who might be willing to help."

At half past eleven, Amber-May huddled on a metal bench just outside the hospital doors. The temperature had dropped some more, so she shoved both hands in the pockets of her jacket and hoped she wouldn't have to wait too long.

She didn't.

At eleven forty-two, a plump black woman in a nurse's uniform and a brown knee-length coat emerged from the sliding doors. Her low-heeled shoes clicked on the pavement as she made her way to the employees' parking lot.

Amber-May followed until they were three hundred yards from the hospital entrance. Then she called out the woman's name.

Jolene Lee turned and peered at her. It was obvious she didn't recognize her. Which was no surprise. The last time Jolene had seen her, Amber-May's face was all bruises and swellings and cuts.

"It's me. Amber-May Jackson. Do you remember me?"

Jolene gaped at her. "My God, it is you! You've had surgery done, haven't you? Remarkable." Then her expression changed. She frowned. "What are you doing here?"

"I've come to see you."

Jolene cast her eyes around. The parking lot was well lit, so she could see they were alone. Still, it was nighttime. It was only natural that she'd be wary.

"Why?"

"To say thank you. And to explain why I lied to the police detective."

"You don't have to explain anything to me. You made your choice. It was your right to make it." It was clear by her tone that she disapproved of that choice and perhaps also resented the fact that Amber-May had made a fool of her in front of Detective Sanchez.

"But it wasn't my choice. I was forced to lie."

"What do you mean? Who forced you?"

"Let me buy you a cup of coffee and I'll tell you all about it."

It was easier telling Jolene everything than it was Martha. Jolene already knew about the rape, the injuries Amber-May had sustained, how close to death she'd come. She didn't have to show her the scars the plastic surgeons had hidden behind her ears.

She told her about Pickens's visit, his threats, the agreement he'd made her sign. "That's why I lied to Detective Sanchez. I had to. For my grandmother's sake."

She and Jolene were sitting in the rear booth of an all-night diner. The place was nearly deserted. No one occupied any of the booths within earshot. They had complete privacy. Still, they kept their voices low. The gravity of what they were discussing demanded hushed tones.

Jolene took a slow sip from her coffee cup. She set it down and looked into it. "I was mad at you, you know. Mad that you'd let the people who'd done that to you get away with it."

"I hated myself for the same reason. But I didn't have a choice."

"No. I suppose you didn't. I should apologize. I thought uncharitable things about you after your talk with the detective. When I came in to work the next day, I was planning on asking you why you lied, but you were gone."

"Pickens arranged to have me moved to another hospital. That's where they fixed my face. It was part of the deal he and I made."

"Whoever worked on you is very good. If I hadn't recognized your voice, I wouldn't have believed you were the woman I treated all those months ago."

"I'm not. That woman was resigned to letting the men who raped her get off scot-free. I'm not going to do that."

"Good. So you're going to talk to the police?"

"No. The police can't help. The forensic evidence was useless. Pickens paid someone to tamper with it. All the police would have is my word, and I'm already on record as saying I didn't remember my assailants. If I said differently now, who would believe me? Any defense attorney worth his salt would find it easy to get a jury to doubt my word. Besides, things have changed too much for that." Amber-May told Jolene about how close she'd come to being abducted. "The police can't protect me. They can't protect my grandmother. And they can't convict any of them."

"So what are you going to do?"

"I'm going to take care of them myself," Amber-May said flatly. "I'm going to kill them all."

Jolene stared at her, shock written all over her face. "What?"

"It's the only way to get my life back. It's the only way to prevent them from doing to other women what they did to me. Before, I agreed to keep my mouth shut for my grandmother's sake. That's not an option anymore. Once they catch me, or kill me, they won't keep paying for her stay in the nursing home. She'll be out on the street. And she won't have me to take care of her."

"You can't be serious."

Amber-May fixed her gaze on Jolene. "I am. Completely."

"You're crazy. You're out of your mind."

Amber-May shrugged. "Maybe. But I don't feel crazy. I feel as sane as I've ever been."

"You're talking about murder."

"I'm talking about justice. And there isn't any other way to get it. Can you think of one?"

Jolene thought for a long while. She started talking a couple of times, but stopped in mid-sentence and fell silent again. Finally, she shook her head. "But just because I can't come up with anything doesn't mean there are no other options."

"Believe me, if there was any other way, I'd have thought of it. And I'm not just thinking of myself. I'm thinking of all the other women these men would harm in the future. I'll be doing this for them. You understand that, don't you?"

Jolene finished her coffee, then chewed the inside of her cheek. "Why are you telling me all this?"

"Because I need a nurse," Amber-May said. "And you're the only one I can think of."

They drove to Martha Mitchum's house, Jolene in her car and Amber-May in Martha's Mazda. Martha was waiting for them, looking nervous as she let them in. Amber-May made the introductions, and the two women nodded slowly to each other. Amber-May had told each of them about the other, and now they exchanged appraising looks. Jolene said, "You don't look like someone who'd be persuaded to take part in something as crazy as this."

Martha chuckled. "Neither do you."

Martha gave them a tour of the house, showing them the room where Grandma Betsy would be staying. "It used to be my daughter's room. It looks out onto the backyard. No neighbors can see in." Then she took them to her son's old room. "You can sleep here, Jolene, when Amber-May's grandmother is also asleep. She sleeps many hours each day and, all in all, is easy to care for."

After that, they sat in the kitchen, drank tea, ate cookies, and talked. Martha made a list of things they'd need. Jolene said she'd bring over a bag with a change of clothes and some toiletries the next day. Amber-May watched and listened to the two older women, her body warmed by the deep affection she felt toward them both.

At two in the morning, they all fell silent. They had planned all they could. Now it was up to Amber-May to take the next step.

She looked at the two nurses. "You can still back out, you know. It's not too late. I won't think less of either of you if you do."

Martha and Jolene exchanged glances. Both shook their head.

"I must be as mad as a hatter," Jolene said, "but I'm in this thing all the way."

Martha nodded to Amber-May. "So am I. Now go get the bastards."

39

Martha asked Amber-May when she planned on bringing Grandma Betsy to her house.

"Maybe as soon as two days from now. I need to get something before I can start going after them."

"What?" Jolene asked.

"A gun. Something the police won't be able to trace to me."

Silence fell in the cozy kitchen. Each of the three women was absorbed in her own thoughts.

It was Martha who spoke next. "Do you know where to get a gun like that?"

Sounding more certain than she felt, Amber-May said, "I'll find one. Somehow."

Jolene said, "I may be able to help with that."

She took a pen and a scrap of paper from her purse and jotted something down. She handed the paper to Amber-May. An address was written on it. Amber-May frowned.

"This is in Roxbury, isn't it?"

Jolene nodded.

"What's there?"

"A bar. Or maybe a dive is a better word for it. Called The Black

Steel. Not the sort of place nice girls tend to frequent. Or nice boys for that matter. At least not the sort of girls and boys we're used to thinking of as nice. Frankly, I'm not sure you should go there alone. I can come with you if you like."

Amber-May shook her head. "No. I don't want either of you more involved than you have to be. Not in anything that can't be denied if the police come calling." She looked at the paper. "What am I supposed to find in The Black Steel?"

"A man called Leroy. He owns the place, works the bar."

"And he can sell me a gun?"

"Or direct you to someone who can," Jolene said. "At least, I think he'll be able to do that. Leroy was in trouble with the law when he was younger, did time more than once. Burglary, car stealing, that sort of thing. He's been out more than five years, has cleaned up his act—or if he hasn't, at least he hasn't gotten caught. Either way, he knows people. Once you're in that world, you never get out of it completely."

"How do you know him?"

"I grew up in Roxbury. I lived three buildings south from Leroy. When he and I were fifteen, we were sweethearts." Jolene blushed a little. "He was my first real boyfriend, and I was his first real girlfriend."

Amber-May and Martha exchanged a glance and a small smile.

Jolene noticed. "Did I say something funny?"

Amber-May shook her head. Martha said, "I just didn't figure you for the kind to fall for bad boys."

Jolene stared at her for a second. Then she laughed. "You may think it's funny. My daddy sure didn't. He forbade me to see Leroy, and he had a long talk with him, told him to stay away from me or there'd be trouble. Not that it made much difference. Leroy and I still met in secret until he got busted the first time and went away." Jolene's face turned somber. "That neighborhood doesn't fit the image Boston portrays to the rest of the world, with its universities and parks. Those are rough streets. They breed hard men and women. And crime. It's not easy to get away from that world."

Martha reached over and gave Jolene's hand a squeeze. "You did."

Jolene nodded. "I had parents who pushed me hard. Leroy was not as fortunate. His mother had him when she was sixteen. She couldn't take care of him properly. It's no wonder he got tangled up with the wrong people." She looked at Amber-May. "You sure you don't want me to tag along?"

"I'm sure."

"Then just tell Leroy you know me. That'll make him more cooperative. I haven't seen him for a while, but we remained friendly over the years. We still have a warm spot for each other."

"Why would he believe me? How would I prove I really know you?"

Jolene thought for a minute; then an abashed, schoolgirl smile twitched across her lips. "You tell him that the lion from the Franklin Park Zoo sends his regards."

"What lion?"

Jolene's smile broadened. "The one that nearly bit his hand off when Leroy tried to act all fearless in front of me and stuck his hand through the bars of the lion cage. He'll remember."

"Okay," said Amber-May with a nod, tucking the piece of paper into her pocket. "I'll also need a car."

"That's no problem. You can borrow mine anytime you want," Martha said.

"I don't think so, Martha. Remember what I'll be using it for. If anyone sees your license plate number as I'm leaving a scene, the police will come knocking on your door."

"Oh, of course. Silly me. Well, you can't buy or rent one, as your name will be attached to the car. What's the solution, then? Steal one?"

"I wouldn't know how." Amber-May turned to Jolene. "Can Leroy get me a stolen car?"

Jolene pursed her lips. "I'm sure he can, but I don't think it's a good idea."

"Why not?"

"Because you don't want a stolen car. Stolen cars get reported to the police. Then the police look for those cars and for their plate numbers. That's a fast way of getting caught."

"What about a car that won't be missed for a while?" said Martha. "From long-term parking at Logan Airport, for instance."

"Those places are usually monitored by video cameras. Besides, you'd have no way of knowing when the owner was coming back."

"So what do you suggest?" Amber-May asked.

Jolene thought for a long moment, running her fingertip around the rim of her tea mug over and over. Then she suddenly stopped and a slow smile spread across her face.

"What is it?" Amber-May said.

"A week ago, the oncology department at the hospital was unexpectedly shorthanded, so they asked me to pitch in. I did a weekend shift and met a patient by the name of Franklin Duckworth." She made a face. "Most patients are nice, grateful for what we do for them. Not Duckworth. He's one of those patients who can turn an already challenging work environment into hell. He enjoys making snide remarks to the nurses, complains about the smallest things, and generally behaves like an ass. He also enjoys talking about himself as though he were the most interesting man alive."

"So?"

"So during that weekend shift, in spite of my total disinterest, I got to learn quite a bit about him. That he's a widower, that he lives alone in a house in Newburyport, that he's a retired professor of sociology. And that he owns a twelve-year-old Honda. He was quite proud of that fact."

"Why?" Amber-May asked.

"Professor Duckworth likes to think of himself as thrifty, not a slave to consumerism like everyone else. He says people throw their money away on new cars and all sorts of gadgets, but not him. He still uses an old mobile phone, watches an old-style TV set, and drives a twelve-year-old car. It makes him feel better than the rest of us, a man above materialism. Like I said—he's an ass. But that's not the important thing. What's important is that he's expected to remain hospitalized for at least another month. During that time, his car is just sitting there at his house with no one to drive it."

"You want me to steal his car?"

Jolene shook her head. "Even if you knew how, his neighbors might notice it gone. What you can do is steal his plates. It's perfect. He won't be around to notice the switch, and if the police come asking questions, he won't get into trouble. He has the perfect alibi."

Amber-May smiled. "You're a regular criminal mastermind, aren't you?"

Jolene smiled back. "Honey, where I grew up, it comes with the territory."

Jolene left at two thirty after explaining the rest of her idea and exchanging warm hugs with both Amber-May and Martha that said much more than words ever could.

Amber-May said to Martha, "For this little errand, I think I could use your car. It will only get dangerous once I start hunting them down."

Martha said, "You're welcome to it. Be careful."

Before Amber-May started the Mazda, she did a search on her phone and managed to find Franklin Duckworth's address. But she didn't go there directly. First, she entered the town of Topsfield and cruised its abandoned nighttime streets until she found a Dodge sedan parked in the shadows of an alleyway.

Armed with a screwdriver she had borrowed from Martha, she exited the Mazda, crouched before the parked Dodge, and proceeded to remove both license plates. She didn't feel good about this part of Jolene's plan—it was a hassle to get new license plates, and the owner of the Dodge had done her no harm—but she knew there was no escaping it.

"You can't leave Duckworth's car without plates," Jolene had said. "A neighbor might notice it and alert the cops. Then they'll be on the lookout for them. But a neighbor won't notice if Duckworth's car has a different set of plates."

My father would have, Amber-May had thought with a pang of loss and longing. But Jolene was right; most people wouldn't.

With the Dodge's plates in her possession, she drove the rest of the way to Newburyport. Duckworth's house was conveniently located in the middle of a large lot, well back from the road. Amber-May parked some distance away and entered his property on foot. The Honda was parked beside the house in a wooden carport.

In the darkness of night, it was difficult to undo the screws holding the Honda's plates in place, and even harder to screw them back on, this time to secure the plates she'd taken from the Dodge. Despite the chilly air, Amber-May was sweating by the time she completed the switch.

Finally, it was done. No one saw her. No one yelled at her to stop. She returned to the Mazda and drove back to Boston. It was nearly five a.m. when she arrived at Martha's house and found the nurse waiting at the door for her.

"I couldn't sleep," Martha explained. "I was so worried that some-thing might have happened to you."

"You needn't have been," Amber-May said, entering the house. She was moved by Martha's concern. "It went fine."

Martha locked the door and turned to see Amber-May yawning without bothering to cover her mouth. "No wonder you're exhausted, with all you've been through lately. Come with me. You can sleep in my daughter's old room."

Amber-May was about to say it would be wiser if she didn't stay at Martha's house a minute longer than necessary, but she suddenly realized that she was too tired to start looking for a hotel. She recalled that the last time she'd slept was two nights ago. Since then, she'd been on the move, with hardly a moment of rest.

Adrenaline and fear had kept her alert and awake till that moment. But now she felt drained of energy. A deep, encompassing fatigue had come over her. She wanted nothing more than to close her eyes and shut off her mind for a few hours.

Feeling as though her weight had quadrupled in the blink of an eye, she shuffled after Martha upstairs to the bedroom and watched as the older woman quickly made the bed. Then Martha led her to the bathroom and gave her a toothbrush and a tube of toothpaste.

"I start work tomorrow at noon," Martha said. "So I'll likely be out when you wake up. There's food in the fridge. Help yourself to whatever you want." She patted Amber-May's arm, bid her goodnight, and walked down the hall to her own room.

Yawning, Amber-May brushed her teeth and splashed a little cold water on her face. She felt grubby, the dust of the road clinging to her skin, but she didn't have the energy to take a shower. Instead, she removed her shoes and clothes, got into bed, and fell asleep.

In her dreams she saw the faces of the four men who had raped her. Each of the faces was grotesquely large, with huge bulging eyes that flashed red and yellow fire, and hungry mouths that gaped as wide as sinkholes and were full of long sharp teeth. Their skin was translucent, their facial bones glowing bleach white underneath. The stench of sulfur and burnt ash floated thickly off them.

The four faces hovered before her eyes like demons, cackling and laughing raucously. One of them said, "You think you can harm us, little girl? You think you can touch us? That's not how it works."

"No," another said, giggling maniacally, "it's the other way around. *We* touch *you*. Anywhere we want, as much as we want."

The face of Emmett MacBaxter, the largest and most demonic of the lot, added, "You must have enjoyed it to come back here. To us. Maybe we'll have another party, what do you say, guys?"

The other three hooted and cheered. They began telling her in graphic detail what they planned on doing to her the next time they saw her. Much of what they said went far beyond what they had done to her all those months ago. Some of it was unnatural, impossible, like some demented fantasy brewed in the warped mind of a rabid psychopath.

She opened her mouth to scream back at them but found herself voiceless. She tried flailing her arms to swat them away, but her limbs did not obey her commands. It was as though she'd been paralyzed. She could do nothing but watch as the four monstrous faces swooped and glided in front of her eyes, stabbing her to the core with their obscene threats, injecting her with a terror so cold that she felt as though she were freezing on the inside.

She'd never had a nightmare of such ferociousness. Not even on the nights soon after the rape. What made it even worse was that this dream seemed to go on forever. Unlike normal nightmares, the moment when she could exert her will and snap into wakefulness took a very long time to arrive. This nightmare had ensnared her like a hunting trap. She was unable to escape, no matter how hard she tried.

When she finally awoke, her skin was soaked with perspiration, her hair clinging wetly to her neck. A sweaty, sour smell rose from her skin. Her heart was galloping. She could hear it pounding in her ears like war drums. All her muscles felt tight, as though they'd been flexed continuously for hours. For a few minutes, she lay motionless in bed, body aching from head to toe, not sure she could actually move.

After she managed to summon the strength to swing herself, groaning, to a sitting position, she remained perched on the edge of the bed for a long while with her eyes closed and her head lolling. Fear was pulsing through her, making her shudder uncontrollably. Her breathing was shaky. With a trembling hand, she picked up her phone and saw that it was two p.m. She'd slept for nine hours straight. Had the nightmare lasted that long? The mere thought was terrifying.

What message was her psyche trying to send her? That she was indeed crazy? That what she planned on doing was doomed to end in failure? That she should turn around and run?

She gritted her teeth, shaking her head. She couldn't accept that. She wouldn't. She wasn't going to live the rest of her life in fear of being abducted. She wasn't going to let those four monsters get away with what they'd done to her.

No, she told herself. They were not monsters. Monstrous, yes, but not monsters. They were just men, no more powerful than her. In fact, she was going to show them just how much more powerful she was compared to them. She was going to make them wish they'd never set eyes on her, let alone laid their hands on her body. And that would be the last thing they ever wished for.

Her resolve restored, she rose from the bed, went into the bathroom, and washed off the sour sweat produced by her nightmare. Then she picked up her phone, opened up Craigslist, and checked the listings of cars for sale in the Boston area. She was looking for a specific model, a twelve-year-old light-gray Honda—just like the Honda whose license plates she'd stolen a few hours earlier. There were three such listings. One of these cars she had to buy today.

She made herself some toast and coffee in Martha's kitchen, then called for a taxi and went shopping for a vehicle.

The first car she saw was in much worse condition than was advertised—its engine rattled loudly. The second was a darker shade of gray than Duckworth's Honda. The third was perfect. Not a mark on her except a slight dent in the rear bumper. The owner, a grandmotherly type with ample hips and an easy smile, was overjoyed when Amber-May did not haggle over the price and offered to pay cash. She even invited her in for cupcakes and tea, both of which Amber-May declined politely, pleading a prior engagement.

The Honda lacked most of the modern gadgetry of newer cars, but it was a few steps up from her old Ford. The previous owner had taken good care of it; it ran smoothly and easily. Amber-May was very pleased with it. She drove it to a nearby shopping center, descended into the lowermost level of the underground parking lot, and there screwed on the stolen license plates.

The plates would not save her if she got pulled over—she had no insurance or registration—but no one would report them as missing. And should a policeman run them through the police computer system—as Jolene said they routinely did—they would match the make and model of the car and so would not arouse suspicion.

Satisfied, Amber-May bought herself another set of clothes—jeans, shirt, socks, and underwear—and a bag in which to stow them all. Then she found a cheap hotel by the train station and paid for three days in advance.

In the tiny hotel room, she sat on the narrow bed and began doing research on her targets.

The thing she needed to decide was which of the four she would go after first.

The answer came to her almost immediately. She only knew where one of them lived. She would start with him.

But before that, she had to see a man called Leroy about a gun.

40

That night, Amber-May sat in her car across the street from The Black Steel. The place was indeed a dive. She could tell that just by looking at its exterior.

The bar took up the ground floor of a five-story building whose brickwork was stained by wide damp patches of brownish-gray. There was no awning. No neon flickered invitingly. Just an old sign that was nailed above the grimy window. Black block letters on a white background proclaimed to the world the name of the establishment therein. A crack slashed through the letters of the word *STEEL*, bisecting them like a scar, and the top-left corner of the sign had been chipped away as though some animal had taken a bite out of it.

The bar fit the street around it. The road was potholed. One in three streetlights wasn't working. The buildings looked weathered and beaten and past their prime.

Dim lighting glowed through the bar's front window, and through it Amber-May could see the shadows of people moving about. She rolled down her window. City noise rushed in. But she didn't hear music pulsing from the bar.

As she sat in her car, dawdling, two large men emerged from the bar. Both looked like they could crumple her in one fist. They were laughing. One clapped the other on the back. They didn't look her way. They walked down the street and out of sight.

On the street corner a block north from where she sat, a lanky teenager slouched against the side of a building. She watched a car approach him slowly, then wind down to a stop. The teenager pushed himself forward, and he and the driver exchanged a few words through the passenger's side window. She saw a hand peek out the window and give the teenager some bills. The teenager's hand dipped into his pocket and came out holding a small bag, which he handed to the driver. The car rolled away, and the teenager returned to his slouching position.

A drug buy. The first she'd ever seen in real life.

She'd never been in this part of Boston. It was a place she'd been advised to avoid. As Jolene had said, this street, this neighborhood, would not appear in any tourist brochure. No bus filled with sight-seers armed with cameras would ever rumble down this road.

"Not a place for nice boys and girls," Amber-May muttered to herself, rooted to her car seat, still staring at the bar's window, at its closed gray door.

But was she still a nice girl, given what she planned on doing? Maybe this was where she now belonged.

She smiled a tight-lipped smile, let out a pent-up breath, and tugged the door handle. The door swung open with a squeak and she stepped out onto the street.

It was chilly. She zipped her jacket all the way up to her throat and stuck her hands in its pockets. A tiny red glow flared on the street corner. The drug peddler lighting a cigarette. Was he looking at her? It was hard to tell with his face in the shadows.

No cars drove by. No pedestrians traversed the sidewalks. The street was as quiet as a big-city street could be. Knowing that to wait is to lose heart, Amber-May plunged herself forward, crossing the street in a determined stride, not stopping until she opened the bar's door and stepped inside.

She found herself in a rectangular high-ceilinged room partially lit in a soft amber glow. The walls were festooned with pictures of boxers duking it out in the ring or working their craft in the gym. The only one she recognized was Mike Tyson. A bar took up the left side. A neglected pool table stood at the rear. The rest of the space was home to about fifteen square wooden tables, a third of which were occupied.

The customers were all men, all black, all tough looking. None looked younger than thirty. Some were a stone-hard fifty or more.

There had been loud, manly conversation when she had entered the bar. Now the only noise was the low jangle of a blues song thrumming from the scratchy sound system.

All eyes were on her. A dozen flat stares and inscrutable expressions aimed right at her like gun barrels. She realized how out of place she was. A young white woman in a black male space.

For a few seconds, she stood frozen just past the threshold, her eyes jumping about the room, from one face to another, unsure of what to do. Unsure of what they'd do. If what Jolene had said was true, there was a good chance these men, at least some of them, were hardened criminals.

Then a voice, deep and rolling: "Lost, miss? Looking for directions?"

It belonged to the man standing behind the bar, leaning his large hands on it. He was tall, broad-shouldered and deep-chested, with a wide face squatting atop a powerful neck. His eyes were a rich, oak brown.

Amber-May licked her lips, did her best to ignore the eyes fastened on her—all except the barman's—and strode toward him. Now her back was turned to the customers. There was no mirror behind the bar. She couldn't see them eying her from behind. But she could feel their gazes.

Up close, she could see the barman had tattoos inked onto his knuckles. Crude letters in blue ink. His nose was large and flat. It had been broken at least once, she thought. In the boxing ring, perhaps, or in a jail scuffle. He was wearing a long black T-shirt spread tautly over his muscular chest, and a shallow frown across his tall brow. It was a face that could look menacing, but it didn't look that way now. His expression was mild, gentle, without a hint of animosity.

"What's on your mind, miss?"

Keenly aware of the silence behind her, as well as all those eyes and ears trained on her, she said, "Are you Leroy?"

His frown deepened, and his voice dropped in pitch. "And if I am?"

She licked her lips again. There had been a tinge of a threat in his tone. It was clear that he didn't like her knowing who he was, since he didn't know who she was.

"I want to buy something from you."

"What? A beer? A shot of bourbon? We don't serve no cocktails here, I'm afraid. Nothing with a little umbrella in it."

He said this with a tiny smile on his lips, but his eyes were scrutinizing her closely.

"I'm not thirsty."

"What is it, then?"

She glanced over her shoulder. As she expected, all of the patrons were watching her. She turned back to Leroy. "Maybe we can talk someplace private?"

He shook his head slowly. "Right here is fine."

She leaned forward over the bar and lowered her voice to a shade above a whisper. "A gun. I want to buy a gun."

He raised one eyebrow, his smile widening. "You guys on the force used to be more subtle than that."

"I'm not a cop," Amber-May said.

"You don't look like one, I'll give you that."

"I got your name from Jolene Lee. She said you might be able to help me."

That made him blink. The smile went away from his face. He gave her a long, narrow-eyed stare. "You know Jolene? How?"

"She was my nurse when I was hospitalized a while back."

"And she just happened to tell you I'd sell you a gun? I don't believe that for one second."

"It's true."

"No, it's not. Listen to me and listen good: I don't know who you are or how you know about me and Jolene, but I don't believe she ever gave you my name. She wouldn't do—"

"She told me to tell you the lion from the Franklin Park Zoo sends his regards."

Leroy blinked again. Then he just stared at her for a moment, not a single muscle in his face moving. Finally he drew in a breath and ran his tongue over his lips.

"You'd better go on home now, miss," he said.

"But I need—"

He held up a hand. "I know what you need. You told me. Only you're not going to be getting it from me. Understand?"

He wasn't saying he couldn't help her, only that he wouldn't. Amber-May scoured her brain for something to say, something that would change his mind. But all she came up with was: "Please. It's important."

He shook his head like the slow pendulum of a grandfather clock. "You go on now."

He stepped back from the bar, grabbed a washcloth, and started wiping glasses, ignoring her.

Amber-May stayed put for a few seconds, but it was clear by his words, tone, and demeanor that he would not be swayed. He would not sell her a gun.

With the eyes of the patrons latched to her back, she walked to the door and stepped outside. She stood on the sidewalk for a minute, disappointment pressing hard around her chest.

Maybe she should try the drug dealer on the corner. Maybe he knew someone who'd sell her a gun.

No. That was stupid. She didn't know him. He might be an undercover cop. And even if he wasn't, what was to keep him from simply robbing her?

She would have to think of another way. Maybe Jolene knew someone else she might approach.

She crossed the street and reached her car. She was pulling out her keys when she heard footsteps approach from behind. She spun.

A man was standing there. Six foot four, wide shoulders, huge arms, shaved scalp. She retreated a step, her rear end now pressed against the closed car door. The man must have read her fear, because he raised both hands, palms out.

"Whoa. Calm down. I'm not about to jump you."

She waited, saying nothing. Her fist was bunched around her keys, and slowly she shifted them so they protruded between her fingers. If he attacked her, she'd go for his eyes and hope her aim proved true.

But he didn't attack her. Instead, he lowered his hands to his sides. "I hear you're in the market for a weapon."

Amber-May frowned. She recognized him now. He had been in the bar, seated at one of the tables. Not close to the bar. Not close enough to hear her and Leroy's hushed conversation.

"What makes you think that?"

He jerked a thumb over his shoulder, in the direction of The Black Steel. "Leroy told me."

"Leroy?"

"Yeah. Just after you left. He said you could be trusted."

She took a second to absorb this. "Why wouldn't he sell me one himself?"

The man shrugged. "Leroy's gone clean. Straightened out. He doesn't do that kind of stuff no more. But I know someone who can set you up. Tonight."

41

The man from The Black Steel said his name was Dwight. The man he could take her to, the one who could sell her a gun, was called TJ.

"He's my cousin."

"Your cousin?"

"Yeah. We live in the same house, too. If you want, we can go see him now."

"Where is he?"

Dwight pointed south. "About a mile down that way. We can ride there."

It took Amber-May a second to realize Dwight was talking about riding in her car. With her. She hesitated. In the car, she'd be helpless if he started something. Out here she could fight back. Or run away.

"Why don't you call him? Ask him to come meet us here?"

"He won't come. You can either come with me or not. I don't care. Maybe you don't really want a gun."

Amber-May swallowed, then nodded. "Okay. Let's go."

She got in the car quickly before she could change her mind. Dwight slipped into the passenger seat. In the confines of the vehicle, his advantage in size was more pronounced. She tensed as he yanked the door shut with a clang, knowing that now, with both of them inside the unmoving car, was the perfect time for him to assault her. But he just sat placidly in his seat, hands on thighs, waiting for her to start the car.

She did, then turned the car south and followed his directions.

They drove deeper into Roxbury, entering a street of identical low residential houses crammed close together on miniature lots.

"Here we are. The one on the left."

Amber-May parked the car and followed Dwight to the house.

It had two floors and a stoop. It had to be at least forty years old and was showing it. Paint was peeling off its facade, which was well on its way from white to gray. The tiny yard was chock-full of weeds. A tire lay in the undergrowth. Beer bottles were scattered here and there. The remnants of cigarettes littered the small path leading from the street to the house.

The three steps rising to the stoop creaked under their feet. The second one sagged in the middle. Dwight took care to climb on the side. Amber-May stepped where he did.

She realized she might be walking straight into disaster, into a trap. The rational thing to do was turn around, run back to the car, stomp on the gas, and get the hell out of there.

She did not know Dwight. She did not know the man he was taking her to see. If indeed there was such a man. For all she knew, there was no TJ. For all she knew, there was no one in that house who would sell her a gun. Dwight might have other ideas.

Like rape, for instance.

She shuddered. So hard that she gasped. Dwight was at the doorway, hand rummaging in a pocket. He turned to her, frowning.

"You all right?"

She gulped, nodded, and ran a hand over her face. Her brow was clammy with sudden sweat.

"You don't look so good."

She cleared her throat. "I'm fine." And judging solely by her voice, she was. It was strong and steady, unlike how she felt.

"Okay," Dwight said, turning back to the door. He produced a set of keys, picked one, slid it into the lock, and pushed the door open.

A television sounded from deeper inside the house. Hip-hop music was playing loudly. She followed Dwight down a short hallway, past a kitchen with a counter heaped with empty take-out cartons, and into a living room. On the sofa lounged a wiry black man in his mid-twenties, dressed in a white undershirt and loose blue jeans. He was barefoot and clasped a cigarette between two long fingers. The other hand was holding a remote.

"Hey, TJ," Dwight said.

TJ turned to look at them. His eyebrows shot up at the sight of her. He straightened and clicked the remote to turn off the TV. He sucked on his cigarette and discharged a jet of smoke, regarding her with keen interest. She returned his stare without shifting her gaze. She needed to appear confident. She needed to hide the fact that fear was making her heart stutter.

TJ's hair was high and flat in the middle, like a mountain plateau, and shaved on the sides. His face was long and lean, with eyes that were two narrow slits on either side of a sharp nose. A thin scar gouged down from one corner of his mouth to the tip of his chin. A heavy linked-metal chain hung at his neck, drooping to the middle of his chest.

Without looking at Dwight, without taking his eyes off her, TJ said, "What's this, Dwight? Who's this white girl?" He had a thin voice, like a taut guitar string being strummed.

Dwight opened his mouth, then seemed to remember he did not know Amber-May's name.

She wasn't about to reveal her true name to these two men. She said, "My name's Jackie and I'm—"

TJ cut her off. "I was talking to him. Not you."

Dwight shifted his feet. He was taller and wider than TJ, but it was clear that, among the two, it was TJ who called the shots.

"This girl wants to buy something from you."

TJ didn't say anything for a second. He looked her up and down, like he was appraising her.

Amber-May felt her skin prickle and turn cold. If this was indeed a trap, she was in a much worse position than she'd been two minutes ago. Now she was inside a house with two strange men, both of whom looked stronger than her, both of whom were criminals.

Then again, the four men who had raped her, she bet none of them was a criminal. At least not officially.

TJ said, "What you want to buy from me?"

"A gun."

TJ simply stared at her. Then he turned his gaze on Dwight. "You know this girl long?"

"Just met her tonight."

"What? Why'd you bring her here for? You crazy? She might be a cop."

"Leroy said she was cool."

"Leroy? That old man? Why should I trust anything he says? Tell me, does this look cool to you? Does this look normal?"

He was gesturing at Amber-May with the hand holding the cigarette. Smoke whispered from its tip. Its scent filled the living room.

"I'm not a cop," she said.

TJ mimed wiping sweat off his brow. "Whew, well, that settles it. Now I'm reassured." He glared at Dwight, who lowered his gaze to his shoes.

"I asked Leroy if he was sure she was cool," he said sheepishly. "One hundred percent, he said."

TJ still glared at his cousin. Then he took a drag and crushed out his cigarette in a bowl brimming with stubs. Rising from the sofa, he stood with his hands on his hips, turning his eyes back to Amber-May.

"You need a gun, why not go to a store? A nice white girl like you, they'd sell you one, all legal."

"I don't want it registered to me."

"Why not? You're planning on doing something nasty?" He dragged out that last word, his tone pure mockery.

Amber-May kept her eyes fixed on him. He was trying to ridicule her—or maybe that wasn't it, at least not entirely. Maybe he was also testing her.

"I'm going to kill four men with it," she said, in a tone so free of inflection and emotion that it stunned her to hear it.

Apparently, it had a similar effect on Dwight and TJ. The first, standing to her left, sucked in a breath. TJ just froze, the mockery wiped from his face, replaced by a look of surprised uncertainty. He rubbed his chin, brow furrowed, looking at her as though seeing her for the very first time.

"Why? Why you want to kill these men?"

"That's none of your business," she said, expecting him to tell her that it most certainly was.

He didn't. Instead, he rubbed his chin again, clearly thinking, weighing his options. His narrowed eyes never left her, probing her, trying to reach some conclusion.

Finally he said, "You could be setting us up. You could be wearing a wire."

"I'm not. You heard what Dwight said. Leroy vouches for me."

TJ sneered. "That tells me nothing. You could have something on him. That old man, he's more scared of going back to prison than anything else. Take off your jacket."

She stared at him. Her chest felt tight, constricted. Her heart rate jumped.

"Do it. I want to see if you've got a wire. Take it off and toss it to me."

Still she didn't move.

"Fine," he said, smirking. "You can go now, officer. I don't know what led you to believe you might find illicit firearms here, but I assure you my cousin and I are both law-abiding citizens."

He bent down to pick up the remote, but Amber-May stopped him. "Wait. Okay."

With a tremor in her fingers, she unzipped her jacket, shucked it off, and threw it at him. He caught it, spread it on the sofa, and patted it. In an inside pocket, he found the wad of bills she'd brought with her in order to pay for the weapon. He showed it to Dwight, who gave a grunt whose meaning Amber-May could not decipher. It might have been approval. Or maybe it was a signal that now that they had her money, they didn't need to give her anything in return.

TJ started counting the bills.

"There's three thousand dollars there," Amber-May said.

He flicked her an annoyed glance, then resumed his count. When he was done, he nodded to Dwight, then looked thoughtfully at Amber-May.

"Okay," she said, "so now you know I'm not wearing a wire."

"I know it's not in your jacket," TJ said.

Amber-May frowned at him. Then the import of his words dawned on her. She shook her head and hugged herself. "No. No way. I'm not taking off any more clothes."

TJ shrugged. "We have to be sure. We can't take chances." He laid the wad of cash on top of her jacket. "It's either that, or I gotta pat you down. Or you turn around and walk out of here. Your choice."

She glanced at Dwight, hoping he'd say something. But he just stood there, big and hulking and silent. He wouldn't help her. TJ was the one in charge. TJ made the final decisions.

A minute passed in which no one spoke. Amber-May noted that TJ did not say that she'd be leaving with her money. He didn't say otherwise, either, but it was possible he planned on keeping it even if he ended up selling her nothing.

What he said was true. She had a choice to make. She could walk out of there empty-handed, or she could suffer some indignity and maybe emerge from this night with the means to exact her revenge. If she chose to leave, it would likely mean postponing her plan for an unknown length of time. Because she didn't know anyone else from whom she could buy a weapon illicitly and discreetly. She was not part of this unlawful world. She knew no criminals. And now she realized that without the right connections, and sometimes even with them, purchasing an illegal weapon was not a simple task.

So she had to stay. And that meant either getting naked in front of these two strange men or having one of them pat her down. As a stripper, she'd done the former many times. It should have been the obvious choice. The easier one. But she found herself unable to do it.

She could not expose herself that way. Not now, maybe not ever again. Certainly not with men she didn't know, for whom she felt nothing but fear. Not after what had happened the last time.

With a voice that sounded firmer than she felt, she said, "You need to pat me down, so do it. Let's get this over with."

TJ gave a tiny nod and stepped toward her. She watched him, watched his face, waiting for the leery grin, for the lascivious glint in his eyes. But there was nothing. His face was blank, his eyes flat, his mouth closed in a straight line. He showed no sign of arousal or lewd anticipation. Still, as he drew closer, a cold current of shame and anger swept through her, coursing through her blood vessels like a wintry river filled with sharp shards of ice. The degradation she'd suffered the night of the rape was not over. It just kept building, adding to itself. An ongoing, expanding nightmare. She clenched her teeth, trying to prevent them from chattering.

The anger she felt was not directed at TJ, but at the four men whose crime had led her to this house, to this low point. Getting back at them was worth a little more suffering.

"Spread your arms wide," TJ said, now standing a foot in front of her.

He smelled of cigarette smoke, beer, and cheap cologne. Up close she could see tiny acne scars dotting his cheeks. She did as she was told, holding her arms like a scarecrow. He reached for her, and she hissed in a breath and shut her eyes as she felt his cool fingers on her skin.

He began with her wrists, then ran his hands up her arms to her shoulders—first the left, then the right—feeling her through her shirt. He did not miss an inch, nor did his hands linger at any spot more than was necessary.

Amber-May kept her eyes shut tight. She held her breath as TJ's hands slid up her legs, over her knees, and onto her thighs. When his fingers reached her groin, she bit her lower lip hard enough to hurt. She barely noticed when she began trembling. TJ paused, withdrawing his hands.

"You all right?"

She didn't open her eyes. Her ears told her he was crouched down before her, his body close to hers, his head at about the height of her groin.

She gave a jerky nod. That was all she was capable of doing. A few seconds later, his hands resumed their journey along her body.

Finished with her groin, the hands roved up her belly, pressing the cloth of her shirt against her skin. They moved over her flanks and up into her armpits before descending to her chest. Her trembling intensified. Now she was shaking. She could no longer keep her teeth from chattering. Her stomach was flip-flopping. Bile rose into the base of her throat. She retreated into a place deep inside her mind, where the sensation of TJ's hands was distant and the fear and revulsion that gripped her were muffled. She pictured a beach, tranquil waves frothing on the sand, a light breeze carrying the tangy scent of the sea. She lay on a beach towel, warmed by the hot sand beneath her and the sun's rays above. Other than the whisper of the surf, there was no sound, no danger. No strange hands roaming her body. No fingers probing her. She was utterly safe.

She didn't notice when TJ finished his frisk and stepped back from her. Only when he spoke, loudly, did she realize he was done and had probably already said something to that effect without her registering it.

She cracked her eyes open. A cold, slick sweat covered her forehead and cheeks. Her back and belly and armpits were damp. Her shirt stuck to her skin. It took a conscious effort for her to stop shaking. She swallowed, pushing the bile back down to her stomach. It burned her throat as it descended.

Glancing around, she saw that Dwight and TJ were both staring at her. Dwight's mouth hung open. His eyes gave clear evidence that he did not begin to understand what he'd just witnessed.

TJ said, "What the hell happened to you?"

She heaved a breath. A final tremor slithered up her back. Sweat dripped from her forehead, stinging her eyes.

"What did they do to you?" Dwight asked.

She ignored both their questions. She fixed her gaze on TJ. "Satisfied? Do you now believe I'm telling you the truth?"

He nodded his head slowly. "Yeah. You're okay. You wait here. Be back in a minute."

He was gone at least twice that. Meanwhile, Amber-May had slipped on her jacket but left the money on the sofa.

When TJ returned, he held a blue gym bag in one hand, a rolled-up white towel in the other. He handed her the towel. Without thanking him, she proceeded to dry her face. She felt a bit better, stabler. Her stomach had settled.

TJ laid the bag on the scratched coffee table and unzipped it. He pulled out three handguns. One revolver and two pistols.

"You know guns?"

Amber-May shook her head.

He pointed to the smaller one. "That's a .22. That's the caliber. It's small, will make a small hole. But you can fit this in your purse, jacket pocket, no problem. And if you hit your target in the head or heart, it will kill like a bigger piece."

His finger moved to the revolver. It was the longest weapon of the three.

"A .357 Magnum. Very powerful gun. Will blow a hole the size of a large fist in someone. You don't have to be accurate with this one to put someone down. You just need to hit them. Problem is, it's got a massive recoil. It can jump in your hand if you're not strong enough to handle it, which means you may be less accurate with it. It also makes a pretty big bang. You fire it, people will hear it three blocks away."

He gestured at the third and final gun. "This one's a .38. Midsized caliber. Not too big, not too small. Nothing close to the Magnum in terms of stopping power, but still packs a good punch. Louder than the .22, but nowhere near the Magnum. The magazine holds eight rounds. I think this is what you need."

Amber-May picked up the gun. It was midnight black, without a scratch on it. Heavier than it looked, a solid piece of metal, cool to the touch. Scotch tape had been wrapped around the grip. She ran her fingers along the grip, barrel, and sight, realizing how little she knew about how this tool worked.

TJ seemed to sense this. He held out his hand for the gun. "Let me show you some things."

He pointed out the safety catch, the magazine release button, showed her how to load the magazine and how to chamber a round. "Here's how you hold it." He held the gun in both hands, arms straight in front of him, elbows locked. "Not like some dumbass wannabe gangster in a movie. And this is how you stand."

She watched and listened carefully, making sure to memorize every word.

TJ handed her the gun. "Now you show me."

He had her go through the entire process: loading the magazine, pushing it into place, cocking the gun, flicking off the safety. He adjusted her stance and grip, told her she had to keep both eyes open and not to flinch just before pulling the trigger. "If you do, your bullet will go nowhere near where you expect."

He had her pull the trigger on an empty gun a few times but warned her that firing for real was an entirely different experience.

"You in a hurry to get these guys? Even if you are, take an hour and go to a range or the woods somewhere isolated and fire a couple of magazines just so you get a feel for how the gun shoots." He scratched his head. "What else? Oh yeah, the scotch tape around the grip is to lower the chance of your fingerprints getting on the gun. But just to be on the safe side, you rub everything down before you go shoot someone, including the bullets, and when you load up, wear gloves. This gun is clean, okay, so you have nothing to worry about in that regard."

"What do you mean, clean?"

TJ rolled his eyes. "It's never been used in a crime; that's what clean means. So if you get caught with it on you, the police won't be able to charge you for anything else." He paused, head tilted slightly, scrutinizing her. "You get caught, we never met. Am I clear?"

She nodded. "Yes. Don't worry about that. I won't tell anyone about you." He did not look convinced, so she added, "If things turn sour, it's more likely that I'll be dead or missing than arrested."

TJ frowned, and so did Dwight. They exchanged a glance; then TJ returned his gaze to her. "You sure you want to go through with what you have in mind? Killing a man, not to mention four of them, ain't no walk in the park, especially if you've never killed anyone before."

"I'm sure," Amber-May said.

TJ gave a short nod, then leaned down and stuck his hand inside the gym bag. He pulled out a small box and handed it to Amber-May. "Ammo for the .38. Fifty rounds. You need more, you'll have to go buy them in a store. No one has you sign papers to buy bullets."

Amber-May put the box in her jacket pocket. "How much for the gun and ammunition?"

TJ looked at Dwight, who shrugged, then at the wad of cash on the sofa.

"Twenty-five hundred," he said. "I'm giving you a discount."

That was probably bullshit. Amber-May guessed he was gouging her, but she didn't care. She just wanted the gun.

"Fine."

TJ peeled off ten fifties from the wad and gave them to her. The rest he stuck in his pants.

"Anything else?" he asked.

"No. That's all. Thank you."

He seemed a bit embarrassed by her thanks. Maybe he hadn't expected it. Or maybe he was ashamed of overcharging her. Either way, he gave a quick nod and muttered, "You're welcome."

Amber-May put the five hundred dollars in the same pocket as the box of ammunition. The gun went into the waistband of her jeans, the jacket covering it. She turned to leave, thanking Dwight for his help, saying goodbye. She had taken three steps when TJ spoke.

"Yo, girl."

Amber-May turned to face him.

"These four dudes, are they black?"

Amber-May shook her head. "All white."

TJ's face broke into a grin. He chuckled, clapped his hands once, then told her to hold on a second.

"In that case, take this as well. On the house."

He gave her the smallest gun, the .22; a magazine; and a small holster, which he said she could strap around her ankle. Still smiling, he added, "I hope you make it, girl. I hope you pay those four bastards back for whatever they did to you."

42

Emmett stared at his phone. It was three twenty-five p.m., and he still hadn't heard from Freddie Sheehan. He had called him twice today already, but neither call was answered. This was unacceptable. It made him worry that something had gone wrong.

He was sitting in his father's old office, at the old man's desk, in the very same chair he had once occupied, from where he had run his business empire—the empire that was now Emmett's. He was immaculately dressed in a dark-blue tailored suit and a carefully knotted burgundy silk tie. He was perfectly groomed—not a hair out of place, his nails manicured, his face carefully shaved. He looked like a million—no, scratch that—like a *billion* dollars.

This was fortunate, and a testament to his good genes and toughness, because another man, a lesser man, would have looked like a train wreck considering that he had barely slept the past week.

This wasn't due to the pressures of his new position and the volume of work it entailed, though these were considerable. He could handle all that. It was what he had been born to do.

Nor was it due to guilt over the fact that he had murdered his father. That did not bother him in the slightest. The old man had it coming. The old man had hung around for too long. And besides, he had threatened Emmett. That gave Emmett the right to dispose of him.

No. The reason he had hardly slept a wink this past week was entirely different.

It was the girl. Amber-May Jackson.

His eagerness to see and lay his hands on her was so great, it was like an electric current was running continuously through him, keeping his entire body wired, on edge. He was like a junkie, strung out, knowing that the biggest fix of his life was just around the corner. His craving for that heavenly high was keeping him awake with overwhelming anticipation.

Today, Freddie Sheehan had promised, he would deliver Amber-May Jackson to him. Today, he would start enjoying her, all by himself. Emmett smiled as he began picturing what he would do to her once she was safely locked away in the bomb shelter. He instantly turned hard, his cock pushing uncomfortably against the fabric of his underwear.

He had his hand wedged inside his shorts, adjusting himself, when a knock sounded on the office door. Before he could open his mouth, or withdraw his hand, the door swung partway open and his secretary—the same old maid who'd worked for his father, and whom Emmett was considering replacing with a newer, prettier model—stuck her wrinkled, birdlike face inside.

Her expression was nearly always reproachful, as though she kept finding fault in him. And he disliked her habit of opening his door without waiting for permission. His father, for whom she'd worked for over thirty years, apparently had no problem with that, but Emmett most certainly did. Yes, it was high time to give her the boot. She annoyed him, and she didn't fit his image. She was too old, too ugly, too wrinkled to be his secretary. He'd get someone who was younger and more pleasant to look at. Someone who knew her place.

The secretary's name was Matilda. She looked even more judgmental than usual as she squinted at him through a pair of old-fashioned glasses. Emmett tensed. She couldn't see he had his hand in his shorts, could she?

No. There was no way. The desk was blocking her view. He gave his cock a final surreptitious nudge, then pulled his hand out and casually laid it on the desk next to the other, interlacing his fingers on the blotter.

"Yes, Matilda," he said evenly. "What is it?"

Her voice was especially dry, like a desiccated cracker.

"Miss Angela Lieu from *Finance Markets Monthly* is here to see you."

Ah, the interview. Emmett had almost forgotten about it. He nodded to Matilda and asked her to show the reporter in and to bring them both coffee. Matilda gave a quick nod, her thin lips set in a disagreeable line, and opened the door wider. Inside stepped a trim Asian woman in a gray sheath dress, black pumps, and a navy blue waist-length jacket over a cream-colored blouse.

Emmett smiled in welcome and rose from his chair, buttoning his suit jacket. His eyes roved over the reporter's slim, well-proportioned figure, starting with her finely shaped calves and ending on her smooth, doll-like face.

He liked what he saw. She was one of those Asian women who would always look five to ten years younger than her real age. Angela Lieu must have been in her late twenties, several years older than Emmett, but she looked no more than eighteen. Emmett found that incongruity very appealing.

She was crossing the office to his desk with a determined stride, a briefcase in her left hand, the consummate professional, when for an instant her gaze dropped a bit and her step faltered. Her air of professionalism vaporized and a subtle blush rose in her porcelain cheeks. Her eyes quickly flicked upward to his. It took him a second, but then Emmett realized that she had noticed the bulge in his trousers.

Did it make her uncomfortable? And was it in a good or bad way? Was her mind now filled with sexual images of him?

Emmett's smile widened. It was odd, but he was not in the least bit embarrassed. He would have been if the person eying his covered erection was the old secretary. But when it was this young, very attractive woman, it actually made him feel good. No, more than good. He felt powerful, virile, in his prime.

Puffing out his chest like a peacock, he circled the desk, holding out his hand. When Angela Lieu's delicate little fingers disappeared inside his larger grip, he gave the back of her hand a small caress with the ball of his thumb and kept hold of her, his eyes never leaving hers. She did not attempt to withdraw her hand. He enjoyed seeing her blush deepen.

Still holding her hand, he gestured toward the seating area. There was a two-seater and a couple of armchairs arranged around a glass-topped coffee table. He led her to the sofa, giving her a little nudge to make her sit, and sat down close beside her.

"I'm very happy that we're having this little talk, you and I," he said in a suave tone. "I look forward to answering all of your questions."

Angela Lieu opened her mouth to speak, but then Matilda entered bearing a tray holding a pot of coffee, two cups, and a plateful of pastries.

"I'll pour, Matilda. Thank you," Emmett said when the secretary deposited the tray on the coffee table. "And please hold my calls. I want to give Miss Lieu my undivided attention."

Matilda nodded and turned to leave, but not before Emmett saw a small frown of disapproval crease her aged brow.

Yes, he would have to get rid of her soon. He couldn't have this judgmental dried-up spinster around. Who was she to judge him? She was a lowly secretary; he was president and CEO of MacBaxter Holdings, a rich man.

Besides, this was his company. He could do whatever he wanted. Any employee who rubbed him the wrong way would get the ax.

He would fire her tomorrow, he decided. Send the old bag packing. Just one change in a whole sea of changes he planned on making in the company. To remake it in his image.

With this happy thought, he turned his attention back to Angela Lieu. What a lovely specimen she was. Five six and femininely thin. Brilliant black hair that fell to her shoulders as straight as a waterfall.

Face that was symmetrical and smooth, with a button nose, a small mouth, and a pair of very large and elegant brown eyes.

She had a long, graceful neck, very pale, and a pair of tight legs that were now crossed, with very thin, fragile-looking ankles.

She was sitting primly, hands clasped over her knee, trying to regain the professional look with which she had entered his office. He smiled at her as he poured the coffee, handed her a cup, and leaned back on the sofa, legs spread wide so that his knee touched her thigh.

The way he was sitting, she could hardly avoid noticing that he was still hard. Enjoying the moment, he took a slow sip, watching her over the rim of his cup. Her eyes met his and darted away.

Yes, dirty thoughts were definitely swirling through her little head. And through his as well.

A sequence of vivid images, like a movie clip, flashed in his imagination. He saw himself bending the sexy reporter over his desk, stripping off her dress and panties, and taking her from behind, one hand gripping her hip, the other clamped over her mouth to muffle her moans so that Matilda the secretary wouldn't hear them.

It couldn't be, of course, and not just because of Matilda.

He might fail to perform, either adequately or at all. Unless he was rough with her, as he had been with Linda the high-end call girl. But Angela Lieu was no prostitute. She was a business reporter. You couldn't just do whatever you wanted to someone like that.

Even if he could, he wouldn't get the same level of pleasure he craved. For that he needed Amber-May Jackson. Suddenly, his erection wilted. The rich taste of the coffee turned bitter in his mouth.

Goddammit, what was keeping Freddie Sheehan? When was he going to call him with the news that he finally had the girl in his possession?

"Is everything all right, Mr. MacBaxter?"

Snapping back into the present moment, Emmett saw Angela Lieu sitting with a worried little frown on her brow. She must have read the anguish, the burning impatience, on his face.

He smoothed his features, refocusing on the task at hand. The interview. "Oh, I was just thinking of my father."

Now she looked sad, her eyes rounded, her lower lip pushed out.

Emmett almost burst out laughing. It was so easy to fool these women. They were so dumb. Even someone like this reporter, who'd graduated college and now held a job at a prestigious magazine, was easy to manipulate.

"I'm sorry," she said. "It must be hard."

He took a deep breath, looking at his hands. "Yes. It is." He raised his eyes, putting on a brave smile. "I just hope to follow in his footsteps. If I do that, I'll know I have lived a good life."

What horseshit! But it flowed so easily from his lips.

And so the interview went. She asked general questions; he gave the answers he knew would make him look good.

When she asked him about his future plans for the business, he talked at length about wanting to expand and grow the company, to make his father proud of him. "So that he'll smile on me from heaven," Emmett said, marveling at the way Angela Lieu lapped up all the nonsense he was spewing.

They talked about the various charity organizations and causes the late Patrick MacBaxter had backed, and Emmett said he would continue that tradition. "A commitment to help others is part of who we are in MacBaxter Holdings, part of who I am. I believe that is what makes us successful."

The interview was not recorded, so Angela Lieu jotted his answers in a little notebook that she balanced on her knee. While she wrote, Emmett examined her more closely.

Her breasts were perky and firm, her waist very narrow. Her ears were small, almost like a child's, and studded with tiny silver earrings. She'd applied a rosy lipstick and a touch of makeup to her cheeks and eyes. Her eyelashes were very long. When she spoke, he noted that her teeth were very white and straight.

There was something very alluring about her, something fragile, like a twig that you simply had to snap just to hear the sound it made as it broke. She struggled hard to appear mature, businesslike, serious—the modern professional woman. But her youthful appearance made that task challenging, making her resemble a teenager dressed up in her mother's clothes.

The more they spoke, the more Emmett pictured how she would look naked, in various poses and positions. It was an enticing set of images, even though he knew they would not be realized.

But then again, maybe one day they would.

He would not attempt to have her today. He could not risk it. He could not bear the thought of being impotent or less than his former self. Especially not with someone who traveled in business circles and was, by her profession, a gossip.

Besides, he had his heart and mind set on the upcoming subjugation of Amber-May Jackson. For the moment, she was all he really wanted.

But that would not be the case forever, surely. There would come a time when the novelty of Amber-May would wear off, when he would tire of her, when he would crave something else. Then he would seek a new woman on which to feast.

This reporter, this delicate China doll, was a prime candidate.

He envisioned her chained to the wall of the bomb shelter after he had had his fill of Amber-May and gotten rid of her. She would not look so serious then. Her pretty face would be contorted in pain. Her big eyes would leak tears. Her small naked body would tremble. She would look like the world's most terrified teenager.

God, that was something to look forward to.

Lost in these tantalizing thoughts, he failed to register what Angela Lieu had just said.

He smiled with charming sheepishness. "I'm sorry. You were saying..."

She smiled back, her notebook closed on her knee. "Only that I think we've covered everything. Unless you wish to add something."

"No, I think you're right."

She slid the notebook into her briefcase and clasped it shut. They rose from the sofa. She smoothed her dress, ran her fingers through her hair, and gave him an expectant look.

After a brief moment in which neither of them spoke, she reached into a side pocket of her briefcase.

"Here is my card," she said. "It has my cell number. You can call if you think of anything you wish to add to the interview or—" there was that blush again "—in case you want to talk to me about something else."

It was as audacious a come-on as a woman like her could make. Smiling, he tucked the card into a jacket pocket. He walked her to the door and opened it. "Thank you for a lovely interview."

Standing in the doorway, she looked at him, puzzled. She had obviously read his interest in her, and now she couldn't understand why he was ignoring her clear signals that she was available.

"Good day, Angela," he said. "I look forward to reading your piece. And perhaps we shall talk again soon."

Still puzzled, she gave a short nod, mumbled a quick goodbye, and walked off across the outer office, toward the elevators.

Yes, Emmett thought, eying the way her firm little ass shifted as she walked. *We shall talk again, lovely Angela. Soon.*

43

Freddie was getting restless.

He'd spent nearly all day yesterday and most of today in the nursing home's parking lot, sitting in his car, hoping Amber-May would show up.

She didn't.

His butt and lower back ached from sitting for so many hours. The interior of the vehicle smelled like an ash heap from all the cigarettes he'd smoked. He'd eaten so many salty snacks that his mouth was constantly dry no matter how much water he drank.

Drinking all that water had one unpleasant side effect. He had to piss quite a few times. Since he didn't dare leave his post, not even to find a restroom, he had to improvise. That was where the water bottles he'd drained came in handy. Now empty of water, the bottles became repositories of a different liquid, carefully capped in the rear footwell.

Normally, this kind of stakeout should have been carried out by more than one person. As Pickens had suggested, Freddie could have called in a buddy to spell him for a few hours, but he knew that was a terrible idea. He wanted as few people as possible to know about

Amber-May so that when she disappeared, no one would connect him to her. Emmett MacBaxter knew, of course, and so did Pickens, but that couldn't be helped. Freddie wasn't worried about either of them.

Pickens would be easy to handle. Freddie would simply tell him he didn't see the girl after leaving Crumley Creek. And as for Emmett, well, Freddie got the feeling that once he'd brought Amber-May to him, she would never be seen by anyone else again. And Emmett would have no reason to tell anyone he had her.

Poor girl. It was too bad that this was her destiny, to become the plaything of some demented rich-boy lowlife. But that's the way the dice rolled sometimes. Some people got lucky and others got very unlucky. Besides, her pain was the key to his happiness. It was just the way it had to be.

The only person he was worried about was Sergeant Leonard Malone. Freddie had asked him specifically about Amber-May. If the fact of her disappearance became public, Malone might come asking him questions. Freddie couldn't let that happen. He would have to get rid of Malone. He didn't like the idea of killing a cop, but he didn't see that he had any choice.

First, though, he needed to get Amber-May.

He had come prepared. Besides his gun and knife, he also had a leather sap filled with lead pellets. He had used saps many times back when he'd worked as a bouncer. They were very effective, even against burly, rage-filled men. If you weren't careful, you could crack a skull with one. A single tap to Amber-May's head and she'd go down like a felled tree. Poetic justice for how she'd knocked him out back in Crumley Creek. He couldn't wait to pay her back for that.

He was taking another sip of water when his phone rang. He knew who it was even before he glanced at the number on the screen.

Emmett MacBaxter.

Freddie cursed. Emmett had called five times yesterday. Freddie had disregarded the first two calls. After the third, he'd texted a quick message to Emmett, telling him that he was working on his "project" and couldn't talk right then. This hadn't stopped Emmett from calling again two minutes later and again three minutes after that. The bastard wasn't used to waiting.

Emmett had called again twice earlier today, and Freddie had ignored both calls. He was about to ignore this one, too, but he feared the potential repercussions. What if Emmett got pissed off and decided to hire someone else to go after the girl? Freddie would lose his chance at a million bucks. He couldn't risk that. He'd have to take the call and lie through his teeth, buy himself some more time. He tapped the green circle on the screen, bracing himself for an unpleasant conversation.

"Yes?"

"Freddie?" Already, on the first word, Emmett sounded irritated.

"Yes. Is that you, Mr. MacBaxter? How nice to hear your voice."

"Cut the crap, Freddie. I want to know what's going on. I want to know why you've not been answering my calls."

Freddie took a stick of gum from his pocket, folded it in half, and stuck it in his mouth. *Keep calm*, he told himself. *Don't let this asshole rile you up.* Chewing vigorously, he said, "I've been working on your behalf, Mr. MacBaxter. That's why I couldn't talk."

"Working on my behalf? Does that mean you still don't have the girl?"

"Not yet, unfortunately. But soon I will have."

"But three days ago you told me you'd have her that night." Emmett's voice had risen half an octave in pitch, stabbing at Freddie's eardrum.

"Well, things didn't turn out that way. Why and how isn't important."

"Don't tell me what's important. I'll decide what's important and what isn't. I want to know what went wrong three days ago."

Freddie ground the gum between his molars, wishing it was Emmett MacBaxter's pinkie. The image filled his mouth with a bad taste. Rich-kid bastard. He spat out the masticated gum, enveloped it in a tissue, and tossed it over his shoulder to the backseat.

Despite his earlier resolution to keep his cool, Freddie's voice came out stone hard. "You want to know what happened? Fine, I'll tell you. The reason it's taking longer than I predicted is she's on the move. Wanna guess where she's going?"

"No, goddammit, I don't want to guess. I want you to tell me."

"She's coming to Boston. Hell, she might already be here."

Emmett was silent for a few seconds. "You sure about this?"

Freddie wasn't, but he wasn't about to share that with this prick. "Yeah, I'm sure."

"Why the hell is she coming back here?"

"I don't know yet. When I catch her, I'll make sure to ask."

"You know where in Boston she plans on going?"

"Yes," Freddie said, staring out his windshield at the sprawling structure of the nursing home. Christ in heaven, when was that stupid girl going to show up? "I'm staking out the place right now."

Again there was silence. Then Emmett said, "Just in case you're wrong, I'll make a call to a security firm I know, get some more people to scour the city for her."

This was exactly what Freddie wanted to avoid. He bared his teeth at the phone. "No, you won't. No fucking way."

"Hey, you don't tell me—"

"This is my gig. I'm running it. No one else."

"I'm paying you. You work for me. I decide who—"

Freddie gripped the phone tight to his ear. "Listen to me and listen good. I know you're used to getting your way, that everyone is supposed to kiss your ass and do your bidding, no questions asked. This time, though, you're going to have to let someone else—me— call the shots, understand? I don't know what you have planned for the girl—and I don't care one bit—but whatever it is, you don't want a lot of people to know about it. *I* don't want a lot of people to know about it. Just you and me. No one else. Anyone else who knows is a danger to you and me both, you get it?"

Freddie could hear Emmett breathing on the other end. Angry breaths, air snorting out of his nostrils.

"I still think—"

"Then don't. Let me make this clear to you. I see anyone else nosing around, I'll kill him, all right? And that would make a mess you don't want."

Freddie stopped to take a calming breath, knowing he had crossed a line, knowing he needed to placate Emmett quickly in order to keep him from bringing more people into this. When he spoke next, his tone was meek and subservient. "Mr. MacBaxter, I'm sorry if I sounded blunt or impolite, and I hope you forgive my tone a moment ago. I was out of line. I sincerely apologize. It's just that I know what trouble can arise when too many people are in on this kind of operation. It's the sort of trouble not even a lot of money can solve. The fewer people in the know, the safer it is. Trust me on this."

After a moment, in a voice husky with frustration or desire or a blend of both, Emmett said slowly, "I want the girl."

Yeah, Freddie thought. *Tell me something I don't already know.*

"And you'll have her, I promise you that. It'll be even easier now that she's heading to Boston. Once I get her, it'll be a short drive to your place up north."

"When? I want to know when you'll have her. And just to be clear, if you fail to deliver this time, I will be making that call."

Freddie thought quickly. He wanted four days, maybe five, to be on the safe side, but he knew Emmett would have a fit if he asked him to wait that long. He needed to give him a lower number and hope the girl showed up by then.

"Two days. Three max."

This time the silence was longer, and weightier too. Freddie could imagine Emmett fuming. The guy was so insanely hot for the girl, he was liable to burst into flame at any moment.

At long last, Emmett exhaled heavily. "Fine, fine. Just so you know, Freddie, I'm not too happy with you right now. You'd better succeed this time. Last chance. You got it?"

"Yeah," Freddie said, half-relieved, half-wishing he could one day slap all the imperiousness right out of Emmett MacBaxter.

Without a word of farewell, Emmett ended the call. Holding the phone before his face, Freddie launched into a long series of profanities.

So focused was he on the phone that he failed to notice a light-gray Honda slide into the parking lot and drive around to the back of the nursing home, about where a service entrance would be.

44

Amber-May drove around the side of the nursing home, through an open gate, and into the small rear lot. Visitors and staff did not park here. The handful of automobiles on this side of the building were service vehicles—a couple of vans, a panel truck, and an ambulance in case one of the elderly residents needed to be hospitalized. There were no people about.

Amber-May parked her car as close to the back of the building as she could. It had drizzled throughout the night and morning, but now the sky was a clear, beautiful blue, and the afternoon sun shone especially bright. Pulling out her phone, she tapped a short message, "I'm here." Then she removed her cap and sunglasses and placed them on the dash, climbed out of the car, and hurried to a metal door painted white and marked with the legend "Service Entrance."

She pulled it open and found herself in a long and musty corridor. Gray floor and gray walls, lit by a line of bright fluorescent bulbs that stretched along the ceiling. Empty apart from herself. From somewhere to her left came a rumbling, mechanical sound. A boiler? A laundry room?

Walking quickly, she passed by a number of closed doors—some labeled as storage units, others unmarked—and pushed through another door, arriving at an intersection.

Per Martha Mitchum's instructions, she turned right and walked down a short hallway. At its end she took another right and traversed another hallway that culminated in a single service elevator.

Amber-May pressed the button and waited. She could feel tension mounting inside her. When she and Martha and Jolene had discussed how she would get Grandma Betsy out of the nursing home, Amber-May had surprised the two nurses by saying it had to be done as stealthily as possible.

"Whoever is looking for me might have someone on the inside. A nurse, a receptionist, a guard—maybe all three. The longer no one knows I've come for Grandma Betsy, the better."

It would have been best if she hadn't needed to set foot inside the building at all, if Grandma Betsy could have waited for her in the rear parking lot. But that wasn't possible.

Grandma Betsy was in no condition to walk by herself all the way to the exit, and Martha Mitchum could not escort her without her complicity being exposed.

Amber-May had to go inside and get her grandmother herself. She wanted to get it done as quickly as possible.

When the elevator door opened, she stepped inside and pressed the button marked 4. The elevator whined as it ascended. It stopped with the indicator panel flashing the number 2.

Inside came a short and stocky man dressed in paint-speckled jeans and work-shirt and carrying a bucket and some brushes. He pressed the number 6 button, and then he noticed her presence. His face showed surprise. He obviously knew she was not one of the maintenance staff, and this was not an elevator visitors used.

"I got lost looking for the bathroom on the ground floor," Amber-May explained in an embarrassed tone. "I just hopped on the first elevator I came across."

The man still frowned at her, and Amber-May felt a prickle of panic. Did he know who she was? Was he about to call someone and tell him she was here?

The elevator pinged when it reached the fourth floor. The door slid open. Amber-May stepped out, feeling a swelling sense of urgency. She did not need to look behind her to know that the maintenance man was still eying her. He did not follow her. The elevator door closed and she could hear the humming of machinery as it resumed its ascent.

If he was indeed going to inform on her, she could do nothing to stop him. All she could do now was get Grandma Betsy out of the building as fast as possible.

She walked quickly down the hall, took a left, and soon could see the nurses' station. Martha was there, writing on a whiteboard. Another nurse, Emily Watts, was talking on the phone.

Martha finished writing just as Amber-May reached the nurses' station. Affecting surprise, she said, "Amber-May, long time no see. You here to visit your grandmother?"

"Yes. Is she in her room?"

Martha made a show of glancing at her watch. She knew what time it was. She had told Amber-May when to come. It was five fifteen, a time of day when Grandma Betsy was always awake, just about when she went down to the dining room for her dinner. "Yes. She should be there now."

Amber-May thanked her and continued on, but not before noticing that Nurse Watts had paused in her conversation when she and Martha had spoken and was now trailing her with her eyes. Was she simply curious, or was she tasked with reporting Amber-May's arrival?

With even greater urgency, Amber-May walked to Grandma Betsy's room and found her seated in an armchair by the window.

A wheelchair stood outside the room. Martha had left it there, just as they'd planned. Grandma Betsy could still walk, but only slowly. Using a wheelchair would allow Amber-May to get her out of the building much faster.

Grandma Betsy's face broke into a smile at the sight of her granddaughter. "Amber-May, how lovely to see you."

Amber-May clasped her grandmother's hands. "How are you,

Grandma?"

"Fine. Better than fine now that you're here. Sit down beside me."

"I have a better idea. Why don't we take a little trip together?"

Grandma Betsy's face lit up. "A trip? Where?"

"I'll tell you on the way. Come on."

Grandma Betsy didn't need much coaxing. She trusted Amber-May implicitly. With Amber-May's help, she rose from her seat, exited her room, and lowered herself into the wheelchair. Then she peered closely at Amber-May's face. "What's wrong, dear? You look worried."

Amber-May forced a smile. It felt unsteady on her lips. "Everything is all right, Grandma. Let's go, okay?"

Without waiting for a reply, Amber-May began pushing the wheelchair down the hall toward the service elevator.

As she passed by the nurses' station, Nurse Watts leaned on the counter and said, "Taking your grandmother down to the dining hall, Amber-May?"

Before Amber-May could reply, Grandma Betsy piped up with obvious delight. "No, we're going on a trip."

Amber-May cursed inwardly. The one time her grandmother's brittle memory might have come in handy, and it had to pick this particular moment to put on a display of rare clarity.

"A trip?" Nurse Watts said. "Where?"

"Just to grab a bite and maybe drive around for a while," Amber-May lied, smiling to mask her nervousness.

Martha Mitchum, who'd been listening to this short exchange, broke in. "Don't let her eat anything too salty, okay, Amber-May?"

"I won't. I Promise. See you."

Nurse Watts was about to say something else, but then the phone rang, and Martha told her to get it. Amber-May moved off quickly, her pulse loud in her ears.

Rounding the corner, she glanced back the way she'd come. Nurse Watts was staring at her, eyebrows knitted close together, speaking with clear impatience into the phone.

Amber-May rolled Grandma Betsy to the service elevator and

pressed the button. Tapping her foot, she mumbled, "Come on, come on, come on." Every second that passed felt endless and heavy with potential disaster.

Grandma Betsy said, "Amber-May? Did you say something?"

"What? Oh, no, Grandma. I was just thinking out loud."

Glancing at Grandma Betsy in her wheelchair, Amber-May noticed how frail she looked and felt a pang of doubt and guilt.

Could Grandma Betsy handle being moved from what was now her home to a strange place? And what if she suddenly had a medical emergency while she was at Martha's house?

A ping announced the arrival of the elevator. The door whooshed open. Amber-May shook away the negative thoughts and wheeled Grandma Betsy inside. She'd done the best she could and had arranged two qualified nurses to care for her grandmother, one of them a woman Grandma Betsy knew and liked. Grandma Betsy would be well taken care of while Amber-May did what she had to do.

Besides, she had no choice. If she were abducted or killed, Grandma Betsy might well find herself evicted from the home. This was the only way to secure not only her future, but Grandma Betsy's as well.

That was what Amber-May kept telling herself as the elevator descended to the ground floor.

Once out of the elevator, Amber-May rolled Grandma Betsy down the empty corridors back the way she came. The air was cool, but she felt sweat gather at her armpits. Her scalp tingled. She couldn't shake off the feeling that time was rapidly running out.

Perhaps it was nothing but paranoia, but she thought Nurse Watts had been just a little too eager to know where she was taking Grandma Betsy.

Rounding the corner to the last hallway, the one with the exit door at its end, she found herself facing an orderly exiting one of the storage rooms. He was tall and heavyset and bald, with small brown eyes under thin eyebrows. He looked from her to Grandma Betsy with suspicion.

"You lost, miss? This isn't the way to the lobby."

Amber-May considered feigning surprise, turning around, and coming back down this way after the orderly had gone, but she wasn't sure there was time. "It's all right. I know where I'm going."

The orderly's skeptical expression did not change. He was standing in the middle of the hallway, his big arms folded across his thick chest. She could not get the wheelchair past him.

"Where are you taking her?" he said, gesturing with his chin at Grandma Betsy. It was clear by his tone that he thought there was something fishy going on, and that he wasn't about to let her through.

Amber-May opened her mouth to answer him, though she had no idea what to say, but before she could utter a syllable, Grandma Betsy began talking.

"Young man, I may be old, but that doesn't mean I appreciate being talked about as though I were not present, do you understand?"

The orderly looked surprised that Grandma Betsy had spoken. His lips parted a little. "Ma'am, I meant no disrespect. I was just—"

"I know what you were just doing. I was here. I heard every word. For your information, this young lady is my granddaughter. She and I are going on a drive. Please let us through. We are in a hurry."

Grandma Betsy had used her teacher's voice, the one that got schoolchildren, obedient and unruly alike, to do her bidding for over forty years.

And it worked. The orderly's arms unfolded themselves. He stepped aside, mumbled an apology, and stared at his shoes. Amber-May hastily pushed the wheelchair past him.

"Thank you, young man," Grandma Betsy called over her shoulder. "I do appreciate it. Have a good day."

"Good day, ma'am," the orderly replied in a chastened tone.

Amber-May had to struggle to keep from laughing. As she opened the door that let onto the rear lot, she said, "That was magical, Grandma."

Grandma Betsy waved her hand. "Nothing to it, dear. Nothing to it. Now let's get out of here."

45

Freddie was still fuming over his talk with Emmett MacBaxter when his phone rang again.

He glanced at the display, thinking that if Emmett was calling him again, he might not be able to contain his rage.

But it wasn't Emmett. It was Garland Pickens.

Freddie collected himself and answered the call. "How you doing, Mr. Pickens?"

Pickens's voice, usually smooth and calm, now held a sharp edge. "Are you by any chance keeping watch at the moment on the nursing home where Amber-May Jackson's grandmother resides?"

Freddie thought quickly. Where did that question come from? Instinctively, he decided to lie.

"No, Mr. Pickens. I brought in an associate, as you suggested. He's now watching the place."

"And has he contacted you in the past few minutes?"

A prickle spread along Freddie's nape. His eyes began darting left to right and back again, scanning the parking lot. Nothing seemed amiss, yet something was definitely wrong. Slowly, he said, "No, he hasn't. Why?"

Pickens sounded as though he was speaking through gritted

teeth. "Because I just got a call from a nurse who works there. Amber-May Jackson just walked into the ward and a minute later walked out. With her grandmother. Wasn't your man supposed to inform you if she made an appearance?"

Freddie sat bolt upright in his seat, thoughts flurrying through his head. How was this possible? He hadn't moved from his car since before six in the morning. He'd been watching the front doors nonstop. He wouldn't have missed Amber-May Jackson. No way.

"Are you sure about this, Mr. Pickens?"

"Of course I'm sure." Pickens was talking loudly now, louder than Freddie had ever heard him. "Now call your man and tell him to follow her. I want to know where she goes, who she sees. If he loses her, Freddie, I'll hold you responsible. Do you understand?"

"I understand," Freddie said.

He had the car door open and one boot already on the parking lot pavement when he stopped abruptly. What the hell did he think he was doing? He couldn't just charge into the nursing home and search for Amber-May. There were people there. Security cameras, too— maybe not everywhere, but certainly in the lobby, and probably in the main areas of each floor as well. Even if he found her, he wouldn't be able to do anything about it. Not without attracting a lot of attention. Not without plenty of witnesses around.

No. He couldn't do that. He needed to remain outside, where he could see Amber-May when she came out, and follow her wherever she went next.

Only there was one problem: If she hadn't gone into the nursing home through the front doors, and Freddie was sure she hadn't, she must have used another entrance. She would likely depart the same way.

A back door?

Freddie had done a circuit of the parking lot three days ago when he'd returned to Boston. He'd found no way to directly access the rear lot from the street. It was surrounded by a wire fence. To get there, you had to go through the front parking lot and circle the building. It was why he could handle doing the stakeout by himself. All he needed to do was keep one eye on the front doors and another eye on the narrow access road to the left of the building that went to the rear lot. It was rarely used. The only vehicles he'd seen go on that road that day were a couple of vans and a truck. No private vehicles. The drivers were all men. No Amber-May Jackson.

Could he have missed her somehow?

He didn't think so. Unless...

"Fucking Emmett MacBaxter and his whining," he muttered, pulling his foot back into the car and slamming the door shut. According to Pickens, Amber-May had gotten into the building at about the same time when he had been trying to keep Emmett from inviting more people into their little party. He'd been distracted by the need to keep Emmett placated. Sufficiently distracted to miss a car slipping into the rear lot?

Or maybe there was a way to get there from the street after all. Something he'd missed.

Cursing, Freddie fired up the ignition. No way was she getting away from him a third time. No way in hell.

The access road to the rear lot was seventy feet away. He could get there and see what was going on in less than a minute. Freddie put the car in gear and stepped on the gas pedal.

And immediately stomped on the brakes.

A light-gray Honda had just nosed out of the access road. The car was old, but looked in okay condition. Both the driver's and front passenger seats were occupied. Freddie didn't need to squint to see that in the passenger seat sat an old woman, and that behind the wheel was Amber-May Jackson.

She had on sunglasses and a baseball cap, but he knew it was her. No doubt about it. The elegant line of her jaw, the sexy shape of her mouth, the perfect nose—all these were imprinted on his mind.

He grinned, his bandaged hand dipping into his pocket, his fingers caressing the creased leather of the sap. He inclined his head downward in case she cast her eyes his way, but she didn't. She simply drove straight to the exit and took a right. He eased his foot off the brake pedal and followed.

Trailing her was easy. She drove at a moderate speed, giving no sign that she suspected anyone was following her. The road they were on was wide, three lanes, and there were more than enough cars around to ensure his wouldn't stand out. Traffic flowed and Freddie kept one or two cars between himself and Amber-May at all times. No need to crowd her. He was a good driver. He'd done this sort of thing before.

As he drove, he started thinking what he would do with the grandmother. He assumed that was who the old woman in the passenger seat was. The question was whether her being there constituted a problem.

After a minute of pondering this, he decided it didn't. In fact, her presence might make his job easier. Amber-May would likely be more cooperative if her grandmother's life was threatened. Freddie might not need to use any force on Amber-May to get her into the trunk of his car. All he would have to do was put his knife to the old woman's throat and Amber-May would climb into the trunk as docilely as a lamb.

Freddie chuckled. Things were finally going his way.

But what would he do with the grandmother once Amber-May was safely stowed away in the trunk? He couldn't take her with him; he had no use for her. And he couldn't leave her behind, either.

Freddie's chuckle died. He found the notion of killing an old woman distasteful, but it seemed to him that there was no other option. She was a witness. He couldn't risk letting her live.

He resolved to make it as painless and fast as he could. A slash of his knife across the throat. A quick death to end a long life.

The matter decided, he focused once more on the task at hand: not letting Amber-May out of his sight and taking advantage of the first opportunity to grab her that presented itself.

When Amber-May made a turn, he followed. He still didn't crowd her. There was one car between them.

The street they were on was lined on either side with six-story buildings, with shops and businesses on the street level and apartments above. The road was wide enough for two vehicles. Foot traffic was heavier than he would have liked. Too many potential witnesses for his purposes.

Amber-May was driving slower now, and Freddie got the sense that she was looking for something, an address maybe. He tensed in his seat. He hoped she wasn't about to stop here, with so many people about.

She didn't. She hooked a left to a side street. The car between them kept going straight. When Freddie turned, he was directly behind her, fifty feet or so between them.

Soon, he thought. *Wherever she's going, she's going to get there soon.*

"Come on," he whispered, impatient and eager. He felt the bulk of the sap in one pocket, the sleek shape of the knife in the other. His palms were damp around the steering wheel. Adrenaline surged through his system.

Amber-May took a left, a quick right, and six blocks later another left. Freddie gave her more space, coasting into the last turn behind her. He was gratified to see a green Kia hatchback slide away from the curb and into the road between them. A little cover was welcome.

They were in Roxbury, a low-end residential area. Old blocky buildings, three or four floors, red brick turning gray with soot and grime. Buckling sidewalks, almost deserted. Black metal trash cans, some canted and some broken. No trees to enliven the place. No color apart from crude graffiti.

He couldn't see any reason for Amber-May to stop anywhere around here. But then again, he couldn't see any reason for her to go through this neighborhood in the first place, especially not with her grandmother. He readied himself. She might stop at any moment. When she did, if there were no people around, he would make his move. He would have to be quick. Grab the grandmother, threaten her, get Amber-May into the trunk, cut the old woman's throat, deliver Amber-May to Emmett, and collect a million in cash. A good plan. Now all he needed was the right time and place.

Ahead of him, he saw Amber-May make another turn, this time to a street a little wider than an alleyway. The Kia turned after her.

Freddie followed, eager to see where Amber-May was going, eager to spring his plan into action.

Suddenly, the Kia jolted to a stop. Freddie slammed on the brakes in surprise. Ahead of the Kia, Amber-May's car kept rolling forward. The street was too narrow to bypass the Kia, not even if he put two wheels on the sliver of sidewalk. Freddie waited for a second, but the Kia didn't budge. What the hell was going on? He hit his horn and, to his dismay, saw Amber-May's car round the corner at the next block and disappear to the right.

He was out of his car like a shot. He sprinted to the Kia in less than two seconds. The driver was a pudgy middle-aged black woman, her hair tangled and messy. She had one hand pressed to her chest, her mouth hanging open.

The woman jumped in her seat and gave a little squeal when Freddie jerked open her door.

"What's the idea, lady? Get this stinking car moving!" He was shouting, anger making his voice raw. He needed to get this stupid cow out of the way right now or he'd lose Amber-May.

The woman was staring at him wide-eyed and fearful through very thick glasses. They magnified her eyes to the size of cupcakes. It was a wonder she was allowed to drive with those things. Even with the glasses, she had a face that screamed moron-level intelligence. She was right to be scared. She was blocking his path to a million bucks. Freddie felt like yanking his knife out and sticking it in her eye, right through one of those thick lenses. Only that wouldn't help him get her car out of his way.

"I—I don't know what happened," the woman stammered. "A cat ran across the street, and I stopped to avoid hitting it, and now the car's stalled."

Freddie hadn't seen the cat, and he didn't give a damn about it. He felt the pressure of his teeth grinding along his entire jawline. His hands were clamped into fists. They itched with his desire to punch this woman right in her doughnut of a face.

He willed himself to stay calm, to keep his eyes on the prize. He leaned into the car, causing the driver to shrink back in her seat, and scanned her dashboard. No warning lights were flashing. He shifted his gaze and let out a sound that was something between a grunt and a roar.

"You stupid retard. Your car's in neutral." Before the woman could react, he reached over and tugged the gearshift into drive. Then he grabbed the woman's upper arm, squeezing the soft flesh so hard that she cried out. "Now drive. First corner, you take a left. Got it? A left."

He let go of her arm and slammed the door shut so hard the Kia shook. He kicked the closed door as though prodding an obstinate mule into movement. The driver didn't dawdle, which was good since Freddie would have likely beaten the crap out of her if she had. As the Kia began moving forward, Freddie allowed himself a quick glance after it, thinking that he would like to pay this dumb woman a visit sometime just to teach her a lesson. Then he rushed back to his car, jumped in, and floored the gas pedal, all thought of the Kia and its driver erased from his mind.

The Kia took a left, Freddie a right. Amber-May's Honda was nowhere in sight. Freddie cursed loudly. His lips were drawn, his teeth bared. His entire body was coiled tight. This wasn't happening again. It couldn't. She wasn't slipping through his fingers a third time. He wouldn't let her.

He drove on, crisscrossing the neighborhood, searching for the Honda on every street and alley, doing his best to ignore the defeatist voice whispering in his ear that she was long gone.

When he saw pedestrians, he stopped and asked whether they'd seen a light-gray Honda cruising past. Some people just shook their heads, others said no, and there were those who simply gave him a funny look and walked off without answering.

After two hours of searching, the sky darkening with night, Freddie finally gave up.

Amber-May was gone. She had eluded him yet again.

46

When Amber-May and Grandma Betsy arrived at Martha Mitchum's house an hour later, Jolene Lee was there waiting for them.

"How did it go?" Amber-May asked after she'd shown Grandma Betsy into the living room and fetched her a glass of cool lemonade.

"As well as it could, I suppose. How about you? You didn't see any more sign of him?"

She and Jolene were standing in the kitchen. Jolene's wild head of curls was kept in check by a blue headband. A pair of very thick glasses lay folded on the kitchen table. Through the kitchen window, Amber-May could see a green Kia hatchback parked at the curb outside.

"No. I drove straight out of there, then took my time getting here. I didn't see his car once."

"Good," Jolene said. "That's good." She rubbed her upper arm, her forehead creased.

"What is it?"

"Nothing to worry about. He just grabbed my arm real hard before he went back to his car. He was so angry I was sure he was going to hit me."

Amber-May touched Jolene's shoulder. "I'm so sorry you had to go through that. I was worried sick about you the whole way here."

Jolene smiled faintly. "Hey, I volunteered for this. I must admit, I didn't really think there would be anyone waiting for you at the nursing home. I thought you were exaggerating. I don't think so anymore. That man—he scares me."

"He scares me too."

"And you think that once you finish, once you take care of these four men, he'll go away?"

Amber-May nodded. "I think he works for money. He was hired to find me and kidnap me and hand me over to one of them. Once they're all dead, he'll have no reason to pursue me."

"I hope you're right," Jolene said, shivering despite hugging herself.

Amber-May said nothing for a moment. She was hoping the same thing.

"You think he suspected anything?"

"You mean, did he suspect that I'd stalled the car on purpose?" Jolene said. She removed the headband and tousled her hair around until it looked as though she hadn't brushed it for weeks. Then she picked up the eyeglasses and slipped them on. Her eyes looked huge and oddly unfocused behind the thick lenses. When she spoke, it was with a tremulous tone and accent that made her sound unintelligent.

"I don't know what happened. A cat ran across the street, and I stopped to avoid hitting it, and now the car's stalled."

Amber-May burst out laughing. Jolene joined her. After a solid, liberating minute of belly-shaking laughter, Jolene removed the glasses and rubbed her eyes. "I can barely make out anything through these. Half the time, I was looking at him over the rim. I pray to God I never lay eyes on him again."

"Me too," Amber-May said. "Let's go and get you and Grandma Betsy better acquainted."

The sharpness of mind Grandma Betsy had exhibited when she and Amber-May were making their exit from the nursing home had dissipated shortly after they got in Amber-May's car. On the ride over to Martha's house, Amber-May had told her where they were going and that she would be staying there for a few days, but Grandma Betsy's debilitated memory did not retain the information. Consequently, Amber-May had to remind Grandma Betsy where they were and for what purpose.

"This is Martha's house. You know her—Martha Mitchum, the nurse. She'll be taking care of you for a few days. She and Jolene."

Amber-May had introduced Jolene to her grandmother when they'd arrived at the house. She did not need to do so again. For some reason, Grandma Betsy had no trouble remembering names.

Grandma Betsy smiled at Jolene, said it was nice to meet her, and turned her eyes to Amber-May. Despite her illness, they still held a good dose of shrewdness. "Why am I here, dear? What's going on?"

Amber-May sat down beside Grandma Betsy on the living room sofa. In addition to the lines old age had carved into her grandmother's thin face, she could see other lines now. Lines of worry. Worry for her.

Amber-May again felt a stab of guilt for dragging her grandmother into her vendetta. But, she reminded herself, Grandma Betsy had been in it from almost the beginning, from the moment Garland Pickens had used her continued welfare as leverage to bend Amber-May to his will.

"I just have to take care of something for a few days, and it's better that you stay here while I do."

Grandma Betsy's eyes probed hers, and Amber-May got the urge to tell her everything, to just spill it all out. She refrained for the same reason she had done so thus far: it would only cause her grandmother grief.

"It's serious, isn't it? I can see it in your eyes."

"I can handle it. Don't worry."

"It's my duty to worry about you. Tell me how I can help you."

Amber-May leaned over and kissed her grandmother's cheek. "You already have. More than I can ever explain. What I need you to do now is stay here for a few days with Jolene and Martha. I'll take care of everything else."

She and Jolene showed Grandma Betsy around the house. Earlier that day, Martha had gone shopping for new clothes for Grandma Betsy, and these were already hanging or lying folded in the closet of her new room. She'd also bought her toiletries and smuggled all the medication Grandma Betsy would need from the nursing home. It appeared that Martha had thought of everything. Amber-May was pleased.

Back in the living room, Amber-May turned on the television and flipped to the TCM channel. Grandma Betsy loved old movies, and she had passed on that love to Amber-May. *Laura* was on, Dana Andrews playing the lead role of the detective investigating the death of a young woman. It was a movie she and Grandma Betsy had watched together more than once when Amber-May was growing up. They both loved it.

Grandma Betsy smiled at her. "Got time to watch an old movie with an old lady?"

Amber-May glanced at her phone. It was past seven. The gloom of evening had begun blanketing the street outside. Soon she would need to go. But she had a little time to spare for her grandmother, a little time to be normal.

"Yes, Grandma. I do."

47

Freddie sat in a run-down bar, nursing a scotch and his frustration. It was a quiet joint, no music playing, no loud conversation. Apart from himself, there were just two other patrons and the aging bartender. Over the bar hung an old television showing a football game. The sound was muted, so the game did not intrude into Freddie's gloomy thoughts.

He thought about Amber-May. He thought about having a million bucks and then losing it. He thought about the lump on his head, the cut on his hand, his wounded pride. He sat there simmering in anger, wondering what he was going to do next.

One thing was certain. He wasn't about to give up. He wasn't a quitter. Not with a million bucks on the line.

He belted down the scotch and signaled the bartender for another. The bartender poured without saying a word. He could probably tell Freddie was in no mood for chitchat. Freddie sipped his new drink and thought some more.

There was one piece of information that might still lead him to Amber-May. Her license plate number. The light-gray Honda was either hers or she'd borrowed it from someone. Either way, there'd be a name attached to it. And an address.

You could find this information if you knew where to look, how to use your computer to sift through the ocean of data on the internet. Freddie didn't know how to do that, but he knew someone who did. He didn't like the idea of talking to anyone about Amber-May Jackson, but he was getting desperate. The plate number was the only link he had left. Besides, the guy he was going to call made most of his money illegally, which meant he'd have little incentive to go snitching to the cops.

He rose from the barstool and, taking his drink with him, trudged over to a table at the rear.

After settling onto a hard wooden chair, he fished out his phone, searched his contacts list, and picked the number of Alvin Greenberg.

"Alvin, this is Freddie Sheehan," he said after Greenberg picked up.

On the other end of the line, Freddie could hear people cheering and the voice of an announcer booming excitedly. He flicked his eyes to the television over the bar. The Patriots were playing the Eagles and had just scored a touchdown. The guy who scored was doing a little celebratory dance in the end zone. And why wouldn't he? He already had his million bucks and probably a good deal more.

Gritting his teeth, Freddie shifted his gaze away from the screen. "I didn't figure you for a football fan, Alvin."

"Oh, why not?"

"Let's see: you're five four and weigh about a hundred and thirty. Not exactly the football type."

"Hell, Freddie, I'm only watching the game, not playing it." Greenberg lowered the volume on his television. "What can I do for you?"

"I've got a plate number I'd like you to run. I want a name and an address."

"Okay. Hang on a second. Let me get a pen...Okay, give me the number."

Freddie gave it to him.

"All right," Greenberg said. "I'll get you your info tomorrow."

"No. I want it tonight. Do it now."

"I'm watching a game, Freddie. And it's only the second quarter."

"I don't care, Alvin. I want the information right now."

"It will cost you an extra hundred. These are the Patriots we're talking about here. My team."

Freddie grunted. With all he had spent on gas and motels, not to mention that bottle of contraband anesthetic, this whole business with Amber-May was starting to cost him serious money. The two grand he'd picked up in the motel where he'd lost her would not come close to covering his expenses, especially considering the near certainty of not getting paid by Garland Pickens.

Well, in for a penny, in for a pound. He had to be willing to spend a little if he wanted to earn a million bucks.

"Fine. When can I expect the information?"

"Give me ten minutes," Greenberg said.

Freddie drained his scotch. He still had three days to deliver the girl to Emmett before he called in other people. So for the time being, that end was covered. Garland Pickens, however, needed to be dealt with right now, and Freddie knew the only way to do that was by lying.

He took a minute to arrange his thoughts, then called Pickens.

The lawyer answered after a single ring. As Freddie expected, he did not sound pleased. "You certainly took your time to call me."

"Yeah. Sorry about that, Mr. Pickens. The girl's been on the move all this time. I figured I'd wait until she stopped for the night before I called you."

"Well? Where is she?"

"At a motel, about sixty miles north of Boston."

"With her grandmother?"

"So it seems. My guy says she's traveling with an old woman. I guess that's who she is."

"Where is this motel exactly?"

"In New Hampshire, a little south of Concord."

"Did they meet anyone?"

"No. They ate dinner, then took a room. Haven't been out since. My guy thinks they're settled in for the night."

A pause. Then: "What is she doing there?"

Pickens sounded like he was thinking aloud, so Freddie said nothing. He wanted to get off the phone, but he had to make sure Pickens wasn't about to involve anyone else in this affair.

Pickens said, "Tell your man to stay on her. I want to know where she goes and who she sees. Something isn't right about this whole thing."

Tell me about it, Freddie thought, his mood so sour putting one over on Pickens did not even engender the faintest of smiles. "I'll keep you informed."

"You do that, Freddie. And next time, don't take so long. I want regular updates. Call me tomorrow morning or during the night if anything happens, all right?"

"All right, Mr. Pickens. Good night."

Freddie went to the bar with his empty glass and raised his eyes to the television as the bartender refilled it. The Eagles' running back cut through the Patriots' defense as though they weren't there and managed to sprint to within three yards of the end zone before being tackled. Freddie almost smiled, imagining Alvin Greenberg groaning in front of his television.

He had just returned to his table with a fresh drink when his phone rang. It was Greenberg.

"You got a pen?"

"I've got a memory," Freddie said, dimly aware that he was slightly slurring his words. He downed half of his drink. "Tell me what you got."

Greenberg said the car was registered to a Franklin Duckworth and gave Freddie his address in Newburyport. "The car's twelve years old. Duckworth is the original owner. A former college professor. Seventy-three years old. What's going on, Freddie? Times are so lean you're out chasing senior citizens?"

Yeah, thought Freddie sourly. *One particular senior citizen and her granddaughter.*

"You mind your own business, Alvin," Freddie said. He considered asking Greenberg if he could find any connection between Franklin Duckworth and Amber-May Jackson but decided against it. He would do a little snooping himself first and see what he could learn. Maybe there would be no need to mention Amber-May's name to Greenberg. It was better that way.

He finished his drink, settled his tab, and went to his car. He leaned his ass on the hood and lit a cigarette, the smoke filling his chest with warmth. He was tired and drunk. He knew he shouldn't be driving, especially not out of the city, but he decided to do so anyway. He had a lead. An address in Newburyport. Amber-May might be there. He wasn't about to risk waiting till tomorrow. The way his luck was going, she might be gone by then.

He drove slowly out of the city, up I-95, until he got to Newburyport an hour later. He meandered about a bit, driving along Hale Street and then Ferry Road before finally locating Franklin Duckworth's house.

It was set back from the road, and a driveway led up to it. The house was dark. Freddie could see a carport to its side, with a car parked within it, but he couldn't make out the model.

Afraid that driving up to the house would alert whoever was in it that they had company, he parked further up the road and crept back on foot. He had no definite course of action. First he would see whether Amber-May was indeed there, and if she was, he would then determine the best way to subdue her. Either he would threaten the grandmother or he would use force.

Night insects hummed around him. Otherwise, there was no noise. The house loomed dark and silent ahead of him. He first went to the carport to check the car. His heart leapt. A light-gray Honda. She was here.

He skulked to the side of the house and peered through a window. A darkened living room. No sign of people. He looked in more windows. A deserted kitchen, an empty den, a bathroom. He found a back door and used his knife to get it open.

Inside, the house was silent and musty. It gave a vibe of emptiness. Freddie toured both floors and found no sign of Amber-May or her grandmother. The single bedroom contained a double bed, which was neatly made. Men's clothing hung in the closet. In the kitchen, he discovered the refrigerator had been disconnected. A thin layer of dust coated the counters. It appeared that no one had lived in the house for at least two weeks. Then what was the light-gray Honda doing here?

Frowning, Freddie exited the house and made his way toward the carport. He looked through one of the Honda's windows. There was no one inside. No bags either. He circled the car, puzzled. Catching sight of the rear bumper as it glinted in a shaft of moonlight brought him up short. It was in perfect condition, not a scratch on it. He stared at it for a full minute. The Honda he had followed, the one Amber-May had been driving, had a dent in the rear bumper. He was sure of it.

Fearing his eyes were playing tricks on him, Freddie hunkered down and ran his hand over the bumper. Smooth. No dent. His frown deepened. What the hell was going on? Then he turned his eyes to the license plate above the bumper.

He read the number twice, scarcely believing the message his eyes were sending to his brain.

It was the wrong number. Not the one he'd seen on Amber-May's Honda. Not the one he had Alvin Greenberg check.

He called him.

"Yeah?" Greenberg sounded groggy, as though he had been sleeping.

"Wake up, Alvin. I've got another plate number I want you to run."

"Who is this? Freddie?"

"Yeah. It's me. Here's the number I want you to check. Right now."

Greenberg grumbled and groused a bit, but Freddie was having none of it. Finally Greenberg said, "Fine. Fine. Give me the damn number."

Freddie did, then waited a few minutes in the dark next to the Honda for Greenberg to call back.

"It's a Dodge," Greenberg said. "The owner is Garth Balderson. Lives in Topsfield. Here's the address."

Greenberg read it to him, but Freddie wasn't listening. He had no use for Garth Balderson's address. He did not think Amber-May was in Topsfield. He knew what was happening. He knew what she had done.

"Damn," he mumbled, awed by Amber-May's cunningness.

There could be but one reason for her to go to the trouble of replacing one set of plates for another and then taking the second set of plates and putting them on another car. She knew or suspected he would be watching the nursing home. She knew he would note the license plate number on the car she was driving. She wanted to make sure that, once she managed to lose him, he couldn't use it to track her.

"Damn," he said again, but this time, rather than in awe, it was in anger and frustration that she had fooled him.

He returned to his car and lit a cigarette, reluctant to admit to himself that there was nothing more he could do tonight, knowing that time was rapidly running out.

He thought again about the route Amber-May had driven earlier that day, from the nursing home and into the crummy neighborhood where he'd lost her.

What had she been looking for in that seedy part of town? Was she still somewhere in that neighborhood? Did she know someone there, a friend who was willing to put her and her grandmother up for the night?

For a fleeting moment, Freddie thought about driving back to Boston and making another tour of those decrepit streets. But then he sighed loudly, flicked the still-smoldering butt out the window, and started driving in search of a motel. He was dead tired. His head was heavy with alcohol, making it hard to think straight. He needed to sleep. He would resume the hunt in the morning.

48

It had been six weeks since Shane Erickson last ventured outside his house.

His retreat from the world had been gradual. After the rape, after finding out the girl was still alive, he started having nightmares. In them, the girl would appear, naked and pale, battered and bloody, and wail at him. Her tone was high-pitched, painful on the ears, and she would level a crooked, broken finger at him, as though pointing him out to a vengeful jury.

She never said a word. She didn't need to. In her bloodshot eyes he could read the accusation, the burning hatred. Her message was clear. She would haunt him till his last breath.

Once, he awoke in the dead of night, sweating and cold, and pleaded with the darkness around him. "It wasn't my fault. I didn't want to do it. The other guys—they made me, they forced me."

The excuse rang hollow. He wanted to believe it, but he couldn't fool himself. He knew the truth. He had not instigated the rape, but he had been a willing participant in it.

He could tell himself that he had simply succumbed to peer pressure, but the fact was that he had wanted the stripper the instant she began her dance routine. She was the sort of girl he could fantasize about but never get. He was short and a little paunchy, had a weak chin and a slight overbite, and his hair had started to thin, even though he was just twenty-three. Girls, the sort he wanted, did not give him a second glance. So when Emmett had told the rest of them to help him subdue the stripper, Shane had hesitated only for a couple of seconds. And when his turn with her came up, he didn't hesitate for even that long.

He had enjoyed it far more than he cared to admit. There had been something intensely erotic about the sight of her naked body lying there on the floor, vulnerable and exposed. Even with her injuries—the blood seeping out of her nose, her skin beginning to purple with bruises—she was gorgeous. And though he knew it was wrong and depraved, the prospect of having her against her will excited him tremendously. Only after he was done did revulsion wash over him. Bile had clawed up his throat and he'd barely made it to the toilet before he threw up.

After they had dumped her in the woods, thinking she was dead, he had returned home and spent two long hours cleaning the living room, where the rape had taken place. He swamped the floor with bleach, then used a full bottle of floor cleaner, washing the floor four times. He had no idea if that got rid of all traces of blood the girl might have left, but it was the best he could do.

He'd taken a long shower, scrubbing his body raw. He wanted to remove all trace of her from his skin. Then, though bone-tired, he stayed up all night, surfing from one local news site to another. He wanted to know the instant someone found the dead girl.

Sitting in his desk chair, refreshing his browser twice a minute, he had been gripped by a sharp fear. They'd been stupid. They must have left a ton of evidence. Hell, none of them had used a condom, and the girl had fought them like a cornered cat, scratching and clawing. She likely had skin and blood under her nails. Their skin. Their blood. The police knew how to process such evidence; he'd seen them do it on numerous television shows.

It had been too late to do anything about it. He wasn't going back to those woods. No way. The police might already be there.

Any moment, he had been sure, the police would come bursting through the door and arrest him. Fear made his stomach cramp. His nerves got so tight that a small muscle under his eye began twitching uncontrollably. It still did, on occasion, months after that night.

When he'd read that the girl was alive, his panic mushroomed. Now it wasn't merely the possibility of forensic evidence that might prove their undoing. Now there was a live victim who could identify them. That was when he called Emmett. He'd seen the look Emmett had given him when he'd returned from the bathroom after throwing up. The contempt in his eyes had been unmistakable. He didn't want to talk to Emmett—not at that moment, not ever again—but Emmett was the richest of the four of them, and he'd been in trouble before, trouble that had been taken care of somehow, without the police ever getting involved.

A few days of fearful near sleeplessness followed. Then Emmett had called to tell him everything was taken care of. The girl was paid off. She would not breathe a word of what had happened to anyone. Shane felt a relief so overwhelming it made him weep. He managed to fall asleep easily that night.

Things should have been back to normal, but they weren't. The fear remained with him, like a worm burrowed deep in his gut. He found that he was easily spooked by the sound of young female voices, as though it were the girl approaching. The sight of a policeman or cruiser made him break out in a cold sweat. And in his sleep, the girl would visit, tormenting him with her wounded body and pointed finger and keening wail.

He'd managed to keep himself more or less together till the end of the academic year. He graduated, though only barely. His concentration was fragile, his attention span truncated. It was a miracle that he passed his final exams.

The only one of the other three guys he still spoke to was Billy Raddick. He didn't want to see Emmett, and he and Russ had never been that close to begin with. Billy was his only friend, and even he had begun distancing himself from him. They still spoke on the phone, but they hadn't seen each other in more than six weeks.

The same six weeks Shane had spent in his house, away from the world.

His mother hadn't noticed his distress. It wasn't surprising; she was never an attentive parent. And after divorcing his father eight years ago, she became even less so. Now her days were filled with shopping, aerobics and yoga classes at her gym, and long expensive lunches with her friends. Her nights were dedicated to dinners and parties and dates with a string of men, all of whom were dark, attractive, and two decades younger than her. Shane had met some of them and liked none. It was clear what they were, what they were after. His mother paid for everything. All they needed to do was please her. They made him sick, and so did his mother.

Her current boyfriend, Julio, was Shane's age. Tall, muscular, with a chiseled face and a shock of full black hair that fell playfully over his forehead, Julio was precisely what Shane wanted to be. A hunk. He hated him.

For the past month, Julio and his mother had been away on vacation. His mother had said they'd be gone six weeks. Shane wasn't sure where they were. Hawaii, perhaps. Or was it Jamaica?

Shane had considered telling her how he was feeling, but he knew it was pointless. She was not the helpful sort. At best, she would offer to pay for a psychologist. But Shane didn't want to talk to a psychologist. He didn't even want to talk to his mother, really. Because he couldn't bear the thought of telling anyone about that night, about the rape, about the bruised and battered girl they'd left for dead. The girl who was now haunting his dreams.

He couldn't bear much of anything anymore. Now that he didn't even have schoolwork to occupy his mind, he began to suffer from hallucinations. The last time he'd gone outside, he kept seeing the girl in the periphery of his vision, pointing her busted finger at him. But when he had turned his head to face her, there was no sign of her.

The only place he felt somewhat safe was in his house. With his computer, his video games, and the large-screen television. He ordered in all his food and accepted no visitors. When the maid arrived twice a week, he let her in and then made sure not to be in the same room with her. The only person he wanted to see was Billy, but Billy was too busy, so he said, to come visit him. So Shane was alone with his fear and nightmares, hoping that the girl would disappear from his life.

He did not know that late one night, six weeks into his self-imposed house arrest, she was sitting in her car, on his street, watching his house and planning her revenge.

49

Amber-May watched Shane's house for over two hours that night. It felt more like twenty.

A small part of it was the boredom of sitting alone in a car on a quiet upscale residential street in the middle of the night. A bigger part was seeing that house again. This was where the four men had held their party. This was where they had raped her. This was the place where her life had irrevocably changed. She felt nauseated just looking at it.

Mostly, though, what made time move painfully slow was the tension that gripped her like a tight fist. Knowing what she was about to do, she was tenser than she'd ever been in her life. It was almost like a paralysis, keeping her rigid and motionless in her car seat.

A timid, nagging voice in her head told her it was not too late to stop this madness. She could still back out of her crazy scheme. *"You're not the sort of person who does something like this,"* the voice said. *"You're not a criminal. You're not a killer. You'll screw up somehow. You'll get caught. Or shoot yourself in the foot."*

"No, I won't," she said softly, her voice sounding strange in the enclosed interior of the car, as though it belonged to another person entirely.

"You'll never be able to actually do it. You'll freeze with your finger on the trigger."

"No, I won't," she said again, acutely aware of the lack of conviction in her voice. The truth was, she had no idea what would happen when it finally came time to shoot Shane Erickson. Maybe the voice was right. Maybe she wouldn't be able to go through with it. Still, her mind was made up. She knew she had no choice but to proceed.

Oddly, once she told herself this, she felt the tension dissipate. Not entirely, but enough so she could breathe more easily and know that she would be able to move when the time came.

Amber-May knew that tonight was an opportunity. Shane's mother, Brenda, was a very social person. Her Facebook profile was far more active and revealing than her son's. It told Amber-May that Brenda was a divorcee and that the only person with whom she shared her house was her son. It also revealed that Brenda was currently on vacation. Photos of her with a handsome young man at her side littered her Facebook feed.

So tonight was the night. But Amber-May had no idea how to go about it. She was utterly clueless when it came to the commission of a crime. She knew Shane was inside; an hour ago she'd seen a shadowy figure move beyond the drawn curtains on the first floor. But how was she to get to him? Bust in through a window? Try to jimmy the door? The first would make a lot of noise, alerting Shane to her presence, and she had no idea how to do the latter.

So she waited, watching the house, hoping an idea would come to her.

It would have been better if she'd had more time to scout the place. But she knew that was a luxury she couldn't afford. Once she'd taken Grandma Betsy out of the nursing home, the clock had begun ticking. Pickens probably already knew that she was back in the city. He'd be wondering what she was up to. He would be looking for her, and maybe other people would be too. She had to move fast.

The house was three stories tall, with a peaked roof, arched windows, and a tall brick chimney, through which no smoke was billowing. It was big enough for ten people to live in comfortably.

Light shone in windows on all three floors, making it impossible to guess where Shane Erickson currently was.

An experienced criminal probably would have known multiple ways to gain quiet entry to the house, but Amber-May knew none. There was probably a back door and maybe a side door as well. Should she creep up the side of the house and look? Maybe she would get lucky and find an unlocked door. But what if the door she tried turned out to be locked after all? And what if Shane Erickson happened at that moment to be near that door and heard her jiggling the handle?

Gripped by hesitation, she stayed put, nibbling her lower lip, wondering again whether she had what it took to go through with this.

A little before midnight, she heard the buzzing whine of a scooter approaching. It whizzed past her car, then circled around before coming to a stop in front of Shane's house. It bore the logo of Domino's Pizza.

The rider dismounted, took off his helmet, and removed a black pizza delivery bag from the storage compartment at the rear of the scooter. Cradling it in his arms, he walked up the path bisecting the wide expanse of lawn that fronted the house and pressed the doorbell.

Amber-May scooted lower in her seat when the front door was opened. Light spilled from within. From where she was sitting, all she could see was a slice of Shane Erickson's face. But that was enough. She knew it was him. Her hands bunched into tight fists, fingernails digging into her palms hard enough to hurt.

The sight of him banished all trace of doubt. She would go through with it. She would kill him tonight.

After slipping on a pair of thin latex gloves she'd picked up at a pharmacy earlier that day, she dipped her right hand into the pocket of her jacket and gripped the .38 tight. Its grip felt smooth and solid. It made her feel strong, the opposite of a victim.

As Shane handed the delivery guy some money and took the pizza box from him, an idea came to her. She waited five minutes after the delivery guy had driven off. Then, seeing no one out and about, she exited her car and crossed the empty road to Shane's house, her sneakers thudding softly on the tarmac. Apart from a cat meowing from one of the yards, the street was quiet.

Amber-May wore a short dark jacket, blue jeans, and a black baseball cap pulled low over her eyes. She had pulled her hair back and tied it with a black band, slipping the ponytail through the hole in the back of the cap. The cap had no markings on it. Neither did her clothes. She wanted to give potential witnesses as little as possible by which to remember her.

She strode up the path to the front door and pressed her forefinger to the doorbell. A tinny ding-dong sounded from within. She made sure to stand a little to the side and angle her head low so that the peephole would afford but a partial view of her.

She waited a minute, her nerves tingling, her heart thundering in her ears. Inside the latex gloves, her palms were slick with sweat. The gun felt foreign in her right hand, an alien object. She adjusted her grip, forefinger tracing the slim arc of the trigger guard.

Again that voice came, exhorting her to turn around, retreat to her car, and drive away before it was too late. It was no longer merely timid. Now it sounded on the verge of panic. Its shrill warnings were cut off by the sound of a shaky voice coming from the other side of the door.

"Who is it?"

"I forgot to give you your complimentary garlic bread when I delivered your pizza," she said, lowering and thickening her voice in an attempt to sound male.

She cringed when she heard herself. She didn't sound like a man. What she sounded like was a woman trying to fake a male voice. Silently she berated herself for her stupidity. Why hadn't she taken a minute to practice? Now she'd blown her chance.

She was still scolding herself when the door swung open.

50

For a moment neither of them moved.

Shane Erickson stared at her with obvious shock, a half-eaten pizza slice in one hand, the other still on the inside door handle. Amber-May stared back at him, her face hot with anger and fear. And hatred.

It was the hatred that broke her paralysis before he managed to shut the door in her face. Raising the gun to her waist, holding it close to her body, she took a forceful step forward.

"Step back," she said in a voice as hard as stone. "And don't make a sound."

Wordlessly, Shane staggered backward, nearly tripping, all the color drained from his face. He kept retreating, barefooted, until he bumped into a side table, knocking the silver bowl that topped it clattering to the floor. He still clutched the partially consumed pizza. His other hand hung limply at his side.

Amber-May crossed the threshold, shut the door, felt behind her for the key and turned it. Only then did she allow herself a good look at Shane Erickson.

He looked different than she remembered him, and nothing like the demonic face that had plagued her sleep. Nothing intimidating about him at all. Pale, pudgy, with a week's worth of uneven stubble grassing his cheeks and chin. Hair thinning and messy. Small bloodshot eyes bottomed by purple half circles. His posture was bent, his shoulders rounded and slumped. His lower lip was trembling and a muscle near his eye kept twitching. On his face was an expression of abject shock and horror. He showed no sign of having noticed the gun in her hand. His eyes were locked on her face, barely blinking. *He's afraid of me*, Amber-May realized with astonishment. *Of me.*

A wave of relief washed over her, and she realized how much she had dreaded this moment in which she would stand face-to-face with this man who had defiled her. A part of her subconscious had been certain she would crumble at the sight of him. But he was the one who was trembling in terror. Not her.

"You remember me, don't you?" she asked.

He didn't answer. All he seemed capable of doing was gulping. They stood six feet apart, but she could still smell him. Stale, unwashed skin, sweat at least three days old. A sour, acrid odor.

He wore baggy black sweatpants and a rumpled blue shirt. Something red had stained the shirt over his heart. The stain looked old. How long had he been wearing these clothes?

Studying him, she was struck by how bad he looked. Sick even. His pallor was that of a man who hadn't been in sunlight for some time. If she hadn't known better, she might have guessed he was in his early forties. Was this truly one of the men who had haunted her nights, her dreams? It seemed incredible, unbelievable, preposterous.

She could shoot him where he stood, end it right here. But she hesitated. She'd expected a monster, not this stooped, pathetic creature who gazed upon her with such naked fear. It seemed wrong, somehow, to shoot such a man.

"Are you alone here?" she asked, partly to postpone the moment in which she would have to act and partly to make sure there were no witnesses around.

He gave a shaky nod and gulped again, his prominent Adam's apple bobbing.

When he spoke, his voice was thin, awed. "You're really here? I'm not imagining things?"

Amber-May frowned. What was he talking about? Was he drunk? On drugs?

Again she thought of shooting him right then and there, and again she faltered. She realized once more how out of place she was. The role of the avenging assassin was alien to her. Like a mismatched piece of clothing made for a person of different size and tastes.

She motioned him back with the gun. "Let's go into the living room. And walk slowly. No sudden moves."

For the first time, Shane Erickson noticed the gun. His breath vented from his mouth with a hiss. His lips turned downward and his eyes watered. "Please," he mumbled.

Amber-May could hardly bear to look at his miserable face. In a soft voice she said, "Just do as I say. Into the living room."

He turned and walked ahead of her, head bowed, through an open doorway and into the spacious living room.

It was almost exactly how she remembered it. Closed French doors overlooking the back garden. Bland landscapes on the walls. A dormant fireplace. Tall potted plants in two of the corners. And, taking up much of the space, a seating area consisting of two sofas and three padded armchairs arranged around a large oval coffee table. The only difference from when she'd last been here was the position of the coffee table. On that fateful night, it had been pushed aside against one wall, to give her space in which to do her strip routine, while the men lounged on the sofas.

Amber-May stared for a moment at the spot on the floor where she'd been pushed off her feet, held down, beaten, and raped. Her temples throbbed as she recalled with excruciating vividness everything that had been done to her there.

There was no trace of the struggle she'd put up, the blood she'd shed, the pain. The floor gleamed under the bright glare of the ceiling lights. The cleanliness seemed to mock her, reminding her how the events of that night had been expunged, erased, covered up. The villains allowed to remain free.

Her teeth clenched, she turned her gaze on Shane Erickson. He stood before one of the armchairs, one arm looped around his midsection, looking at her fearfully. He cringed under her withering stare and lowered his eyes. The half-consumed pizza slice slipped from his hand, landing facedown on the floor. He didn't seem to notice.

Amber-May raised the gun and aimed it at his chest.

Eyes the size of dinner plates, Shane brought his arms up before his body like a shield. "Please. Please." He collapsed into the armchair and leaned forward, face in hands, sobbing. "I'm sorry it happened. I'm so sorry."

Amber-May's finger trembled on the trigger, but she couldn't bring herself to shoot him. Not the way he was, weeping, all bent over like that. What's more, he sounded truly remorseful.

"I didn't want to do it," he wailed. "I didn't. I swear."

"Then why did you? Why didn't you stop them?"

Lifting his head, he ran his forearm over his nose and looked at her, face wet. "I should have. I know I should have. But I'm weak. I'm pathetic. I hate that about me, but that's who I am. I couldn't do anything against the three of them."

That may have been true, Amber-May thought. The man before her certainly seemed incapable of standing up to anyone. But that didn't mitigate his guilt.

"But you didn't just fail to stop them. You took part in it. You raped me."

Her voice vibrated with shame and rage. Her hand shook, the gun wavering. What was happening to her? What was she doing? Why didn't she just get on with what she was there to do?

Because she was not a cold-blooded killer. She couldn't just shoot him where he sat. Slowly, she lowered the gun, unsure of what to do next. She'd been so certain of her decision, but now, when the moment came, she was incapable of taking the final step, of pulling the trigger.

Shane was blubbering now. "I know I did a terrible thing. An awful thing. And I've been agonizing over it. I barely sleep. My dreams are terrible. I can't bear to go outside. I haven't left this house in weeks. I wish I could undo what happened that night. Believe me, I do." He paused, tears streaming down his pale cheeks. "I'll make it up to you. Please, I'll do anything."

Amber-May felt a glimmer of hope. Maybe there was a way out of this mess that didn't involve her becoming a killer. "You can go to the police, turn yourself in, tell them everything."

Shane looked appalled. "They'll lock me up. They'll throw me in prison. There has to be something else I can do. I can pay you. I've got money. I'll give you all I have."

"I don't want your money. All I want is justice."

"But I don't want to go to prison," Shane whined, his voice climbing in pitch and volume. He sounded like a spoiled child who'd been told he had to visit a boring aunt. His face rippled in agitation. He pushed himself to his feet, the muscle under his eye twitching even faster than before. "I won't survive there. It's not a place for people like me. I don't deserve that. Not for making one stupid mistake. Can't you see that?"

He was no longer crying. It took a second for Amber-May to interpret the new look in his eyes. Gone was the pleading, imploring, round-eyed stare. What had taken its place was the sharp, narrow-eyed gaze of incredulous accusation. *Why are you doing this to me?* Shane's eyes seemed to ask. *Why are you being such an unreasonable bitch?*

"I get it, okay?" he said, beginning to pace the room, his voice sharp and tinged with irritation. "I did a bad thing. And I'm sorry about it, I told you that already. I wish I'd never done it, okay? But it's not like you suffered permanent damage. Look at you; you're all fixed up. You can't seriously believe I should go to prison. I don't belong there. I'm not a criminal."

"Yes, you are. You raped me."

"But that was a one-time thing. I've never done something like that before, and I never will again. I promise. I swear to God."

His pacing had taken him around the armchair, toward a side table laden with a stack of magazines and a tall and thin metal statuette of a robed woman. Amber-May took a few steps toward him. A moment ago, she'd been sure he would agree to come with her to the police, to tell them the truth. Now the moment appeared to have slipped away. She desperately wanted to bring it back, to get Shane to agree with her. It was her chance to make things all better without spilling a single drop of blood.

"I'm giving you the chance to come with me to the police. To come clean. They'll go easier on you than the others if you do."

He shook his head, his lower lip sticking out—the sullen, recalcitrant child.

She took two more steps toward him. "Don't you see? It's the only way to ease your conscience."

He gave her a long baleful look. His face molded itself into an ugly, hateful mask. "I won't go to prison. I won't let you do that to me. You've already done enough. All my nights are hell because of you."

Then he whipped around, snatched up the statuette off the side table, and spun toward her with it raised above his head.

Amber-May barely had time to register the glinting metal of the statuette poised high above before Shane was closing the distance between them and the statuette was streaking down toward her head.

She'd been holding the gun by her thigh, pointed down, sure that he posed her no danger. Now she jerked the weapon up, certain that she was already too late. Her finger pulled the trigger just as Shane's forward momentum brought his torso into contact with the muzzle.

The recoil punched its way up her forearm. The blast was largely muffled by Shane's body. His face, twisted in rage, turned slack as surprise invaded his eyes. The statuette slipped from his fingers, grazing her shoulder as it fell to the floor.

He teetered back from Amber-May, stood stock-still for a second, peering down at the red stain blossoming just under his breastbone. He placed one hand over the wound then lifted the reddened palm before his eyes, as though examining a piece of art. His face held no hint of understanding. Then his knees buckled and he fell rightward, landing on his side and rolling onto his back.

Amber-May's hand shook. She could feel her heartbeat in her

head. She stepped closer, standing over Shane, looking down at him. Blood was oozing out of the hole in his torso. Some of it was dripping onto the floor. A dull, metallic smell wafted from the wound, mixing with the scents of spent gunpowder and singed cotton and skin. His hands lay slack, his breathing was ragged and scratchy. He didn't move. Nor did he look at her. His eyes stared vacantly upward. Then the light faded from them, and a final breath bubbled out of him.

She knew she should have been horrified at the sight of him. She knew she should have felt shock at what she'd done. But she felt neither.

What she felt instead was searing anger. At herself.

Her hesitation had nearly cost her everything. If she'd been a little bit slower, or Shane a little bit faster, she would have been the one lying motionless on the floor, her head caved in by the statuette.

Her feeling sorry for Shane, her unfounded belief that he could be expected to do the right thing, and her reluctance to see her plan through had brought her to the edge of disaster.

And this was not the first time this had happened.

The first time the man in the blue Toyota attacked her, she'd managed by sheer luck to get the better of him. She knocked him out with a pipe. Then, instead of making sure he was dead, she fled. This had allowed him to follow her to the motel room, catch her off guard, and overpower her.

If that stack of bills hadn't been lying there on the bed, if he hadn't gotten distracted by it, she would not have gotten away from him. She would have been unconscious in the trunk of his car, en route to who knows where. She shuddered at the thought of what might have awaited her at the end of that journey. Whatever it was, she feared, was likely worse than death itself.

In each case, her cowardly inability to act forcefully in her own defense, to punish her enemies as they deserved, had almost proved the end of her. It was her old self that had held her back, the civilized, lawful woman she'd been before the rape. The woman who knew that bad things happened to good people, but had never really believed those things could happen to her. The woman who had always assumed that if, by any chance, she fell victim to a crime, the police would be there for her.

That woman had revolted against the possibility that she would become a killer, a criminal herself. That woman had clung to the flimsy hope that Shane Erickson would agree to turn himself in. That woman had nearly gotten her skull bashed in.

Once again, she'd been lucky, but she couldn't count on luck any longer. She had to change who she was. Because now she was a killer, and if she wanted to kill again and get away with it, she could not let her old values, norms, and boundaries hinder her.

Amber-May closed her eyes and inhaled deeply. The toxic smell of death rising from Shane's corpse filled her nostrils, infiltrating her lungs. The stench sickened her, but she forced herself to inhale again, to hold the smell inside her. She could not be squeamish. She could not avoid any aspect of the dirty work she'd taken upon herself. She had to accept it all. She had to be strong.

A bubble of sadness filled her chest. She realized that being forced to kill these men meant that she had to commit one more act of murder. She had to kill off her old self. She could not afford to let the woman she'd been before the rape get in her way. It was too risky. She had to eliminate her as surely as she had to eliminate the men who had raped her.

A slow tear wriggled out of the corner of her left eye and trickled down her cheek. She didn't wipe it off. She let it work its way to the corner of her mouth. Then, with a flick of her tongue, she tasted it. The taste of mourning, for the woman she'd been and could never be again.

Because, though she still drew breath, though her heart still beat, though her memories remained intact, the old her was no more. And that was heartbreaking.

The old her would have wept openly at such a loss. The new her allowed herself that single tear. Still feeling the cold, slick trail the tear had left down her cheek, Amber-May considered her next move.

She should get out of there right now before someone called the police. Before they swarmed the house and found her in it, standing over the dead body with a smoking gun in her hand.

But after taking a moment to contemplate this, she concluded that there was a good chance that no one had heard the gunshot. Shane's body, pressed against the muzzle at the instant the gun had discharged, had swallowed most of the noise.

And this might present her with an opportunity.

But first she had to make sure. As sure as she possibly could.

Walking into the kitchen, she peered out a street-facing window and saw no sign of agitation outside. No lights in the houses across the street that hadn't been there before. No neighbors exiting their homes to investigate the sudden noise. The street was quiet. Not even the sound of a dog barking.

She was safe. At least, that was what her instincts told her.

Taking a quick tour of the house, she found Shane's laptop in an upstairs bedroom. She tried logging in, but couldn't guess the password. She had better luck with his mobile phone. He had left it on when he had come to answer the door.

Amber-May scrolled through the list of contacts and located the names and numbers of Billy Raddick, Emmett MacBaxter, and Russ Koenig. She entered the numbers into her own phone, then checked the log of calls and messages that Shane had made and received. There weren't a lot of either. It appeared that he hadn't had much contact with other people over the past few weeks. There were calls to his mother and to various take-out restaurants, but nothing to Russ Koenig or Emmett MacBaxter.

Billy Raddick, however, was another matter.

51

Billy Raddick was in his bedroom, watching the latest episode of *The Big Bang Theory* on his laptop, when his phone buzzed. Without taking his eyes off the screen, he reached for the phone, drew it closer, and flicked a glance at it.

A message. From Shane Erickson.

Billy's lips curled. Shane and he used to be good friends, but Shane had changed in the months since the night the four of them had raped the stripper. Changed for the worse.

At first it was subtle. A frightened, haunted look in Shane's eyes. An edginess, nervousness. The way he would suddenly whip his head around, as though trying to locate someone who was stalking him. Then it got gradually worse.

Shane's hygiene began to deteriorate. He wouldn't wash for days, came to classes with dirty clothes, neglected to shave. In class he would sit with a harrowed look on his face, a muscle under his eye twitching like he had brain damage or something. People noticed. And they noticed who he hung out with. Which was Billy.

So when they began to steer clear of Shane, they also distanced themselves from Billy.

And this Billy did not want. Especially when he began dating

Emma, a cute anthropology student from Florida he'd met at a student bar.

It took Emma a single chance encounter with Shane to form an opinion of him. She found him repulsive. "A total weirdo," she said. "Gross."

She didn't understand why Billy was hanging out with someone like him, and was shocked to learn the two were longtime friends. Billy didn't like the thoughtful look that came into Emma's eyes when she had learned this, as if she was seeing him in a new, unfavorable light and was asking herself whether he was a weirdo, too. He explained that Shane hadn't used to be like that, but he could see that didn't change anything as far as she was concerned. So he told her he was fed up with Shane as well, and that he was going to stop hanging out with him. He didn't feel good about it, but, the way he saw it, Shane had brought it upon himself.

It had come as a relief to Billy when Shane's college attendance began to slip, and things improved further once the academic year had ended. Now he and Shane no longer had classes together. He didn't have to actively avoid him. Billy started working at a brokerage firm, and Shane, well, Shane continued spiraling downward.

He still called Billy on occasion. Their conversations were invariably short and shallow and always ended by Billy. He'd asked Billy to come over several times, explaining that he couldn't leave his house. *He's finally lost it*, Billy thought. *He's gone over the edge.*

He didn't want to see Shane, so he always made up some excuse as to why he couldn't come. Busy at the new job. Out with the new girlfriend. Car trouble.

Shane probably didn't buy all that, but Billy was slowly learning not to care so much what Shane thought. He didn't hate the guy. Actually, he still liked him and hoped he would get better. But he couldn't let Shane's problems disrupt his life. He was young and wanted to take care of no one but himself.

He knew what had made Shane go off the deep end. At least, generally.

It was that night. The rape.

About a month ago, during one of their increasingly brief phone conversations, Shane had asked him, "You ever think about her?"

"Who?"

"The girl. The stripper. Because I do. All the time. I have nightmares about her every night. Do you?"

Billy gripped the phone tight. He couldn't believe Shane was talking about this, about her. Once Emmett's lawyer had paid off the girl, they agreed to never again talk about her and what they'd done to her. And what was this bullshit about nightmares? For Christ's sake, Shane was even worse off than he thought. And over what? One goddamn time they got carried away with one lousy stripper?

Billy wasn't proud of what they'd done to her, would never have done such a thing if Emmett hadn't sort of pushed him to participate. But let's be real, she was a stripper, a hooker too, most likely. It probably wasn't the first time she got roughed up. Only this time she got a nice, fat payment to soothe her wounds.

He didn't like to think about that night. He remembered feeling scared at the sight of her bloodied body lying there in Shane's living room. He remembered the shock and terror when he had learned she wasn't actually dead. And the relief that followed when Emmett informed them the problem had been taken care of.

But he didn't feel guilty. The more he thought about that night—which he tried to do as little as possible—the stronger his conviction became that it was the girl's own fault that it had gone as far as it had.

If she hadn't been stupid enough to struggle so hard, if she'd just let it happen, they wouldn't have gotten physical. She would have gone home that night maybe a little sore, but no more worse for wear than that.

Again, she was a stripper. Used to taking her clothes off in front of men. Used to flaunting her nakedness, her sexuality, dangling it like bait. She wasn't just asking for it; she was practically begging.

Still, hearing Shane mention her had made Billy flare up. "Shut up, all right? Just shut up! I never want to talk about that night. You hear me? Never."

And he'd hung up the phone in anger. The next time Shane

called, he didn't say one word about the stripper, but Billy could tell she was still very much on his mind. He could also tell by Shane's wavery voice that he was nowhere near close to recovery and might, in fact, have gotten worse. Still, it was not Billy's problem.

Now, Billy reread the message Shane had just texted him.

"Dude, you awake?"

Billy considered not answering him. Hell, Shane had already given him the perfect excuse. He could say he was asleep. But that would only mean he would have to get back to him tomorrow. Better to get it over with now.

"Yeah. What's up?"

Ten seconds later came Shane's response.

"Can you come over? I really need to talk to you."

Billy checked the time on his phone. It was after midnight. Christ, Shane *was* crazy.

"It's late. I'm tired. I got work tomorrow."

"Please, dude. I gotta see you tonight. It's important."

Billy rolled his eyes, sighing. He rang Shane's number. Shane didn't pick up. A few seconds after Billy reached voice mail, another text message arrived.

"Sorry. Can't talk about this on the phone. Not right now. It's about that girl, remember? The stripper? We may have a problem. Come on over, okay? And don't tell the other guys."

Billy sat up straight when he read the message, pausing the sitcom playing on his laptop. Now what was Shane talking about? What problem? And why shouldn't he tell Russ and Emmett about it?

Billy considered disregarding Shane's last request. Russ was pretty much useless, but if there really was a problem, Emmett should know about it. He checked the time again, frowning. He didn't want to call Emmett this late, not when this could—was likely to— turn out to be nothing more than some fevered delusion on Shane's part. Emmett was volatile, and Billy didn't want to be on the receiving end of his temper.

Pursing his lips, Billy drummed his fingers on his knee. This was probably nothing. What problem could there suddenly be with the stripper? And if there was anything, why would Shane be the only one of the four of them to know about it?

Still, it was better to play it safe.

"Shit," Billy muttered. He didn't relish the idea of driving out to Shane's house in the middle of the night and was already planning the verbal ass-whipping he would administer to Shane for making him come all that way. But he got off the bed, pulled on his jeans and sneakers, and headed down to the garage.

"On my way," he texted while bounding down the stairs. *"See you in half an hour."*

52

It was the most excruciatingly tense half hour of Amber-May's life.

She stood in the shadows of Shane's kitchen, in a spot that afforded her a view of the street. She tried hard not to check the time, but did so every one or two minutes.

Every cell in her body was screaming at her to get out right now. Was she insane? There was a dead body in the living room no more than thirty feet away, and she was holding the murder weapon in her hand.

No, she corrected herself. *Not a murder weapon, but an instrument of justice. A means of execution of the guilty.*

Not that it changed anything. The police wouldn't see it that way. Neither would a prosecutor, and likely not a jury either. The safe play was to leave before it was too late.

But Amber-May was done playing it safe. She knew that was no longer an option. She—the new her—knew she must take risks in order to complete her mission. Come tomorrow, or whenever Shane's body was discovered, her situation would likely get even riskier.

But tonight she still had one advantage. Her targets didn't know she was coming for them. Which was why this was the only night she could lure them to her. At least one of them.

As she stood staring out at the street, she wondered whether Billy Raddick had actually believed it was Shane who had sent him those messages? Had he seen through her ruse? Had *he* been playing *her*?

Nibbling her lower lip, Amber-May could only hope that wasn't the case. If it was, she would soon find herself in deep trouble.

Thirty-five minutes after Billy's last message, twin beams of light speared the darkness outside. Amber-May retreated further into the gloom of the unlit kitchen. The lights approached, slowed, halted. Amber-May saw that the source of the lights was a dark, expensive-looking vehicle. It stopped right in front of Shane's house.

For a moment, nothing happened. Then the headlights were turned off, and she saw a man emerge from the driver's seat. She recognized him instantly. Billy Raddick. He was wearing jeans and a tan jacket over a white shirt. On his feet were a pair of blue and white sneakers. She let out a breath when she saw he was alone.

Billy tucked something into his pocket—a phone or car keys, Amber-May thought—and began trudging up the path that led to Shane's house, looking like a man who wanted to be someplace else. Amber-May exited the kitchen and strode down the hall toward the front door, drawing out the gun. On the way, she passed by the living room and caught a glimpse of Shane's body lying sprawled on the floor in the center of a pool of blood.

She averted her gaze and continued on, walking quickly but softly toward the front door. Her heart was beating fast and every nerve ending felt primed.

With her finger on the trigger, she leaned forward and peered through the peephole. Billy Raddick was just five paces away, his head looking big and fuzzy around the edges, distorted by the glass of the peephole. Amber-May took a step back, held the gun firmly in her right hand, and reached out for the door handle with her left.

Two seconds later, when the doorbell rang, she was as ready as she would ever be. With a swift tug she jerked the door wide open and stuck the muzzle of the gun three inches from Billy Raddick's nose.

"Hi, Billy," she said, her voice as calm as standing water. "Thanks for dropping by."

Billy Raddick gaped at her. He had almond eyes with long eyelashes, flanking a narrow nose with a slight bump on its bridge. His oval face was topped by light brown hair parted on the side, a few strands falling fashionably over his forehead. His thin-lipped mouth hung open, giving him a slightly idiotic look. His shock at seeing her was so intense, it appeared that he forgot how to breathe.

Amber-May, on the other hand, was oddly cool. Somewhere deep inside her, she felt something simmering. A cauldron of hatred, hot to the touch but under her control. Unlike the moment in which she'd first laid eyes on Shane Erickson from up close, the sight of Billy Raddick's face did not stun her into momentary paralysis.

"Step inside," she said. "And keep quiet, or I'll shoot you in the face."

Keeping the gun leveled at his nose, she stepped aside, pressing her back to a wall, allowing Billy to step inside and past her.

He hesitated, and she could read the thoughts of escape rushing through his brain.

"If you try to run, I'll put a bullet in your back. I'm a good shot." Then she added, a bit softer, "I want to talk to you. Answer my questions and I'll be on my way."

He licked his lips, then did as she said, apparently not noticing that she hadn't promised not to shoot him if he obeyed.

Crossing the threshold, he ran a nervous hand over his mouth. Sweat beads sprang up along his hairline. His steps were a bit wobbly, like an old man's. His eyes stayed on her as he passed where she stood. She told him to stop when he was five feet further into the house than she was. Now she was between him and the door.

Without taking her eyes, or the gun, off him, she swung the door shut and locked it. Her muscles, tighter than she'd realized, relaxed slightly. So far, so good. He was here. He was alone. It appeared that no one outside had seen them.

She took a longer look at Billy. Average height, slim build, a notch in an otherwise unimpressive chin. Not an intimidating man, but, she reminded herself, she had nearly been undone by Shane Erickson, and he had seemed about as threatening as a sick puppy.

Billy was looking right back at her. No, he was looking at the gun. He seemed transfixed by it. He licked his lips again and said, "Listen, I'm sor—"

"You're sorry, I know," Amber-May said. "You wish it never happened."

He frowned, unsettled by her cutting him off. "That's right. Truly I am."

She smiled faintly, feeling strangely, perversely playful. She was a bit dismayed to realize she was enjoying his discomfort. "Tell me how much."

"What?"

"Tell me how sorry you are."

Billy frowned again, shifting his weight from his right foot to his left as he worked out his reply. "I'm one hundred percent sorry," he said at length, seemed to realize how stupid he sounded, and quickly added, "I've thought about you every day. Wishing, hoping, praying you were all right. I'm glad to see that you are. Is this what you wanted me to say? Is this what you wanted to know?"

He sounded hopeful. And deceitful. She knew he was lying through his teeth. The only reason he regretted the rape was the fact that she had a gun on him. He was scared, not repentant. Now she hated him even more than she had before tonight. At least Shane had true regrets. At least Shane had suffered a bit.

Billy did not appear to have anguished. He showed no sign of lack of sleep or bad health or mental deterioration. His conscience was not bothered by what he'd done to her. The only thing bothering him was the prospect of being made to pay for his crime.

She was about to play with him some more, but caught herself before saying another word. This was no time for games. She had to focus. She had to move this along.

"No, that was not it at all. I have another question. What's the name of the man you sent to kidnap me?"

Billy looked perplexed. "What? What man? I don't know what you're talking about, believe me."

She did. Unlike his remorse, his bewilderment looked genuine. It would take a world-class actor to fake something like that.

So it wasn't Billy. And she was sure it hadn't been Shane. That left the other two rapists. And Pickens, of course. There was always Pickens.

She realized now that she might have to kill him, too. But she'd save him for last. In case it turned out that it was indeed he who had hired the man to kidnap her.

"Where's Shane?" Billy suddenly asked, a quaver in his voice.

Amber-May didn't answer for a moment, then decided it might be to her advantage if she did.

"He's in the living room. You remember the way, don't you? That's where the four of you raped me. Come on. Let's go see him."

As Billy walked ahead of her, she kept the gun pointed at the center of his back. She heard him gasp when he got to the entrance to the living room, saw his shoulders tighten. When he turned his head to look at her, his skin was gray.

"He attacked me with a statuette," Amber-May answered the question in his eyes. "I had to shoot him."

Billy swallowed. Unlike Shane's, his Adam's apple was barely noticeable. His eyes were turning wet. He opened his mouth to speak, but no words came out.

She motioned forward with her chin. "Go on. Inside. Take a seat on the left sofa. That's where you were sitting that night, remember? Before you turned into an animal."

He hesitated, clearly not wanting to go into the room where his friend lay dead. A glance at her gun persuaded him. He walked stiffly to the sofa, casting a single quick look at Shane's corpse before jerking his eyes away. When he sank onto the sofa, he looked sick to his stomach. Maybe it was the smell. It was unlike anything Amber-May had smelled in her life. Ripe and tangy and raw. She had no doubt it would get much worse over the next few hours.

Billy sat slightly hunched over, his hands clasped between his knees. He gave her a beseeching look. "Listen, you've got a right to be angry, to hate me even; I understand that. Just don't...you don't have to do this."

Amber-May ignored him. "I have a question: Where can I find your friends Russ Koenig and Emmett MacBaxter?"

"They're not my friends. Not anymore. We sort of drifted apart."

"Be that as it may. Tell me where to find them. What are their addresses?"

Billy didn't hesitate, which made her think he had told her the truth about no longer being friends with Russ and Emmett. He recited two addresses, which she committed to memory. "I don't know if they'll be there now. I don't know where they spend their time. Like I said, I'm not friends with either of them anymore."

"All right. I get it."

"And I don't think Russ will be at his house. Last I heard, his father kicked him out a few months ago."

Amber-May studied Billy. He seemed earnest, eager to please. She realized he was trying to save himself by cooperating with her as fully as he could.

"Why did he kick Russ out?"

"Russ is a dopehead. He didn't even graduate because he was always wasted. But from what I hear, the reason his dad threw him out was that Russ had also started dealing on the side."

"And you don't know where he's living these days?"

Billy shook his head emphatically. "No. I swear I got no idea."

"Okay," Amber-May said, believing him. Her arm was starting to get tired from the weight of the gun. Was there anything else she needed to learn from Billy? She didn't think so.

Perhaps reading her frame of mind, Billy said in a rush, "I promise I won't tell them I saw you. I won't tell anyone I was here." He paused, then added with a bitter edge to his voice, "It was Emmett. Weren't for him, none of us would have laid a finger on you. He's to blame."

"You could have stopped him. There were three of you."

She could see him search for the right words. It didn't surprise her when he failed to find them.

"I know. I got carried away. I lost my head. Emmett...it's not easy to say no to him."

"I did," Amber-May said, feeling that cauldron of hatred inside her begin to boil over. "Again and again. Not that it made one lick of difference to you."

She squeezed the trigger.

The bang was louder than she'd expected, like a hard slap on the inside of her ears. Early the previous morning, before she got Grandma Betsy out of the home, she'd gone to a firing range, as TJ had suggested. Now she understood why the shooting instructor there had stressed the importance of wearing earmuffs.

Her aim was off. The bullet punched a hole in the sofa two inches to Billy's left. He jerked in terror, eyes so wide they looked about to pop out of his head. Raising one hand before his face, he opened his mouth and managed to get one word out, "No!" before she fired again.

She had overcorrected, but not by much. She'd aimed for his chest, but the bullet chewed into his right shoulder instead. The impact knocked Billy backwards into the sofa cushions. Blood surged out of the wound, darkening his jacket and shirt. He groaned, then began to wail, but Amber-May could barely hear him over the ringing in her ears.

Too much noise. The neighbors must have heard the shots. Time to get out.

She took a step forward and allowed herself an extra second to aim.

This time, the bullet went where it was supposed to. Right into Billy's face. His head was thrown backwards, and his body gave a final jerk before turning still.

Amber-May didn't need to check his pulse to know Billy was dead. She could tell that by what remained of his face. Stuffing the gun back in her pocket, she hurried to the front door, opened it a crack, and peered out.

Lights that she was sure hadn't been on when she'd entered Shane's house were now blazing in one of the houses across the street, but no one was out and about. Somewhere close by, a dog was barking furiously. Lowering the bill of her cap and keeping her gaze pointed downward, she hastened to her car, resisting the urge to break into a run.

She kept expecting someone to shout at her to stop, but no one did. Heart pounding, she opened the car door and slid inside. Adrenaline was coursing through her body, making her hands shake a little, but she managed to slip the key into the ignition on the first try.

She started the car and drove slowly, keeping her headlights off. It was only after she had turned the nearest corner that she switched them on and accelerated.

If someone had called the cops, Amber-May was long gone by the time they arrived at the scene. In fact, she didn't hear a single siren all the way to her hotel.

53

Amber-May was sure she would not be able to fall asleep after killing two men, but when she returned to her hotel, locked the door, and got into bed, it took her less than a minute to drift off.

She slept like a stone, and when she awoke, sometime after nine in the morning, she could remember no dreams.

She showered and put on fresh clothes and called Martha Mitchum.

"How's Grandma Betsy?" she asked after Martha answered.

"She's doing well. She seems to have settled in without a hitch. We played a little cribbage and now she's watching a talk show. She told me it felt nice being in a house again." Martha's tone shifted to a blend of curiosity and concern. "And how are you?"

"I'm okay. It's begun. I got two."

"Two? How did you—never mind, I don't want to know right now. Are you all right? Physically and emotionally?"

Amber-May did not need to think about her answer. "I'm fine, Martha. Not a scratch on me, neither on my skin nor on my psyche."

They talked some more, mostly about Grandma Betsy, and Amber-May said she'd call again later that day.

"I'd like to come by and see her, but I think it's better if I don't."

"I understand," Martha said. "You take care of yourself. Be careful."

"I will, don't worry," Amber-May said, and was about to hang up when she heard Martha's voice.

"Amber-May?"

"Yes, Martha. I'm here."

"I just want to tell you that I'm proud of you for what you did. Real proud."

Amber-May felt her eyes moisten. She had no qualms about killing Billy and Shane, no doubt that she had done the right thing, yet Martha's approval meant the world to her.

"Thank you, Martha. For saying that, and for everything else."

"Think nothing of it. You take care. And call again soon so we'll know you're all right."

"I will," Amber-May said and ended the call.

Drying her eyes, she thought about Susie back in Crumley Creek. She had called her the morning before and explained that she'd had a family emergency and had to leave in a hurry. Susie had sounded worried and more than a little hurt that Amber-May had left without a word, and their call had ended on a sour note. Amber-May felt bad about that and promised to herself that she would find a way to make it up to Susie when her mission was complete.

Across the street from her hotel was a diner whose sign boasted of cheap breakfasts and fast service. Amber-May walked there, planning to have some toast and juice for breakfast, but when the scent of bacon and eggs hit her nostrils, her stomach rumbled so loudly it surprised her that none of the other patrons turned their heads to see where the noise was coming from.

She ordered a triple omelet with bacon and hash browns and didn't leave a trace of food on her plate. Her unusual hunger had to be related to her deeds of the night before. Perhaps, she thought, the taking of a life made you more aware of your own.

After breakfast, she got in her car and drove past the apartment building where Billy Raddick had said Emmett MacBaxter lived. It was a gleaming tower, shiny and modern. According to Billy, Emmett lived in the penthouse.

Amber-May parked across the street from the building and studied it for a few minutes. She didn't like what she saw. The underground parking garage was closed off by an electric gate. In the lobby sat a beefy security guard. There were cameras mounted at the entrance to the parking lot, on the exterior of the building overlooking the lobby doors, and probably inside as well.

It would be difficult to gain access to the building and impossible to do so undetected. Maybe an experienced criminal could do it, but she certainly couldn't. Even after killing two men, she was an amateur at all this. She would need to get to Emmett MacBaxter someplace else.

Lacking a clear next step, she drove aimlessly until she arrived at a strip mall on the outskirts of the city. There she parked and turned on the car radio for the first time that day, choosing a local station. With a knot of anxiety in the pit of her stomach, she waited for the news to come on.

When it did, she had the bizarre experience of listening to a radio report of a crime that she herself had committed. How many similar reports had she heard and almost immediately forgotten in her life? A thousand? Even more than that?

None of those other reports had touched upon her life. But this one did much more than that. It didn't merely touch her. She was at the center of it.

The report did not include the names of those the reporter dubbed "the victims." It merely stated that they were two young men and that both had been shot dead. Other than that, the report conveyed the bare facts of the killings, as much as was known to the media, and that the police were investigating the crime. There was no mention of suspects. No mention of anything that would indicate that she'd been spotted entering or leaving Shane's house. All in all, the report lasted under thirty seconds.

When it ended, Amber-May switched off the radio and sat still in her car for a long while. She took deep breaths and exhaled slowly, trying to calm her nerves. She knew the police might have information they hadn't shared with the media. She could not be certain that there was no evidence that might lead them to her.

And she was anxious for another reason. Soon, if he hadn't already, Garland Pickens would learn of the deaths of Billy and Shane. There was a good chance he would suspect she was the killer. She didn't think Pickens would alert the police; that would require him to supply her motive for killing Billy and Shane, and he couldn't do that. In fact, the last thing Garland Pickens would want was for her to be caught by the cops. That would bring everything out—the rape, the cover-up, every nasty detail.

What was likelier was that Emmett MacBaxter and Russ Koenig would take precautions that would make killing them more difficult. It might also mean that soon she would have more than just the man in the Toyota on her tail. Because once Pickens realized what she was up to, he might send more people after her. This meant she had to move fast.

She couldn't think of a way of getting at Emmett MacBaxter, but perhaps she could do something about Russ Koenig.

She had copied his number from Shane's phone. Now she called it. It rang eleven times, and she was about to hang up when a sleepy male voice came on the line.

"Hello...yeah, hello?"

"Is this Russ?" Amber-May said, pitching her voice slightly higher and injecting a little quaver into it so she sounded like a nervous college girl.

He cleared his throat. "Yeah. Who's this?"

It wasn't sleepiness that was slurring his words, Amber-May decided, at least not exclusively. Russ Koenig was either drunk or high, or recovering from one of the two.

An image of him flashed before her eyes. Long stringy hair, sharp chin and nose, dark narrow eyes, a creepy leer on his face. She felt the urge to scream at him, but she forced the anger down, reminding herself that she would get just one shot at this.

"My name's Ashley. I got your number from a friend of mine. She said if I ever needed to, you know, score some stuff, that you're the guy who can hook me up. So I was wondering if we could meet, if I could buy a little from you."

She expected him to ask for the name of her friend, but he didn't. He was either stupid or thought laws and rules simply did not apply to him. And why wouldn't he think that? Hadn't he gotten away with rape and attempted murder? She felt her anger flare up. She gripped the wheel with one hand, squeezing hard. She fought to keep the anger bottled up, at least for now.

Russ cleared his throat, sounding a little more alert. "Yeah. Sure thing. I can hook you up. What do you need?"

Amber-May chided herself for not asking Billy Raddick what sort of drugs Russ sold. Now she'd have to pick one and hope she got it right. But then Russ sniffed wetly in her ear and a memory of him from the night of the rape came to her. He was sitting on one of the sofas in Shane's house, watching her dance and repeatedly rubbing his nose, like he'd just snorted something.

"Coke," she said into the phone, hoping she'd guessed right. "You got some, don't you?"

"Yeah, sure. I'm your guy. I got the best stuff there is. But it will cost you."

"Don't worry. I got money."

He named a price and she didn't bother haggling.

"Okay, cool," he said. "Why don't you come on over here tonight and we can make the exchange?"

He gave her an address in Brockton, a southern suburb of Boston, and told her to come by at 10 p.m. "The house has a black shingle roof. You can't miss it."

"Okay," Amber-May said. "Thanks. Oh, just one thing: you're going to be alone, right? I don't want anyone to see me, you know."

He chuckled. An intrepid man amused by her fearfulness. "Yeah. I get it. No problem. I'll tell my girlfriend to take a hike someplace while you're here. No one will see you. Just make sure to have the cash on you. I don't sell on credit to nobody."

She assured him she would have the money and hung up. The car clock said it was just past twelve thirty. She had nine and a half hours to burn.

On her phone, she searched and found the address of the office building where MacBaxter Holdings was headquartered. It took her nearly an hour to get there through midtown traffic. Disappointment awaited her. This tower looked even more secure than Emmett's apartment building. There was a guard in a shack at the entrance to the underground garage and two more in the lobby. Even worse, when she exited her car and chanced a closer look through the lobby's floor-to-ceiling windows, she saw a line of turnstiles stretched across the breadth of the lobby. These, no doubt, could only be opened if you possessed an employee's card of some kind.

She returned to her car and mulled her options. She could wait for Emmett MacBaxter at the end of the workday and follow his car. Only she didn't know what sort of car he drove, what time he finished working, or whether he was even at his office that day. And even if she learned all these things and managed to follow him, it didn't mean she'd get a chance to shoot him. Certainly not if he drove straight home, and probably not if he went anywhere else, like a restaurant or a gym. Neither of those places offered the seclusion she needed to have any hope of killing him and getting away with it.

She suddenly felt very foolish. What had led her to believe she could kill four men without getting caught or killed herself? The very notion seemed preposterous.

Yet she had already killed two of them. She had eliminated fifty percent of her targets. Was it really ridiculous to believe that she could somehow finish the job?

"I can do this," she told herself. "I'm going to do it no matter what it takes."

Her spirit fortified, she drove back to her hotel to eat and rest. She needed to be at her best tonight when she went to kill Russ Koenig.

54

Freddie rose early in the morning and called Garland Pickens.

"Nothing new," he told the lawyer. "My guy says Amber-May and her grandmother are still in their room." He promised to call Pickens later with an update. Then he got in his car and drove back to Franklin Duckworth's house.

Something was bothering him. Namely, he wanted to know where Franklin Duckworth was. He wanted to know what made Amber-May decide to steal his plates specifically.

The light of day did not reveal anything new about Duckworth's house. It still gave off an aura of recent disuse. Freddie was wondering what to do next when he heard a female voice behind him.

"Can I help you with something?"

He turned and saw a plump woman in her mid-sixties with chin-length silver hair and rimless glasses stuck on the end of a sharp nose. She wore white slacks and a long-sleeved sky-blue blouse. A thin metal bracelet that was supposed to help with arthritis encircled her left wrist. She had gray eyes, both of which were busily assessing him.

"I'm looking for Professor Duckworth," Freddie said. "I see his car is here. I knocked, but there was no answer."

"He's not at home," the woman said, her tone a bit cautious. He wondered what about him was making her wary. His clothes? The four-day stubble on his face? Or just the fact that he was unknown to her?

"You're his neighbor?"

"Yes. I come here every day to water his plants while he's gone."

"He's away on a trip?"

The woman's eyes narrowed. "Why do you want to know?"

He had come prepared and delivered the lie smoothly. "I'm a former student of his. I was passing through town and I thought I'd drop by to say hello and see how he was doing."

All trace of suspicion fell away from the woman's face. She smiled brightly. "Oh, how nice of you." Then the smile was supplanted by a look of sadness. "I suppose you haven't heard."

"Heard what?"

"About Professor Duckworth. He's in the hospital in Boston. He has cancer, the poor man. It's very serious."

Freddie feigned shock. "How awful. How long has he been hospitalized?"

"About three weeks. Like I said, I come here to water his plants in his absence."

"That's good of you," Freddie said, wondering how in hell Amber-May knew that Duckworth was hospitalized and it was safe to steal his license plates.

"If you're headed for Boston, you can visit him in the hospital," the woman said. "He's in St. Augustine's."

"I'll do that," Freddie said.

Back in his car, he lit a cigarette and let the smoke fill his lungs. What was the next step? What was he to do now?

He had no intention of visiting Duckworth. He doubted Amber-May really knew him. If she did, she wouldn't have needed to steal his plates. She could have just borrowed his car.

He swore, realizing this lead was dead. He had driven all this way for nothing.

He drove back to Boston, feeling dejected. Back in the city, he wound about aimlessly for an hour and a half as his mind roamed, trying with mounting desperation to latch on to some course of action that might lead him to Amber-May.

Nothing came to him. He had no idea how to proceed.

His head throbbed, and so did his cut hand.

He felt like screaming, like sinking his fist into a random person's face again and again until that face turned to pulp, to kick someone and hear their ribs crack one by one. He wasn't one of those people who had uncontrollable violent impulses, but right now he felt the undeniable desire to inflict pain on someone as a means of alleviating his own.

Because he was in pain, and he didn't mean the physical pain in his head and hand. That he could deal with. What tormented him was the pain of losing a fortune. A million dollars that had been as good as his, but which now seemed forever out of his reach.

To make things even worse, Freddie knew that the lies he'd told Garland Pickens would soon be exposed. When that happened, his reputation would be in tatters. He wouldn't be able to land any decent investigation jobs in Boston, maybe in the whole of Massachusetts. He would have to leave Boston and set up shop someplace else, start over from scratch.

And all because of one girl.

No. It couldn't end this way. He wouldn't let it.

The idea he'd had last night of going back to Roxbury, where he'd lost Amber-May, returned to him. He had nothing better to do. He drove there and started scouring the streets. He rode slowly, examining every building, every alley, every parking lot.

No light-gray Honda. No Amber-May Jackson.

Driving around, he noted the bleak buildings, the dirty sidewalks, the worn-out faces of the pedestrians. Again it struck him that this was the wrong neighborhood for a girl like Amber-May to take her grandmother to. Was she holed up someplace close by, or had she simply been passing through? What had she been looking for when she rolled through here, with him on her tail? Because he remembered thinking that she had been looking for something. He was sure of it.

He made a turn and then another and suddenly came upon the narrow street where the stalled Kia had blocked him. "Stupid woman," he muttered, thinking of the driver of the Kia. Of all that could go wrong, to lose a million bucks because a dumb woman had put her car in neutral, that was almost... "Unbelievable," he completed the thought out loud.

And then it dawned on him that it was, in fact, exactly that.

Unbelievable.

The realization hit him with such force that he instinctively hit the brakes, bringing the car to a sudden, jolting halt. A car horn blared behind him. In the rearview mirror he could see a blue sedan mere inches from his rear bumper, the driver holding up his hands in a what-the-hell gesture.

Freddie eased up on the brakes and moved the car forward. After making a right, he pulled into the first available parking spot and turned off the ignition. Then he sat perfectly still and let his mind work.

Amber-May was not in Roxbury. And she hadn't driven through Roxbury to another neighborhood. She had come here with another purpose in mind.

To lose him.

He felt like smacking himself for not realizing this yesterday. After all, she had switched license plates because she knew he might be watching the nursing home. She wouldn't just let him follow her and hope for the best. She would make a plan to lose him. A plan that involved leading him into a narrow street and having another car block the road while she made her escape.

The green Kia.

"Son of a bitch," Freddie whispered, angry at himself. He had been fooled, and it was his own damn fault for allowing it to happen.

But now wasn't the time to beat himself up over his mistake. Now was the time to correct it.

The Honda was a dead end. Switching the license plates had made sure of that.

But had Amber-May taken a similar precaution with the Kia? Maybe not. Maybe she hadn't expected him to figure out the trick she'd pulled.

He had glanced at the Kia's license plate before it had driven off, half-thinking it would be nice to pay the stupid driver a visit some-time in the future. What was the number?

The memory was there, elusive and faint, like a faded signature, just beyond his mental reach. Freddie closed his eyes, breathed deeply, and focused, directing all his concentration on this one problem—trying to recall the Kia's license plate number.

Eyes closed, breathing slowly and deeply, Freddie sat utterly still, groping for the memory.

It was there. He could feel it, sense it; he almost had it.

But just almost.

He couldn't grasp it, couldn't see it clearly. The memory remained hazy, indistinct, indecipherable. Freddie cursed loudly. "Come on," he grunted. But that only chased the memory away completely, leaving his mind blank.

He cursed again, opened his eyes, and pounded his fist on the dash. He closed his eyes again, willing the memory to resurface, this time with clarity, but it was no use. It was gone.

Freddie buried his face in his hands, then ran them over his hair and face so hard that it stung. He couldn't believe it. He was positive that if he had the Kia's plate number, it would lead to Amber-May. But his brain betrayed him. It wouldn't supply the information he needed. He would have to come up with another idea.

His stomach grumbled, distracting him, and he realized he hadn't eaten all day. Ten minutes later he entered a Burger King, ordered a meal and a large Coke, and settled into a booth.

He was halfway into the meal, slowly chewing a cheeseburger, trying to think of nothing but the food before him, when, like a bolt of lightning, the plate number popped in his brain. Freddie swallowed, dropped the rest of the burger on his tray, and repeated the number three times to himself in order to imprint it on his memory, fearing it would soon disappear again. With fingers that trembled slightly, he whipped out his phone and typed in the number, letting out a pent-up breath the instant he hit SAVE.

He stared at the plate number on the screen, the corners of his lips curving into a feral smile. He picked up the burger and wolfed it down in two large bites. God help him if it wasn't the best damn cheeseburger he'd ever had.

He guzzled the Coke, wiped his mouth, balled the napkin, and left it on his tray. He quickly exited the restaurant. Back in his car, he called Alvin Greenberg.

No answer. Just a series of rings and then Greenberg's annoying voice telling him to leave a message.

Freddie ended the call and forced himself to wait three minutes before calling again.

This time Greenberg picked up. His curt hello made him sound as impatient as Freddie felt.

"Alvin, I called a couple of minutes ago. Where the hell were you?"

"In the can. Not that it's any of your business. What do you want?"

"I got another plate number I want you to run."

"You still haven't paid me for the two I ran last night, Freddie."

"I'll pay you. You know I'll pay you. Have I ever not paid you for a job?"

"Relax, relax, okay? Jeez, you sound as wired as hell. All right, give me the number and I'll run it. But if you want another rush job, it will cost you extra like last night, okay?"

"Fine. Whatever," Freddie said, and read Greenberg the plate number off his phone.

"Got it. Ten minutes," Greenberg said, hanging up.

Freddie remained in his car. He turned on the radio, found a station playing music that didn't irritate him, and waited. Doubt started to creep in after a couple of minutes. Maybe he had jumped to the wrong conclusion. Maybe the thing with the Kia had been nothing but bad luck. Maybe having Greenberg run the plate was simply throwing good money away on a false lead.

Well, it was too late now.

Greenberg was punctual. Ten minutes exactly had elapsed before he called again.

"Okay, Freddie. I got your info. You ready?"

Freddie was indeed ready. His left hand held a piece of paper spread out on the dash; his right gripped a ballpoint pen. "Shoot."

"The registered owner of the Kia is one Jolene Lee. Female, in case the name didn't already tell you that. Forty-six years old. You need an address?"

Freddie said that he did and jotted it down when Greenberg read it to him.

"You got a picture of her?"

"Yes."

"Is she black?"

"Yes. Is that important?"

Freddie didn't answer Greenberg's question. "Can you send her picture to my phone?"

"Sure. It'll just take a minute."

It took slightly less than that. Freddie tapped his finger on the fuzzy image file and watched as it became clear and focused. The woman on the screen looked very different from the driver of the Kia —her hair was neatly held back by a red headband, she wore no glasses, and her eyes glinted with bright intelligence—but it was the same woman nonetheless.

Freddie smiled in triumph. Not a dead end. Not even close. "I got you now," he whispered.

"What's that?" asked Greenberg.

"Nothing, Alvin. Tell me, anyone else live with her at the address you gave me?"

"No one's listed. Lee's a single mom. One daughter, Crystal, but she's in college in Illinois. Anything else?"

"No, that's it. Thank you, you did good, buddy. I'll get you your money in a couple of days."

"Looking forward to seeing you with it, Freddie. Bye for now."

Freddie was suddenly struck by another thought. "Hold on, Alvin, maybe you can answer one more question for me."

"What?"

"What does she do? Jolene Lee, I mean."

Greenberg tapped some keys. "She's a nurse."

Of course she was. Amber-May would need a nurse, wouldn't she? To take care of her grandmother.

"A geriatric nurse?"

"No. Just a regular nurse."

Not what Freddie expected, but it hardly mattered. A nurse was a nurse. And it wasn't as though Amber-May was in a position to be picky. Freddie remembered the money Amber-May had withdrawn from the bank, two thousand of which had tripped him up when he'd attacked her in the motel. Was that why she had withdrawn that money, to pay this nurse? It made sense. He knew full well why she'd gotten her grandmother out of the nursing home. It was because of him. Once Amber-May knew someone was out to kidnap her, she knew she could be gotten to through her grandmother. Freddie shook his head ruefully. That was what he should have done to begin with —go after the grandmother and make Amber-May come to him.

Well, he'd rectify that mistake soon enough.

He was about to end the call when another question came to him.

"Alvin, does Jolene Lee work at St. Augustine's hospital?"

Greenberg confirmed that she did. So that was how Amber-May knew about Duckworth. Jolene Lee had told her.

Freddie thanked Greenberg and hung up. Then he started laughing. He laughed for one minute straight. Big laughs that made his abdominal muscles ache and his eyes water. He wiped his eyes and said, "You dumb woman. Seems like I'm going to be paying you a visit after all."

55

It was one in the afternoon by the time Garland Pickens got the bad news.

It came in the form of a telephone call from one of his police contacts. The lieutenant informed Pickens of the shooting of Shane Erickson and Billy Raddick and said detectives from Homicide Division would be dropping by to ask Emmett a few questions.

"Not that we suspect him of anything, of course," the lieutenant explained. "It's just that we understand he was friends with both victims. It's routine to talk to people who were close to the victims."

"Of course," said Pickens, aiming for a tone of vague indifference, even as his mind was churning, processing the news. At that moment, he was quite thankful for his long and varied business experience. Over the years, he had grown quite adept at masking his emotions when receiving unwelcome news. Still, it was fortunate that the lieutenant could not see his face. "Quite understandable. Thank you for letting me know. Mr. MacBaxter has a busy schedule, as you can imagine, but he would gladly assist in any investigation. Are there any leads so far?"

"Nothing concrete. The old lady who called us said she heard a loud bang and saw a figure hurrying away from the house where the shooting took place and into a car parked nearby. But she can't identify the car nor give much of a description of the figure. She did say it was a woman, though the only reason for that is that she thinks the figure had a ponytail. Even if that's the case—and this witness is eighty-two, so I'm guessing her eyesight isn't what it used to be, especially at night—it could be a guy with long hair. There are more than a few of those around."

"Indeed." Pickens considered prying some more, but worried it might arouse the lieutenant's suspicion if he seemed too interested. He thanked him for the tip and hung up. Then he sat for a moment, tapping his lower lip with a forefinger.

It couldn't be her. She was miles away at the time, in a motel room with her grandmother.

But the coincidence was too big to ignore.

Very soon after Amber-May Jackson returned to Boston and removed her grandmother from the nursing home, two of the men who had raped her were shot to death. And the only witness so far claimed that the purported shooter was a woman.

The witness might be wrong, or the woman she saw could be someone other than Amber-May, but Pickens's gut told him neither was the case.

But this could only be if what Freddie Sheehan had told him was false. Pickens dropped his hand to his desk and drummed his thick fingers on the blotter. He picked up his phone and called Freddie's number.

"Hello?" Freddie said. "How you doing, Mr. Pickens?"

Freddie sounded upbeat, almost cheerful. He hadn't sounded this chipper when they spoke earlier that day.

"I'm fine, Freddie. Have you been in touch with your associate recently?"

"Not since this morning. I plan on calling him in an hour to hear what's up. Why do you ask?"

Pickens pondered what to tell Freddie. Obviously, he couldn't tell him about the rape; that was not something Pickens intended to share with anyone. Likewise, he couldn't tell him that he suspected

Amber-May Jackson had shot two men to death last night in Boston. Freddie would be able to learn who they were from the news. Pickens didn't want that.

"Because I got word she was seen last night in Boston. Around midnight. Which means she could not have been in a motel in New Hampshire."

There was a pause, and Pickens could feel the weight of it. Then Freddie said, "Where was she spotted exactly? Which street?"

"That doesn't matter, Freddie. What matters is you told me she was nowhere near Boston. What I want to know is whether that's the case or not."

"That's what my guy told me. Give me two minutes, Mr. Pickens. I'll call him and get right back to you."

Freddie hung up and Pickens lowered the phone slowly to his desk. He rubbed his chin thoughtfully. When he had told Freddie Amber-May had been seen in Boston last night, Freddie's immediate reaction was not surprise but a desire to know exactly where *in* Boston she had been seen. Not what Pickens would have expected under the circumstances.

His phone rang. Freddie calling back.

He sounded sheepish and more apologetic than Pickens would have thought possible. "This is very embarrassing, Mr. Pickens, but I just confronted my guy with what you told me, and he admitted that he lied to me. He lost Miss Jackson yesterday while following her from the nursing home and was hoping he'd be able to pick up her trail before I found out he messed up. I don't know what to say. I trusted him and he screwed me over. He's never done something like this before. I take full responsibility, Mr. Pickens, and I apologize this happened. I'd like to try to rectify the situation if you'd let me. If you tell me where Miss Jackson was seen last night, I'll do my very best to locate her."

Pickens had his lie ready. "She was spotted near the State House."

"Around midnight, you said?"

"That's correct."

"By who? I'd like to talk to whoever saw her."

"That I cannot tell you, I'm afraid. The gentleman in question would not talk to you, anyway. And he has no idea where she is now. Freddie, I must say I am very disappointed in you. I expected better results. I appreciate that you were misled by your associate, but that doesn't change the fact that you've failed me."

"I'm sorry, Mr. Pickens. Believe me, I am. If you give me another chance, I'm sure I can find her again." Freddie sounded sincere, truly anxious to do better, but Pickens wasn't buying it.

He said, "I hope you can, Freddie. Because I don't know if I would ever hire you again if you don't."

After ending the call, Pickens reclined in his swivel chair, lacing his fingers across his bloated stomach. He had no doubt that Freddie Sheehan had lied to him, but he had no idea why.

There was no associate. No one had told Freddie Amber-May was in New Hampshire. He knew she was in Boston. Only he didn't know where.

Freddie had some other agenda besides what Pickens had hired him to do. Pickens wondered what it was, but he couldn't even venture a guess. This made him uneasy. He did not like being in the dark under the best of circumstances. And these were far from the best of circumstances.

He unlaced his fingers and brought his right hand up, using it to forcefully rub his bald scalp and the nape of his neck. He shook his head in disgust. He couldn't believe how badly he had played this.

Yesterday, when he'd learned that Amber-May Jackson had taken her grandmother from the nursing home, he had been sure she was about to go to the media and tell the world about the rape. He had reached out to his media contacts with instructions to let him know the minute they caught whiff of any story involving MacBaxter Holdings. Then he began strategizing his moves for when some media organization contacted him or Emmett for a reaction. He would threaten them with legal action and hope to smother the story before it broke. In case that didn't work, he'd written a strongly worded denial and prepared a detailed plan of attack to discredit and smear Amber-

May, to destroy her reputation and shatter her credibility. He'd been confident he could minimize whatever damage her going public might cause. He was experienced at such matters, and she was decidedly not. He'd almost felt sorry for her, for the destruction he was about to unleash upon her, but she deserved it for breaking their bargain.

But he hadn't anticipated, hadn't even for a second imagined, what her true intentions were. And now two men were dead.

And they would not be the last to die if this crazy girl had her way. Her hit list contained two more names—Emmett MacBaxter and Russ Koenig.

Emmett. He had to be protected. He needed to be shielded until the threat posed by Amber-May Jackson was eliminated.

Pickens pursed his lips and blew out a long stream of air. Then he called Samuel Vaughn, head of security for MacBaxter Holdings. He told Vaughn he wanted four armed men to guard Emmett at all hours, day and night. "Hire the best, Samuel. They need to be qualified and able. Not some retired police officers looking to supplement their pension."

Vaughn didn't ask why Pickens wanted extra security. That wasn't his job. He simply said he'd take care of it. "I know just who to call. Good people. Know how to keep their eyes open and their mouths shut. This is urgent, I take it?"

"It is."

"I'll tell them to have the first shift over to Mr. MacBaxter's office within the hour."

With that arranged, Pickens turned his mind to the issue of finding and dealing with Amber-May Jackson.

He could not go to the police. They must never know why Amber-May had killed Shane Erickson and Billy Raddick. They must never know about the rape.

Amber-May must never be caught by the police. She had to be dealt with outside the boundaries of the law. Pickens didn't much like the thought of what had to be done, but he had made an oath to Patrick MacBaxter to serve his son and his company. Doing so demanded that Amber-May be stopped. No matter the costs or the means.

But first, he had to talk to Emmett. He had to tell him what was going on and warn him that the police wished to interview him. He rose from his chair, went out into the hall, and walked to Emmett's office.

Stepping into the outer office, he was surprised to see Matilda Miller sitting at her desk, weeping.

"What is it, Matilda?"

She turned her red-rimmed, wet eyes his way. "He fired me."

Pickens stared at her. "Who did? Emmett?"

"Who else?" Matilda clutched a tissue in one bony fist, but did not seem to be doing much with it. Her cheeks were slick with tears. Her thin shoulders were hunched forward, quivering.

"Why? What reason did he give?" Pickens couldn't imagine Matilda Miller gone. She was as much a fixture of the management floor of MacBaxter Holdings as he was. In fact, she preceded him in the company, had greeted him on his first day of work so many years ago.

"He said I didn't fit the new MacBaxter Holdings," Matilda said bitterly. "He said I didn't fit *him*." She looked beseechingly at Pickens. "Maybe you can talk to him, make him reconsider..."

Pickens went around her desk and awkwardly patted her shoulder. He found it hard to see Matilda crying, but he also wanted her out of the office. It didn't do to have a secretary weeping openly. "I will, I promise. But for now, Matilda, I think you'd better head on home. I'll call you later today after I talk with Emmett. I'll do my best for you."

Matilda nodded shakily, and Pickens helped her out of her chair, into her jacket, and out the door.

"I'll be awaiting your call," she said, and he was happy to see that she'd ceased crying, at least for the time being.

"Good. Talk soon," he said, and watched her walk away toward the elevators. He had been truthful when he said he'd talk to Emmett on her behalf, but that would have to wait until after he'd informed him about the deaths of his two friends.

He crossed the outer office, now empty with Matilda gone, knocked once on Emmett's door, and allowed himself in. Emmett was reclining in his chair, feet on his desk, perusing the contents of a folder. He raised one eyebrow at Pickens. "Next time you knock, Garland, wait for me to invite you in, all right?"

Pickens blinked, caught off guard by Emmett's admonishment, and also by the stark unfriendly tone with which it was delivered. He had been striding towards Emmett's desk, but now he faltered, suddenly apprehensive of how his boss would receive the bad news he had come to deliver. There was a tightness to Emmett's expression, a barely repressed—what was it? Hostility? No, surely not that. A taut impatience, perhaps.

Maybe Emmett was simply in a bad mood. Maybe that was why Matilda Miller got the ax.

"I'm sorry for interrupting you, Emmett, but something important has come up. Something very urgent."

Emmett gave a loud sigh, flipped the folder closed, and tossed it on his desk. He did not lower his feet. "What is it, Garland? What is it that simply cannot wait?"

Was there a mocking edge to Emmett's tone? Pickens could not be sure.

He stopped before the desk but did not sit down. Emmett looked up at him, now with both eyebrows elevated.

"Well?" Emmett asked.

Pickens told him. Not everything, not even close—nothing about Freddie Sheehan, the time Amber-May spent in Crumley Creek, her grandmother, or the details of the agreement Pickens had had her sign all those months ago. None of that was relevant to the issue at hand.

What he told him was that Billy Raddick and Shane Erickson were dead, that both had been shot to death last night, and by whom.

"She likely wishes to do the same to you and Russ Koenig. I've already arranged for extra security to protect you until she is dealt with. You'll have personal bodyguards with you around the clock. She won't be able to touch you. Since, for obvious reasons, we can't tell the police about her, I'll personally manage the effort to find her." Pickens paused, watching Emmett process what he'd told him. After an initial flash of surprise, Emmett's eyes narrowed menacingly and a strange light entered them. His lips parted, and Pickens could see his teeth clenched together. Pickens was about to continue, but Emmett held up a hand.

"No, Garland, you will do no such thing."

"But—"

"Shut up, Garland." Emmett finally lowered his feet to the floor and rose to his full height. He glowered down at Pickens, his lips curling into something between a smirk and a sneer. "This is a disaster. An unmitigated disaster. Because of your mishandling of this whole affair, two of my friends are dead and I am in danger. I can't believe you've put me in this position. There can be but one consequence for such incompetence." He pointed at Pickens. "You're fired, Garland. You're done with the company."

Pickens gaped at Emmett, shell-shocked. His heart began hammering so hard he thought he was having a heart attack. Not that it would have made much difference to him. All of a sudden, life did not seem all that important.

With his mouth devoid of moisture, Pickens rasped, "Emmett, this is not—"

Emmett cut him off. "That's another thing that annoys me, Garland: you calling me Emmett. I'm not a child anymore, goddammit, nor am I your friend; I'm your boss. You should be calling me Mr. MacBaxter or sir, just as you called my father." Emmett's voice had risen a notch, and tiny specks of spittle dotted his lips. After wiping the back of his hand across his mouth, he seemed to compose himself. "Not that it matters now, since I won't be your boss for much longer. In fact, I'd like you to clear your office by the end of the day." Emmett sat down in his chair, smoothed his tie, and did a little dismissive wave with his fingers. "If you like, we can throw a little retirement party sometime next week, in appreciation of all the years you've been with us. I'll have my new secretary call you with the details."

Pickens didn't react. In fact, he barely breathed. He simply stood there in Emmett's office—the office of Patrick MacBaxter—and tried to come to terms with Emmett's decision. It proved difficult; his mind rebelled against the notion that his time with the company was at an end. He felt weak; his legs were threatening to fold under his weight. With his left hand, he steadied himself on the backrest of one of the chairs that stood before the desk. Still, he felt as though he were falling from a great height. He closed his eyes and forced his lungs to pull in a regular dose of air. It helped. He felt a little better, a little more stable.

He opened his eyes and, in a pitiful voice he didn't recognize as his own, said one word, "Please..."

Emmett's lips twitched. His eyes twinkled. "It's over, Garland. You're over. Done. Accept that." He opened the folder he had been reading earlier. "Now leave. I'm busy."

Pickens flailed for another appeal but could come up with nothing. Not that it would have made a difference. He had fired people many times. He knew a final decision when he heard it.

He had been dismissed, but he still had one service to perform. He marshaled his strength enough to say, "The police will likely pay you a visit later today or tomorrow. They know nothing; they just want to talk to whoever knew the victims."

Then he turned and, on shaky feet, made his way back to his own office. There he sank into his chair and covered his face with his hands.

It felt as though he sat that way for hours, though in truth it was but a few minutes. He felt unmoored, untethered to anything real and tangible and familiar. He recognized the sensation for what it was—a death. Not a physical demise, but the end of his life as he knew and loved it.

For MacBaxter Holdings and his position in it were his life. The reason he woke up each morning was to further the company's fortunes. He had never married, had never fathered children. He had no other goal, no other aspiration, and got scant pleasure from anything else. His service to the company, to Patrick MacBaxter and later to Emmett, was his purpose in life.

No. A correction: had been his purpose in life. Because his services were no longer wanted. He had been cast out.

Pickens wondered whether his office ceiling had begun to leak. Then it dawned on him that his cheeks were wet with tears.

At that moment, he missed Patrick MacBaxter more than at any other time since his funeral. Yet he felt no resentment toward Emmett. He knew he had earned his dismissal. He had screwed up royally. He had misread Amber-May Jackson. He'd thought she could be bought off like most other people. And even when he had sensed something unbending, unyielding inside her, he had not allowed it to trouble him for long. He had simply demanded that she leave town and felt that was sufficient precaution. It was one of the biggest mistakes he had ever made.

With his handkerchief, he dried his eyes and cheeks, then took a slow glance around his office. So many memories, so many challenges vanquished, so many triumphs. Close to three decades of his life, virtually his entire adulthood. He couldn't believe it was all coming to such an ignominious end.

Pickens sighed, only it came out sounding like the whimper of a starved cat. He wondered what he'd do now, with what he would fill his days. It was likely that once his firing became public, he would be offered any number of lucrative positions in other corporations, but he knew he would not work for any other company. Doing so would be a betrayal. He might have been cast out of MacBaxter Holdings, but he was still full heartedly loyal to it.

He swore. First at nothing in particular, then at the person at the heart of his downfall. Amber-May Jackson.

A part of him could not fault her for desiring vengeance. She had been wronged. It was only natural that she would want to pay back those who had harmed her. But she had also agreed to put her mistreatment behind her and move on with her life. He had kept up his end of the bargain; she hadn't hers. That was despicable conduct on her part. It infuriated him.

He wished he knew where she was. He wished he was given the chance to personally see to it that she was hunted down and disposed of. Because that was what it would take now. Amber-May could not be bought off. She had to be found, and she had to be killed. Before she got to Emmett.

He recoiled at the idea. As Patrick MacBaxter had told him months ago, they did many things, but killing women was not one of them.

But he couldn't see any way to reconcile that policy with maintaining the oath he'd made to Patrick MacBaxter. Amber-May had forced the issue. She'd left him with no other choice.

Then it struck him—the perfect way, indeed the only way, in which he might reverse Emmett's decision. If he could engineer the elimination of Amber-May Jackson, and do so in a way that did not draw the attention of the police, he might be forgiven and reinstated.

He straightened in his chair, buoyed by renewed hope and determination.

Yes, it might do the trick. It was by no means certain; it wouldn't erase his earlier failure, but it might persuade Emmett to give him another chance. It was worth a shot.

Pickens brightened. He felt reinvigorated. He had a goal, and he was going to achieve it.

But where should the search for Amber-May begin?

He ruminated on this for a couple of minutes, then realized it was the wrong question.

Amber-May could be anywhere. An apartment, a cheap hotel— heck, she was young enough to find the backseat of a car an acceptable place to sleep.

Her grandmother, though, required a certain level of care. She could not sleep in a car. Even a hotel might fail to meet her needs. Her condition demanded that she be closely looked after. Which meant that when Amber-May wasn't around to do so, someone else was.

Who?

There wasn't any family around, and the research done on Amber-May all those months ago had turned up no close friends.

Someone else, then. Someone willing to care for an old woman with dementia.

No. Not simply willing, but also able. Pickens might have misread Amber-May on certain fronts, but one thing he was certain of. She loved her grandmother more than life itself. She would not leave her with someone who was not fully able to provide the care she needed.

A professional caregiver, then. A doctor? A nurse?

It had to be someone like that.

A slow smile spread across Pickens's chubby face. He reached for his phone and tapped the number of Nurse Emily Watts.

"Emily? This is Garland Pickens. Are you free to talk? I have a few questions for you."

56

The moment Pickens left his office, Emmett closed the folder he'd been holding and dumped it on his desk. Then he rose, went to the drinks cabinet, and poured himself a tall glass of vodka with ice from the mini-fridge.

He sipped it as he stepped over to the southern windows of his corner office. The drink felt good and cold. He himself was hot.

This was partly due to his anger at Pickens for having failed him so spectacularly. But it was mostly due to excitement. He was excited to have finally gotten rid of the old windbag. He could have done so at any time for any made-up reason, but it was much better to do it when he had just cause. He knew that would hurt Pickens all the more. Emmett laughed. The anguished look on Pickens's face had been priceless. He wished he had a picture of it. He would have blown it up and framed it and hung it in a prominent spot.

He was even more excited by what Amber-May had done. She was proving to be even wilder than he remembered. He was going to enjoy breaking her will and owning her body.

He felt no sorrow over the deaths of Shane and Billy. Emmett couldn't care less about them. In fact, it was probably better that they were dead. He had come to realize that the fewer people alive who had witnessed one of his indiscretions, the better. Besides, he was no longer friends with either of them. They were unimportant.

He took another long sip of the vodka, rolled the cool liquid around his mouth, and swallowed. He had told Freddie Sheehan he would wait before he hired other people to search for Amber-May, but things had changed. She needed to be found quickly. Emmett wasn't worried about his safety; that was what bodyguards were for. What worried him was the police. The murder of two young, high-status men—it was the sort of case the police would investigate hard. Who knew what evidence that stupid girl had left at the scene? If Emmett didn't catch her soon, the police might beat him to it. Then he would never have her.

Where could she be?

His gaze traveled downward thirty-nine floors to the street below. She might be down there right this second, casing the building, waiting for him. Well, they would soon meet again, just not the way she envisioned.

She might also be hunting for Russ Koenig. Which made wherever Russ was a good place to lay a trap for her.

Emmett phoned Russ. The call went straight to voice mail. It hadn't rung once, which suggested the phone was turned off or its battery had run out. Knowing Russ, it was likely the latter. The guy was so wasted he was liable to forget to put his pants on before leaving the house.

Emmett called Russ's home number. No answer. Wait a minute, hadn't he heard something about Russ getting kicked out of the house by his dad? Yes, he remembered now. People at school had talked about it shortly before graduation.

Still, his father might know where to find him. Emmett called him and learned Russ's father did not know where his son was—and by the tone of his voice, did not much care.

Emmett tried Russ's number again. Voice mail. For all he knew, Amber-May might have gotten to him already. Still, it was worth finding out where Russ was, and, if he was still alive, to have someone close by to grab Amber-May if she showed up.

Should he tell Freddie?

No. Freddie was out of the picture. If he managed to find Amber-May, then good for him. But Emmett recalled Freddie's threat to kill anyone he hired to find Amber-May. The guy was obviously a loose cannon. Emmett was not about to give him any information.

So who should he use instead?

He knew of only one outfit. They had failed him before, but perhaps that was not due to any fault of theirs. And besides, he had no other options.

He called the number of Folssom Investigations & Security and told the receptionist he wished to speak with the CEO, Nicholas Brunnert.

Emmett explained the situation and what he wanted. Brunnert balked at first, but Emmett interpreted his reluctance as a mere bargaining tactic; he was well aware of the man's reputation. Emmett soon overcame Brunnert's objections—real or manufactured—with the offer of an extravagant fee and the promise of many future assignments. Brunnert assured Emmett that a special team would be assembled and that Amber-May Jackson would be found and delivered to him, whatever the means.

Emmett poured himself another vodka, sat in his chair, propped his feet on the desk, and waited for the good news of Amber-May's capture.

57

Freddie parked across the street from Jolene Lee's house and eyed the place. It was a modest, one-story white-trimmed house with a porch and a small neat lawn. It stood in Brookline, a town on the western border of Boston. The lots weren't large, but each looked well-tended. The sort of place people are proud to call home. A good place to raise kids.

Conveniently for him, the house stood adjacent to a small playground. A couple of swings, a metal carousel, and two slides, one red and one green. It was four thirty, and five children were cavorting around. On a bench nearby, three mothers sat chatting.

The house looked empty. No car in the driveway, no movement beyond the windowpanes. He wanted to take a closer look, but that was impossible with those mothers around.

Freddie drove off, found a shopping mall with a pizza parlor, and ordered three pepperoni and olive slices. He took his time with them, perusing a *Boston Globe* while he ate. It turned out the Celtics had lost their third game in a row, a state senator had been accused of sexually harassing one of his aides, and the governor was vowing to fight crime with what he termed "compassion and belief in the goodness of humanity." Freddie chuckled. Good luck with that, Governor.

After the pizza, he returned to his car and dozed for ninety minutes. Oddly, despite what he planned on doing, he felt completely relaxed. He was in control again. He had a target, a plan of action. He was back on the hunt and had the scent of his prey.

He got back to Jolene Lee's street shortly before eight and cruised past her house. It was dark by then, the playground deserted. No light shone in any of the windows. The driveway was empty. Freddie parked three blocks away from the house and ambled back, just a guy out on an evening stroll.

Scanning the street, he saw no one about. He entered the playground, scaled the low fence that separated it from Jolene Lee's property, and slunk to her kitchen window. It was dark inside and empty. No noise, either. Freddie crept through the backyard, found the rear door, and had it open in less than two minutes.

Closing the door softly behind him, he stood still while his eyes adjusted to the gloom. It wasn't completely dark. Faint light from the street outside filtered through the windows. Pretty soon, he could make out the shape of furniture and doorways, of pictures on the walls.

The house was quiet. Just the soft hum of a refrigerator. Freddie sniffed the air. The sweet scent of flowers. He found the source of it a minute later—a tall vase standing at the center of a dining table. Fresh roses and carnations.

Walking through the house, Freddie quickly determined that no one apart from Jolene Lee resided there. One room was obviously the daughter's, but its extreme tidiness was proof enough of its current disuse. No young person was that neat.

He was disappointed to find no sign of Amber-May or her grandmother. It was clear they had not been staying there. He swore softly, then told himself it didn't matter. He would soon learn where they were.

He pulled open drawers, peered into closets, and checked under the bed in the main bedroom. No sign of a gun safe or a weapon. Good. He didn't ransack the place. He didn't need to. He wanted nothing from the house. What he'd come for was in Jolene Lee's head.

The layout was simple. The front door opened onto a short hall-way, a living room to its left and the kitchen and dining area to its right. The bedrooms and bath were at the rear. Right by the front door was a small bathroom. It smelled of air freshener. Freddie swung down the toilet seat and sat, his gun held loosely in his right hand across his thigh.

He waited in darkness and silence. He did not even dare to smoke. Periodically, he checked the time. To keep boredom at bay, he imagined what he would do with his million bucks. It made him smile.

Every so often, the headlights of a passing car would bathe the bathroom windowpane, and Freddie would tense. But then the car would continue on, and he would allow himself to daydream some more.

Around nine fifteen, new headlights painted the bathroom window yellow. Only this time, the lights did not quickly vanish; instead, their angle changed, the lights cutting through the glass, and Freddie heard the purr of a car engine grow near and abruptly die, along with the lights. He realized a car had swung into the driveway and been turned off.

His grip tightened around the gun. He rose to his feet, careful to steer clear of the window. He'd left the bathroom door open a crack. He stood close to it. And waited.

He didn't have to wait long. Less than a minute later, he heard the tinkle of keys outside the front door, followed by the soft scrape of a key sliding into the lock. Then came a click, and the door swung open. Through the crack, he watched.

Jolene Lee entered the house and flicked on the hallway light. He recognized her instantly from her picture, but it was still strange to see her like this, so different from the woman in the green Kia. She was alone. She wore a dark blue jacket over a white shirt, blue jeans, and black shoes. Softly, she was singing a tune he didn't recognize. Something jazzy. She had a good voice, warm and full. She kicked off her shoes and hung her jacket and handbag on wall pegs by the door.

She began striding deeper into the house. As she did so, she moved her hand toward the bathroom door, and Freddie was certain she was going to push it open right into him. But she simply pulled the door closed, leaving him inside, unseen.

He let her proceed five or six paces further into the house, then pressed down on the handle, pulled open the door, and stepped into the hall.

The door moved silently, and so did he, but something made her turn all the same. Her singing died and her eyes got big. Her body stiffened with fear. He pointed the gun at her and held a finger to his lips.

"Remember me? You make a sound and I'll put a bullet in you. Understand? Nod if you do."

She swallowed and nodded. Her fear was palpable, but she was doing a good job of keeping herself together. No crying. No fainting. No weak knees.

"Good. That's good. Now put your hands over your head and turn around. Then walk slowly toward the bedroom on the left."

She made no move to obey him. Her intelligent eyes were busily assessing the situation, assessing him. Defiance shone in them. "What do you want?"

"You'll find out in a minute. Now do as I say or I'll shoot you."

"The neighbors will hear. They'll call the cops on you."

Goddammit. First Amber-May and now her. Why did all these women have to be so difficult?

He shrugged, though he knew she was right. He moved toward her, halving the distance between them, knowing that proximity enhanced fear and that fear bred obedience. She stood her ground, not retreating a step.

He said, "I'll be gone before they get here. You, on the other hand, will still be here. With two or three bullets in you."

"That won't do you any good. I know why you're here. I can't help you if I'm dead."

He nodded slowly, as though agreeing with her. He marveled at her spirit; this woman was tough. Fortunately, he had the perfect way to shatter her resistance.

"Maybe. But being difficult only means you'll die slower than you have to. And you know where I'll go once I'm finished with you? I'll head on over to Illinois to pay your daughter a visit. I'll spare you the details of what I'll do to her, but when she screams for you, I'll tell her that all the pain she's feeling is your fault."

His threat struck her like a hammer blow. She staggered, putting out a hand to brace herself against a wall. Her chin began trembling, and of the defiance that had shone in her eyes a moment ago, not a trace remained.

"And..." she began in a voice half as full as before, "and if I tell you what you want to know, you'll leave my daughter alone?"

"Yes. I got no cause to hurt her. All I want is Amber-May Jackson. Tell me where she is and your daughter will never know I exist. Lie to me, and I'll be the last person she'll ever meet."

He watched as tears sprang from her eyes and rolled down her cheeks, how she finally crumpled to her knees and wept. She did so quietly, as though mindful of the fact that she must not arouse the attention of her neighbors. Freddie knew he had her. He gave her a minute to cry.

"Well? What's it going to be?"

Jolene Lee began talking.

58

When Pickens finished talking to Emily Watts, he had a list of five names scrawled on a legal pad before him. Tapping the end of his pen on the desk blotter, he read the names again. Five nurses, all of whom worked at the nursing home. All five were potential accomplices of Amber-May Jackson. But one name drew his attention more than the others.

He had asked Nurse Watts to relate to him, without omitting a single detail, her encounter with Amber-May at the nursing home when she'd taken her grandmother away.

His experience as a lawyer had proved invaluable, as he knew when to dig deeper and when to let his interlocutor talk freely. He'd had to occasionally guide Nurse Watts in her narration, but eventually he felt that he'd gotten everything—the complete sequence of events, every word spoken, and Nurse Watts's impressions.

At first, she didn't even mention the fact that another nurse had been present at the nurses' station at the time, that said nurse had also exchanged words with Amber-May. But he'd managed to coax the information from her, and as he did so, a tingle had climbed up his spine and spread over the back of his neck and scalp. He had stumbled onto something.

With one hand supporting his chin, Pickens examined his thinking process. There was no evidence that Martha Mitchum was caring for Amber-May's grandmother, but his gut told him that she was. Her being in the nursing home when Amber-May had gone there only served to make her more suspicious. If he were in Amber-May's shoes, that was what he would have done—have a person on the inside at that critical moment, to warn her off in case something felt wrong.

Add to that the fact that, according to Watts, Martha Mitchum and Amber-May had had a cordial, almost friendly relationship back when Amber-May used to visit her grandmother regularly, and Mitchum was looking like a very viable candidate for the role of the grandmother's caregiver.

Pickens gave a little nod to himself and scratched a circle of dark-blue ink around Martha Mitchum's name.

Then he made a call. It was time to see if his hunch was right.

Three rings later, a smooth male voice with a crisp New England accent sounded in his ear.

"Garland, so nice to hear from you. How long has it been?"

"Too long, Nick. Way too long." Pickens did not have much patience for small talk, but it was part of the ritual of doing business. So he suffered through two minutes of chitchat before cutting to the chase.

"Nick, I have a job for you. A very delicate job."

"I'm all ears, Garland."

Pickens began telling him, but he didn't get far before he was cut off.

"But we're already looking for her."

"What?"

"We're already looking for Amber-May Jackson," said Nicholas Brunnert, CEO of Folssom Investigations & Security. A different firm had done the research on Amber-May soon after the rape, but for what Pickens now had in mind, he needed an outfit like Folssom. "Mr. MacBaxter talked to me about it personally no more than an hour ago."

Pickens felt a stab of panic. Was he too late? If Folssom found Amber-May without his assistance, Emmett would never reconsider his firing.

In a carefully controlled voice, he said. "How is the search going, Nick? Are you close to finding her?"

"We've only just started, Garland. We're good, but we're not miracle workers."

Pickens let out a breath. "So it's good that I called, after all. Because I got new information that might help you locate her very quickly."

"Oh?"

Pickens told him about Amber-May's grandmother and his suspicion that Martha Mitchum was caring for her. "I'd check Mitchum's house if I were you."

"I'll pass it on to my men. Thank you for the tip, Garland." In a humorous tone Brunnert added, "You're not about to ask for a discount on our fees, I hope."

Pickens didn't care about money. All he wanted was to get his job back. And he wanted it done in a way that Patrick MacBaxter would have approved of.

"Nick, this is important: I don't want the grandmother harmed, nor Martha Mitchum. The only target is Amber-May Jackson. And, Nick, you are to report only to me, not to Mr. MacBaxter. All right?"

Brunnert was silent for a moment. "Just so we're clear, Garland, you're telling me to kill Jackson? Because the instructions I got from Mr. MacBaxter were quite different."

Pickens frowned. What was Brunnert talking about? What besides death could Emmett possibly intend for Amber-May Jackson? He did not like to appear out of the loop, but he had to know. "What instructions?"

"To bring Miss Jackson unharmed to the family estate in Maine. It was my impression that Mr. MacBaxter would personally be waiting for us—for her—there."

Were it not for the suggestive undercurrent to Brunnert's tone, Pickens might not have grasped Emmett's true intent. As he did so, he leaned back in his chair as though pushed by a powerful hand and sucked in a breath that Brunnert would likely have caught if he hadn't been talking.

"You know, Garland, it's a shame Mr. MacBaxter pulled us off the search for Miss Jackson shortly after his father died. We might have already found her."

Now Pickens was truly stunned. His fine mind revolved like an accelerated assembly line, pulling in this new information, processing it, and spitting out conclusions. He had been blind, utterly blind, but now he could see the truth. And the truth he saw was as ugly as it got. It made him queasy and nearly robbed him of the power of speech. He had to swallow hard a couple of times before he managed to say, "Water under the bridge, Nick. Water under the bridge."

Pickens did not believe he knew everything, or even most of it, but the overall shape and form of recent events, and the people involved in them, was clear to him. He now knew why Amber-May had returned to Boston. He knew why she was targeting the men who had raped her. And he thought he knew why Freddie Sheehan had lied to him.

It also dawned on him that this situation presented him with a remarkable opportunity. Not simply a chance to get his job back, but a certainty. Because if he succeeded in this, there was no way Emmett would not be grateful enough to give him his job back. For a split second, he asked himself how Patrick MacBaxter would have reacted to what Pickens had learned about Emmett, but he quickly pushed this question aside. Thinking about it only aggravated his queasiness. Besides, hadn't MacBaxter made Pickens take an oath to serve his company and his son? He needed to get his job back to do that. To achieve that, things had to happen a certain way. And Nicholas Brunnert was key to that. "As for the current, and final, instructions, let me spell them out for you so there's no confusion." And Pickens proceeded to do just that.

59

Russ Koenig did not often think about the night he and three friends had raped a woman. But when he did, he viewed it in much the same way as a dozen other drug-fueled episodes of the past two years of his life, ever since he first started doing hard drugs. Like the night he and some of his junkie buddies broke into a house and frolicked the night away in the inside pool, leaving a mess behind. Or the time he borrowed his father's car and ran it into a fence, miraculously emerging without a scratch, giggling hysterically as he stared at the damage. Or when, during a house party, he had sex with a sixteen-year-old girl whose name he did not know while she was too wasted to tell the day of the week.

All these events were simply things that happened. They belonged in the past. Their only importance had been in the moment. They did not leave much of an impression on his memory or conscience.

This was more a reflex than a philosophy. He did not have to justify to himself the things he did; the drugs had obviated that need.

So he refrained from thinking about the girl he and three others had raped and nearly killed not due to a guilty conscience or a depraved mind. She was simply not something his brain paid attention to. She was all but forgotten. She was unimportant.

What was important was the little business he had established for himself. From a consumer of drugs he had become a dealer of them. This was relatively new. He'd only started selling six months ago, which was the reason his father had kicked him out of the house, warning that he'd call the police on him if he ever showed his face around again.

So he'd moved to an old and rather run-down house in Brockton, where he'd set up shop. The house belonged to his girlfriend. Her name was April. She was nineteen, a college dropout like himself, who did nothing but lounge about the house, drink beer, take drugs, and watch television. She wasn't pretty, but she never turned him down when he wanted sex and usually did as she was told, which was good enough for him.

He was a small fish in the big ocean of drug dealing, and this was also good enough. He had no aspiration for greatness; that would require too much work. He was okay with the way things were. He was doing very little and making okay money, enough to pay for cable and buy all the pizza and booze he and April could consume. The drugs he got free. It was one of the perks of being a dealer.

A few times a day, people would come to the house to buy from him. Sometimes he noticed their emaciated faces, their shaking hands, the way they couldn't stop sniffling, and he would know these people were sick and needed help. But he sold them their next hit all the same, pocketing their money without giving one thought to where it had come from or what they had done to get it.

He himself was in good shape. The drugs he took had not afflicted his body in any noticeable fashion. He did not look like the stereotype of a junkie. Sometimes he worried this would not last, but only rarely.

Where the drugs did have an effect was his mental faculties. His memory was shaky, his ability to focus his mind pitiful. He had tried to graduate, but he wasn't able to write coherently for more than ten minutes straight. He couldn't come close to passing an exam.

He often forgot things. Like paying bills or charging his phone, which he had only discovered had run out of power at nine that night. If he hadn't written down the appointment he had scheduled for ten, he likely would have forgotten it too.

The name beside the time was Ashley. He had a vague recollection of their conversation. She had asked to see him alone, hadn't she? He glanced toward the couch, where April was sprawled, watching a reality show. Her mouth hung slightly open, her eyes half-closed. She couldn't go out in this state.

"Yo," he called. "Go into the bedroom, will ya? And stay there till I tell you to come out. I got a customer coming."

At first, it seemed like she hadn't heard him. Then her eyes twitched tiredly his way, and she pushed herself up from the couch and dragged herself into the back of the house. He heard a toilet flush and running water, followed by the sound of bedsprings as April plopped down on the bed. She'd left the television on. He let it play.

Five minutes later came a knock at the door.

60

Amber-May arrived in Brockton at nine forty. She took ten minutes to locate the address Russ Koenig had given her and spent another ten circling the block, familiarizing herself with the surroundings and the house itself.

The house was one and a half stories, with dirty white trim and a black shingled roof. It squatted like an old and weary animal in the middle of a large uncultivated lot that was more weeds than grass. Lights shone in the front windows behind blue curtains. A red Suzuki was parked crookedly up front, one of its wheels sunk in the weeds beside the driveway.

Glancing around, Amber-May saw neglect everywhere, but also clear signs of habitation. Cars in driveways, lights in windows. There were neighbors here. Plenty of them. And Russ Koenig's house did not look like it had walls as thick as those in Shane Erickson's house. She would need to be careful and as quiet as she could. Recalling the loud bang of the .38, she reached down, pulled up her pant leg, and unholstered the .22 TJ had gifted her. It was quieter than the larger gun.

Unlike the previous night, she did not dawdle in her car. The new her heard no doubtful voices. The new her did not rebel against the idea of taking the life of an evil man. The new her just wanted to get the job done.

The sidewalks were empty, and so was the road. She crossed it quickly, her baseball cap on as yesterday, her head tilted low, her latex-gloved hands stuffed in her jacket pockets. Her right hand gripped the .22.

She went straight to the door and knocked. From inside came the sound of a television.

A breeze carried with it the scent of grass and ripe leaves. It cooled her skin, but inside she was hot with impatience for the door to open, to face another of her tormentors.

She almost smiled as she envisioned Russ Koenig's reaction upon seeing her on his doorstep. Rounded eyes, gaping mouth, the shock of knowing justice had finally come calling. Fear, horror, futile denial.

But when the door was pulled open and Russ Koenig stood before her, his face registered none of that. Bizarrely, he smiled.

"Hey, how you doing? Come in, come in." He ushered her inside with a hand, and she was so stunned that she actually accepted his invitation, stepping over the threshold and into the hall, without saying a word.

Russ looked much as she remembered him. Five nine, lean, with long, stringy dark hair. But now he also sported an untidy beard and mustache. He wore low-slung jeans and a T-shirt with a dragon emblazoned on it. White sneakers covered his feet.

"You found the way okay?" he asked, still smiling. His eyes ran the length of her, and his smile turned lascivious. "Glad you made it," he added before turning and motioning her to follow him into the living room, keeping up a patter of words that she failed to register due to how incredulous she was that he didn't recognize her.

She could have pulled the gun from her pocket and shot him in the head right then, but she held back. What kept her from firing was not doubt that he deserved to die and that she would be justified in killing him, but a desire for him to know why she was here, why she was about to end his life.

"You brought the money?" he asked, rubbing his hands on his jeans.

He stood before a ratty leather two-seater. On the coffee table, next to an ashtray heaped with crushed joints, was a quintet of empty beer bottles; two more stood on the floor by the couch, along with a short stack of pizza boxes. The thick scents of pot and melted cheese pervaded the room.

"You don't remember me, do you?" she asked.

Russ furrowed his brow. He was still smiling, and his eyes held a mischievous twinkle. "We ever hook up or something? I must have been way high to forget someone as hot as you, babe."

He licked his lips, his eyes fastening on her chest. Her stomach lurched. Her ears turned hot—not from embarrassment but from anger. This lowlife had raped and nearly killed her, and now he didn't even remember who she was. She was nothing to him. She did not even merit a memory.

At least it answered an important question. It told her that Russ Koenig had not hired the man in the Toyota. That left only Emmett MacBaxter and Garland Pickens.

"Something like that," she said, in answer to his question.

His grin widened. "Sorry for forgetting. I get that way sometimes. I live in the moment, you know? Nothing personal. Don't mean to imply you're lousy in the sack or anything, okay?"

"Okay," she said, feeling so sick her stomach hurt.

"Later, if you like, we can maybe get to know each other again. Have a little party."

Gritting her teeth, she barely managed a tight nod and a tighter smile.

Oblivious to her discomfort, Russ rubbed his hands together, eager to do business. "Let's get you stocked up first. You got the cash on you?"

"No," she said, pulling out the .22 and leveling it at his face.

His smile deflated, leaving his lips curled crookedly. He reminded her of some of the sick old people at the nursing home, those who had suffered a stroke and could not fully control their facial muscles anymore. But most of those people still had intelligence in their eyes. At that precise moment, all she could see in Russ Koenig's was dumb confusion.

"Sit down on the couch," she said.

He started to say something, but she shushed him. "Do as I say. Right now."

The sudden steel in her voice prodded him into action. He dropped onto the couch, sitting stiffly, staring at her with narrowed eyes.

"I got protection," he said. "You rob me, there'll be people after you."

"I'm not here for your money or your drugs. Let me tell you why I'm here. You remember a night a few months ago, a party at Shane Erickson's house?"

She watched as recognition slowly infiltrated Russ Koenig's addled brain, followed closely by his eyes. Now came the reaction she had pictured earlier. His mouth came open, his eyes grew huge. But then he did something unexpected. He called out, "April! Yo, April!"

Surprised, Amber-May looked past Russ to an open door, beyond which stretched a dark hallway. A drowsy female voice wafted over from there.

"What, baby? I'm sleeping, okay?"

They weren't alone in the house. A woman was back there. And this bastard had no qualms about involving her in this regardless of the risk this put her in.

With his head turned over his shoulder, taking his eyes off Amber-May, Russ called again—not for the woman to run, but for her to do something else. "April, get my gu—"

Amber-May did not let him finish. In one fluid movement, she stepped forward, pressed the muzzle against his hair, and pulled the trigger.

His body flopped onto the couch and didn't move. There was surprisingly little blood. The bullet evidently had not exited his skull.

The .22's report was much softer than the .38's and muffled further by being pressed to Russ's head. The scent of singed hair and burned skin rose sickeningly. Amber-May heard the thud of feet on wooden floorboards, then hurried footsteps approaching.

Whoever this April person was, Amber-May had no intention of shooting her, not even if she saw her face. Which meant she had to get away right now.

Close to panic, she hurried out of the living room and into the entry hall. Behind her came a choked cry, which, by the time she got to the front door, had blossomed into an incoherent series of screams.

The good news was that it sounded like April had stopped by Russ's body and was not coming after her. Head down, Amber-May ran toward her car, April's screams reaching after her like tentacles, clawing at her ears. She jumped in the Honda and tore away, hands gripping the steering wheel as though trying to choke it. A glance in the rearview mirror showed no one following her.

61

Amber-May drove away from Russ Koenig's house with the echoes of April's screams in her ears. She had never seen April, of course, but her mind conjured the image of a waif-thin young woman on her knees beside her dead boyfriend, her vocal cords being shredded by shrieks of disbelief, denial, and shock.

When she had set out on her vendetta, Amber-May had not given any thought to those who would discover the bodies of her tormentors and the anguish this might bring them. Apart from herself and her four assailants, she had not considered other people at all. She had only thought of her desire for vengeance and the need to stop whoever was pursuing her.

She realized now how self-centered this was. Punishing the guilty brought much pain to the innocents who were close to them. Like April had been to Russ Koenig. And this made Amber-May feel guilty.

Immersed in such thoughts, she arrived at Martha Mitchum's house. The hour was close to midnight. A light shone in the kitchen. All other rooms were dark.

She parked her car and crossed the street. She felt exhausted. She should have gone to her hotel for the night, but she felt an irresistible urge to see Grandma Betsy, even if she was asleep. Before the Alzheimer's had struck, it had been Grandma Betsy to whom she'd turned whenever she felt bad or moody. Invariably, Grandma Betsy had helped her feel better. She hoped that simply seeing her grandmother would have a similar effect on her now.

Martha had furnished her with a key. She unlocked the door and stepped inside.

The house was quiet and still. She walked into the lighted kitchen, finding it empty. She filled a glass with water from the tap and drank it in one long pull. She hadn't realized how thirsty she'd been. She splashed water on her face and that helped blunt the sharp edge of her exhaustion. Then she heard a strange noise coming from somewhere to the back of the house. It sounded like a muffled cry.

Frowning, Amber-May padded over to the kitchen's entrance. There she paused and peered into the dark hallway, holding her breath. The noise came again, this time a bit more shrill and urgent. It was coming from the living room.

What remained of her tiredness dissipated as fresh adrenaline coursed through her. She was about to call out Martha's name, but stopped herself. She felt a prickle of anxiety. Something did not feel right. The house gave off a bad vibe.

She'd returned the .22 to the ankle holster after driving away from Russ Koenig's house. The .38 was in her pocket. She pulled it out and held it before her in both hands, her finger on the trigger.

She stood stock-still, her ears pricked. Silence reigned for a solid minute, then was broken by another muffled moan and the scrape of wood on floor tiles.

With all her senses on high alert, Amber-May crept down the dark hall until she arrived at the living room. She peeked around the door frame.

Martha Mitchum sat in a wooden chair, illuminated by moonlight slanting through a rear window. Her arms had been tied to the armrests, her feet were strapped to the chair legs at the ankles and just under her knees. A strip of black duct tape sealed her mouth.

Something bulged beneath it. As far as Amber-May could see, Martha was all alone.

With panic turning her skin to ice, Amber-May glanced down the hall toward the stairs. Grandma Betsy's room was up there. Had someone harmed her? Was the person who had tied and gagged Martha up there right now? She was about to go and check, but Martha drew her attention by letting out another moan. Her eyes latched on to Amber-May, huge and urgent. She flexed her fingers as best she could with her wrists immobilized, motioning for Amber-May to approach.

Amber-May ran to Martha and as gently as possible eased the duct tape off her mouth. Martha winced. A sock had been jammed between her teeth. Amber-May yanked it out, and Martha took a heaving breath, coughing and retching.

"Are you okay, Martha? What happened here? Is Grandma Betsy all right?" Amber-May asked, putting the gun back in her pocket and trying to free Martha's arms. Like her legs, they were bound with zip ties. No matter how hard she pulled, Amber-May could not wrench them open.

Martha's voice was thick with despair. "They got her, Amber-May. Dear God, they took her."

A sense of helplessness spread throughout Amber-May's body. She did not need to ask who had been taken. That left just one mystery. "Who took her, Martha?"

"Three men. They came in about two hours ago. Didn't make a sound. I just looked up one moment and they were standing there. All three were dressed in black with ski masks on their faces. All had guns." Martha shook her head as though trying to erase a bad memory or undo a terrible reality. "They asked if you were here. When I said you weren't, they pushed me into this chair and one of them tied me to it. They wanted to know where you were, and I told them I didn't know. I was sure they were going to beat me, but I guess they could see I was telling the truth. Then they asked where your grandmother was. I tried to act like I had no idea what they were talking about, but it was pointless. They found her, and they took her away."

"Did they hurt her?"

"No. She looked confused, scared, but I don't think they hurt her. They injected her with something—a powerful sedative, I think—and carried her out of the house, through the back door. Then they gagged me and left me here." She looked at Amber-May. "They left a message for you."

"What message?"

"You're to call a number. It's written on a piece of paper on the coffee table. They said they'll give you further instructions then. They told me that if either of us breathed a word about this to anyone, they'll come back and kill me." Tears spilled from Martha's eyes in a thick stream. "I'm sorry, Amber-May. There was nothing I could do."

Amber-May squeezed Martha's hand. "I know. It's not your fault. It's mine. Give me a second. I'll go get a knife and cut you free."

Rising to her feet, she heard Martha gasp and saw the nurse's eyes stare over her shoulder, full of sudden fear.

62

Freddie had been on Martha Mitchum's street for less than five minutes when he saw the light-gray Honda roll to a stop in front of the house.

He laughed. No doubt about it, his luck had definitely turned. Through the windshield, he watched Amber-May climb out of the car, trudge toward Martha's house, and let herself in.

She looked tired, lost in thought. "Well, sweetheart," Freddie said to himself, "I hope you're ready for the surprise of your life."

He got out of the car and made his way to the house. He walked up the driveway, skirting the house, looking for the easiest way to make his entrance. In the backyard, he paused for a second in surprise. The back door hung open, and so was the screen door. The room beyond them was dark.

He minced forward, pausing in the doorway, listening and giving his eyes a moment to adjust.

It was a multipurpose room. Washer and dryer, shelves loaded with gardening implements and cleaning products. A broom, a mop, and a rake leaned against a wall.

At the far end was a door. Freddie eased it open. A deserted hallway. Female voices in conversation from somewhere toward the front of the house. Amber-May and her grandmother having a late night heart-to-heart?

He moved forward, keeping his steps light and his gun ready.

As he drew nearer, he recognized one of the voices. Amber-May. No doubt about it. The other voice was unfamiliar and older. They were coming from a room to his left.

Coming into the doorway, he saw them. Amber-May sat on her haunches, blocking most of the other woman from sight. Freddie could see her face, though. She wasn't Amber-May's grandmother. She had to be Martha Mitchum.

As soon as he saw her, Martha saw him, too. Her reaction made Amber-May turn her head around sharply. She froze, pure shock on her beautiful face. Freddie smiled, pointing the gun at her.

"Hey, sweetheart. Third time's a charm, am I right?"

Amber-May didn't answer. Instead, her hand went toward her jacket pocket. Freddie shook his head, stepping to the side to gain a clear line of sight at Martha Mitchum. "Don't you move or I'll shoot her dead." It was only then that he saw that Martha Mitchum was tied to her chair.

Freddie frowned. What the hell had happened here?

He'd worry about that later. First, he needed to subdue Amber-May. Her hand hovered near her pocket. Her expression was one of tormented indecision. She looked breathtakingly beautiful, even when she was in anguish. Freddie could understand Emmett's obsession.

Martha Mitchum gazed at him in horror. Perhaps she knew what was to be her fate.

"Reach into your pocket slowly and take out whatever you've got in there," Freddie told Amber-May. "Be nice and your friend here will live."

Lips tight, eyes blazing with impotent hatred, Amber-May did as she was told, her hand coming out holding a gun by its barrel. Freddie's eyebrows shot up.

"You got yourself a piece? You even know how to shoot that thing?"

"You'd be surprised how good I am with it," Amber-May said, her voice strangely flat.

Freddie was indeed surprised—by the fact that she'd spoken at all, by her tone, and by her words.

"Drop it on the floor and kick it this way."

Amber-May obeyed. "Who sent you? MacBaxter or Pickens?"

Freddie was impressed. "MacBaxter. He wants to meet you again. I'm here to make that happen." From his pocket he brought out a pair of handcuffs. He tossed them to her. They landed at her feet. "Put them on. No games, or I'll kill your friend and your grandmother, too."

Amber-May winced. "You're too late for that," she said almost inaudibly.

"What was that?"

"Nothing." Amber-May gave Martha a long look and said, "Sorry for getting you into this," before lowering her head and then crouching and clicking the handcuffs closed around her wrists.

As she began rising, Freddie stepped forward, shifting his gun to his left hand and ramming his right fist into Amber-May's belly. She crumpled to her knees, trying to suck in air and, by the sound of it, not having much luck.

Freddie stood over her. "That's for what you did to my hand and head. Trust me, you got off cheap. At least from me."

"Hey!" Martha Mitchum called from his right. "You leave her alone."

Freddie gave her a withering look. "You shut your mouth. I'll deal with you soon enough."

He turned back to Amber-May. She had rolled over on her side, her shackled hands pressed to her belly. Freddie grabbed the chain of the handcuffs and yanked hard, wrenching Amber-May's arms violently upward. She cried out. He yanked her to her knees, but not too hard. He didn't want to pull her shoulders from their sockets. She deserved it for all the trouble she'd caused him, but it was best that he get her to Emmett in as good a shape as possible.

Her face was twisted in agony. Still, she was beautiful. Maybe Emmett was shortchanging him by offering just a million.

"Come on. Let's go," he said, and was about to pull Amber-May to her feet when something crashed into his legs from the right, knocking him off balance. He went down hard, his gun slipping from one hand, the handcuffs from the other. It was Martha Mitchum. She had toppled herself into him, chair and all. She lay helpless on her side, blood pouring from a cut on her temple.

"You bitch," Freddie muttered and reached for his weapon.

"Hold it right there, you bastard."

Freddie froze with his fingers mere inches from his gun. Amber-May was sitting with her legs straight before her, one pant leg pulled up her calf, exposing an ankle holster. The holster was empty. Her hands weren't. They gripped a gun, and it was pointed right at him.

63

Amber-May sat holding the gun on the man, each breath eliciting a sharp pain in her abdomen. Several strands of hair had fallen across her face, partially obscuring her view. With her hands shackled, she could not brush them away without taking the gun off the man who, incredibly, had once again found her.

"Where is my grandmother?" she asked. "Where did you take her?"

The man looked bewildered. "I got no idea what you're talking about."

She believed him, mainly because if he had her grandmother, there was no need for him to break into Martha's house to kidnap her. She would have gone to him.

So who were the men who had taken Grandma Betsy? Who had sent them? How had they known to come to Martha's house?

Martha. Amber-May flicked a glance at the fallen woman, noted the blood on her head, and felt another stab of guilt. Another innocent person she had dragged into her vendetta. Another person traumatized and hurt. April, Grandma Betsy, Martha. Was this as long as the list would get? Or would more names be added to it?

"Are you okay, Martha?"

"Yes. I'm fine, Amber-May. Don't mind the blood. Just mind him." Martha motioned with her chin toward the man.

He lay on the floor like a coiled snake, ready to strike at the earliest opportunity. His dark eyes shifted from hers to the gun she held, and she could guess his thoughts. Should I go for my gun? Will she shoot? Is she capable of pulling the trigger at all?

"How did you know to come here?" she asked.

"Your car. I followed your car," he said, but only after the slightest of hesitations.

"Liar. You had no idea where I was after I gave you the slip the other day."

"You're right, I didn't. I was just cruising around when I spotted your car. It was dumb luck."

She scrutinized his face. He was a good liar, adept, but he couldn't fool her. He hadn't found her by accident. So how?

Sickening horror twisted her stomach as the answer dawned on her.

"Jolene," she mumbled, and saw the man's eyes twitch. "You found Jolene, didn't you?"

Martha gasped, and the man affected an air of perplexity. "I don't know any Jolene."

Amber-May felt like weeping, but she knew she must not allow tears to cloud her vision. "What did you do to Jolene? How did you make her give you this address?"

"I'm telling you, I don't know any Jolene."

Amber-May pulled the trigger. She'd aimed over the man's head, and the bullet flew past him, chewing into an armchair across the room. Martha yelped. The man flinched, pressing himself into the floor. The gun's report echoed around the room, hard on the ears, but all the windows were closed, containing the noise. Amber-May did not think much of it got out.

"What did you do to Jolene?" Amber-May asked again. "No lies, or next time I'll aim lower."

The man's tongue moistened his lips. "I went to her house and made her tell me where your grandmother was."

"How did you know where she lived?"

"From the license plate of her car. I figured out she and you were working together."

It was like another blow in the pit of her stomach, much harder and deeper than the one the man's fist had delivered. The list just got longer. All because she couldn't take care of her own affairs without drawing others into them.

"How did you force her to speak?"

"I threatened to hurt her and her daughter. She talked without me laying a finger on her."

Amber-May studied his face. She thought he was being truthful. Poor Jolene. She must have been terrified out of her mind. Otherwise, she wouldn't have talked.

"What did you do with her afterward?"

"Left her tied up in her bedroom," the man said, but again there was that slight hesitation. It was enough for Amber-May to know the man was lying, even though she desperately wanted to believe him.

But the truth was undeniable for the simple reason that, unlike the men who had taken Grandma Betsy from Martha's house, this man did not wear a ski mask. Which meant that Jolene would have seen his face. She would have been able to identify him. He could not afford to let her live. So now Amber-May had the death of Jolene on her conscience.

She should never have returned to Boston. She should have kept running. If she had, Jolene would still be alive and Grandma Betsy would not be a hostage.

And the worst thing of all was that it had all been for nothing. She had failed to carry out her mission. True, she had killed three of the four men who had raped her, but Emmett MacBaxter, the most vicious of the four and the one who had sent this man to kidnap her —the one who was probably in possession of Grandma Betsy—was still alive.

For a moment, she wondered whether she could use this man to get to MacBaxter. But it didn't take her long to realize how unlikely this was to succeed. Her hands were shackled and he had the key. She could get him to toss her the key, but she wouldn't be able to unlock the handcuffs without relinquishing her hold on the gun. Similarly, she could not undo the ties that bound Martha to the chair.

She could threaten to shoot him and thus get him to take her to MacBaxter, but she knew that the first chance he got, he would attack her. She had no faith in her ability to thwart him. And if he overpowered her, he would return to kill Martha as he had Jolene. One innocent life on her conscience was more than enough.

"Tell me you killed her quickly," she said to the man. "Tell me she didn't suffer."

The man didn't answer for a long moment, obviously weighing his words and wondering how she would take them. Eventually he said, "She died instantly. Hardly no pain."

Amber-May nodded. "At least that's something."

Then she shot him in the forehead.

64

Blood dripped from the hole in the man's forehead, dribbling over one open eye and onto the living room rug. There was no doubt that he was dead.

It was a moment that should have birthed a sense of deep relief, but there was none. Amber-May was still in deep trouble. The death of this man did not change that.

Martha had started sobbing—whether from shock at witnessing a violent death or from grief over Jolene, Amber-May could not say. She went over to the dead man and rummaged in his pockets for the key to the handcuffs.

After freeing her hands, she went to the kitchen and returned with a steak knife. She severed the zip ties binding Martha and helped her to her feet. The gash on her temple had ceased bleeding, but it was likely to swell. Amber-May led Martha to the couch, returned to the kitchen, gathered ice cubes in a towel, and gave it to Martha, who pressed it to her head.

"Poor Jolene," Martha muttered. "I can't believe it."

Amber-May couldn't believe it either. She went to a street-facing window and peered out. No commotion. No sign that anyone had heard the shots. Maybe the neighbors thought a car had backfired. Still, it would be best if they hurried.

"I need your help, Martha. We need to get rid of the body."

Martha looked confused, and Amber-May worried she might be going into shock. She went to her, clasped her free hand, and said, "Help me roll him up and load him in my car. We need to hurry."

Martha gave a shaky nod and got to her feet. Together they rolled the living room rug around the dead body and dragged it to the backyard. Amber-May drove Martha's car out of the driveway and parked it at the curb. Then she backed the Honda up the driveway as far as it would go, into the shadow of the house, where no one could see it from the street.

They loaded the corpse into the trunk and reentered the house. In the living room, Amber-May picked up the note the three abductors had left for her. A phone number was typed on it.

"They said you should call them as soon as you got this, and no later than noon," Martha said.

Amber-May nodded somberly, pocketing the note.

"What are you going to do?"

"I'll dump the body somewhere, and then I'll call them. I'm pretty sure they'll want to make an exchange: me for Grandma Betsy."

Martha stared at her. "You're not about to go through with it?"

"I have to."

"But...but..." Martha was unable to finish her sentence.

Amber-May saw how pale Martha was, how distraught. She tried to offer her a comforting smile but wasn't quite able to pull it off. She struggled to keep from thinking of the future that awaited her. She might fall apart if she did. She couldn't allow herself that. She needed to keep Martha from doing something that would jeopardize her safety. She owed her that much and more.

"I've got no choice, Martha. If I don't do as they say, they'll kill Grandma Betsy and you, too. I've already got Jolene on my conscience. I won't have you and Grandma Betsy on it as well."

"What happened to Jolene isn't your fault. You hear me, Amber-May? It isn't."

But Amber-May merely shook her head. "You're very kind, Martha. You're one of the kindest women I've known. I wish I'd never gotten you involved in all this. I've put you in grave danger. You need to promise me something. Don't call the police. Don't talk to the media. You'll be dead if you do."

"And what makes you think they won't kill me anyway once they have you?"

Amber-May had thought about that when they were hauling the corpse into her car. She didn't know why the three men had spared Martha's life, but she was sure it had been intentional.

"Because they could have killed you when they got Grandma Betsy. They didn't need you to pass on their message. They could have left me a note with their instructions. They let you live because they were told to do so. I believe that if you stay quiet, you won't be harmed. Promise me you'll say nothing."

Martha raised her chin. "That's my choice to make."

Amber-May nodded. "It is. But then what I'm about to do will have been for nothing."

"I can't let you sacrifice yourself for me."

Amber-May grabbed her arm. "You have to. You need to be around to care for Grandma Betsy."

"You don't even know if they'll let her go."

"You're right, I don't. But I think they will. She's no threat to them, not with her memory being what it is. I don't know why they didn't kill you, but I think—I hope—that they'll do the same with Grandma Betsy. But just in case I'm wrong, let's agree that if they return her to the nursing home, you'll stay quiet. If they don't, you're free to talk to anyone you wish. All right?"

Martha merely looked at Amber-May, her face showing her turbulent emotional state. "You expect me to just go on with my life while you're...I can't even bring myself to say it."

"Maybe it's better that you don't," Amber-May said. Fear of what lay in store for her gripped her innards, making her chest ache. She pulled Martha into a tight hug, and both of them began weeping in unison.

They held each other for a long time, crying on each other's shoulders. They would have kept on crying for much longer if Amber-May hadn't forced herself away from the solace of Martha's embrace and back into the bleak reality that was her life.

After kissing Martha on her tearstained cheek, she said, "Thank you for everything." Then she walked out the back of the house and into her car and drove away.

She made her way down to the docks, into dark and deserted streets and alleys. In one, behind a loaded dumpster, she stopped, heaved the rug-encased body out of the trunk, and rolled it free onto the tarmac. She stuffed the rug back into the trunk and drove clear across the city, to another empty alley, where she disposed of the rug. By then it was past 2 a.m., and she was exhausted. Her body craved nothing more than to curl up in a bed and sleep. But knowing her resolve might crumble at any moment, she denied herself even a short rest. Instead, she pulled to a stop near Fenway Park and called the number on the note.

A man with a gruff voice answered, "Yeah?"

She identified herself. The man exhibited no emotion. He simply gave her an address, told her to come alone, and said, "You'll see a blue van parked by the fence. Walk up to it and knock on the back doors." She began to ask about Grandma Betsy, but the man had already hung up.

She drove to the address he'd given her. It was a shopping center near the southern border of Boston with an outdoor parking lot. Near the perimeter fence stood a navy blue van.

Amber-May climbed out of her car and, with a step as heavy as a life sentence, plodded toward the van.

There was no indication that the van was occupied. Its lights were off, its engine silent. Amber-May halted before the closed rear doors and girded the courage to raise her hand and knock.

They must have seen her approach because as soon as she knocked, the van's doors swung open and a stony-faced man with a crew cut motioned wordlessly for her to enter. She did, climbing into the claustrophobic compartment. In addition to Crew Cut, there was another man present, this one with a shaved scalp. Both were dressed in black.

If she had harbored any hope of appealing to their conscience, that hope was dashed at the sight of their emotionless expressions.

Crew Cut ordered her to remove her jacket and spread her arms wide for a search. She suffered through it with clenched teeth and crawling skin. He found nothing. She had disposed of both her guns on the drive over there. She knew she could not save Grandma Betsy by force.

Satisfied that she was unarmed, he motioned her to sit in one of the four seats bolted to the floor.

"Where is my grandmother?" she asked.

"She's fine," Crew Cut said. "She'll be released once we reach our destination."

"Which is?"

He didn't answer. He simply prodded her to sit. Once she did, he produced a pair of handcuffs and shackled her hands before her. Then he buckled her seatbelt.

The shaved-headed man rose and approached her. He held a black cloth in his right hand, and it took her a moment to realize what it was. A hood. He pulled it over her head, completely blinding her. The acrid stink of cotton ingrained with old sweat and fear clogged her nostrils.

"Stay quiet," he said, his voice weirdly amplified as her ears tried to compensate for her blindness. "We got a short ride."

She couldn't say whether he was truthful or not. In addition to sight, the hood deprived her of the ability to gauge time. It also made breathing difficult, trapping the air by her face, making her skin excruciatingly hot.

Sightless and disoriented, the fear struck her hard, an onslaught of panic and terror that made every muscle in her body ache. The fear painted lurid pictures across the backdrop of utter darkness—all portraying nasty, depraved, unspeakable horrors that were like doomsday prophecies of her near future. She cringed in her seat as the van rocked around her, shut her eyes and balled her fists and pressed her teeth together so tight her jaw hurt—but the fear and the images it conjured were relentless. They kept coming, faster and sharper, stabbing at her mind's eye. Cold sweat covered her skin, and her heartbeat was like a bombardment in her ears. Her mind was under assault, and she felt madness about to engulf her.

She called upon her visualization technique to repulse the fear, to calm her body and mind. She tried to imagine blue skies and tranquil meadows, placid seas and calm lakes, a field of wheat fluttering in a faint breeze, children and puppies playing on a verdant lawn, a sunny hilltop filled with fragrant flowers around which butterflies circled. Above them all she strove to picture a glowing sun, warm but not scorching, and birds swooping above luscious treetops, their branches laden with succulent fruit.

But she managed to complete none of these images. Just a few stray lines of color and contour. Then the fear would erase them, trample them to nothing, and sink its claws deeper into her soul. She struggled to escape to a peaceful, safe place in her mind, the way she'd done countless times before, but it was no use. There was no escaping her grim reality, her abject terror. She could not find solace even in her own imagination.

She was lost, forsaken, body and soul.

She barely noticed when the van finally stopped, when the engine quit rumbling. In the blackness of the hood there was nothing but the fear.

A hand gripped her arm and pulled her to her feet. She was led out of the van and for a distance she could not estimate before being told to stop. Shortly after, there was a ping followed by what sounded like an elevator door swooshing open. The elevator ascended—she could not say how many floors—and she was led down a carpeted hallway and pushed into a chair. Her handcuffs were removed for a brief and blissful moment, but were soon refastened, this time with her arms behind her back and secured to the chair upon which she sat.

Her hood was yanked off and light stabbed her eyes, bringing forth tears. She heard the sound of retreating footsteps and a door closing behind her. Blinking rapidly, she slowly grew accustomed to the light—and saw Garland Pickens standing in front of her, dressed immaculately in a three-piece suit and tie, his hands clasped before him, a curiously mournful expression on his face.

The dapper bald lawyer shrugged his rounded shoulders. "I'm sorry it had to come to this," he said. "But this is my duty, and I must do it."

65

Shortly after, the hood was placed once more over her head and she was taken away from Pickens's office. A few minutes later, Amber-May was back in the van, once again in total, disorienting darkness.

This time the drive took longer, though she couldn't begin to speculate exactly how long. Judging by the van's speed, she knew they had driven out of the city and along a stretch of highway, but whether north, east, west, or south, she had no clue.

At times she thought the drive would never end, that she would be forever imprisoned in this absolute blackness. Eventually, though, the van slowed and began meandering along a winding road before finally coming to a stop.

When the doors opened, her ears told her she was no longer in an urban environment. There were no automobile sounds, and she could hear nocturnal insects whispering to each other, as well as what sounded like the distant hoot of an owl. It was colder here than in Boston, but it made no difference to her. She was already freezing from the inside out due to terror.

One of the men grabbed her by the forearm and led her out of the van and across a stone path. A moment later they halted, and over her booming heartbeat she heard the faint ring of a doorbell.

A door was opened, and a man spoke. Young, breathy, eager, frightening beyond all imagination. "You're finally here. Good. Bring her inside."

Nine or ten paces forward. Stop. A few seconds of silence. Then the same voice, "Give me the keys to the handcuffs," followed by the tinkle of keys and, "You can leave now. I'll make sure you get a bonus." The scuffle of shoes, followed by a door being shut, and, a moment later, a car engine revving and gradually growing distant.

Then silence once more.

Except for her rapid, choppy breathing. And the heavy, excited breaths of the man.

They were alone. She could feel that. The darkness of the hood seemed to deepen around her, as though she were stuck in an oubliette, cut off from the world. Her hands were handcuffed behind her back. She could not fight if she chose to. Her fear was so encompassing that her bones ached and she felt as though she might shatter to pieces.

A hand suddenly grabbed her breast, squeezing roughly. She gasped in surprise and pain. The hand moved, stroking, pinching, oblivious of her discomfort—or uncaring. Her legs felt wobbly, but she forced herself to remain standing. She still had her dignity. For the time being, at least.

The rough hand released her and the hood was pulled off. As before, the sudden shift from total darkness to light hurt her eyes. It took a few seconds before she was able to see clearly.

Emmett MacBaxter stood before her, a demented leer carved on his face.

He looked nothing like the demon from her nightmare of a few days ago. The real him was far scarier. It was the insane fire in his eyes, the manner in which his hungry smile twisted his facial features. He was a monster, yes, but not of some myth or night terror. He was real, flesh and blood and cruel intent—the sort of evil that you never suspected was close by until it chose you for its victim. And now she was at his mercy.

In his left hand he held a black device the size of a TV remote. He pressed a button. The device let out a crackle. An electric shocker. He waved it before her eyes.

"Behave," he said, still leering. "Be a good little girl and do as you're told or you'll get a taste of this."

Slowly, he ran his tongue across his lips as his eyes ate her up. His cheeks were flushed a lustful red, his nostrils flaring wide with each inhalation. "How I waited for this moment, you have no idea." His voice was breathy, but suddenly it hardened, as did his eyes. "You should not have kept me waiting this long. You'll have to be punished for that."

He looked at her, waiting, perhaps hoping she'd start begging for mercy. But Amber-May kept silent. She would deny him any satisfaction she could.

His jaw tensed, and his free hand moved so fast she barely saw it. His open palm struck her cheek with a loud clap. The slap sent her reeling, and she only barely managed not to fall down. Her cheek felt as though a burning torch had been pressed to it.

Emmett threw his head back and laughed. The sound echoed around the spacious foyer. Amber-May blinked back tears and stood straight. This was nothing compared to what he had planned for her. This was but a mosquito bite. Much worse was to come.

"Let's go," Emmett said gleefully, grabbing her arm and jerking her forward. "Let's get you settled into your new home. You'll love it."

He pulled her down a hall and through an open door, and together they descended a long staircase into a deep basement.

The room they were in was large and well-appointed. She expected him to throw her down on one of the couches, but he dragged her past them, down another staircase, through an open doorway, where a foot-thick steel door stood ajar, and into a windowless room that had to be a bomb shelter.

Then she saw the wall shackles and understood everything. It was much worse than she'd imagined. She'd allowed herself to hope that Emmett MacBaxter merely wanted a repeat of that dark and awful night a few months ago. She suspected it would not be a one-time torment, but she thought that after a few days, a few nights, he would simply dispose of her. She had reconciled herself to that fate. But this was not something she could stand.

This was a prison, an underground dungeon. It was to be her cell. She would be kept here for months, perhaps years. Repeatedly molested. Forever.

A sharp tremor cut through her, from the crown of her head to the tips of her toes. She stiffened and, for the first time since entering the house, refused to budge, even as Emmett's pull on her arm intensified.

He grinned at her, and she smelled alcohol on his breath. He was much stronger than her. He could have dragged her easily enough against her will. But he chose another course of action. Amber-May heard a crackle, and a searing, convulsing pain shot through her entire body, causing her teeth to clank hard and every muscle to seize. He had used the shocker on her.

Unable to move a finger, she became as limp as a rag doll. Laughing, Emmett hauled her to the wall, removed the handcuffs, and shackled both her hands to the wall chains. Then he let go of her. With her legs unable to bear her weight, she hung by her arms, the metal bracelets biting into the soft flesh of her wrists.

Raising her head, she saw Emmett approaching with a pair of long-bladed scissors. He slit her shirt and bra open, tore them off her body, and tossed the remnants aside. He stepped back and began unbuttoning his shirt, ogling her ravenously.

Here it comes, Amber-May thought. The thing she feared most, that was worse than all her nightmares combined. Being raped again by this psychopath.

Emmett removed his shirt, exposing his muscular chest. Grinning at her, he unbuckled his belt, unzipped his trousers, and had pushed them halfway down his thighs, exposing a pair of underwear bulging with his erection, when a sudden loud ringing sound stopped him.

Through the haze of terror that enveloped her, Amber-May at first did not place the sound; but when it came again, she recognized it for what it was. A doorbell, ringing insistently.

"What the hell?" Emmett said. He didn't move for a moment, but the bell wouldn't stop ringing. "Shit!" he growled, giving her a venomous look, as though she were to blame for this interruption. "I'll be back with you shortly. Then we'll have us a nice, long reunion." He refastened his pants, but did not bother putting his shirt back on. He exited the bomb shelter, swinging the heavy door shut, cutting off the sound of the bell, leaving Amber-May in total silence.

She wondered who had rung the doorbell, but decided it wasn't important. Emmett would soon get rid of that person and return to her. She did not have much time.

She pulled on the shackles, but they were bolted fast to the wall. She tried slipping her hands free of the bracelets, but they were too tight. She gazed around the austere room, knowing that soon she would know every damned inch of it, that this was to be her world, her universe.

How long would her sanity hold? Would it be better to simply let go of it and retreat into madness?

There were no weapons she could use. No means of escape. She could fight him, but she knew she would lose.

With each passing second, her terror mounted until she was shivering all over. She did not scream, knowing it was no use. Just as the sound of the doorbell did not penetrate the closed bomb shelter, so would her screams not pierce its thick walls and door.

She nearly screamed, however, when a metallic grinding noise came to her ear. Then the door began to open slowly, whining on its axis.

66

Garland Pickens stepped into the bomb shelter and stared at her with an expression of awkward horror.

He still had on his suit and tie. His shoes were polished. He looked ready for a fruitful day at the office—except for the gun in his hand and the sweat covering his face and bald scalp.

Upon seeing her, he cleared his throat and lowered his eyes. His face turned beet red—with embarrassment, Amber-May thought, not lust.

"I hope I'm not too late, Miss Jackson."

Amber-May was so stunned to see him that she was unable to formulate a reply.

Pickens walked forward and stopped where Emmett had dropped his shirt. He picked it up and handed it to her with his eyes averted. "Please."

She held the shirt to her chest, covering her breasts, and Pickens raised his eyes to hers. He noted her reddened cheek.

"He struck you?"

"It's no big deal," Amber-May said, still overcoming her shock at seeing him.

"That despicable madman."

"Don't worry about it. Where's Emmett?"

"Dead. I think he's dead."

"Think?" Amber-May's eyes went frantically to the entrance to the bomb shelter, fearing Emmett would walk in at any second.

"I shot him three times. There's a lot of blood. He did not move. I'm pretty sure he is dead."

Amber-May gave Pickens a close look and realized he was partially in shock. She had to snap him out of it. "Mr. Pickens, can you unlock these chains, please?"

Pickens blinked as though he had only just noticed that she was chained to the wall. "I'll go find the keys."

It took him a few minutes. A few agonizing minutes in which she was once again alone in the bomb shelter, though this time with the door open. Still, her anxiety remained elevated until Pickens returned with a set of keys in his hand.

When he had her free, he said, "I apologize it took me this long to get here." He turned his back while she put on Emmett's shirt.

Amber-May rubbed her wrists where the skin was ringed an angry red. "What made you come at all?"

"You did. It took me a while to realize that what you told me in my office was the truth. I could not allow Emmett to continue to head the company."

Amber-May gave him a frown, baffled by his unorthodox motivation and skewed morality. Yet, at that moment, she did not care why he had come to save her, only that he had.

Two hours earlier, when they were alone in his office, with her chained to a chair, he said, "I'm sorry it had to come to this. But this is my duty, and I must do it."

"Your duty?" Amber-May replied. "It's your duty to procure young women for your boss to rape?"

Pickens's face twitched in distaste. "I have never done such a thing before. I do not particularly wish to do so now. But it's the only way for me to...I am oath-bound, you see."

"Oath-bound? What the hell does that mean?"

Pickens explained. Amber-May wasn't sure why, but it seemed as though illustrating for her why he had sent men to kidnap her grand-mother, why he would soon dispatch her to Emmett, satisfied some need of his.

It infuriated her to hear him attempt to justify what he was about to do to her, but she kept her temper, remembering that he had Grandma Betsy. She listened as he explained about the dual oath he had made to Patrick MacBaxter: to serve the company he led and to serve his son, Emmett.

"That is why I must do this to you," Pickens concluded with a shrug of finality.

She stared at him, incredulous. "You truly believe having a man like Emmett MacBaxter at the head of your company will serve its best interests? Don't you know that his kind of evil can never be satis-fied? You think I'll be the last woman he targets? One day, he'll be exposed as the man he truly is—then what would become of your precious company?"

Pickens frowned, but otherwise it appeared that her words had no effect on him. Raising his voice, he called for the men standing in the hall outside his office to enter and take her away.

"You cannot serve your company and Emmett MacBaxter at the same time," she said just before the hood was placed once more over her head.

Now, in the house where Emmett MacBaxter had planned on imprisoning her, Pickens said in an introspective tone, "I should have seen it right away. I think I was out of my head there for a while, unable to think clearly." Closing his eyes, he shook his head. "Mr. MacBaxter would have had harsh words for me if he were alive to witness my behavior and lack of judgment. He would never have allowed something like this." Pickens gestured at the walls of the bomb shelter. "Never. Not even for his son."

They exited the bomb shelter together and ascended to the ground floor.

Pickens said, "Ten minutes after they took you, the idea came to me: this was the perfect time and place to get rid of Emmett. The perfect time to kill him. He would want to be alone with you. He would send his bodyguards away. I decided to come because you were right. I could not possibly serve the company and him at the same time. Not in the way Mr. MacBaxter had intended. But it occurred to me I might be deemed to have kept my oath if I served the company by serving Emmett...to you." He smiled faintly. "It's the sort of logic only a lawyer can fully appreciate."

They walked toward the entrance hall. Sprawled on the floor by the front door was Emmett MacBaxter.

"I suppose that means you should have been the one to finish him off," Pickens said thoughtfully. "But this will have to do, won't it?"

Emmett lay on his back, blood pooling around him, three holes marked in his torso. His mouth hung slack, his eyes were vacant and open. He was undoubtedly dead.

Amber-May stopped when she saw him. She felt light-headed, dizzy with relief. Tears began streaming down her face. Pickens shifted his feet awkwardly, unsure of how to react to her emotional outburst.

That was all right. She did not want him to comfort her. She and Pickens were not friends. At most they were momentary allies. She would find comfort elsewhere.

"Where's Grandma Betsy?" she asked.

"Asleep. Safe. I've arranged for her to return to the nursing home in the morning—unless you have other arrangements, of course."

"No. That's fine. And Martha Mitchum?"

"As long as she keeps quiet, she will come to no harm."

Amber-May told him about Jolene and the man who had killed her.

Pickens's face darkened at the news. "His name was Freddie Sheehan. I hired him to follow you when you left Boston, but somewhere along the way, he became Emmett's man, charged with kidnapping you. I am sorry about your friend. I'll see to it that her daughter is amply compensated. It's the best I can do."

Amber-May took this in silence. There was nothing that could make up for Jolene's death. No compensation would fill the void left by her murder. Money would not alleviate the pain that Jolene's daughter would experience. Amber-May felt the weight of guilt on her heart. For Jolene, and for her daughter as well.

But she also knew that Pickens was correct. There was nothing more to be done. Freddie Sheehan was dead, and so were the four men who had raped her. All the guilty parties had paid with their lives. All except Garland Pickens.

He had played a part in all this. A small part, but one nonetheless. And he had been willing to leave her to her fate, to give her to Emmett. But he had also saved her life. In the end, he'd done the right thing, even if it was for his own peculiar motives.

She felt no affection toward him, but she bore no desire to hurt him as she had the others. In truth, she had no energy for more fighting, no stomach for additional violence. She wanted nothing more than to sleep. And to see Grandma Betsy and Martha Mitchum.

She asked Garland Pickens if he would take her back to Boston, and he said he would. Together they left the house, leaving Emmett where he lay.

67

The following night, Amber-May sat beside Grandma Betsy on the window-facing couch in her room in the nursing home. They drank tea and ate cupcakes that Amber-May had brought with her. They watched an old movie on the television and talked of this and that.

Grandma Betsy had no recollection of her abduction, and for this Amber-May was grateful. Oddly, Grandma Betsy did remember visiting Martha Mitchum's house, but she thought it had been an afternoon visit. She did not remember sleeping there.

Grandma Betsy glanced sideways at her. "You look better, dear."

"Better? How?"

"You seemed so troubled lately and now you look as though your mind is free from worry."

For what had to be the millionth time, Amber-May marveled at the bizarre manner in which her grandmother's condition affected her memory. Some things she recalled perfectly, some not at all; others, she made a jumble of. But her perception was as keen as always.

"I've had a lot on my mind lately," Amber-May said. "But not anymore."

"Good. That's good. Worrying too much is not healthy. Take it from me, things have a way of working themselves out in the end." Grandma Betsy sipped her tea and sighed. "This is lovely, dear, and the cupcakes are delicious. Thank you for bringing them and for coming to see me."

"It's my pleasure, Grandma."

Grandma Betsy frowned as she groped for an elusive memory. "Lately, we haven't been seeing each other as regularly as before, or am I mistaken?"

"You're not. But don't worry. I plan on coming to see you so often you'll be sick of me."

Grandma Betsy smiled. "I very much doubt that is possible." After a minute, she asked, "What are your plans for tomorrow?"

"Rest. Just rest. I'm very tired."

"And later this week?"

Amber-May didn't know. She had no immediate plans. For now, she was still recovering mentally from all that had happened. In a few days, she'd start thinking of the future. Pickens had told her she would still be paid the annual sum they had agreed upon all those months ago in the hospital. She had not protested. That money no longer felt tainted. She had earned it.

She'd go to college, that much she knew. And later? Law school, probably. With the goal of eventually becoming a prosecutor and making sure people like the four men who had raped her would be removed from the streets.

For now, though, she was content to be sitting here with her grandmother. Later, she and Martha would have dinner together. They would eat and drink and laugh and wish with all their hearts that Jolene was there with them.

Martha had offered to put her up for a while, until she found a place of her own. Amber-May had gratefully accepted. She needed a place to sleep that felt safe, with at least one person around who cared about her.

She sipped her tea, holding the warm cup close to her chest. She gazed at the window and beyond it at the night's sky. So many stars, bringing light into darkness.

She focused on those stars, on that light, and felt for the first time in a long while that things would get better from here on out, and that happiness was within her grasp.

68

Garland Pickens stood in his private bathroom and examined himself in the mirror. His maroon bow tie was perfectly knotted and centered. The collar of his shirt lay symmetrically on either side of his jowly neckline. His navy blue suit jacket was unblemished by either lint or trace of dandruff. His hair, what little of it remained, was neatly trimmed and combed. He had shaved with particular care that morning, and now, tilting his head from side to side so he could inspect every inch of his cheeks and jawline, he was pleased to note that not a hint of stubble could be seen anywhere.

It was a shame, he reflected, that his waistline was so expansive, but that could not be helped at this point. Still, he attempted to suck in his belly but soon realized that was an exercise in futility.

All in all, though, he was satisfied with what he saw. He looked neat, distinguished, respectable. He had never been, nor ever would be, the match of Emmett MacBaxter in the looks department, but there was more to life than appearances. He was most certainly Emmett's superior in other areas. Intelligence for one, character for another. And, of course, there was the minor fact that he was alive and Emmett dead. That thought made him smile at his face in the glass. It was not an entirely happy smile, more a satisfied one, an acknowledgment of an unsavory job well done. "You did well," he said softly to himself. "You did your duty as best you could. For the company's sake." In his heart he hoped that Patrick MacBaxter, wherever he was, agreed.

Buttoning his jacket over his ballooning belly, he gave it a final, unnecessary smoothing brush with his left hand. Then he turned from the mirror and exited the bathroom.

Crossing his office, he was surprised to feel a rising sense of excitement. It began as a flutter deep inside his chest, grew to a vibration, and, by the time he stepped out of his office and began striding toward the boardroom at the end of the hall, blossomed into something approaching an internal quake.

It was an unfamiliar feeling, yet not an unpleasant one. He realized that he was nervous. Reaching the closed double doors of the boardroom, he paused and steadied his breath and heartbeat as best he could before pulling open the right-hand door and stepping inside.

The others were already there, seated around the long table, talking in somber tones. Eighteen men and women in business suits. He knew their names, their work histories, their career accomplishments. He had known each of them for years. And they knew him.

As Pickens entered, conversation ceased and all eyes turned his way. The mood in the room was apprehensive, gloomy, uncertain. Faces were strained, tired, fearful. Perfectly understandable. It was not common for a corporation to lose two leaders in such rapid succession, especially when the latter was murdered by person or persons unknown. The newspapers were filled with lurid speculation regarding Emmett's murder. Journalists were sniffing around for juicy details and innuendo. The internet was rife with conspiracy theories, none of which approximated the truth in any way. Stocks of the various public companies MacBaxter Holdings controlled had nosedived when news of Emmett's death had broken. The men and women in that boardroom knew that the company was now sailing in turbulent waters. Competitors were circling around like hungry sharks. A steady hand was needed at the helm.

Pickens went around the table, pumping hands, patting backs, providing a confident word here and there. He could see it in their eyes—a bewilderment, a desire to be told everything would soon be back to normal. The careers and reputations of all present were firmly and inextricably tied to the condition of the company. If it should happen to fall into ruin, so would they.

At last, Pickens came to a chair situated one place to the right of the head of the table. It was his chair, at the right-hand side of the empty seat that had briefly belonged to Emmett and before him his father.

He sat down and called the meeting to order. There was just one item on the agenda, the appointment of a new president and CEO.

Halfway down the table, a silver-haired director by the name of Bellamy rose and addressed the gathering in his distinct Brooklyn accent.

"At this time of crisis for the company, we need a leader who can start running things from day one, starting today; someone who knows this company inside and out; someone we can all trust implicitly. There is just one man who fits the bill." He turned to look at Pickens. "I move that we appoint Garland Pickens as our new president and CEO."

Pickens sat in silence, on his face an expression of studied humility, as another board member seconded Bellamy's motion. None of this surprised Pickens. He had arranged all of this beforehand with Bellamy and a few of the others.

So he allowed his mind to drift as the matter was put to a vote, and each board member was given the chance to speak his or her piece. Unexpectedly, his thoughts were of the girl, Amber-May Jackson.

What a remarkable young woman. What an angel of vengeance and death. She had nearly ruined everything with her vendetta. But in so doing, she had actually made everything right. For the company, and for him as well.

If not for her, he might never have known the true depths of Emmett's depravity, or it might have come to light in a public way, causing terminal damage to the company. If not for her, he would not have been able to deal with Emmett in a way that complied with the oath he had made to Patrick MacBaxter, even if he'd had to twist and bend the original meaning of that oath to do so.

And if not for her, he would not be on the cusp of being appointed to head the company that he loved more than anything, to which he had dedicated his life.

In truth, this leadership role was not one he had ever aspired to. He had always seen himself as a natural number two, the right-hand man of Patrick MacBaxter. He would have been one to Emmett if he had wanted him to be, and if Emmett had deserved it.

But Emmett was gone and so was his father. All that was left was the company bearing Patrick MacBaxter's name. And there was no one better suited than Pickens to lead it out of its current troubles and into a bright future.

For which he had Amber-May Jackson to thank. A twenty-year-old waitress and stripper. What an utterly ludicrous turn of events.

He shook his head, bemused. Yes, he was grateful to her despite all the trouble she'd caused him. Ensuring the police investigation of all the recent killings would go nowhere had cost him a veritable fortune. He'd had to stretch his influence to its utter limits. He had called in favors, spread bribes, made threats and promises—all so the murders of Emmett and the others would never be solved.

It was the most expensive and difficult to orchestrate cover-up he had ever been involved in, but it was worth it. For the company's reputation and future.

And for Amber-May Jackson as well.

Because she did not deserve to spend the rest of her life in prison. Because she had earned his respect and admiration. Because she had helped him get rid of Emmett and in so doing safeguard the company's future, and nothing was more important than that.

As for Nicholas Brunnert, Pickens was unconcerned. He was relatively certain Brunnert suspected he was responsible for Emmett's death, but Brunnert could hardly go to the police with his suspicions, nor did he have any reason to. Though Brunnert would never have sanctioned or taken part in the killing of an important man like Emmett—men of that status were potential clients, never targets—he had no cause to regret his death. He had been paid in full for his latest assignment, and Pickens had assured him that he would gladly commission his firm again, whenever the need arose. They had always been cordial with one another, so Pickens expected no trouble.

In fact, Pickens had detected a previously absent undercurrent of awed respect in Brunnert's tone when they last spoke, the day after Emmett's body was discovered, as though Brunnert had a new and deeper appreciation of him. Pickens had been both surprised and deeply pleased by that.

Smiling slightly, he became aware of the silence around him.

Breaking his reverie, he returned his attention to his present surroundings and found eighteen pairs of eyes aimed squarely at him. He accessed the part of his mind that had absently followed the voting that had just ended. There had been no last-minute surprises. It was unanimous.

He heaved himself up from his chair and addressed the assemblage in his smooth baritone voice, his tone calm yet determined, designed to banish all apprehension among his listeners.

"My friends, I appreciate your confidence and I humbly accept the post to which you have elevated me. With your help, I will do my utmost to ensure MacBaxter Holdings continues to be an exemplar of what an American corporation should be. Not just a financial enterprise, but a moral one as well. One that advances society, one that holds itself to the highest standards of propriety, one that helps those less fortunate. This is the kind of company Patrick MacBaxter built. This is the kind of company we shall continue to be."

Pickens paused, feeling slightly flushed and breathless. He had rehearsed this brief speech numerous times last night and that morning, trimming a word here, adding another there. Now he waited a loaded second for the reaction of his peers.

It was as he had hoped it would be. One by one, the eighteen board members rose to their feet and began clapping. He could feel the changing atmosphere in the room, the rising spirits. Pickens glowed with satisfaction.

Everything was all right now. Everything was as it should be.

Thank you for reading *The Payback Girl*.

Looking for more by Jonathan Dunsky?

Ten Years Gone, book 1 of the Adam Lapid mysteries series by Jonathan Dunsky, is now available.

Please review this book!

Reviews help both authors and readers. If you enjoyed *The Payback Girl*, please leave a review on whatever website you use to buy or review books. I would greatly appreciate it.

Turn the page for a personal message from the author.

AFTERWORD

Dear Reader,

Thank you for reading *The Payback Girl*. Writing is often rewarding in and of itself, but the best part of it is having your work read by others. I treasure each and every one of my readers, so thank you!

I began writing *The Payback Girl* soon after the publication of *A Debt of Death*, book four in my historical mystery series featuring private detective Adam Lapid. At the time, Adam Lapid novels were not selling particularly well. Partway through the writing of *The Payback Girl*, however, something magical happened. Readers began finding the Adam Lapid novels, and sales of them rose precipitously.

This presented me with a dilemma. Should I set the book I was writing aside to write the fifth Adam Lapid novel? Economically, it was a no-brainer; readers were clamoring for more Adam Lapid mysteries. But I was already committed to finishing *The Payback Girl* and plowed ahead, now doubly motivated. I not only wanted to see *The Payback Girl* through to completion, but I also wanted to get back to Adam Lapid as soon as possible.

The Payback Girl was not an easy book to write, and it took me a good deal of time to complete. I'm quite happy with how it turned out, and I can only hope that you, dear reader, feel the same way.

If you enjoyed *The Payback Girl*, could you do me a favor and review the book on whatever website you use to buy or review books? Good reviews are very important. They help persuade potential readers to try out new books. I'd be grateful if you could spare a moment to write your review of The Payback Girl.

I love hearing from readers, and I answer every reader email I get. If you have any feedback, questions, or you simply want to reach out and say hi, write to me at jonathan@JonathanDunsky.com.

I hope to meet you again soon in another one of my books.

Yours,

Jonathan Dunsky

P.S. You are also welcome to contact me on Facebook: facebook.com/JonathanDunskyBooks

ABOUT THE AUTHOR

Jonathan Dunsky lives in Israel with his wife and two sons. He enjoys reading, writing, and goofing around with his kids. He began writing in his teens, then took a break for close to twenty years, during which he worked an assortment of jobs. He is the author of the Adam Lapid mysteries series and the standalone thriller The Payback Girl.

Printed in Great Britain
by Amazon

45639680R00219